Mrs Ramsay

A Summer in Spain

Mrs Ramsay

A Summer in Spain

ISBN/EAN: 9783337237974

Printed in Europe, USA, Canada, Australia, Japan

Cover: Foto ©Andreas Hilbeck / pixelio.de

More available books at **www.hansebooks.com**

A SUMMER IN SPAIN.

RAVINE BETWEEN THE ALHAMBRA AND GENERALIFE.

A SUMMER IN SPAIN.

BY

MRS. RAMSAY,

AUTHOR OF A

'TRANSLATION OF DANTE'S DIVINA COMMEDIA.'

AT TORTOSA.

LONDON:

TINSLEY BROTHERS, 8, CATHERINE STREET, STRAND.

1874.

A SUMMER IN SPAIN.

BY

MRS. RAMSAY,

AUTHOR OF A

'TRANSLATION OF DANTE'S DIVINA COMMEDIA.'

LONDON:

TINSLEY BROTHERS. 8, CATHERINE STREET. STRAND.

1874.

PRINTED BY TAYLOR AND CO.,
LITTLE QUEEN STREET, LINCOLN'S INN FIELDS.

CONTENTS.

CHAPTER V.

CHAPTER VI.

CHAPTER VII.

CHAPTER VIII.

CHAPTER IX.

CHAPTER X.

CHAPTER XI.

CHAPTER XII.

CHAPTER XIII.

CHAPTER XIV.

A SUMMER IN SPAIN.

CHAPTER I.

Doubts and Difficulties—Custom-house—Troops at Zumarraga—Arrival at Burgos—Las Huelgas—Cartuja of Miraflores—Tomb of the Cid—Cathedral.

Often had we wished to make a tour in Spain, but, unfortunately, it had never happened that the country was quiet when we could go. After the accession of King Amadeus, we, believing in the rose-coloured view of things at that time prevalent in Italy, thought the suitable time had come. But one's Roman winter home is too pleasant a thing to leave without due consideration ; and we greatly dreaded carpetless rooms, chimneyless houses, and discomforts in general. There was our bright Roman life on the one hand ; on the other, the glories of the Madrid gallery ; the Moorish memories of Cordoba ; the orange-groves of Seville ; Cadiz, rising like Venus from the sea ; the palm-forests

B

of Elche; our own Gibraltar, and, fairest of all, the Arabian Alhambra.

But the cold of travelling in Spain in winter! What was to be done? It is so pleasant to see things! Yet it is so disagreeable to be uncomfortable, and especially to break up one's winter home one's house, to the manifold inconveniences of which one has got accustomed; one's old and trusty servants, to whose shortcomings one has become positively attached! . . .

At length the idea occurred to me, "If it be objectionable to go in winter, why not go in summer?" Certainly, in that case, we should not suffer from the cold, whatever else might be our miseries. But, then, it might be too hot. Well, we had spent summers in Italy, and it was rather hot; yet I don't think we ever regretted it. We could go to the Pyrenees if Spain were too hot. At least, I said so; but privately I had it in my mind to spend the hot months quietly at Granada; only I did not say so, for fear of being told it was impossible. Why, it was almost Africa.

Accordingly, we decided that we should leave Rome soon after Easter, 1872, and take advantage of the apparently peaceable state of the country. We sent for a Spanish master; and were provided, by the kindness of our friends, with letters of introduction for Madrid and elsewhere. All was prospering, when just as our things were packed up, came the news of the Carlist insurrection.

It was exceedingly provoking; and we were obliged to delay our departure a little. If they would only have kept quiet for six months more! We very nearly abandoned our project; but a friend, who had lived long in Seville, advised us to take courage, saying, "If you don't like revolutions, why did you ever plan a tour in Spain?"

At last we determined to go on and trust to Fortune. We might possibly be able to get in if we went to the frontier; at any rate, it was quite certain that unless we went there, we had no chance. If things were very bad, we could stay at Biarritz, or go to the Pyrenees for the summer; and perhaps in autumn we might get across the Bidassoa. And there was always the hope that the newspaper accounts might be exaggerated; which, as we afterwards found, was very far from being the case.

On the 25th of April we started, and got on prosperously till we arrived at Bayonne, where the news greeted us that the rails were cut, there was fighting along the line, and nobody could go into Spain. At the station no tickets were issued.

Next day it was reported that the way was clear. But the accounts were so conflicting that we went to the English Consul to ask his opinion. He prudently said he did not exactly like to advise people to go on, when the country was in such a state; but it certainly was possible to pass, others having gone without meeting with any inconvenience. On further inquiry, he said that one of the stations, Zumarraga, was in the hands of the Carlists; but that there seemed to be a kind of understanding that as long as the trains brought only passengers, and not troops, nor material of war, they would be allowed to pass.

That evening, however, the trains were again at a standstill. We therefore thought it best to go on to Biarritz, and wait for calmer times. There we were fortunate enough to meet friends coming out of Spain, who said they had found no difficulties to signify, and strongly urged us to go on.

We were quite willing to follow this advice; the only obstacle was, that the trains did not go. There was nothing for it but to enjoy ourselves at Biarritz. Sketching, scrambling about the cliffs, and walking on the sands by that delicious green sea. So pleasant was it, that I think we were almost sorry when we were told that we could now have tickets for Spain.

Tickets for Spain! How strange it sounded! We started for Burgos on the 15th of May, by the midday train, and almost immediately, as it seemed to me, crossed the Bidassoa. Of course, we were stopped at the frontier to have our luggage examined. The solemnity of the Custom-house officers was something appalling; my heart died within me as I advanced with my keys.

The boxes were opened, and the douanier very gravely and very slowly drew on a pair of perfectly clean white gloves, and then proceeded to turn over my dresses with the utmost care and minuteness. No waiting-maid could have handled them more daintily.

But everything was examined: what he expected to find I don't know; he made no remark, replied only by a bow to my attempts at Spanish conversation, and when he had carefully looked at everything in my box, he motioned me to open my bag. I did so; and the same process was gone through. At last he drew out a new sponge-bag which I had bought at Bayonne, and holding it cautiously between his finger and thumb, asked what it was. I explained as best I could. He looked graver than before, and politely requested me to open it. I did so; and he shut one eye, and looked in with the other, holding it, however, at arm's length, as if he feared it would explode. Seeing that he was not satisfied, I offered to take out the sponge, that he might examine it at his ease. "It would be better," he said. On the sponge being extracted, he asked "of what use that could possibly be?" I tried to explain the use of a sponge, as well as my limited command of Spanish would permit. He listened courteously, but with evident disbelief, saying, "It might be so; but he had never seen such a thing before."

However, he did not confiscate the article, perhaps because he was so persuaded of its uselessness; and at last I was allowed to depart.

We should have much liked to stop at San Sebastian, and also at Pasajes, where the harbour is exceedingly curious; it is like a Scotch loch or a Norwegian fiord, only more completely landlocked. But, in the present state of things, we thought it wiser to pass through the Carlist bands as quickly as possible, and go straight to Burgos.

The sky was grey, the country was wooded, the trees just breaking out into their first fresh leaf, little valleys lay quietly among the hills, little clear streams ran sparkling below the green boughs; all was cool, not to say cold; and the roads, when there were any, were exceedingly muddy. There was no dust, no glare, no sun ; nothing that one had been accustomed to think Spanish ; not even a donkey to be seen. The Pyrenees had disappeared in a most extraordinary manner ; indeed, of all the mountain ranges I have ever encountered, they are generally the most persistently invisible.

Those green valleys must be most excellent cover for Carlists and other guerilla bands. No regular troops would have a chance there. We now understood why it was that the Carlists kept appearing and disappearing, never any the worse for being defeated ; if, indeed, they were defeated.

We went on slowly, but comfortably enough, till past five o'clock, when I knew we ought to be approaching the dreaded station of Zumarraga. At first, we had been so triumphant at crossing the Bidassoa, that we were recklessly indifferent to what might happen next. Now, however, we began to wonder how it might be ; and just at that moment we perceived a small hole, the unmistakable mark of a rifle bullet, in most unpleasantly suggestive proximity to the passengers' heads.

While we were considering attentively the mark of the bullet, and wondering if it had passed through the carriage yesterday or the day before, and whether it had done mischief or not, the train slackened speed ;

we were coming to a station. I looked out, it was the dreaded name Zumarraga, and the platform was crowded with very dirty soldiers. However, they turned out to be the royal troops, who had re-taken the station the night before. It was well we did not arrive in the midst of the fighting.

Some of the soldiers were wounded ; and all looked disconsolate and much dilapidated. None of them had stockings, nor shoes either, in our acceptation of the word. They had only sandals ; not the picturesque sandal of the Abruzzi peasant, but simply a very ill-shaped bit of leather (or rather of the skin of some animal, for it scarcely merited the dignity of being called leather), caught up, toe and heel, with a dirty rag, and tied round the ankle. We were told that this was a classical and historical *chaussure*, and exceedingly comfortable besides : it certainly was particularly ugly.

We went on again, much faster than before. I fancy they had feared being thrown off the rails, as was often done by the Carlists, and had therefore gone very slowly ; consequently, we were a good deal behind time. Away we went through the gathering dusk ; the scenery grew magnificent ; extraordinary peaks and pinnacles seemed about to fall on us : it was like the chaos of an unfinished world.

But soon it grew too dark to distinguish anything, and at 11 P.M. we found ourselves in Burgos.

That same arrival in Burgos was rather more alarmingly Spanish than anything we had as yet met with. What a dirty omnibus it was! In Spain, as in some parts of the south of France, the hotels have not yet reached the luxury of a conveyance of their own; and private carriages are, as a rule, even more unattainable; so the only means of getting to or from the station is the common street omnibus, which is far from select in its inmates, as we perceived on this occasion. However, we were really exceptionally fortunate, for in one corner was an English lady travelling quite alone. This greatly reassured us, as she had fearlessly come up through. the whole of Spain in perfect safety, if not always in absolute comfort.

The hotel (Fonda del Norte) did not look very inviting; the stair was dark and dirty; and, as is always the case in even tolerably good Spanish inns, nobody came out to meet us, far less to relieve us of our hand-luggage. With difficulty somebody was found, who looked a good deal surprised to see us, but at last showed us a very wretched bedroom. We were too tired, however, to care much, and soon were asleep.

It is a curious sensation to waken for the first

time in Spain, in Burgos, the very name of which brings grand old memories of Edward the First of England, and his heroic wife, his *chère reine* Eleanor, or, as I suspect she was called in Spain, Leonór: and longer ago and grander still, the tales of the Cid himself, Ruy Diaz of Vivar, the Campeador of Spain. But on first opening your eyes in this chivalrous city, it is more curious than pleasing to observe the many specimens of entomology which have been familiarly associating with you during the hours of darkness. It was fearful! The floor was black with beetles, one of which ran out of the sleeve of my waterproof cloak when I put it on. The walls were spotted with yet more evil insects. I am bound to state, however, for the honour of Spain, that this, as it was the first, was also the last really dirty inn we suffered from in the whole of our Peninsular travels. In fact, on the whole, Spanish inns are cleaner than Italian ones used to be in old vetturino days. Even here, there was next our bedroom a tolerably clean and comfortable little sitting-room, where they said we might have our chocolate. Accordingly, we had some of that excellent chocolate, which is the staff of life in Spain, and set off in a curious, old-fashioned, high-hung hackney coach (the only vehicle in the

town except the railway-omnibus) to the tomb of the
Cid, and other interesting places round Burgos.

We first went to Las Huelgas, where Edward of
England was knighted by Alonso the Wise, the
astronomer-king, who ventured to doubt the sun
moving round the earth, and was very nearly struck
by lightning in consequence; so say the monkish
historians. Dante, too, blames this learned monarch,
not on account of his lax astronomical opinions,
but because he neglected the earth for the starry
heaven.

Las Huelgas was, however, not the scene of
Alonso's astronomical studies, nor of any such heterodox theories. All here was most orthodox, most
Spanish: the nuns in their black and white robes,
sitting on the floor and listening in that icy cold
church to a solemn reading; the crucifixes clad in
blue or pink silk petticoats; the represention of Santiago on his white horse, as he appeared fighting
against the Moors at Clavïjo, when the worthy
chronicler, Bernal Diaz, who fought in the same
battle, remarks, "No doubt it was so; but it was
not given to me, a sinner, to see him."

Some of these nuns wore a very peculiar head-dress,
like horns; it put me in mind of the crescent moon
on the forehead of the Egyptian goddess Athor.

We asked why they were not all dressed alike; and were told that those with the moonlike tire were the original nuns of Las Huelgas, and were of high rank; they, therefore, walk into the choir before the hornless ladies, who were not noble, and had been brought here from another convent.

Apart from historical interest, there is not much to see at Las Huelgas, and we went on to the Cartuja, or Carthusian convent, of Miraflores, with its exquisite alabaster monument of John the Second, the founder, and his Queen, Isabel of Portugal, the father and mother of Isabella the Catholic. It is impossible to imagine anything more fairy-like than the delicate carving; one could have spent months in studying those lovely designs. The vine-foliage encircling the kneeling figure of their son, the Infante Alonso, is also especially beautiful. But the alabaster blossoms and leaves within the church are all that now entitle the place to the epithet of Miraflores; without, it is desolate and absolutely flowerless.

Next we went to San Pedro de Cardeña, where the bones of the Cid once lay, and where his tomb still remains. What a strange, dreary wilderness that country is round Burgos! The fields were brown, and the sky was black, and the road (when there was one) blinding white; while the wind howled wildly over the wide treeless plain. And yet this was in what elsewhere would have been the merry month of May! But can any month be merry in Old Castile?

I wonder if it looked like that when the dead Campeador was brought here on his war-horse, Bavieca. Certainly, the road, when we saw it, was much fitter for a horse than for any sort of carriage. No words can convey an adequate idea of the state it was in. Between the deep ruts and the high wind, I cannot think how we escaped being upset. However, we arrived in safety at that lonely church in the desert.

There lies the armed figure of the Cid on his now empty tomb; and in truth the sacristan, and an old friar aged eighty-eight, who showed it to us, seemed scarcely more alive than he. They were anxious for news from the outer world; but were rather behind in foreign politics. The friar was surprised and grieved to learn that the house of Bourbon did not now reign in Naples. We, on our parts, were equally surprised to hear that the Carlists were in the Sierra, close to us, marching upon Burgos, which was to rise next day. Upon this, we reproached our guide with bringing us into danger, saying, he ought to have informed himself before coming. The reply was, " Madame, I was perfectly aware of it ; but I am a Carlist captain, and you are safe with me." How it would have been had the Carlists appeared, I don't know. Probably, we should have met with perfect politeness ; and I really believe, even without the Carlist captain, we ran no risk whatever ; but, as it was, we saw no Carlists, nor indeed any other living thing, the whole way (five miles) back to Burgos. There, too, we were much struck with the utter loneliness and silence of the streets. On asking why there was nobody visible, the answer was, " Because all the Carlists are obliged, on pain of a fine, to keep within doors." The inference was that the whole population were Carlists, which we were assured was really the case.

In the afternoon we went into the Cathedral, that gorgeous Cathedral, too rich, too sumptuous, bewildering in its variety of ornament. It is a pity that here, as almost everywhere in Spain, the choir so completely blocks up the interior that no good general view can be obtained. The plan of a Spanish cathedral is a house within a house. But the details are exquisite, especially in the chapel of the Condestable, built for Don Pedro Fernandez de Velasco, hereditary Constable of Castile.

This chapel was built in 1487, by John of Cologne, who also designed the Cartuja of Miraflores, and the west front of the Cathedral, with its delicate spires. The tombs of Don Pedro and his wife are very beautiful. Yet, after walking through all those gorgeous chapels, one leaves them with eye and mind weary rather than satisfied. Outside, however, the Cathedral is perfect, especially when seen in the early morning from the railway station.

We went also to the Casa de Ayuntamiento (Town Hall), to see the bones of the Cid and of Ximena, which are kept in a glass case. Better had they been left in his beloved San Pedro de Cardeña, in the tomb erected for them, six hundred years ago, by Alonso the Wise.

On the whole, Burgos, with all its dreary desolation, its strange, bleak loneliness, exceeded my expectations. I had been told it was quite a French-looking town, and so perhaps it may appear to those who come from quiet old Cordoba, where it is difficult to believe that Abdarrahman is dead; or from that Oriental bazaar, the Alcaiceria of Granada. To us, who had just left comfortable Pau, the very perfection of dull luxury, and bright little brisk Biarritz, the contrast was striking; and the silent streets, with their projecting miradors, seemed quite Spanish enough. It was the old story of the two travellers, one ascending, the other descending the mountain.

However, as before our departure we heard that the Carlists really arrived at San Pedro de Cardeña a few hours after we left it, I think we were rather glad to leave Burgos behind us.

CHAPTER II.

WE left Burgos at 5.30 A.M., after having the unfailing cup of chocolate, which there is never the slightest difficulty in procuring, however early the hour. In this respect Spain is much more comfortable than Italy, or France, or indeed any other country I have ever travelled in. Whether you are leaving a large hotel, with waiters on each floor, as at Madrid, or the smallest wayside Posada, without waiters at all, as at Elche, your chocolate, with a bit of excellent bread, is brought to your room half an

c

hour before you wish to start, even if it be 4 A.M., and so sustaining is this delicious chocolate that you can travel on for half the day without wishing for anything more.

How unlike the miseries of an early start in most countries, where the orders you have given the night before are never attended to till you grope your way into the *salle-à-manger*, and find all the chairs on the top of the dining-table, while a sleepy, cross waiter looks injured because you ask for a cup of coffee; which is at last brought, along with the bill full of mistakes, and the announcement that the omnibus is at the door! All this annoyance is obviated in Spain, partly by the prompt chocolate in your room, and partly by the very convenient system of paying so much a day, agreed on at the moment of entering the hotel. The sum varies much, and there are sometimes a few extras, always ascertainable beforehand. As a general rule, the higher the charge, the more extras one has to pay; if the prices are very low, there are no extras at all. At the Fonda de Paris, in Madrid (the dearest hotel we were in), we paid sixty reals a day each person, a real being about twopence-halfpenny of English money, or a quarter of a French franc; thus the price was about fifteen francs a day each, or indeed rather more, as the peseta (four reals), which answers to the French franc, is really a more valuable coin; add to which that the rate of exchange is always very much against English travellers in Spain. This sum of fifteen francs included only a very large and beautifully furnished bedroom, with windows on the Puerta del Sol; breakfast *à la four-chette*, with tea or coffee and wine, and dinner at *table d'hôte*, also with wine, which is everywhere comprised in the daily charge. In some parts of Spain you have to pay for water (that is, if you are particular, which all Spaniards are, about having it very good), for wine, never; every inn gives that at discretion; sometimes good, sometimes bad, but always abundant. Generally speaking, the wine is said to be best in out-of-the way places, where there are few travellers except the muleteers, who won't drink it unless it is good, and where there are so few English that it is not worth while to keep bad wine for them.

In Madrid, the morning chocolate (one franc each), service, and lights were extra; also tea or coffee, if taken at any time but breakfast. At Elche, where the prices were lowest of all, we paid fourteen reals a day, everything—chocolate, lights, and service, included. At Segovia, twenty reals, also everything included. The usual price, however, all over Spain, except in Madrid, is thirty reals a day; that is what one ought to offer, on entering most hotels. At the Hotel Siete Suelos, at Granada, we paid thirty-five; but there we had a very pretty little suite, consisting of two bedrooms and a sitting-room, and there were no extras, except the large marble plunge-baths; they gave us small baths in our rooms without additional charge. At Malaga, also, thirty-five was the price; but there too we had a large sitting-room. In all hotels, even when service is charged in the bill, it is necessary to give something to waiters, chamber-maids, and everybody who has or has not done any-thing for you. Also, I may remark, that in Spain, much larger gratuities are expected than in France, Germany, or Italy. Not that the Spaniards are greedy; far from it : they will often give you things for nothing; even an hotel-keeper will sometimes not charge you for some trifle, saying, "It will be for the next time." But they think it beneath the dignity of a Spaniard to accept a small sum, or to work without a large remuneration.

On the whole, the discomforts of travelling in Spain have been greatly exaggerated. In winter I should think cold must be the great evil, judging by what we suffered in that respect in May; while in all the six months of Spanish summer and autumn, we seldom found it very hot, not at all to be compared with the broiling climate of Italy. Of course, if one chooses one's residence injudiciously, and fixes oneself, say at Seville, during the dog-days, it would probably be intolerable; but so it would at Bologna, where St. Dominic, a Spaniard, who should have been accustomed to a good deal of sunshine, died of heat in the month of August. And we certainly found the summer retreats of even the south of Spain cooler than those of the north of Italy.

We had been told that starvation would be our inevitable fate, and indeed travellers whom we had seen coming out of Spain had a sufficiently haggard and hungry appearance to appal the stoutest heart Perhaps the season of the year had something to do with it, for the plentiful supply of fruit and game is a valuable addition to the commissariat, but, to our surprise, we found everywhere, without exception, an abundance of food, generally excellent, of which we were expected to eat a very great deal. A Spanish waiter thinks you don't like the food if you eat little, and is much distressed, often bringing you something else that he supposes you may prefer. This is not so much out of kindness as from a wish to uphold the honour of Spain, the burden of which every Spaniard, waiter or otherwise, believes to rest upon his own individual shoulders.

Another much-vexed question is that of Spanish politeness. We had heard the most contradictory reports, some people saying they were the politest nation in Europe, others that there never had been such a rude set of mortals since the world was created. On asking a friend who had spent many years in Spain, the reply was, "Both accounts are true." However, speaking from our own experience, I should say that, on the whole, the politeness greatly predominates. The graceful courtesy of the upper classes is unrivalled; the middle classes also, shopkeepers, etc., are extremely polite; on the other hand, the lower classes are often exceedingly rough, and sometimes even rude, while the street boys in general may fearlessly claim to be the most teasing in Europe. Their great numbers, and, in summer, completely open-air life, make them the more tormenting; but in some places even they were civil, at Cadiz, for instance. After all, we were really wonderfully little annoyed by them anywhere, but we heard of others who were less fortunate.

The Spaniards are extremely hospitable, much more so than the Italians, partly, in all probability, because there are comparatively few travellers in Spain, but also, I think, in accordance, with the national character. On presenting our letters of in-

troduction some piece of civility immediately followed,
an invitation to dinner, a box at the opera, a ticket of
admission to some object of interest, permission to see
some private palace not usually shown; in short, it
never seemed to occur to a Spaniard not to do something to make a stranger's sojourn agreeable. Their
ideas of hospitality are pushed so far that it is sometimes difficult to prevent a Spanish lady who chances
to be one's fellow-passenger in a railway carriage from
paying for chocolate or any refreshment one may have
taken at a station; they seem to think it quite shock-
ing to let strangers pay when travelling through their
country.

But all this we learnt afterwards. On our way
from Burgos to Valladolid, Spain was as yet an unknown country, and certainly not, for the moment, a
very beautiful one. No object of any interest did we
pass, and exceedingly bleak it was till we drew near
Valladolid, when a few trees in their first freshness
enlivened the scene a little.

At Valladolid we arrived between nine and ten A.M.
The omnibus was rather cleaner than at Burgos,
and there was even some attempt at beautifying it.
My eye was attracted by a sort of glittering star,
dark blue and gold, on the roof. On examination, it
turned out to be the trade-mark of a bale of Man-

chester goods (with the number of yards of muslin stated round the edge) stuck on by way of ornament, in the centre of the omnibus roof.

We had intended to go to the Fonda del Norte; but as it was shut up, we repaired to the Fonda del Siglo, which we found very clean and comfortable. After breakfast we went out to see the town, which is much more lively than Burgos, in spite of its horrible celebrity for burning heretics under Philip the Second.

The Cathedral, planned by that gloomy monarch, is the image of his own disposition—cold, grey, stern, yet not without a sort of icy grandeur. But one of the most beautiful things in Valladolid is San Pablo, built by the terrible Torquemada. Buildings generally bear some impress of the character of their founders. This is certainly an exception to the rule, unless Torquemada was very unlike what the facts we know concerning him would lead us to believe. However, the rich façade, with twining foliage encircling statues and armorial bearings, is said to be of later date. Adjoining it is the Colegio of San Gregorio, even more beautiful, also with its exquisite façade and portal branching out into a tree. The court inside, with the curious staircase, is probably the finest thing of the kind in existence. It is in that peculiar style of very rich ornamentation which prevailed in Spain in Ferdinand and Isabella's time, and was a sort of compromise between Moorish and Gothic. In the reign of Charles the Fifth the German element predominated, and with Philip the Second came the frozen semi-classical architecture so cherished by him. Our guide said that this Colegio of San Gregorio was now the governor's house.

We then went along a silent sunny street (here for the first time in Spain we saw that luminary), and knocked at the door of a small, deserted-looking house. We were admitted into a quiet court, surrounded by low, quaint, picturesque buildings, with wooden balconies full of flowers. Then we were conducted by an old woman through part of this tumble-down house, across a small garden full of weeds ; a door was opened, and we found ourselves in a stately church, where the forms of saints and angels stood in strange life-like beauty, beside the rich altars ; and beneath one of the richest lay the dead figure of our Saviour, so touching in its weary stillness that one could scarce look at it save through tears. This was the Church of the Jesuits, San Miguel.

Of course, we went to see where Columbus died. Strange that his bones should rest far off, in distant Cuba ! Somehow, one wishes it had been rather at

Cogoletto, where his boyhood was spent by the fresh seashore.

Our time was too short to see all the historical houses and sites of this city. Few towns are as rich in interesting associations: Cervantes, Calderon, Gondomar, Alvaro de Luna, Berreguete, Juan de Juni, Hernandez, all those names are connected in life or in death with Valladolid; not to mention Philip the Second, who was born there.

But we went to the Museum, where we saw (besides the most wretchedly bad pictures I have ever beheld) a great number of carved and painted wooden statues, from desecrated or ruined churches; being, many of them, the figures composing the *Pasos*, or representations of the Passion, which are, or were, brought out in Spain during the Holy Week. Some of them are said to be of great merit; and, if seen when properly placed and arranged, possibly they might appear to more advantage. As it was, nothing could be more grotesque; angels, Roman soldiers, disciples, and the Maries, all higgledy-piggledy, and combined in a manner that was ludicrous in the extreme. Add to which, being of colossal size and quite close to the beholder, the effect, when not ludicrous, was terrific. With all allowances, I do not think that any of the wooden figures in the

Museum could ever be so beautiful as those in San Miguel.

The Plaza Mayor, where the first *auto de fe* was held, is now very bright and rather picturesque. The trees were fresh and green, and there was a market going on, with peasant-women in bright yellow and red petticoats. This was the first indication of costume we had seen. About Burgos, the men were dressed either like shabby gentlemen, or like Irish beggars; and I do not remember seeing any woman at all.

Next morning we left Valladolid at 9.30 A.M. Much has been said of the ugliness of the country round; and, in truth, great part of the way had little beauty to recommend it. About Medina del Campo, it was especially bleak, and we could not but be sorry for Isabella the Catholic, and Joanna the mad, and Cæsar Borgia, and everybody else who had the misfortune either to live or to die in such a dismal place. As to poor Joanna, it was not to be wondered at if she tried to escape from this dreary abode, even if she had not had the additional inducement of wishing to rejoin her much-loved and ungrateful husband; nor was it any proof of insanity that she did so. Certainly, however, a long residence in this most depressing " City of the Plain " (as its name signifies in a mixture of Spanish and Arabic) was enough to make anybody low spirited, if not positively crazy.

After we passed Medina del Campo, the scenery improved. We came to refreshing clumps of stone-pines; and presently to rugged, broken ground, ending in a perfect wilderness of huge boulders of every form. We were in the midst of a high table-land, and the view was most extraordinary. We looked down on the Sierra, tinged by the varying sunbeams with every shade of pale yellow and vivid light green; while the flitting clouds threw azure and purple shadows, changing every moment; and in the distance stretched away, away an illimitable depth of blue ether. It was like some of Breughel's wondrous aerial pictures; with the addition of that strange chaos of granite in the foreground. It seemed as if earth were unfinished, without inhabitants or any life; and only air and heaven perfect. Apparently we were hundreds of miles from any town, so utterly wild was it; when all at once, almost close to us, against the sky, rose Avila, many-towered Avila. Never was there a grander position; the Apennine cities shrink into nothing in comparison. It is said to have eighty-six towers and ten gateways. I did not count them, but certainly they formed a " diadem of towers," much more perfect than that of Cortona.

The granite walls are said to be forty feet high, and twelve feet thick; and indeed they look massive enough for anything.

We arrived at Avila about three o'clock, and proceeded to the little inn of the "Dos de Mayo," which did not at first look very promising, the entrance being full of whitewashers. However, we were shown a very clean and comfortable room, arranged in the Spanish fashion, which we now saw for the first time. As the beds were placed each in a separate alcove, which could be closed with glass doors, the room by day became a sitting-room. This is convenient in some respects; but in very hot weather, though the alcove is generally tolerably cool from the darkness and the absence of outside wall, there is less circulation of air, even when the doors are open, than English people like. I used also to suspect the dark corners of sometimes harbouring more and larger spiders and centipedes than could have been desired. This kind of bedroom is, however, by no means universal; in most places one can have it otherwise if one likes; and we never saw it at all in Andalusia. Here all was dazzlingly clean whitewash, above the faintest suspicion of insect life; while the weather was so cold that we were not inclined to quarrel with the snug alcoves.

The landlady made her appearance, and, as we were extremely hungry, I was just endeavouring to muster up Spanish enough to beg that some food might be brought quickly (I had unluckily forgotten the Spanish for " immediately "), when the delightful sounds greeted my ear, " Would you like a *homelette*, ma'am, or shall I send you up some 'am and heggs ? " Never had I heard the English language more agreeably spoken, and soon both dainties smoked on the table.

Our host and hostess were worthy English people, who do all in their power to make travellers comfortable, and succeed admirably. The landlord, John Smith by name, and as complete a John Bull as if he had never left England, was always called Don Juan, and was evidently greatly esteemed and much liked by high and low. He had been employed in making the railway, and afterwards settled at Avila, where his hotel is indeed a boon to English travellers, he himself kindly acting as guide, without making any charge for so doing. We found him extremely well-informed, much more so than Spanish guides usually are.

It had now begun to rain so heavily that we gave up thoughts of going round the town that day, and ran across the Plaza into the Cathedral. Never shall

I forget that sight ! I held my breath for very awe. Grey and dim, with nothing distinctly visible but the glorious, gem-like windows, all dark rich crimson, blue, and orange, giving an impression of colour, glowing colour, *without light ;* it was to me far grander, because simpler, than Burgos. Of course, in saying this I speak only of the interior ; outside, there can be no comparison. Yet even the exterior of the Cathedral of Avila is interesting, being half fortress, half church ; it is plain, at least for a Spanish cathedral, they being usually very richly and lavishly decorated ; and its severe early character is striking. It was founded a hundred and thirty years before that of Burgos, and about a hundred and thirty-four before the present Cathedral of Toledo. In fact, it is one of the oldest in Spain, coming, I think, next to Barcelona, Tarragona, and Santiago, as to date. It is dedicated to the Saviour, whereas most of the Spanish cathedrals are in honour of the Virgin Mary.

It is not very large, but its great height, its twilight gloom, and the forest of columns round and behind the High Altar, give an idea of greater size than it really has. It is also much less blocked up by the choir than is usual in Spain. The walls are very dark grey, and those marvellous windows, reaching far up to the very roof, seem to give, rather than admit, what little light there is. Even if we could have seen the details, I could not have examined them then. We sat down, and vespers began ; a few black-veiled, black-robed figures came in, and crouched low on the floor in prayer. Spanish women always either kneel, or sit on their heels, in church ; they never venture to place themselves on a chair or bench as the men do. Also, in the churches they always wear the black veil, and generally a black or very dark dress ; black being thought in best taste ; and it is well for strangers to do the same, as they thus escape observation.

By the time vespers were over, it was so dark that we had almost to grope our way out of the church. The rain had now ceased, so we walked round the outside, and particularly admired the very peculiar battlements encircling the cloisters. Then we went back to the comfortable little inn to dine and rest.

Our landlady came up ostensibly to see if we had everything we wanted, which we certainly had ; but really to have the pleasure of a chat with English people. She told us that our room had been occupied for a day the year before by the Empress Eugénie, and was full of praises of her kindness, simple ways, and great desire to avoid giving trouble. The little chamber-maid who waited on us, and who was deeply marked with smallpox, said that she had then scarcely recovered from that horrible malady, and that the Empress, so far from shrinking from the frightfully sore and disfigured face, patted her kindly on the shoulder, and said, " Poor thing ! you have indeed suffered much."

Next morning the weather was better, though still showery ; and I rose early to sketch the façade of the Cathedral. Finding that I could not see it all from the window, I hastily tied a black handkerchief over my head, and rushed down into the Plaza, in spite of H.'s assurances that I should certainly be mobbed : firstly, for being such a very extraordinary figure ; and secondly, for drawing at all. Far from it ; the extreme propriety of my appearance, with my head tied up in the black handkerchief, completely neutralized the oddity of sketching, and I was left in peace. Had I gone down in an English hat or a French bonnet, the result would probably have been very different and much less agreeable. I mention this for the benefit of all lady sketchers in Spain.

After chocolate, we started with our friendly host, Don Juan, to see Avila. Most of the churches are outside the town, and the walk round the walls is delightful.

We first went to San Tomas, to see the exquisite

marble tomb of the only son of Ferdinand and Isabella, Prince Juan; who died, aged nineteen, at Salamanca, in 1497, a few months after his marriage. Nothing can be more lovely than the calm, white figure, so touching in its perfect repose. All around is deserted; the court and cloisters grass-grown, the garden full of weeds, with a few sweet-smelling herbs.

Strange, that none of Isabella's children should have had both prosperity and length of days! This prince was perhaps the happiest, dying in all the brightness of youth, having probably never known a sorrow. His eldest sister, Isabel, Queen of Portugal, died also young, of consumption; and her only son, Prince Miguel, heir of Spain and Portugal, was thrown from his pony in the streets of Granada, and killed at seven years old. Poor Joanna's fate is well known; her life was long, but sorrowful indeed; and Katherine, the youngest, the divorced wife of our Henry the Eighth, was scarcely more fortunate, though happier in her own natural disposition.

And Isabella herself—one of the best of Queens and of women, beautiful, talented, and good, a most devoted and affectionate wife, who, even on her death-bed, was more anxious about her husband, then also ill of fever, than about herself—was soon forgotten for the young and giddy Germaine de Foix, Ferdinand's second

Queen, whom, report says, he loved far better than he did the perhaps too perfect Isabella.

But there was the one black spot in her reign, for which neither she nor Ferdinand were wholly nor even greatly responsible. Yet, had she been a less scrupulously conscientious woman, it may have been that much evil would have been spared ; much misery, much bloodshed, much burning of heretics. It is one of those perplexing cases in which one is obliged, unwillingly, to admit that good intentions may be as mischievous as bad ones, if not more so.

Even this church of San Tomas, the quiet resting-place of that calm figure and sweet, still face, was built with money wrung from the oppressed and tortured Jews. In the floor of the church is one black stone, said to be the grave of Torquemada. The common people quite impute its blackness to its covering the bones of the terrible Inquisitor. However, at Toledo, they showed us another tomb of Torquemada ; probably only his empty monument, as it seems likely he should be buried in San Tomas, his name also being Thomas.

The view from the door of the church is very striking. A tall, dark grey cross stands up against the sky ; great masses of granite lie around ; and in the distance the Sierra, all dark blue, and purple, and pale yellow, as the sunbeams come and go.

Next we went to San Segundo, where, just under the walls, is another of those grey crosses, marking the spot where the saint once threw over a Moor, and, some years afterwards, was thrown over himself. Three other crosses stand in front of the church, and we sat on a stone at the foot of one of them, looking at the wide, varying landscape, and waiting for the *guardiano*, who soon appeared with the keys. Inside, the chief object of interest is the kneeling statue of the saint; it is very beautiful, and reminded us much of that of Pius the Sixth, by Canova, in the Confession of St. Peter's at Rome.

Then we went, still following the line of the walls, to San Vicente, with its roofless but still most beautiful and peculiar propylæum, and its subterranean church celebrated for possessing a great treasure : namely, a serpent that generally bites anybody who puts his fingers into a certain hole. We did not try the experiment, so can give no opinion as to the truth of this. But we greatly admired the extreme beauty of the church ; and still more, the lovely view from its entrance. The walls and towers of the town are also particularly fine at this point.

Now we plunged into the streets, in quest of those

very remarkable granite beasts, called bulls, but not greatly resembling any specimen of that quadruped I have ever seen. Some people call them pigs; but there too the likeness is not striking. One that we saw was not unlike a hippopotamus; the smaller ones had perhaps some resemblance to misshapen pigs. They now stand in the courtyard of one of the venerable old houses that abound in Avila.

There has been much dispute as to what these extraordinary creatures really are, and by whom they were made. Some authors consider them to have been in commemoration of Julius Cæsar's victories; but they certainly do not resemble any Roman work of that epoch, or indeed of any other date whatever. Even the bronze Wolf of the Capitol has quite a modern air in comparison. It seems impossible that at a time when Rome already possessed the masterpieces of Greek art, Cæsar could have considered it complimentary to have such uncouth monuments erected in his honour; nor does one see why they should have been in the form of those so-called bulls.

Another view of the case is that they were idols of the ancient inhabitants; and it must be allowed they look old and queer enough for anything. If it be so, the Spanish aborigenes had very rudimentary ideas concerning sculpture. How unlike the mild, beautiful

Athor, the Egyptian Goddess, the Golden Calf, whom one could scarcely wonder that the Israelites worshipped!

Our guide said that the common opinion among the natives was that they had been made in the Middle Ages, and fastened to the doors of those citizens who refused to pay the taxes. It is quite possible that they were so used, though not made for the purpose. However that may be, almost every door in Spain would be thus ornamented at the present day, if this mediæval system were fully carried out. And in Italy also, the same breed of bulls might be introduced with advantage.

We passed through the market-place, where there were most picturesque groups of peasant women in the bright yellow petticoats universal in that part of Spain; even children and quite small babies were attired in the same intensely brilliant hue. The men wore excessively tight black or brown velvet breeches, with dangling silver buttons, extremely shortwaisted jackets, and red sashes. On their heads they had very large, broad, black velvet hats, with a curious point in the middle—genuine *sombreros*—that must have been excellent sunshades. Everybody was either riding on a donkey or driving one before him. It was not a handsome population; the human beings,

I mean; the donkeys were beautiful. The men were all more or less in the style of Don Quixote, with long legs and arms, and dry, hatchet faces; the women burnt almost black, and withered even when young. But they looked good and respectable; and all were politeness itself. Don Juan seemed to know everybody, and was greeted with respect and liking wherever he went.

In the afternoon we returned to the cathedral, to examine it in detail. Behind the choir are most beautiful reliefs in marble and alabaster. The four Evangelists are quaintly treated; they are writing, each with his ink-bottle differently placed; the eagle holds it in his beak for St. John, the lion has it in his paw for St. Mark, while St. Luke had hung his on the horn of the ox, which arrangement, we thought, looked the best of all. We also went into the deserted, grass-grown cloisters, most beautiful in their lonely decay.

Next day we again went out under the same guidance, and saw many fine old houses, with rich gateways and façades, and pillared courts or *palios*. Avila is one of the most perfectly Spanish towns in Spain, being totally unchanged since the middle ages, and quite free from all foreign influences, Moorish or modern. The old house of the Counts of Polentino is one of the finest, the gateway being very richly decorated.

After our luncheon-breakfast, we took leave, with much regret, of our kind host and hostess, and of the walls and towers of lordly Avila.

CHAPTER III.

The journey from Avila to Madrid is most beautiful;
over, through, and sometimes under the Guadarrama
range of mountains, there being forty-four tunnels.
As we were passing through one of them the train
slackened speed, and then stopped in utter darkness.
We sat quietly and contentedly, never dreaming of
danger, and merely supposing it to be the habit of
Spanish trains to stop suddenly in the middle of
tunnels, without apparent cause. But most of our
fellow-passengers became nearly wild; the men opened
the carriage-doors, and jumped out, shrieking and
gesticulating; a lady in the same compartment with

us scolded her husband vehemently, as if it had been his fault, and exclaimed that she was "suffocating; why had she come in the train? she should die; she must have water; she must be bled!" Water, happily, was forthcoming; but, luckily for us, neither doctor, barber, nor lancets were at hand, so we escaped the sight of the last-named operation. Certainly, she looked very uncomfortable; her face was purple and swollen, but, I think, only from fear; there was really no want of air, for, as it turned out, we were not far from the mouth of the tunnel. Indeed, I don't think she even fancied there was no air, or cared about having any; but terror seemed to have produced a kind of incipient apoplexy.

We looked out to see if anything was really the matter. Everybody was running, shouting, swearing; and the scene looked positively demoniacal in the red torchlight. Nobody answered my questions; and, at last, a Spanish gentleman in the same carriage, who had been looking rather amused at the confusion, and whose coolness contrasted favourably with the prevailing excitement, offered to go and inquire. He came back saying that there was an obstruction at the mouth of the tunnel, but whether purposely put there or not nobody knew. There was no danger, but we must wait.

After a long delay we moved slowly on, and then we could see that large stones and rubbish had been lying at the mouth of the tunnel; but whether they had been put there to cause an accident, or had only fallen from the top in consequence of the late heavy rain, we never could learn. Most probably it was the latter, for this part of the country was comparatively quiet. Had it happened near Burgos, there might have been reason to suspect it of being the work of the Carlists, who very frequently put obstructions on the railway, always, however, signalling the train to stop, for fear of loss of life.

With the exception of this incident, our journey was delighful. The lonely hills were entirely covered with a carpet of wildflowers. Thickets of cistus, not only the little shrub with small blossoms that one sees on the Corniche road, but also the great old-fashioned gum-cistus, with larger flowers than I have ever seen in English gardens; tall purple lavender, golden broom, and splendid clusters of a pink flower that was new to me, and which I should have much liked to examine, clothed the slopes for miles and miles. Then we got to the top, and looked down on the vast blue plain of Madrid. And presently we saw below us a great building, of which there was no need to ask the name, so well does one know it by

drawing and description. It was like what I expected; so like, that I felt as if I had seen it every day
of my life; yet unlike, too, for with all its grand
solitude, its cold severe Spanish aspect, the Escorial
looked, on that bright May afternoon, rather a cheerful place than otherwise. The trees surrounding it
were dazzlingly green; the pure, bracing air swept
across the flower-clothed hills, laden with the sweet
perfume of lavender and other aromatic herbs; and
over all was the golden sunlight. What it may be
on a wet winter day, I don't know nor even much like
to imagine; certainly, I shall never endeavour to find
out by personal experience. As it was, it was delightful, and, as I before said, decidedly exhilarating
to the spirits. We a little regretted not having
arranged to stop there before going on to Madrid;
but, as letters awaited us in the latter place, we had
decided rather to make a separate and luggageless
excursion to Segovia, La Granja, and the Escorial.
Thus, about 8.30 P.M., we were comfortably settled in
the Hotel de Paris, in the gay and brilliant Puerta del
Sol.

Our first impression of Madrid next morning was,
indeed, very brilliant, very gay. No traveller should
ever be beguiled, under any pretext whatever, into
establishing him or herself elsewhere than in that

world-famous Puerta del Sol. Other hotels may possibly be better than the Hotel de Paris; many, if not most, are, in all human probability, cheaper; they could not well be dearer. But it is worth it all—worth the extortionate prices, the scanty civility of the waiters, the enormous cheating of the Greek porter, who speaks every European and Eastern language, and the truth in none; in spite of the incessant noise that keeps you awake all night, and the roasting sun that attacks you the moment you cross the threshold, yet go to the Hotel de Paris if you wish to be amused and to enjoy Madrid. The Hotel des Princes is also in the Puerta del Sol; the prices are about the same, and it is said to be rather quieter, and perhaps better in some respects; but the position is scarcely so fine. Of course, it is necessary to have windows to the front; the rooms on the side streets, though also cheerful, have not the *coup d'œil;* and, as the court is occupied by the café of the hotel, the rooms that look in that direction are unendurable from noise and heat, besides having no view whatever. We had three windows commanding the whole of the Puerta del Sol; and so lively was it, that we could have been very well amused all day if we had never gone out at all.

We had been told that Madrid was thoroughly

modernised, that it was quite a French town in fact; we were, therefore, agreeably surprised to find how unmistakably Spanish it is still. If one were dropped from a balloon in the midst of Madrid, it would be quite impossible to suppose oneself to be in France, or in any country except Spain. Modern, of course, it is; for Madrid is not an ancient city, nor indeed a city at all, properly speaking. Yet it is not all absolutely of yesterday: the Plaza Mayor, more than two centuries and a half old, has its historical associations; most of them of rather a bloody character, to be sure. Executions, *autos de fe*, bullfights, those are the memories of the Plaza Mayor; the most interesting, to English people, of the last named, being the one given in honour of the royal knight-errant and Prince, Charles the First of England when on his romantic journey in quest of a wife. When the marriage was broken off, the Spanish Princess said, "If he had loved me he would never have left me." Very likely she was right; for he, with the well-known preference of the Stuarts for dark beauty, and his head probably full of ideas of the black eyes and raven locks of Spain, must have been woefully disappointed when he saw the vacant Flemish face, light, unmeaning eyes, and fair hair of this, in reality, Austrian princess; the "very comely lady," so much admired in Spain,

where they do not seem to have disliked the projecting under lip inherited from her ancestress, Margaret
Maultasch, Princess of Tyrol. It may well have been
also that he, a Protestant, did not much care about
having Philip the Fourth for a brother-in-law; nor
can one see how Philip could have consented to
give his sister to a heretic, whom, indeed, it
would have been much more agreeable and meritorious to have burnt in that very Plaza. This
question of religion was the real obstacle to the
match; but Charles, who, a true Stuart, had no great
liking for the trammels of kingly etiquette, must
have been fearfully bored with the dull regulations of
the Spanish Court. It is related that when he wished
to talk French with the Queen, sister-in-law of the
young princess he had come to woo (and sister, by the
way, of his future wife), she said she would ask permission to do so, otherwise it was contrary to rule!
And afterwards he was warned that if he persisted in
speaking to the Queen, his life would not be safe!
No wonder he preferred marrying the beautiful and
accomplished Henrietta Maria.

This Plaza Mayor strongly resembles the old Place
Royale in Paris, of the time of Henri Quatre; having
been built in 1619, probably under the influence of
Queen Isabel, Henry's daughter.

Everywhere in Madrid, even in the most modern parts, one sees Spanish costume; it being by no means true that French fashions are universally adopted. Black is certainly no longer necessarily worn, except in Lent, or early in the morning, to go to church; but the veil is commoner than the bonnet for all ranks. Young ladies sometimes wear fashionable hats; but more among the bourgeoisie than the upper classes. The veil is almost universally worn by old ladies; by very old ones, the ancient mantilla, which is no longer in use among the younger women. Generally speaking, it is considered in best taste, if on foot, to wear the veil or a black lace bonnet somewhat resembling it; in a carriage, fashionable and very gay French bonnets are often seen; but quite as often the veil with a bright carnation or a rose in the hair. This we thought much the prettiest. Foreigners are, however, not expected to follow the Spanish fashion in Madrid, except at the theatre, where the black veil is quite necessary, unless one has a private box.

We were told that, at the time we were in Madrid, all the old national costume—the veil, the high comb, and the flower in the hair—had been more adopted than usual by fashionable people; and that it was a protest against the Italian dynasty, so universally detested. Be this as it may, we saw far more of it in Madrid than we did in Granada, where French fashions prevailed to a lamentable extent.

In the Prado, even handsome carriages were often drawn by mules, fine velvet-coated animals. Long strings of mules are also constantly seen passing through the Puerta del Sol and the adjacent streets, driven by men in the costume of the district to which they belong, all which gives a much more peculiar and Spanish character to the town than we had been led to expect.

We had heard, too, that there were no trees in or about Madrid. It is not in the midst of a forest, certainly, like Baden-Baden; but neither is it in a barren wilderness. It is true that south of Madrid, after Aranjuez is passed, is a bare and absolutely treeless plain, which reaches to the frontiers of Andalusia, so that to those arriving from the south, especially from Granada, it must have rather a bleak appearance. But Madrid itself is completely encircled, outside the walls, by a sort of boulevard, shaded by trees; at many points this boulevard expands into a net-work of public walks, the Paseo de la Florida, Paseo de la Virgen del Puerto, Paseo de Atocha—all those are shaded by tall trees, which in May are in the freshest and greenest leaf; so that as we approached from the north it seemed quite surrounded with foliage. Of course, in winter there is none of this; but it is not only in Spain that deciduous trees lose their leaves in winter.

The Prado, in May, is very pretty. Again, in contradiction to most travellers, I must say that it is green, exceedingly green, with plenty of shade, many flowers, especially roses, and *no dust*. In fact, the Prado, the Puerto del Sol, and the principal streets, are almost too much watered; in the Prado, mud is the evil to be dreaded, even in the driest weather; and the inhabitants say that fever, which never formerly existed in Madrid, now prevails and increases, owing to the damp thus produced. We never saw dust at all within the walls; outside there certainly is a good deal, but it generally lay quietly on the road and did not blow about much.

Another surprising thing was, that there really was some water in the Manzanares. This was probably in consequence of April and May having been unusually rainy.

As to the climate, it is the one drawback to an otherwise very pleasant place; but so fearful is it that it is an all-sufficient objection to Madrid as a residence. I use the expression *fearful* advisedly, as of a thing really to inspire fear. It is not that it is

very disagreeable—at least, we did not find it so—
but it is exceedingly dangerous. What it is, and
why it is so, no one knows; some people say it is
because it is changeable, but during our stay there
was but the one change, from winter to summer,
which took place very suddenly indeed. Before that,
it was steadily cold; afterwards, steadily hot. Others
say it is the difference between sun and shade, but
we did not find that greater than in most parts of
Italy. The air feels pure and clear; there are no
evil odours; in all the latter half of May and beginning of June there was no wind; a light might
have been burnt in the street without flickering: yet
this subtle air, which, as the Spanish proverb truly
says, kills a man and can't put out a candle, is perhaps the deadliest in Europe. It is not at all depressing though; very much the contrary: when you
are so ill that you can't move, nor even raise your
head, you feel quite cheerful, and think it an exceedingly nice place. Perhaps this was the reason the
gloomy Spanish sovereigns liked it so much.

With all its disadvantages of climate, we found
Madrid a most agreeable sojourn, owing, in a great
measure, to the very great kindness and courtesy of
those Spanish families to whom we had letters.
Nowhere is society pleasanter than in this little

capital. Once properly introduced, there is no stiff-ness; all is the frankest cordiality, the kindliest hos-pitality, and it must be allowed that the Spanish ladies have a grace and charm quite peculiar.

The houses of the upper classes in Madrid are very much more comfortable than Italian dwellings gene-rally are; in cold or even chilly weather a bright fire blazes on the hearth, and there is a look of occu-pation that is quite English. Books in abundance, drawings, music: I do not think sketching is much cultivated among them, but the ladies frequently copy the paintings of the old masters very well indeed. One lady, whom we knew, had her whole drawing-room hung round with the copies she had made, in oil, of the paintings in the Museum.

Almost all spoke English; most of them extremely well, often better than they spoke French. In some families the children's governess had been English, and English ways seemed to prevail to a greater extent than among the Romans or Florentines. We were much surprised when paying a visit a few miles out of Madrid to be offered a cup of tea. However, I do not think this was usual, but done solely out of com-pliment to our insular prejudices. When we refused the tea, wine was next offered, and when that too was declined, azucarillos (a sort of very light, sugary, foam-like substance, flavoured with lemon), and deliciously cold water appeared instead; a much more Spanish refection. This was served in the garden under the shade of tall trees, and surrounded with roses, the most beautiful of which were gathered for us in handfuls, while our kind hostess, the Countess M., repeated, "Take all the prettiest; take as many as you like." In the meantime our carriage was sent away, and we were detained to dine and spend the evening.

If you admire a flower, it is always given you. Even when out at dinner the finest roses were pulled out of the bouquets on the table and given to us; and on one occasion the entire bouquets were sent down and put into the carriage when we were going away.

It has been said that Spanish civilities are merely verbal, that it is not intended one should avail oneself of them. Of course, some are forms of politeness in the same way as in English one signs oneself " truly yours " to people one does not care a straw about, or perhaps even dislikes. For instance, the Spanish expression, " This house is your own," is of this kind; you do not proceed to act upon it. Also, when a peasant asks you to share his breakfast of bread and grapes, or if the conductor of the diligence

offers you a piece of raw sausage before he begins to
eat it himself, it is not supposed you will accept it.
In other respects, it is in Spain as elsewhere; when
people invite you to their house, they expect you to
come, and are sorry if from any cause you cannot accept their attentions; and they would be especially
vexed if you refused to eat and drink what is offered
you.　This latter is a remnant of Orientalism.

Even without society, however, Madrid would possess quite sufficient interest.　The great attraction is,
of course, the Picture Gallery.　It is not only one of
the finest, but one of the pleasantest in the world;
never too hot nor too cold while we were there; exquisitely clean, well lighted, and well arranged, with
most civil officials, who are always ready to give
information, and, moreover, never object to one's
making little sketches of any picture, though without
special permission, provided that it is done on a small
book or bit of paper, so as not to take up room or
annoy others.　There is also here the great advantage
of plenty of comfortable seats, always placed exactly
where one would wish; not chairs, but benches, so
that a party may sit together, and not be scattered all
about, as in the otherwise perfect Pitti Gallery at
Florence, where one may often look in vain for
a seat of any kind.　The only thing wanting is a

good catalogue, which possibly may now be ready, as one was then, and had been for some time, in preparation. The old one was tolerably correct, but as only two copies existed, was limited in its usefulness; those were lent by the door-keeper to anybody whom he thought likely to give him half a franc for so doing. It did not include all the pictures in the collection, and one of the copies had lost a good many of its leaves; still, it did pretty well, and the officials generally could supply the deficient information.

The first visit to the gallery is indeed a thing to be remembered, ranking with the first time one sees the Vatican, the Pitti, or the Louvre. In one respect, it is superior to any collection in the world; namely, in portraits. Velasquez is the king of portrait-painters: none excel and few equal him; not Vandyke, not Rubens, scarcely even Titian himself. In equestrian portraits especially, he is quite unapproachable; and it is only in Madrid that he can be properly appreciated. Our favourite of all was the portrait of little Prince Balthasar Carlos on his Guadarrama pony. In this wonderful picture, you can *see* the wind, and the rapid motion of the little steed, while the child's scarf flies out in the air, as he seems to dash away with a tiny gesture of right royal command, well befitting the son of the best horseman in Spain, as Philip the Fourth was said to be. The landscape is a sketch from nature of the Guadarrama, behind the Escorial; and its cold blues and greens contrast admirably with the rich, dark, warm brown of the pony, and the fair face of the child. Poor little fellow! he died of smallpox in early youth.

On showing a photograph of this picture to one of the oldest and most eminent of the Roman portrait-painters, he gazed at it in silence for a while, with his aged countenance positively radiant, then exclaimed, flinging his arms into the air, "Away he goes!" And really, as Murray well remarks, he seems to be galloping out of the frame.

In another admirable picture, the same boy is standing, with a gun in his hand, under a tree; the Guadarrama landscape behind, a splendid large dog at his feet, and another, that we used to call "the half-dog," with only its sharp nose and stiff fore paws appearing at the edge of the canvas.

But the dogs of Velasquez are many and beautiful; finest of all, perhaps, the great, powerful, good-natured creature, who is allowing the dwarfs to tease him in 'Las Meninas,' and who looks so very much more intellectual than either the dwarfs or the

Infanta. That of the Archduke Ferdinand is also charming.

Of the series of likenesses of Philip the Fourth himself, it is nearly superfluous to speak, so well are they known. First, one sees him young and almost handsome, with his calm, rather aristocratic bearing: if only he could have looked a little brighter; but that was the difficulty. In middle life, he looks cold, and much more vacant. Then the face grew colder and colder, and duller and duller to the last. The finest of all his portraits is the world-famous equestrian one. That of Queen Isabel, his first wife (the lady who was not allowed to speak French with our Charles the First), is very beautiful.

Two other fine pictures, by Velasquez, are the Surrender of Breda, and Olivares on horseback. Those are the kind of subjects in which he most excelled; the representation of all that is brave and gallant, and royal and courtly. His religious pictures are generally less satisfactory; always excepting the wondrous crucifixion, so grand in its mysterious darkness and hidden face.

From Velasquez one passes naturally to Murillo. He too must be studied in Madrid, or, at least in Spain, to be really understood. Elsewhere, one thinks of him chiefly as the very clever and realistic painter of exceedingly dirty beggar boys, employed, at the best, in eating melons. With the exception of the two splendid pictures in the Louvre, even his Madonnas, out of Spain, are of the earth earthy; she is usually but a dark-eyed peasant woman, with a very fine baby on her lap. But here, I felt as if I had for the first time seen his works. Never did I look upon so ethereally, spiritually lovely a face as one of those in this gallery; those liquid, child-like eyes haunt one with their strange, rapt expression. It is a picture that one places in one's memory beside the Madonna di San Sisto and the Madonna della Seggiola; yet it is very different from both. In the Dresden picture, the Virgin still wears the memory of unfathomable sorrow; in that of Florence, she is the sweet, happy, human mother of a Divine Babe: while in this of Murillo, she is the wondering child-woman, scarcely understanding what is in store for her. She does indeed look not merely pure and innocent, as Raphael and Perugino have so often depicted her, but absolutely and wholly sinless, as the Spaniards have always said she was.

Another exquisite picture by Murillo, is the Infant Saviour, giving the little St. John water to drink out of a shell, with the lamb looking up with a most touching expression of love and reverence. Surely

Murillo painted lambs as never any other artist did! They are as superior to those in the paintings of the Italian school, as the veritable Spanish sheep is to the long-legged, long-nosed, drooping-eared animal whose type may be seen at the present day anywhere between Lombardy and Rome. The perfection of the model may, in a great measure, account for the wonderful beauty of Murillo's lambs; yet he gives them an absolutely human and intelligent look, to which even the Spanish sheep does not attain.

Of other Spanish artists the paintings of Juan de Juanes pleased us most. He has been called the Raphael of Spain; and, in truth, his style combines much both of the Florentine and Venetian schools. The drawing is Florentine; the colouring, Venetian: but the composition, the grouping, remind one more of Albert Dürer and the Van Eycks. Two of Juanes' pictures we especially admired; the Ecce Homo and the Christ bearing his Cross.

There are plenty of terrible Spagnolettos, but the only one I should care to see again is Jacob's Ladder. Jacob is but a Spanish peasant, and a very ugly one too; the same coarse, brutal face that served as a model for many of Spagnoletto's saints: yet there is something about it that rivets the eye; and the expression of sleep and weariness is perfect.

There are also some of Zurbaran's white-robed Carthusians, painted as he, and he only, could; his masterpieces, however, are not here, but at Seville.

We admired Coello's portrait of Isabella, Philip the Second's favourite child; she is very beautiful and graceful, with an expression of much intellect and refinement. The rich and most becoming costume is admirably painted. The portrait of her half-brother, Don Carlos, by the same artist is also interesting.

So completely were we occupied with the Spanish school, that we almost forgot to look for the Raphaels, till, at the further end of the circular saloon, we saw an Enthroned Madonna, with the calm, sweet face and simple majesty, so unmistakably Italian. There was no need to look in the catalogue: it was one of Raphael's masterpieces, the Madonna del Pesce; so called from the fish that Tobias holds in his hand. Critics have said that this picture is too yellow in colour; to me it seemed all bathed in a golden glory, and quite faultless.

Then we went in search of the " Pearl;" and when we found it, were wofully disappointed. The photographs and engravings of this picture are very beautiful, because of the fine composition and correct drawing; but alas! for the colour. It has been so sadly over-cleaned and re-painted

by bungling hands that I am sure Raphael would
be greatly astonished and not at all pleased, could
he rise from the dead and look at it. The shadows
are black, and the light spotty, and all harmony
is destroyed. We were at first rather disappointed
also in the "Spasimo;" it has often been compared
with the Transfiguration, and is in the same style,
and with the same fault of want of concentration
of the light. It has, moreover, too many figures
for the size of the picture, which causes a tendency
to confusion and spottiness. It seemed to us that
it also had been over-cleaned and re-painted.
Yet on a second view one finds out its beauties;
the figure of the Christ is very fine.

From Raphael we turned next to Titian. What
a splendid array is here! First, the magnificent
equestrian portrait of Charles the Fifth; and another,
that pleased us quite as much, where the Emperor
stands with his favourite dog beside him. No wonder
the dog was a favourite; he deserved it, if there
be truth in physiognomy; and he looks up at Charles
with an expression of absolute worship. The portrait
of Isabella, wife of Charles, is admirably painted;
but she was less beautiful than I expected; she
looked careworn and formal. There is another
picture in the Museum at Augsburg, purporting

to be also the wife of Charles, and representing a younger and far lovelier face; but the style of dress is, I think, either of a different date or a different country.

Then come the series of portraits of Philip the Second; even more striking in their chronological debasement than those of Philip the Fourth, inasmuch as the earlier Philip began better and ended worse than the later. First, the handsome face, somewhat like his intellectual and gifted father, and yet more resembling his timid, scrupulous, nun-like mother, who always intended, when her children should be grown up, to leave her husband and end her days in a cloister. You scarcely observe that the under jaw is weak and heavy, the under lip projecting; there is no coldness in the dark eyes: the cruelty has not yet come to the surface. In the next it has; but there is some strength and majesty still struggling out of the gloom. And so on till the last (not, however, by Titian), which is positively awful to look on. Yet Philip is much admired by the Spaniards, who call him Philip the Just. When poor Prince Amadeus first arrived in Madrid, they said, "He might perhaps do; he had a look of Philip the Second."

There are some very fine specimens of Paul Veronese. Of these, we thought Cain the finest. It is perfectly magnificent; even the landscape seems full of remorse and despair. The allegorical picture of Virtue and Vice, too, is splendid.

It is impossible to name all the fine pictures in this superb gallery. One more, however, must be mentioned as being peculiarly interesting to English people, the portrait of Mary Tudor, Queen of England, whom *we* call Bloody Mary, while the Spaniards, taking a different view of the case, call her " Maria la Santa," " Mary the Saint." It is wonderfully well painted, and wonderfully sour in expression, probably true to nature. Some authors have, of late years, laboured to prove that when young, Mary was handsome and sweet-looking. Certainly, if she ever did possess good looks and a pleasant expression, both had totally disappeared before this picture was painted; so much so, that one's chief feeling is compassion for Philip having such an unamiable-looking wife. This portrait was sent over to Spain before the marriage; I should have thought it quite sufficient to put a stop to it.

In the long room is a case of cinquecento jewellery, containing, among others, specimens of Benvenuto Cellini's work; in particular a mermaid with two green tails, said to be of emerald. There are also some caskets studded with exceedingly fine engraved gems. I do not think those are by Benvenuto Cellini, not being in his style of workmanship, but we could get no information respecting them.

Downstairs are some statues, none of them very remarkable. In the middle is a most exquisite pietra-dura table, given by Pope Pius the Fifth to Don John of Austria, after Lepanto. Some stones in it resemble the kind found four or five years ago among the excavations at the Marmorata in Rome, and supposed by some learned men to be the rare and celebrated *myrrha*. There are also in this table some particularly fine cornelians.

Very often did we visit this delightful gallery, and many hours did we spend in it. The last time was like bidding good-bye to a friend, while we thought, " Shall we ever look upon it again ? "

CHAPTER IV.

Except in the Museum there are not many pictures
to see in Madrid; the private galleries being all shut
up, sent away, or dispersed, owing to the troubles
of the times. In the Academy of San Fernando are
three pictures by Murillo. The most remarkable
of those is the celebrated one of St. Elizabeth of
Hungary (here called St. Isabel) washing the head of
a beggar-boy. This, though one of Murillo's finest
works, is by no means one of his most agreeable; the
sore on the boy's head is too unpleasantly natural;
yet it is a wonderful picture. One goes back and
back to it, and can scarcely leave what when first

F

looked at sent one away in a shudder of disgust. The colouring is so splendid as to throw a golden light even on the sores and scabs, and, finally, it is the sweet holy face of the gentle queen that eclipses all else. She is not represented in regal beauty, as I have seen her in other pictures; nun-like, with her black dress and white coif, and kind, pale face, she bends over the wretched, filthy boy, who is really too filthy, too wretched: he is quite brutal, he does not even seem grateful, and the old woman has a greedy, grovelling look that rather detracts from the interest. You feel that St. Elizabeth is quite throwing her charitable deeds away. I suppose the idea is that nobody was too degraded for her kindness. This picture was painted for the hospital of the Caridad, in Seville, where it was singularly appropriate, and must have appeared to more advantage.

The other two Murillos represent the legend relating to the church of St. Maria Maggiore, in Rome. The first of these is the Dream of the Roman Senator; asleep in his easy-chair, and dressed like a Spanish hidalgo, he sees in a vision the Virgin Mary, who points to the miraculous snowfall said to have once taken place in the month of August on the Esquiline, about the middle of the fourth century. The other, less interesting, is his interview with Pope Liberius, in which the foundation of the church on the very spot thus indicated is determined on.

The most beautiful private house we saw in Madrid was the palace of the Duke of Alva. It is not generally shown to strangers, but the ever-kind and considerate Countess M. (mother-in-law of the Duke) thought that we might like to see a fine portrait of Mary, Queen of Scots, which had belonged to Prince Charles Edward Stuart, and had been presented by the Duchess of Albany to the present Duke of Alva's ancestor, he being also a Stuart. In this portrait Mary is sad and faded, scarcely beautiful, but sweet and queen-like. There are several other family portraits of both Stuarts and Alvas, but the gem of all is Titian's of him whom we in England term the ferocious Duke, while in Spain he is called the Great. It is magnificent; one of Titian's very finest works, and certainly the expression is not ferocious, nor cruel, nor bad in any way. He looks a rather proud and very polite Spanish grandee, extremely handsome and dignified, with a long narrow face and tall slight figure. The firmly-closed mouth is the only feature that recalls his character, and yet, though firm, it is not hard, nor even stern. Either his physiognomy belies him, or his cruelties have been exaggerated by unfriendly historians, which is indeed extremely probable.

Even without the interesting portraits the house would be worth seeing, on account of the exquisite taste of its internal decorations. Outside there is nothing remarkable, except that it is prettily situated in the midst of a large garden and surrounded by trees; but inside it is very beautiful. One room in par·ticular is fitted up in imitation of the Alhambra with Moorish stucco work, gilt and painted in rich red and blue; a fountain is in the middle, and Oriental divans round the sides. The day was hot, and the coolness and soft light delicious. Those splendid apartments have not been much used since the death of the Duchess, yet they still had a look of occupation, with plenty of books lying about.

This taste for Moorish decoration seems to prevail a good deal in Madrid, and certainly nothing can be more adapted for comfort in a hot climate. At the Countess M.'s the greenhouse was in Moorish style, its delicate tracery combining beautifully with the green leaves and bright flowers; in the evening it was lighted with lamps, and coffee was served there.

Owing to the disturbed state of affairs while we were in Madrid, it was impossible to obtain permission to see the Royal Palace. Not that they ever refused it; on the contrary, hopes were always held out that next day at the same hour, or that day at a different one, we should get in. The fact was, that nobody ever knew at what hour the King and Queen would go out to drive or ride; it was probably concealed purposely, for fear of assassination; and, of course, visitors could not be admitted till the royal family went out. After all, I believe we did not lose much; most of the pictures being now in the Museum. The palace itself is a magnificent building, dazzlingly white against the brilliant blue sky. The situation is not at all dreary; at least, certainly not in the month of May. It looked quite bright, seen through the fresh green trees of the Plaza de Oriente, and backed by the turquoise blue and crowning snow of the Guadarrama.

In the Plaza de Oriente, in the midst of its flowers and leaves, is the celebrated equestrian statue of Philip the Fourth, said to be one of the finest in the world. It has been well called a Velasquez in bronze. The horse is rearing so high that a real living horse would have difficulty in keeping its balance, and not falling backwards on its rider; yet it looks quite easy and natural, and you feel sure that the rider has perfect command over his prancing steed. Galileo suggested the means of preserving the balance; but I did not find anybody who could explain it satisfactorily.

In the Plaza Mayor, there is an equestrian statue

of Philip the Third, also very good, though not equal to that of his son and successor. I do not think there are any other statues in Madrid which deserve mention, except that of Cervantes, in the Plaza de las Cortes.

The artist, a native of Barcelona, has contrived the drapery so as to hide the want of the arm lost at Lepanto. This is a pity, and not at all as Cervantes would have wished.

The Spaniards do not seem to have possessed, or at least practised, the art of casting in bronze. This statue of Cervantes was cast by a Prussian; that of Philip the Fourth by Pietro Tacca, in Florence; while Philip the Third had the honour, scarcely deserved as far as the character of the monarch was concerned, of being cast by no less a person than John of Bologna himself.

Though we were not shown the interior of the palace, no objection was made to our seeing the Royal Stables and Coach-houses. They are very extensive, and beautifully kept; the horses many of them very fine. The mules, however, interested us most; an exceedingly fine mule being, to us northerns, a much rarer quadruped. And wonderfully fine they were; until one has seen a Spanish mule, one has no idea to what perfection the creature may be brought. Glossy they were not, but looked as if their skins were made

of black velvet, and their size was astonishing. I do
not think they were all very amiable, however; we
were always carefully warned as to which were likely
to kick us, and which were not; and the former
greatly predominated. There were also two tiny
mules like toys, which the young Prince of the
Asturias, Queen Isabella's son, used to drive. It
must have been a charming turn-out; the little
animals were not bigger than Newfoundland dogs.
Perhaps they stood a little higher; but I don't think
they were so long as some Newfoundlands I have
seen. The carriages were innumerable and various.
I felt as though we were walking through miles of
gilt and painted coaches, nodding ostrich-plumes,
and gorgeous hammer-cloths. There was the corona-
tion coach; the coach that went to Atocha on solemn
occasions, the one that went there on lesser festivals,
and the one that went when there was no festival at
all. There also were the plain carriages of King
Amadeus and of his Queen, dark blue, sparingly
decorated with silver. The Spaniards looked scornfully at those, saying, "He does not think *our* carriages
good enough for him; he has brought his own."
This was quite true, and was one of the many mistakes
made by the well-meaning couple who had taken
upon themselves to rule a country with whose tastes

and prejudices they were, to say the least, imperfectly acquainted. The Spaniards, naturally, resented this ignorance, saying, " Why has he come to govern us, when he knows nothing about us, not even our language ? "

And so it really appears to have been; the history, language, literature, tastes, prejudices, peculiarities of the Spaniards were completely ignored. They were at once pronounced "barbarous," "half-civilized," and were to be improved in season and out of season, chiefly the latter. Even granted that the young King was right, and that all Italian ways are better than any Spanish ones, no nation likes to be treated as inferior to its ruler, especially when that ruler is a foreigner; and the Spaniards, of all people, are un-suited to relish it. It was unfortunate that the King always said he meant to devote his life and energies to improving Spain; Spain did not wish to be im-proved, thinking herself already equal to any nation, and superior to Italy.

The Italians have, unluckily, a theory that the Spaniards are like them, but " less civilized." Now, never were two nations so unlike, nor so unsuited to get on well together. In everything, in faults and virtues, talents and defects, tastes and prejudices, they are exactly the opposite of each other, and totally in-

capable of even understanding what each other would
be at. The consequence is, that the Italian looks
upon the Spaniard with conceited contempt, while the
Spaniard regards the Italian with scorn and detesta-
tion. He calls Italian gentleness deceit; the simple
tastes of the House of Savoy, so deservedly popular
in their own country, he considers meanness, while
economy is invariably stigmatized as parsimony. In
Spain, even ordinary travellers who have every wish
to be economical, must not bargain as they would in
Italy; so the horror of the Spaniards may be imagined,
when the new Queen asked the price of everything
before she would buy it. When the King rode through
the Puerta del Sol, attended by only one groom, even
the excellent horsemanship, to which they did every
justice, could not save him from scornful looks, and
exclamations of "Que clase de rey !" "What kind of
king is that !" The upper classes, of course, were too
courteous to make such observations ; if they met the
King or Queen they bowed, for, as they said, "It would
be impolite to do otherwise." But, I think, they
rather avoided coming in contact with them. One
lady of high rank said, "The Queen is a good woman,
I esteem her, but we do not meet—I never see her."
Others said, "She was clever, and had learnt to speak
Spanish very well; but she wanted refinement and

grace of manner." Indeed, they did not scruple to say plainly that they considered her "vulgar." The men generally rather admired the King's appearance; said he rode splendidly, and spoke French beautifully; but that in other respects he was an "inferior man," and they were disappointed in him. The end of it always was, "I *wish* he would go away, and take all his things with him."

The language, of course, was a chief stumbling-block. It must be allowed that the Spaniards are a little unreasonable about their language. They expect everybody, who has been three weeks in Spain, to speak it fluently, and pronounce it perfectly. Now, fortunately, it is very easy; probably much the easiest of European tongues; so that almost anybody of average abilities, who really wishes and tries to learn it, can do so in a month or six weeks, spent in the country and among the natives. But whether it was that King Amadeus did not see the necessity of taking pains, certain it is that he never could express himself correctly and fluently in Castilian; and this was un-pardonable in Spanish estimation, as implying either want of capacity or want of will. The Spaniards themselves say that no Italian can ever speak Spanish well. At first I thought this must be prejudice, the two languages being so exceedingly similar. But I soon perceived that this very resemblance constituted a difficulty, inasmuch as one may fancy one is talking good Spanish while sliding insensibly into Italian ; a most undesirable result in Spain, where "Italian" is a term of reproach. If you refuse to give money to a beggar-boy, he will, in all probability, execute a war-dance round you, in which his friends and companions join, singing "Italians! Italians! Strangers! Strangers!" Consequently, it is quite a serious matter to use an Italian word by mistake for a Spanish one, or to speak Spanish with an Italian accent. Even Castilian politeness can hardly stand that.

Unluckily, too, one of the first and most important words the poor young King had to say publicly, happened to be perhaps the most difficult of all, "Juro," "I swear," with its rough guttural, being considered a crucial test of pronunciation.

Practical people will naturally exclaim that all these things are trifles ; and certainly each grievance by itself seemed comically small. Yet the sum of the whole amounted to a good deal, especially as all those proofs of awkwardness and want of tact were looked upon as a deliberate wish to mortify Spain and magnify Italy.

The Spaniards, as is well known, are proud of their history ; and, that being the case, it really must have been provoking to find that their young sovereign's compatriots knew and cared nothing whatever about the past glories of Spain. The Italians, even in their own home, have only too much contempt for all that belongs to the Middle Ages ; and they were not likely to be more tolerant to mediæval ways and prejudices in a country which they regarded as being peopled with savages: somewhat as we might New Zealand, in fact ; only with much less knowledge of the subject than the English usually possess concerning the Antipodes. The Spaniards, on their parts, are apt to forget (if indeed the idea has ever fairly gained admittance to their minds) that Spain is no longer the greatest Power in Europe, as she was in the years that succeeded the Conquest of Granada, and the discovery of the wondrous Western World. She lives in the Past ; and, in truth, we felt inclined to do so too, as we turned away from those bones of contention, the state-carriages, and entered the armoury.

All there was calm and grand ; with the stately suits of armour, each with a history more romantic than any fiction, ranged solemnly around. There was the armour of Alonso Guzman, "el Bueno," or "the Good ;" which, indeed, the name Guzman already signifies, being Godman, that is, Goodman, in the original Norse. For Guzman el Bueno (a near relation of St. Dominic, by the bye) was of no southern race; his ancestors came from the far north, from the island whose bold outline, dark purple against the sunset, closes the port of Aalesund, in Norway. A long way, in truth, from the wild Scandinavian coast to the sunny shores of Tarifa, where Guzman's glorious deeds were done. But, to be sure, there was the stepping-stone of fair Normandy for some centuries between the barren haunt of the sea-bird and the rich heritage of the Moor. This Alonso Guzman, when besieged by the Moors in Tarifa, was threatened, if he did not surrender, with the death of his eldest son, a boy of nine years old, who had been treacherously given up to the enemy. Alonso refused, and the boy was killed. On hearing the cry of horror on the battlements, Alonso rushed out to inquire what had happened. When told, he said quietly, "I feared the infidel had gained the city." He was indeed a brave descendant of the Vikings, of Ganger Rolf, and of the Dukes of Normandy.

There too is the armour of the "Gran Capitan," Gonsalvo de Cordoba; that of poor Don Carlos, Philip the Second's unhappy son; that of the heroic and equally unfortunate Juan de Padilla, leader of the Comuneros, who was defeated and executed in 1520; that of Fernan Cortes; of

Columbus; and of Don John of Austria, worn at Lepanto.

We looked in vain for the Cid's shirt of mail. I suspect it was hid, for fear of being carried off or injured in those troublous times. But the Cid's sword is there; a plain weapon, with twisted handle. Ill-naturedly accurate people are fond of suggesting that this sword is not the veritable weapon of the Campeador of Spain; but there seems no reason why it should not be, and it is pleasant to believe in things when they are not manifestly absurd. They also point out the weapon of Pelayo, sovereign of the Christians of Spain in the eighth century. Though *called* King of Leon, he did not possess the city, and only a small portion of the territory; his dominions, at his accession, being but twenty-five miles long, and twelve miles broad. He wielded his good blade with such success that, at his death, his kingdom had increased to a hundred miles in length. All else was under Moslem sway, and obeyed the Caliph of Damascus. In this instance, even if the sword be apocryphal, the historical facts regarding the hero are true. Bernardo del Carpio's sword is doubtful; and that of Orlando still more so. But there is quite enough of authentic romance connected with the weapons here displayed, without insisting on the truth of all the wild and wonderful legends of Spanish story. Here is the sword of St. Ferdinand, conqueror of Seville, and that of Garcilaso de la Vega, poet and soldier; that of Isabel la Catolica, and that of Pizarro; besides Toledan blades innumerable, some of the finest having belonged to Charles the Fifth, Philip the Second, and Don John of Austria. There is also a sword of Boabdil's.

Among the helmets is that of James the Conqueror, King of Aragon, the hero-sovereign, whose bones lie at Poblet, near Tarragona, in the once magnificent but now ruined convent where he wished to end his days. Boabdil's helmet, too, is here, of a very curious and exceedingly ugly shape.

One of the suits of armour is said by the guide-books to be unmistakably that of a German elector, being "web-footed and short-legged." Short-legged some of the German electors may have been, though others, including, for instance, Augustus of Saxony, were tall; but they surely are not invariably, nor even frequently, web-footed.

The most curious things in the whole collection are the crowns of the Gothic Kings, found at Guarrazar, in the mountains of Toledo. They are of gold, with pendants of pale sapphires. From the largest of those diadems hangs a cross, in the same style. This crown has an inscription which, though incomplete, may be read thus :—"Svinthilanus Rex offeret." This Svinthilanus, or Suintila, was the twenty-third of the Visigothic monarchs of Spain; and in his time the Greeks of Constantinople were finally expelled from the Peninsula. He reigned from A.D. 621 till 631, being thus a contemporary of Mahomet. We saw also a smaller diadem of similar workmanship, purporting to be the "Crown of the Abbot Theodosius." Another gold and sapphire cross bears an inscription stating that it was "offered by Bishop Lucetius." There were several fragments of smaller golden crowns, some with, some without, the sapphire pendants; but I could learn nothing more about them; probably, however, they were all votive offerings.

These objects were found soon after those of the same kind, also from Guarrazar, now in the Hôtel Cluny, in Paris. Those latter were sold privately to the French government before Queen Isabella heard that they had been dug up. She accordingly ordered further excavations to be made at Guarrazar; and at last they found a *tinaja*, or large jar, containing all the Visigothic jewels now in the Madrid armoury. The crown in the Hôtel Cluny is supposed to be that of Recesuintho, the immediate predecessor of "the good King Wamba," as he is generally called. Recesuintho reigned from 650 to 672, and was one of the most prosperous of the Gothic sovereigns of Spain.

We should have liked to pay a second visit to this most interesting armoury, which indeed deserves more time than we could well give; also, we wished much to see the Archæological Museum, recently arranged.

But by this time the deadly climate was beginning to make itself felt, and we saw that we must leave Madrid before we were quite incapacitated by illness. We spent one day walking and sitting in the quiet, shady gardens of Buen Retiro, as H. said, "just to try our strength." I don't know that the trial did much good, but it ended in our deciding to make an excursion to Toledo and Aranjuez before the weather got hotter.

The last days were occupied with some odds and ends of sight-seeing that, being either inconvenient or less interesting, had been put off from time to time. We went to St. Antonio de la Florida, a little church outside the northern gate, in an avenue of tall, shady trees. It contains some of Goya's best frescoes, and they are really very well worth seeing. The little dome is painted to represent a balcony, and saints and angels seem bending over the balustrade. The figures are very graceful, and the colouring brilliant; not at

all in Goya's usual wild, almost grotesque manner:
but the style is more gay and bright than devotional.

We did not go to the other churches of Madrid; most
of them are modern or modernised, and said to be
nowise remarkable for good taste.   Nor did the history
and legends connected with them attract us, as we
felt no peculiar interest in St. Isidro, for instance, the
peasant-saint—a great favourite in Madrid.   He is
much more highly esteemed than the really great
and learned St. Isidoro of Seville, the " Egregious
Doctor," as he was called in the Middle Ages; while,
as to St. Isidoro of Cordoba, he and his biblical
commentaries have been forgotten long ago.   But the
memory of St. Isidro, the ploughman, still flourishes,
and great respect is paid to him.   We happened to
enter Madrid the day after his *fête*, and, consequently,
the trains that we met were crammed full of peasants
and artisans who had gone there to do him honour,
the majority of whom, unfortunately, had testified
their devotion by drinking a great deal more wine
than was good for them.   To do them justice, however, they were in perfectly good humour, but their
merriment was overpowering; they sang and shrieked,
and always offered to shake hands with the travellers
in the trains that passed them; and we were very glad
that none of them were our fellow-passengers.   All

this, perhaps, rather prejudiced us against St. Isidro, though it certainly was unreasonable to blame the saint for the too great jollity of his worshippers.

One church it was really necessary to see—the world-famous Atocha, and accordingly we went there from St. Antonio, following the line of the boulevard outside the town. We passed the tobacco manufactory, where a tremendous uproar was going on. Some machinery had been introduced, at which the women and girls employed were so enraged that they smashed it all to pieces, and threw the bits out of the windows. They were occupied most energetically with their work of destruction; and we saw the fragments of the machinery flung out with wild yells and laughter. Of course, nobody interfered; indeed, who was there to do so? I don't think there were any police when we were in Madrid, and as to the soldiers, they were not to be depended upon; they would probably have fraternised with the mob. On remarking to a Spaniard that riots like this would not be tolerated in England, the reply was, " Here we are more free." Such are the Spanish notions of liberty.

We did not feel inclined to linger at the tobacco riot, and proceeded to the far-famed Atocha. Of all the many desolate churches of Spain, this is the most utterly forlorn. Not that it is dilapidated; it has not

the picturesqueness of a ruin; and, indeed, even ruin
could not make it otherwise than hideous. The
entrance is grass-grown, but flowerless; the very
weeds looked coarse and dingy. Within, it was in
good enough repair, but gaudy and tawdry, without
architectural beauty, or, indeed, beauty of any kind.
Most of the valuable jewels had been taken away. I
suppose they were concealed for fear of the mob—a
very prudent precaution in those times; but there
was still a good deal of silver and gold brocade, and
some lace about the altars and images. I looked for
some time in vain for the celebrated Virgin; I looked
up and I looked down, and began to think that it, too,
had been stowed away somewhere. I knew it ought
to be above the high altar, before which I was
standing, but still it remained obstinately hidden.
I now supposed there was a screen or curtain before
it, and applied to the sacristan. "No, it was never
covered; does your worship not see it up there?" I
began at last to fear he would think that my heretic
eyes were unworthy to behold this treasure; but he
only lamented the want, not of the true faith, but of
an opera-glass. Making a desperate effort, he exclaimed piteously, "Does your worship not see a brocaded silver robe?" Yes; the brocaded silver robe I
did see. "And the jewelled crown?" Yes, I saw

the crown. "Well, then, was not the face of the most Holy Virgin between the diadem and the robe?" It seemed not unlikely that it should be so, and I strained my eyes to the utmost—this time rewarded by perceiving a black circular object about the size of the palm of one's hand, which proved to be the face of the image. It would be very hideous if it were not so small; as it is, it does not offend the eye much. Artistically speaking, it certainly is the ugliest of the many ugly black images ascribed to St. Luke; but then, being nearly invisible, it does not obtrude itself. It is very strange that this little fetish should have such honour paid it, not merely by the ignorant, but by people of education. I wonder what King Amadeus thought of it when he first saw Atocha; when Prim was lying there dead, murdered for having offered him the crown he had come to take. A sad and ominous reception for the poor young Italian prince.

It is impossible to visit those shrines of Spain without feeling in what a much more degraded state religion has been there than has ever been the case in Italy. Really, when gazing at this black idol of Atocha, it seemed as if there was more difference between Rome and Spain in this respect than between Spain and the interior of Africa. Nothing can be more unfair than to charge the Church of Rome with either the superstition or the cruelty of the Spanish Catholics. If superstition was derived from Rome in the first instance, the scholar has gone far beyond the master; and, as to cruelty and intolerance, these are the dark spots on the otherwise noble Spanish character. The Inquisition was a purely Spanish institution, never so powerful nor so terrible in Italy as in its native country. In Venice it was never admitted at all; and even in Rome its proceedings were comparatively mild. In the Middle Ages it was not uncommon for the persecuted Jews to take refuge in Rome, and sometimes even to be sheltered at the Vatican; and there is one instance of a noble family driven from Spain on suspicion of heresy, and welcomed with honours by the Pope.

Even yet, intolerance is very general among the Spaniards. Some, who have no religion at all, never go to church, and wholly detest their own priests, dislike the Protestants quite as much, and revile them as " wretches who don't believe in the Virgin and saints."

The higher classes are too polite to express intolerance, even if they feel it; but they are very orthodox and strenuous Roman Catholics, whose chief objection to King Amadeus was, that he was " the son of an excommunicated man, who had robbed the Pope of his dominions." The lower classes are exceedingly superstitious, especially the women. Among the middle classes, the men appeared to me very frequently to have no belief in anything, except in the everlasting perdition of all Protestants.

Their irreverence was something perfectly appalling; and their hatred of the priests unbounded. One man, speaking of a murder that had been committed, said "it was of no consequence; it was only a priest who had been killed; and the more of them who were killed, the better." Yet the next minute, he spoke with horror of a Spanish Protestant, calling him a *Jew*, and a *Moor*.

This speech was very characteristic, as combining Spanish indifference to life with true Spanish intolerance. Recklessness of life and of suffering, whether with regard to human beings or to the lower animals, is but too common in Spain. It is not exactly cruelty; for I don't think even Spanish boys torment merely for the sake of tormenting; they are simply perfectly careless about it: if their amusement or advantage is served by cruelty, nobody has any scruples on the subject.

This peculiarity of character explains the otherwise incomprehensible barbarities of the Inquisition. It was not that they enjoyed looking at torture, but it did not give them any pain to see it: they were resolved to extirpate heresy, and cared little or not at all by what means they attained their end, always provided it was attained. Even at the present day, the objections of the Spaniards to the Inquisition are founded much more on its interference with their liberty to do whatever they please, good or evil, than on its cruelty.

In justice to the Spaniards, it must be said that, if they are indifferent to the life or sufferings of others, they are very nearly as careless of their own. Personally, they are exceedingly brave; they delight in fighting for its own sake, without any reference to the cause they are at the moment supporting. They do not wish nor expect to be pitied for any sufferings that may befall them; even a Spanish child does not cry nor lament if he is hurt accidentally, though he bitterly resents a punishment. The contrast between Spaniards and Italians is very great in this respect: in Italy, if a child falls and hurts himself, he sheds floods of tears, and is petted and comforted by everybody; in Spain, he is laughed at, and told to take better care for the future.

No very tender-hearted nation could tolerate, much less enjoy, the bull-fight. It is frequently said that the English love of sport comes to much the same thing. It might be so, in some degree, if the bulls were wild, and hunted as tigers are in India. But in the arena they have no chance : if they are gentle, they are hooted at as being cowardly ; if they are fierce, they are applauded, but tormented and killed all the same. Even if it were not for the cruelty, the unfairness would make it painful to see.

The danger to the men, of course, counts for nothing. It is very seldom that an accident happens : as far as they are concerned, it is not much more dangerous than fox-hunting, and quite as safe as riding a steeple-chase ; and, after all, they need not do it unless they like. But the slaughter of the horses is dreadful : the whole time I was in Spain, I had no pleasure in looking at the beautiful Andalusian steeds ; the horrible bull-ring always rose before my eyes. Englishmen, when they sell their horses on leaving Spain, often stipulate that they shall be shot, when old, rather than sent to bull-fight. Spaniards cannot understand this feeling ; and when you express compassion for the horses, they say, "Oh! but it was an old horse, worth nothing."

I was told that if I went often enough to the bull-fight I should get to like it. I should be sorry to go through such a disagreeable process in order to attain

so undesirable a result. We went once, and stayed
till one bull and three horses were killed, which
occupied about a quarter of an hour. If I could have
got out, I should have come away sooner. Anything
more utterly disgusting and brutal I never beheld,
and hope never to see the like again. The first
entrance of the procession was certainly very pretty,
and the horsemanship wonderful : but the rush of the
bull was less exciting than I expected ; and the clumsy
way in which the poor beast was killed at last, after
repeated failures, was quite distressing. I always
knew I should be sorry for the horses ; but I was
surprised to find how much compassion I felt for the
bull. When he sank on his knees, and looked up
with his great eyes at his butchers, as if wondering
why they tormented him so, I should have liked to
go down into the arena, and wash the blood from his
wounds, and try to save him. The horses I could
hardly look at : one gentle, graceful black Andalusian
started a little, on first entering the arena ; his rider
patted him and spoke to him, and he obeyed like a
dog, arching his neck and looking pleased ; the
animal was evidently accustomed to be caressed : in
five minutes the bull had ripped him up, and the
spectacle was too horrible to look on.

Fórmerly, when, instead of hired picadors on poor

old horses, the Moorish chiefs, and afterwards the Spanish knights, fought the bull, riding their own good steeds, and of course trying as much as possible to save them, it must have been very different and much better. It was always thus, not only in the days of the Arab domination, but even till comparatively recent times.

The people at the bull-fight, though naturally intensely interested, behaved with great order and propriety; much more so than at the *Fête Dieu*, which occurred during our stay in Madrid. As this latter procession was to pass through the Puerta del Sol, we went out to look at it. It was not very well worth seeing, being confused and irregular, with long gaps and breaks, which an exceedingly dirty mob took care to fill up. The priests were quite as dirty as the people, very ill-dressed, and many of them suffering from ringworm, which produced the odd effect of a double or triple tonsure. Very often had we seen the *Fête Dieu*, not only in bright Paris, and grand old Florence, and in Vienna, where the Emperor and all his Court and his glittering Hungarian regiments walked in procession; but also in the quiet valleys of Styria and Savoy, among hardworking peasants. But never, in the poorest country, did I behold anything so squalid and forlorn as in this the capital of Spain. Perhaps things were worse than usual just then, when the country was in a state of half-suppressed revolution. The ecclesiastics seemed uncomfortable and exceedingly cross; the high functionaries of State looked sheepish and rather frightened; there was no police, nobody to keep order, which, accordingly, was not kept at all. A Spanish crowd is always excitable; and they howled, and danced, and went on with all sorts of antics; not in derision, however, but with the utmost gravity and sadness. The women were the worst; they pushed and struck each other, and shrieked and swore, and behaved like furies. This was not a demonstration against the clergy; on the contrary, they were quite pleased with the procession, and some of them threw wild lavender before it.

There were pickpockets among the crowd, but probably not more than in other European capitals. I saw H.'s fan lying on the ground, and, on picking it up, she exclaimed lamentably, "I must have a hole in my pocket!" And sure enough a hole there was, of the very largest dimensions, a sharp instrument having cut open all the lower part of the pocket, and keys and purse were gone. Luckily, there was not much money in the purse, but the keys were a serious loss. On applying to the Greek porter to have the locks forced open, he became so interested in the novelty of this particular style of pocket-picking as to be quite unable to attend to our wishes. He looked admiringly at the devastated pocket, exclaiming, " This is quite new! It has never before been seen in Madrid! It is so beautifully done! No Spaniard is so clever! None but an English thief has sufficient skill for this!" I really think he was sorry he had not had the merit of the invention himself. However, in justice to Spanish honesty, I must say that though we had to leave the boxes open, at the mercy of anybody who chose to enter the room, till the mischief was repaired, nothing was touched.

On the *Fête Dieu*, in the afternoon, it is the custom to walk up and down one particular street, the Calle de las Carretas, above which an awning is stretched, as shelter from the sun. No carriages are allowed to enter, and the street is thronged, The ladies generally wear white blonde veils on this occasion, and all have new dresses of the gayest description. We did not think the white veils so becoming to the dark Spanish faces as the black: besides which, as the white veil is very expensive, it is made to last several years; and, though seldom worn, it gets yellow. I don't think any of the upper classes were among the promenaders; they seemed to belong to the bourgeoisie, who are not nearly so handsome as those of higher birth. They looked hot and tired, which was not surprising; this being the first really warm day we had experienced.

Day by day the sun blazed more fiercely, though the air was still cool; and H.s cough remaining obstinate, we determined to try change of air without further delay. Accordingly, we started at 7 A.M. on the brilliant morning of the 10th of June for Toledo.

CHAPTER V.

Strange, dreamy, magnificent, desolate, tawny Toledo! The very most singular of calcined-looking cities! For that is at first the principal thing that strikes you; it looks like a fragment of a burnt-up world, of which the cinders are by no means as yet cool. In and about Toledo there is no grass, no green thing, except the myrtles in the cathedral-cloister, the vines and the oleanders in that of San Juan de los Reyes, and a few little acacias in the Plaza. The streets, in any other town equally depopulated, would certainly be grass-grown; but here, there being no grass, the crevices between the stones are full of a tiny, bright purple flower, which, in some places, is so plentiful as to shed a bloom over the pavement, if pavement it may be called. All else was like ashes from a furnace. The very cliffs seemed burnt to powder; and, as we stood on the edge, looking down into the rushing Tagus, the stones, or rather hardened dust, on which we stood, began to crumble and slide away from beneath our feet. Yet Toledo is a pleasant place; the steep, narrow streets are clean, and the air fresh and invigorating, though the country round is, on a small scale, more like the moon seen through a telescope, than anything we had hitherto met with on our travels.

The inn being, by all accounts, intolerably filthy, we had been advised to go to a Casa de Huespedes, as it is called. These Casas de Huespedes are private lodgings, which in Spain can be had almost everywhere, and are quieter and frequently cleaner than the inns; the latter, in the smaller and more out-of-the-way places, being the resort of muleteers, who are never admitted to a Casa de Huespedes. These private lodgings may be had without difficulty, even for one night, as well as for a longer period; they are a little dearer than the *Posada* or inn; but they are much more comfortable. Of course, they must be recommended by some reliable person. Those that we had been advised to go to were kept by two old ladies, sisters, and apparently decayed gentle-women, who made us exceedingly comfortable. The house was quiet, clean, and quaint, with large, almost unfurnished rooms, and a cool, silent *patio* or inner court. The cookery was a little oily, and not always quite above suspicion of garlic; but the bread was white and good, the water deliciously cold, and the wine excellent. Besides this, the chocolate was beyond all praise; and the fruit and goat-milk cheese very good. So, as far as food was concerned, we were well off.

We went immediately to the Cathedral, that glorious Cathedral! It is absolutely perfect, outside and in: there is nothing that one could wish otherwise; even the inevitable choir cannot spoil it. Its peculiarity is the combination of exceeding richness of detail with great unity of plan; the general style of the arches being simple, extremely pointed Gothic, quite without mixture of anything Moorish. In one chapel only are some remains of the old mosque.

H

A cathedral is said to have existed on this spot, in the times of the Visigothic kings ; indeed, the Spanish chroniclers assert that a church was built here and dedicated to the Virgin in her lifetime ! Afterwards, here was the great mosque of the Arabians, guaranteed to them by treaty, at the time the Christians took Toledo. Of course, the guarantee was soon set aside, and the Moslems dispossessed. I do not know if any record exists as to its size, as compared with that of Cordoba ; but it was probably smaller and less rich, as Toledo was only the capital of one of the lesser Arab kingdoms, and never of all Spain, under the rule of Islam. At any rate, St. Ferdinand pulled it down, in order to build the present Cathedral ; and whatever the splendour of the mosque may have been, one can feel no regret when standing in the glorious aisles which have replaced it. At first, I could look only at the marvellous windows, with their ruby, amethyst, and sapphire radiance. It was too late to see the Chapel of the Kings that day, and I think we were rather glad simply to feast our eyes, without studying anything.

From the Cathedral we went to San Juan de los Reyes, a Franciscan convent, founded by Ferdinand and Isabella, to commemorate the victory of Toro, which secured the crown of Castile to Isabella. St.

John was ever her favourite apostle, her patron saint; her father was called John, and she gave the same well-beloved name to her only son. There was also a peculiar propriety in consecrating a Franciscan convent to St. John; St. Francis being originally baptized John, and not Francis at all; which latter name indeed did not previously exist, and was only given to the founder of the minor Friars, because he spoke French so well that he was called "the Frenchman."

Without, San Juan de los Reyes is now all desolation—dry, dusty, ashen desolation; but the chains of the Christian captives set free from Moorish slavery still hang on the walls. Within, is the lovely cloister, all sunshine, and green leaves and vine-tendrils encircling the exquisite sculpture. I wonder if anybody ever thought that cloister less beautiful than they expected! The decorations of the chapel, too, are very rich, and in good preservation. Then we went and looked down on the Puerta del Cambron; a few steps further, and we stood on the edge of a cliff composed of tawny dust, and saw the Tagus, sheer down below us. A strange, lonely river it is, as it rushes past this City of the Dead!

From thence we went to the old synagogue, built in the ninth century, on earth brought from Mount Zion, and roofed with cedar from Lebanon. It is now a church, having been stolen from the Jews by Ferdinand and Isabella, and much spoilt by whitewash. It quite deserves its name of Santa Maria la Blanca, or the White. I wish the Spaniards would not wash over all the beautiful Moorish colours. The photographs of this synagogue are finer than the reality; it is so disproportionately high and narrow.

The other synagogue, called El Transito, is also now a church. There they have recently discovered colours under the prevailing whitewash. The roof and cornice are exceedingly beautiful.

The Jews were anciently very rich, numerous, and powerful in Toledo. They claim to have been settled in Spain ever since the days of Solomon; and in Toledo, one of the oldest of Spanish cities, was one of their early colonies. They say, too, that they had no share in the guilt of the crucifixion; that, on the contrary, they protested against the condemnation of an innocent man. This did not, however, save them from persecution, their wealth being a great resource to the Visigothic kings; for was it not always easy to bring some sort of crime home to a Jew? Even if no false accusation were at hand, there was, at any rate, the fact that he was not a Christian, and this was surely sufficient. They did not exactly

endure patiently, but at least they endured ; till that
Palm Sunday morning, when they opened the gate of
this very Toledo, and let in the Moslems, who, after
all, were much more akin to them, in blood and
manners, than the Gothic Catholics. Now, one might
have thought they would have got on peaceably ; and,
indeed, for long they did so. But at last, whether
their riches were too great a temptation even to the
followers of the prophet, as the Jews allege ; or
whether, as is quite as probable, their discontent arose
mainly from their own restless and ungovernable
spirit, they, in an evil hour for themselves, intrigued
with the Christians against the Moslems ; and greatly
helped to bring in Alonso the Sixth, in 1085, after
Toledo had been under Arabian rule for 371 years.
Three hundred years more passed, however, tolerably
comfortably, as far as the Jews were concerned. They
lived on in Toledo, and made money ; of which, as was
natural, they were now and then plundered. Learned,
too, they were in their way ; though, as Jews have
ever been, extremely conservative, and averse to new
theories and discoveries. It was a Jew of Toledo,
Isaac Israeli, who, in the fourteenth century, wrote a
treatise to prove, not that the Ptolomaic system was
true, but that its opponent, Alpetragius, even if right,
should not be listened to, because he was right on
erroneous grounds !

Towards the end of that century the persecutions again became virulent; and, after another hundred years of oppression and spoliation, they were finally expelled. It is curious that, to this day, the Jews seem still to love the architecture of their ancient Moorish home; at Pesth, where they are descendants of those banished from Spain by Ferdinand and Isabella, the synagogue, lately built, is thoroughly Moorish in style.

From the synagogues we went to the fragment of the old palace of the Moorish kings, with its exquisite tracery. It was probably built some time between 1038, the date of the dismemberment of the Spanish Caliphate (and consequent establishment of a separate kingdom of Toledo), and 1085, when the Christians re-took the city. It is now a ball-room.

In walking through the streets, we were particularly struck with the many and fanciful forms of the door-nails. Every door is studded with those nails, and the shapes are very quaint, and often beautiful. Sometimes they have reference to the object or history of the building; for instance, any building in any way connected with Santiago, has nails in the form of scallop-shells.

The handles and knockers, too, are varied and beautiful. I wonder if the graceful devices of door-hinges and handles in the old Imperial Free Cities, as in Nürnberg, for example, were derived from Spanish influence in Charles the Fifth's reign.

We were by this time exceedingly tired of walking up and down the steep streets of Toledo; and, in spite of the guide's entreaties that we should see everything that day ("it would not take more than four or five hours longer," he said), we persisted in going home to breakfast and rest.

At this breakfast or *almuerzo*, as it is called (it being really more luncheon than breakfast), the land-lady brought us a Tagus eel, as a great delicacy. H. at once pronounced it a snake, and refused to have anything to do with it; so I was obliged, unwillingly, to eat her share and my own too, for fear of hurting our kind hostess's feelings. I cannot say it was particularly good, being rather oily, with an exceedingly strong flavour of musk. This latter peculiarity still more convinced H. that the eel was a snake; a water-snake, if I liked, but certainly a snake.

From the very door of our lodgings there was a most beautiful view of the Cathedral spire, with a picturesque bit of street scenery; so, after breakfast, I went out to sketch it. The street, like almost all others in Toledo, was silent and deserted; probably everybody was at that moment asleep, and thus I was tolerably unmolested. It was very, very Spanish; the intense sunlight, and deep, still shadows; the windows, with their dark blue striped blinds drawn outside and fastened to the railings; the flower-filled balconies; the bright yellow and orange houses, with their brown roofs; and, at the end of the vista, the pale, rich, creamy hue of the tall Cathedral spire, with its circling thorny crowns. Presently, one or two solemn figures, apparently but half-awake, came pacing slowly up the street; a priest in his black dress and curiously turned-up hat; a man who might have been a beggar (only he didn't beg), in a rusty brown cloak; then a clatter of heels, and I was nearly swept away by a string of mules coming down; next, a wise-looking donkey, bearing a basket of fruit. At last, unluckily, the Toledan boys roused themselves from their slumbers; and those same boys have the character of being the most impertinent and troublesome in the whole Peninsula, which is saying a great deal. They would be quite intolerable if it were not for two mitigating circumstances: one is, that they are not very numerous; the other, that all the respectable people, and indeed all grown men and women gene-rally, league together in self-defence against them, and are quite willing to extend their protection to the stranger within their gates, who, in this instance, was myself. One imp of mischief, watching his opportunity when a good many of his companions and admirers were present, and when no grown person was in sight, placed himself before me, holding up a large, round loaf at arm's length, and begged me to take his portrait, offering me a *peseta* (tenpence) for so doing. In Spain, if you can turn the laugh against your adversary, the victory is yours; the Spaniards being very sensitive to ridicule, and also about personal appearance. I knew this; so replied coolly, "No; you are too ugly." All his friends instantly turned against him, laughing, and applauding my retort; thoroughly abashed, the boy slunk away, followed by his playmates hooting at him. Fair-weather friends! But I had half an hour's peace in consequence; then they began to collect again; whereupon our hostess emerged from her doorway, and with true Castilian gravity handed H. a stick, without saying a word. The sight of the stick was enough; they fled in terror; and I then observed that everybody, women as well as men, carried a cane or stick of some sort, with which they charged the little ragamuffins when matters became unbearable. In about three-quarters of an hour they returned, in orderly procession, the ringleader carrying a whip which they had manufactured.

By this time, however, the sketch was finished; so, as is often the case in Spain, the opportunity had slipped away while the preparations for war were being made.

After dinner, we went into a pretty sitting-room upstairs, with a view of the Alcazar and the brown roofs of Toledo. There we made acquaintance with a most amiable old black tom-cat. He was suffering from asthma, poor thing; but even that could not irritate his exceedingly sweet temper; and he was kindness itself to two young interlopers of kittens, taking entire charge of them, and always calling to them to come to him, quite unruffled by the practical jokes the ungrateful little creatures too often played on him. There was also a pet turtle-dove, who was very fond of the old pussy, and sat on him, and cooed to him.

The Spaniards are extremely fond of cats and birds, always keeping them together, in a way that I should have thought hazardous; but it was surprising how seldom fatal results ensued. Dogs do not seem so popular, being more rarely kept as pets; perhaps because, in Spain, a quiet, domestic animal that does not expect nor wish to be taken out for a walk, is preferred. However, especially in Madrid and Granada, we saw some very handsome dogs, who seemed much prized, and were treated with great kindness.

Next day we had chocolate very early, and went to the Cathedral, hoping to hear the Mozarabic liturgy there; but the Mozarabic chapel was under repair, and no mass could be said in it. This was disappointing, Toledo being one of the very few places where this ancient ritual is still in use. The Toledans say that the books were buried by the Gothic priests at the time of the Moslem Conquest, and found again when the Christians re-entered the city.

As the Mozarabic mass was not to be had, we went into the Capilla de los Reyes Nuevos, where so many Kings of Castile are buried. Among them lies Catherine of Lancaster, wife of Enrique the Third, daughter of John of Gaunt, and descendant of the Cid. The statue of John the Second, father of Isabella the Catholic, is here; but his bones lie at Miraflores, beneath the exquisite tomb erected by his daughter. The more ancient kings are buried near the High Altar, where also rests the great Cardinal Mendoza, the " third sovereign," as he was called in the days of Ferdinand and Isabella.

We wandered from chapel to chapel, all rich, all beautiful, all interesting; the grand old Spanish names ever recurring, and bringing back historic memories of the Sanchos and Alonsos, each a hero of chivalry. The Chapel of the Condestable, built by the great and unfortunate Alvaro de Luna, is one of the finest; there the scallop-shells of Santiago (he having been Master of that Order) are mixed with the silver crescent moon, his own armorial bearings.

Yet, with all its magnificence, the Cathedral of Toledo does not weary the eye and mind as that of Burgos does. The whole is so perfect that the rich details adorn without oppressing it. It has been said that architecture is frozen music; and certainly, in that Cathedral one *felt* the silent harmony. Alas! it must be owned that *silent* harmony is the only kind one is likely to perceive in most Spanish churches, for ecclesiastical music is at an exceedingly low ebb throughout the Peninsula. If one could but transfer the old Sistine choir to those wondrous aisles!

The door leading to the cloisters was open, so we went in and sat down under a rose-tree, among the myrtles, and the children brought us bunches of flowers. Those Spanish cloisters are always enchanting, and this is one of the most beautiful, with its light Gothic arches and wilderness of bright blossoms. People say that Gothic architecture suits the gloom of a northern climate; to me it seems to harmonize best with the golden Spanish sunlight.

We should have liked to stay there half the day, and spend the other half sitting in the little Plaza, looking at the exquisite portal; but was there not still the Alcazar to see, and many things besides? To the Alcazar accordingly we went, the Amalekite Alcazar. The very name thrilled one, though I must confess to very hazy notions as to how it came to be Amalekite; nor could I exactly explain to myself why, except in point of antiquity, the Amalekites should have such a strong claim upon my affections. What was worse, I could not get anybody to explain to me clearly who those Amalekites really were; were they indeed children of Amalek? The accounts are various: some saying that they were really and truly a heathen tribe of Palestine, driven out by Joshua; others, that they were Hebrews who fled into Spain in the time of Rehoboam, or later, at the period of the Babylonish captivity, and who were called Amalekites, as having come from the same country whence the Phœnicians had migrated. Be that as it may, its antiquity is appalling. How many dominions it has seen! That is to say, its foundations would have seen them, if they had not, unfortunately, been underground; for, truth to say, little else now remains of any edifice more ancient than the time of Charles the Fifth. But Phœnicians, Romans, Visigoths, Arabians, Spanish Goths again, have ruled since the first stone of that grand fortress was laid ; the Moors properly so called, never. One has got so accustomed, in common parlance, both in Spain and elsewhere, to call everything Arab *Moorish*, that this assertion may at first seem strange, but it is really true. Toledo, with Castile generally, was colonized by natives of Arabia and Persia, without any mixture of African blood. It was among the mountains of Aragon that the Berbers settled, and also in the Alpujarras, south of Granada. The Egyptian Moslems took possession of Murcia and Lisbon, but the Moors of Morocco had not yet overrun the country to any great extent. It was not till the latter part of the eleventh century that the great flood of invasion from Morocco took place, just about the time that Toledo fell again into the power of the Christians, after which epoch the Spanish Moslems were usually called *Moors ;* before that, always *Arabians.* Even after that date, the rulers and generals seem to have been almost always of Arabian descent, though the mass of their subjects were Africans of Morocco. However, all over Spain everybody calls everything belonging to the Moslem domination, without troubling themselves about the exact period, indifferently *Moorish* or *Arabian.*

From the Alcazar the view is superb, though the
low hills in the immediate neighbourhood of Toledo
are tawny indeed, consisting of every shade of brown,
from the darkest sepia to the faintest orange ; but the
more distant landscape is in spring streaked with pale
tender green, stretching away to the blue mountains
and white snows, while over all is the dome of azure
that dims even an Italian sky. The curious bend of
the Tagus can be seen only from a height so as to
understand the topography of the place, the whole
town standing on a kind of promontory formed by the
river. They pointed out to us the remains of the
palace of King Wamba, whose reign seems to have
been a Gothic Golden Age. "The time of the good
King Wamba," is an expression used in Spain equally
to signify anything either very long ago or very
peaceful and prosperous, perhaps because there has
not been a great deal of peace and prosperity in that
country of late years. Anyhow, the expression may
be translated into English either by "Before the
flood," or "In Arcadia." The real date of Wamba
is, however, not so very long ago, being from 672 to
687. Wamba's is an interesting story altogether.
His unwillingness to accept the crown, his deservedly
great popularity, and the strange way in which he
was finally deposed read like a romance. His kingdom

extended not only over all Spain, but over the south of France. It was he who equipped the earliest Spanish fleet; the Arabs beginning by this time to be troublesome by sea, though they had not yet effected a landing on any part of the coast. Fifty years later all Spain was under the dominion of Islam. The walls of Toledo were built by Wamba; and history tells us of his triumphal entry into the city after his victories at Barcelona, Narbonne, and Nîmes. In the midst of his glory he abdicated, and ended his days in a monastery. Strange tales were told of how an enemy administered a strong opiate to him, and had his head shaved; for, according to the laws of the Goths and Franks, a head once shaven could wear no crown except the tonsure, which, by the way, if true, shows clearly in what light the temporal sovereignty of any priest would have been regarded in those old days. Others say that, being very ill, he became insensible, and was supposed to be dead; the attendants therefore cut off his hair, and dressed him in the monkish garb for burial; a pious observance common in those times, and up to a much later period. He woke from his trance, and, whether in obedience to the old Gothic laws, or merely impelled by the feeling that one who had so nearly crossed the verge of death should never return to the world again, he voluntarily became a monk and died in the cloister. Another account is that Wamba, weary of reigning, himself contrived the plot which dethroned him.

The Toledans still cherish the Gothic associations of the Alcazar much more than those of Moorish days. The names of Recaredo and Recesuintho are inscribed on its walls, with the dates respectively of 589 and 652. This Recaredo was Recared the First, who reigned from 586 to 601. It was in his time that the whole Peninsula abjured the errors of Arianism and became Catholic. He was son of Leovigild, who removed the capital of Spain from Seville to Toledo. Recesuintho is the same whose crown is in the Hôtel Cluny in Paris. But the proudest memory of all is that of Alonso the Sixth, who was here proclaimed Emperor of Toledo, and who here appointed the Cid its first Christian alcaide.

From the Alcazar we went down into the marketplace, still called by its Arab name of Zocodover. *Zoc* or *Suk* is, at this day, a market-place in Arabic; but, I believe, the original word meant the Moorish summer-houses made of cane, which are often to be seen in southern Spain and in Morocco. Probably the markets were held in summer under this kind of shelter, and hence the name. A fair has been held in this Zocodover every Tuesday for many centuries. It was an ancient custom under the Moslem rule, and the peasants still come in with their wares as they did when Abdarrahman reigned in Cordoba, and his viceroy here in Toledo; and longer ago than that, when the first Abdarrahman was but a viceroy under the Caliph of Damascus, when the Ommiades ruled in that oldest city of the earth, and Bagdad was yet unbuilt.

This being the case, we felt it our duty to buy something at a fair of such respectable antiquity. All the wares were spread on the ground, and the vendors sat among them, also on the ground. Nothing very splendid was displayed for sale: fruit, vegetables, chickens, eggs, little mirrors, brown earthen jars, coarse stuffs, and very pretty fans were the chief things; the latter were astonishingly cheap. I now began to understand how it was that the beggars were always so much better provided in this respect than I could ever contrive to be. So, not wishing to be outdone by them, we each bought a fan, for which we paid the extravagant sum of fivepence apiece; but of course we could not attempt to rival the beggars in the management of the article.

Then we went to the Mezquita, formerly, as the name imports, a mosque, and now a church, called the ' Cristo de la Luz.' Its modern name was given to it from the legend of a miraculous light appearing. Excavations were made on the spot, and a strange, ghastly crucifix was found, with real human hair and beard. This crucifix is still in the church, above the altar.

Long before the Arab invasion, a church is supposed to have existed here. Indeed, fragments of an earlier building are visible in the walls of the present edifice. It has not been altered at all, except of course by a little whitewash (and even that, less than usual), since Moorish days—since Alonso the Sixth, nearly eight hundred years ago, took the city. Here mass was said for the first time, when the Christians entered; for the first time, that is, for three centuries and a half. It is an exceedingly curious and interesting church, or rather mosque. The arches are very peculiar, quite Moorish, and all different; lately, they have discovered frescoes in some of the alcoves; these, of course, date from Christian times, and were probably painted over the old arabesques.

The beautiful Puerta del Sol is very near the Mezquita; so we went and looked down from above on this Eastern gate. There it stands, looking as if no force, no time could overthrow it, nor even chip a morsel off its stately towers; a true Gateway of the

Sun, whose rays lighted up the pale rose-red brick-work into the most glowing flame-colour. I should have liked to go down and see it from below, but the road was totally shadeless, and Spanish noonday is a serious matter in the month of June. So we contented ourselves with the splendid view from the point where we stood, looking over the swift, full Tagus, and the Huerta del Rey; those meadows by the river-side where Alonso held a Cortes to judge between the Cid and his treacherous sons-in-law, the Counts of Carrion, who had married and ill-treated his daughters, Doña Elvira and Doña Sol.

Next we proceeded to the Hospital of Santa Cruz, now a military college. It was vacation-time; so we had all it to ourselves, and could wander about as we pleased. The sculptured tracery is very beautiful, resembling twisted wreaths of double convolvulus, a little in the same style as that round the doorway at Las Huelgas, near Burgos. The Hospital is a Greek cross, and everything in and about it is in the same form; even the very nails of the door have the cross on them. Here we found Roman association; for Cardinal Mendoza, who built it, was titular Cardinal of Santa Croce in Gerusalemme.

But it would take too long to tell all we did and saw in Toledo; how we wandered up and down the

quiet streets, and peeped into dim, cool Moorish
courts or *patios*, with the oriental-looking well in one
corner, and a thick awning overhead; and how
everybody, instead of resenting our impertinent
curiosity, bowed politely, and invited us to come
in 'and consider the house our own; and showed
us Arabian stucco-work, and marvellously inlaid
wooden roofs, and quaint staircases, and room
partly lined with the beautiful azulejos, which we
English call Dutch tiles, though they are really
Moorish. In one house was a Moorish hall (now used
as a private theatre) with very fine tracery. We
went also into the Town-hall, which is wainscoted
with azulejos of majolica patterns.

Very tired we were when we had seen all; and
greatly did we enjoy the next day, spent in thinking of the wonders of Toledo, and listening to the
nightingales and cuckoos, under the shady elms of
Aranjuez.

Really those elms make one have quite an affection for Philip the Second's memory; a feeling
which was previously not by any means habitual
to me. Before he brought them from England,
Aranjuez must have been a much less agreeable
place. To do the Spaniards justice, they thoroughly
appreciate those magnificient trees, and take the

greatest care of them. Little runnels of water flow at their feet, and this, with the hot sun, nourishes them so well that they grow to a size I have never seen equalled before or since. The trunks rise, tall and straight, to an immense height before they begin to branch; then the boughs shoot higher and higher, till at last they meet overhead, in an impervious roof of green; a thing not to be despised when between you and the Spanish sun. Aranjuez is a good deal hotter than Toledo, as we found when walking across the wide, white, shadeless space in front of the palace.

It is an extremely handsome building, and looks as if it would be pleasant to live in, there being nothing dreary about it. There is one very curious room, which, instead of being painted or papered, is entirely lined with beautiful Capo di Monte porcelain in high relief. The gardens, however, are the great attraction; not so much the *Florera*, or flower-garden, which was simply a jungle of luxuriant common flowers, losing itself finally in an immense orchard, where the apricots and cherries hung over the tangled roses. But the shady walks under the elms, oriental planes, and sweet-blossomed lindens were delicious. We sat a long time in the very thickest of the covert, with the nightingales almost deafening us with their song ; and, in the distance, the clear sweet cry of the cuckoo, bringing back memories of primrose banks at home.

There are ponds and rustic bridges and summer-houses in abundance ; and there were once waterfalls and fountains in a small way, when Queen Isabella and her gay Court used to come here every spring, after Easter, for six weeks. The ponds are stagnant now, the waterfalls silent, the fountains dry, but the great glory of the place can never dry up—the lordly Tagus, which rushes in full stately volume right through the garden. Somehow, I could never get accustomed to seeing the Tagus there; though, to be sure, as I had just parted from it at Toledo, I need not have been so surprised. But one always associates the Tagus more with Lisbon and Portugal generally than with Aranjuez or Toledo, or any other Spanish place or thing. There is certainly no lack of water here; for the Jarama (celebrated in Moorish ballads for the fierce breed of bulls reared on its banks) joins the Tagus quite near the palace.

We went to the Casa del Labrador, one of those little Trianon-like palaces at one period so beloved by sovereigns who might have been better lodged in their more regal dwellings. It is a pretty little bird's-nest of a place, in the midst of deep shade, a very wilderness of greenery, which must have been pleasant to eyes weary of the glare at the larger palace. It seemed a kind of playing at being lost in the depths of a forest. French timepieces abound in the house; and in one room was a clepsydra, more appropriate in the vicinity of Toledo, so renowned in the Middle Ages for those water-clocks, that learned men came from distant lands to inspect them. An odd contrast between the gilt *pendule*, suggestive of Louis Quinze and all his surroundings, and the strange-looking instrument which aided Alonso the Wise in his heterodox astronomical calculations!

The gardens are of great extent, and, pleasant as it was, the walk was fatiguing, especially when we had to cross the Tagus by a shadeless bridge, and then traverse an equally shadeless Plaza, in order to get into the Jardin de la Isla, which is quaint and formal, with statues like those in the Villa Borghese in Rome.

Then we went back to dinner, to the little Fonda de los Infantes, where the waiter was greatly distressed that we would not eat more. We apologised, saying that we had breakfasted late, and extremely heartily. He replied: "I do not know about that; I only know that now your worships have eaten nothing, nothing, nothing (nada, nada, nada)," vanishing out of the room with an untouched dish of asparagus and a melancholy countenance. Very soon he returned, with everything he could think of to tempt us to eat, and a request that we would only name anything we fancied. It was really an exceedingly comfortable clean little inn, with very good food and great civility.

In the evening it was very hot in the house, so, though tired, we went out. The road, though pleasantly shady in the day time, looked rather gloomy in the dusk. Accordingly, we coaxed the gate-keeper of the palace-garden to let us in again. This was quite contrary to rule, as people ought to get in only with a *papeleta* or permit, which serves for but one visit, and ours had been already given up in the morning. But I suppose he saw that we would give him a trifle, and therefore admitted us. We went up to the flower-garden, which had been too sunny to linger in at noon. Now it was delicious with all fresh odours, and the song of the nightingales louder and sweeter than ever. Long did we sit there, till we began to fear we might be locked in for the night. I don't know that it would have been any great misfortune after all ; it would have been quite safe, and exceedingly cool and pleasant. But we found the civil gardener waiting to let us out, and receive his half-peseta. It was a well-bestowed fivepence.

The wide dusty street of Aranjuez was suffocatingly hot; thunder was growling in the distance, and, as we entered the inn, one or two great drops of rain fell. Our hopes of a refreshing shower were disappointed, however; for, though the thunder crashed and rolled with blue forked lightning all night, yet there was scarcely any rain, and next morning the sky was cloudless as ever. We were told that those rainless thunder-storms were characteristic of Aranjuez, and that they were extremely dangerous, there being almost always somebody struck by the thunderbolt.

By breakfast-time we were again in Madrid, occupied with preparations for our excursion to La Granja, Segovia, and the Escorial.

CHAPTER VI.

On the 14th of June we left Madrid by the early train for Villalba, on the northern railway; there we were to find the diligence for La Granja, or St. Ildefonso, as it was originally called; La Granja meaning simply the Grange, or farm. Philip the Fifth, who hated the Escorial, was struck with the extreme beauty of the situation and purity of the air at this mountain farm of the monks of St. Ildefonso; he therefore bought it of them in 1720, built the palace, and made the gardens at a great expense.

This was to be our first experience of a Spanish diligence. Now, in no country were we partial to this mode of travelling, always preferring a *vetturino* in Switzerland and Italy, and it certainly did not seem probable that we should here find greater comfort than in those more tourist-ridden countries. To add to our misgivings, we could not get the seats we wanted. The *berlina* is the best place, answering to what is called in France and elsewhere the *coupé;* in it there is room for three, and very amply sufficient room, too. Above this is what in Spain is called the coupé, which is perched at a tremendous height, and, though covered with a hood like that of a caleche, has no glass in front. Sometimes there are leather curtains, sometimes not; but, in any case, they can never be drawn, and are generally wonderfully torn and dilapidated. To get up to this elevated position is not always easy; getting down is less difficult, owing to the laws of gravitation, which, however, by no means ensure your not hurting yourself in the process. At the starting-points from any large civilized town, there is generally a ladder, more or less unsteady, and not invariably long enough; but still it is a great help. In the smaller places there is nothing of the kind; and everybody looks hopelessly, first at you, and then at the height above you, as if this were a contingency that had occurred for the first time. At last a neighbour produces a rickety table, or the sausage-seller on the opposite side of the street brings out a greasy bench, or an official rises grandly from a broken chair, and, with a bow worthy of the Grand Monarque, presents it to you; and by the united exertions, most obligingly offered, of all your fellow-passengers and half the population of the village, you are finally hoisted into your seat.

When we arrived at Villalba, two diligences were waiting, as it seemed to us, in a pigsty; and, truth to say, their appearance harmonized admirably with their surroundings. We soon perceived, however, that the pigs were mere casual visitors, who had come to see the travellers start; and the state of dirt around was but the normal condition of the place. Of course, there was nobody to help us out of the train, nor into the diligence, nor even to tell us which was for La Granja; but it is surprising how soon one learns to be independent, to open the doors of railway carriages, to get out and in when the train is in motion, to find out somehow where one is, and where one ought to be, in order to reach one's destination;

and, in short, to get out of the habit of considering oneself as luggage, to be taken care of and forwarded by the proper authorities. To be sure, some things in Spain are greatly in one's favour : at the station there is never a crowd, and, above all, never a hurry ; the train goes so slowly that getting out when it is in motion can scarcely be dangerous ; and, though no Spaniard ever volunteers information, even when it is his duty to do so, all are most willing to give it when asked, although you may chance to apply to somebody who has no connection whatever with the subject.

We scrambled up like cats into our coupé, having secured the whole of it for ourselves. Once up, it was not so bad, though rather dirty ; there was plenty of room, and the view not impeded by the driver's back, as is sometimes the case in the berlina. There was a little difficulty at the first start, in consequence of two of the mules running backwards, and one attempting to go round and round. But soon we were off ; and, observing a stream and a bridge before us (two things not often found united in Spain, though frequently to be seen separately), we naturally concluded that we were to cross the stream by means of the bridge. Not at all ; whether merely impelled by the force of habit, or whether the bridge was supposed not strong enough for the heavy diligence, we dashed off the road, down a steep bank, plunged with our eleven mules and one horse right through the water, and struggled and scrambled up the still steeper bank on the other side: the *mayoral* or con- ductor shouting, screaming, swearing, and addressing each mule by name, with very uncomplimentary adjectives, while the by-standers helped, to the utmost of their power, by sending a shower of stones after the animals. It was an excellent beginning, inas- much as we saw at once that it was no such easy matter to upset a diligence. After this the road was tolerable, and the scenery lovely. The gum-cistus was in even richer bloom than when we had crossed the Guadarrama the first time in coming to Madrid; the broom was more golden, the lavender more royally purple, and in the diligence, of course, we had more time to observe and enjoy the profusion of wild- flowers. We wound our way up the steep slopes that reminded us of the background of a Velasquez; but instead of his cold greens, here all was brilliant colour, and his dark indigo blues became purest sapphire. Up we went till we got among the snow- fields; and the cool freshness was delicious, after the glare of Madrid and the tawny desolation of Toledo. It was like an Alpine pass, and the road was actually cut through the snow which lay on both sides. Then we descended into a wild valley, full of magnificent pines, where the road skirted a tremendous ravine, and was exceedingly Norwegian in character. In some parts the scenery reminded us of the Bavarian Highlands, near Ammergau; and altogether it had quite lost its Spanish and *Velasquez* look. It was a most delightful drive, and we were quite sorry to emerge from this grand forest into the open country again. Even then, it was very pretty; the ground was beautifully broken with thickets of dog-roses and plenty of oak brushwood; and always the blue Guadarrama peaks and the snowy slopes.

About five hours from the time we left Villalba, we came in sight of a stiff, prim edifice, with high-pointed roofs and pepperbox towers; looking like the palace of some small, dull German princedom, and very unlike the wild Guadarrama scenery. We stopped under a large tree, there being apparently no diligence-office; but luckily there was a ladder, and we descended among the whole population; not very many, to be sure. We had been advised to go to the Fonda Europea; and, on naming it, a bright-looking French youth of fourteen or fifteen came forward, and took possession of our small luggage. It was a most comfortable little inn, kept by a Frenchman and his wife and family, without any waiters or servants whatever. The eldest son kept the principal shop in the place ; the second cooked, and extremely well too, besides playing a great deal on the piano ; the third, Jules, who had received us, was waiter, boots, chambermaid, porter, and *commissionaire ;* in addition to which, he knew exactly the position of the old strawberry beds, now run wild, in the Palace-garden, and how to creep through the fences in order to get at them. The fourth boy was still at his education ; and his father's great ambition was to send him to England to learn the language. The landlady was a nice, motherly woman, who superintended everything, and made wonderful apricot jam. The landlord did not do much except pet his little girls, scold everybody else, rail at the Spanish nation, and press his guests to eat.

Here we should really have felt inclined to stay all summer, had not the Alhambra lain beyond. We rose early, had chocolate, and went into the Palace-gardens. Those gardens are open to the public every day, and all day long ; and as the public, in this instance, consisted exclusively of ourselves, it was most enjoyable. Long, shady elm-avenues stretch in all directions ; the leaves were but just out, and had not yet lost their first fresh green and delicately-crimped edges; and in those thick coverts the nightingales sang all day long. Near the palace all is formal, with stiff gardens, quaintly clipped trees, and splendid fountains; but gradually it becomes wilder and more forest-like, till at last, after many a long, cool alley, where the very air seems of emerald, one enters a little firwood, full of wildflowers. From this one emerges on a little lake, just below a bold bare peak of the Guadarrama, which rises almost sheer out of the water. This lake is in reality artificial; but so wild and natural does it look, that one can scarcely believe it otherwise than a mountain tarn.

The palace itself is a delightful little place; little, that is, when compared with the Escorial, or with the palace in Madrid, or even with Aranjuez; but it is really a good-sized building, with pretty apartments, and the advantage, I should think, of being always cool, even in the hottest weather. In June, when we were there, the ground-floor was quite too cold. The Queen's private apartments are charming, with some good modern pictures. The bath-room is the prettiest I have ever seen, being a mixture of bath, fountain, and conservatory. No wonder La Granja has always been such a favourite residence of the Spanish Bourbons.

In the reserved gardens is a labyrinth, greatly

delighted in by those same Bourbon sovereigns, who
amused themselves by taking people to the centre
and then letting them make fruitless efforts to get out
again. It was not so very difficult after all, not being
nearly so complicated as some other labyrinths I have
seen. We found our way out easily enough, having
only twice to retrace our steps a little way.

Otherwise, there is not much to see in the reserved
gardens; they being chiefly nurseries of young trees
and shrubs. The winters are too long and cold, and
the soil too poor for very fine flowers. However, the
gardener gave us beautiful bunches of roses.

We went also to see the remains of the old chapel
of the monks of St. Ildefonso. The situation is lovely ;
and I think they must have been sorry to sell their
mountain grange to Philip the Fifth.

One day the landlord came to us in a state of great
excitement to say that Marshal Serrano was coming
that afternoon; and if " Mesdames " would go and sit
under the large tree where the diligence arrived, they
would see " Le gentil General." " Is he coming in
the diligence ? " we asked with some surprise. " How
else could he come ? " was the yet more astonished
reply. And it was quite true that, unless he walked
or rode, there was no choice. Indeed, in Spain, even
royal princes frequently travel in this way, from

sheer lack of any other means of conveyance. Once when the present King and Queen of Portugal passed through Spain on their way from Paris to Lisbon, they took the whole diligence on the Badajoz route, and travelled thirty hours in it, in the month of December, the King going outside, and the Queen and little Prince in the berlina. Queen Isabella herself, however, always came from Madrid to La Granja in a *coche*, or travelling-carriage, with relays of mules, forced into so quick a gallop that one or more of the poor animals generally died afterwards.

But the diligence was to be Serrano's conveyance; and the news of his expected arrival having spread, everybody turned out to meet him in gala dress. There were actually some gens-d'armes, the first we had seen in Spain, and they were exceedingly well-dressed, and looked remarkably soldier-like. All the gatekeepers, gardeners, and other officials connected with the palace were there in splendid uniforms; and everybody of consequence, our landlord and his sons included, had on their Sunday's best. There was no rabble; I don't think there are materials for a mob in La Granja, which is essentially an aristocratic and royal place: the crowd seemed composed of officials and shopkeepers. All stood respectfully a little apart; and when the lumbering diligence appeared, those who had arms presented them, and those who had hats took them off. We, of course, expected to see Serrano step out of the berlina. Not at all! He emerged from the dusty, dirty interior, and walked quietly away, carrying an exceedingly small carpet-bag, and acknowledging the salutations of the people.

He looked older than I expected, but walked with a firm, springy step, and his bright, quick eye glanced eagerly round. I could not but contrast his reception here with the cold, slighting manner in which poor King Amadeus was looked at in the streets of Madrid.

The next day we were told the waterworks were to play. "In honour of Marshal Serrano?" asked we innocently. "Not at all, Madame; the fountains play only for royalty," was the reply. "But what royal personage is here at present?" said we. This was a puzzling question; and the only answer vouch-safed was a recommendation to go and see the wonderful fountains. Certainly, they are magnificent; finer than Sydenham, finer than the Grandes Eaux at Versailles; even though the most beautiful of all was, unluckily, under repair. The surrounding scenery, too, is infinitely more picturesque than in either of the above-named places.

When we went into the garden, there was nobody

there except the gardeners and gatekeepers in uniform, as if to receive the Queen. Presently the great palace-entrance to the garden was thrown open, as it used to be for the Queen and her Court, and out stepped Serrano, with two or three gentlemen with him. He bowed royally to everybody, and immediately the fountains began to play

One of them is so contrived as suddenly to increase so much as to drench all the by-standers. We had been warned of this, and stood at a cautious distance; but Serrano, though he must have known it well, was talking at the moment, and had to jump back very quickly to escape being thoroughly wet. Queen Isabella delighted much in this fountain. We were told she used to engage people in conversation, so that they could not escape; and she did not care how wet she got herself, provided she could succeed in drenching anybody else.

The fountains played in succession, each beginning just as Serrano came up; and, indeed, he walked so exceedingly fast, that it was no easy matter to keep up with him, especially as it was the hottest hour of the day, and there is not much shade in that part of the garden.

There was nobody present except Serrano himself, the innkeeper and his family, and ourselves, but they

still asserted that whatever might be the reason of
the fountains playing, it was not in honour of the
Marshal !

After it was over he again bowed, this time taking
off his hat; the officials bowed very low indeed, and
Serrano walked quickly away.

Ten days passed most agreeably in our leafy retreat.
We had got to know all the work-people, the civil
gardeners, and the old woman at the gate, whose
heart we had won in this manner : one day, when we
were walking down the steep street leading from the
palace, we espied a tortoise making its way leisurely
along in the very middle of the road, where a passing
cart must inevitably have crushed it. We did not
know whether, in Spain, tortoises habitually crawled
about the streets in this manner ; but thought it best
to capture it, and carry it back to the palace-gate.
"Does this belong to your worship ?" said H. politely,
in her best Spanish. "Maria purisima ! that's my tortoise," exclaimed the old woman, holding out her arms
to receive the treasure ; and adding, "It is a great
runner (corre mucho)," which is not the usual
character of this animal. She was full of gratitude,
inquired if our worships liked kittens, and, on being
answered in the affirmative, ran into her house,
deposited the tortoise in a place of safety, and came

back with a lapful of cats and kittens of all ages and
sizes, whose different relationships she strove to
explain to us, while a large dog looked solemnly and
respectfully on. The tortoise certainly was a great
vagabond; and several times afterwards we saved it
from destruction. The consequence was that the old
woman was always ready to let us out through her
house, if the great gate was closed, as was sometimes
the case when we stayed in the garden long after sunset. And how magnificent those sunsets were, over
the great plain that stretched away far below us, with
the Cathedral of Segovia standing up like a tall ship
in the midst of the golden sea!

I could never make up my mind whether the
evenings or the fresh bright mornings were the most
delightful. Perhaps the early mornings; for then the
nightingales sang the loudest; but, indeed, they sang
all day long, more or less. The only drawback, the
only thorn on the rose, was the fear of the much-
lreaded asp. One is always told that there is only
one venomous kind of snake in Spain. This is quite
true; but would be even more reassuring, if there
were not so very many of that particularly deadly
species. After all, it is not much consolation, if a
snake bites you, to be told that it is precisely the only
poisonous kind in the country. The common wrig-

ling, dark-coloured snake is perfectly harmless ; and is indeed supposed to be beneficial, being much used, made into broth, as a remedy for consumption. But the grey asp is a very deadly creature, some people even asserting there is no cure for its bite ; while others say it is not always fatal. However this may be, it was not pleasant to see a large asp crawling majestically, with head erect, down the very middle of a broad path, and ensconcing itself behind our favourite seat. The gardeners are exceedingly afraid of them.

But now St. John's Day was at hand, when the nightingales cease to sing, and the heat is supposed to begin ; and we had Segovia and the Escorial still to see, and burning La Mancha to cross, before getting to the pure air and deep shade of Granada. We therefore, most reluctantly, prepared for departure, visited all our favourite haunts once more, and started for Segovia early on " the morning of St. John," so often sung of in the old Spanish ballads. In little more than an hour we drew near the gate, and found ourselves in the middle of a gipsy horse-fair ; the fair of St. John. The gipsies are the great horse-dealers in this part of the world, and they are said to cheat fearfully.

The first object that strikes one at the entrance of

Segovia is the old Roman amphitheatre; it is in good preservation, and is now a bull-ring. We hastened on, however, in order to be in time for High Mass at the Cathedral. It is a grand building, but plain compared with Burgos and Toledo; the position is perfectly superb. We entered, and found it full of peasants, in most picturesque costumes. One very tall, striking-looking man, was attired exactly like a man-at-arms of the olden time, in tight-fitting buff jerkin, broad leather belt, a sort of flounce round the waist, high boots, wide sleeves, and a very high, standing-up ruff. Everybody looked clean and respectable, and extremely devout; the women crouching low on their mats, and the men, with high ruff and short cloak, kneeling on one knee, and looking like Sir Walter Raleigh. The church was exceedingly clean, as indeed, is generally the case in Spain; Spanish churches being very superior in this respect to Roman ones.

Then we went back to the Fonda, to breakfast. It was an exceedingly primitive little inn, in the very picturesque market-place, where every house leant in a different direction from its neighbour, besides being all of various colours; brown, orange, and yellow, being the predominating tints. At first, the people at the inn were greatly surprised to see us, and asked, as they almost always do in small places in Spain, "Who could possibly have recommended this hotel?" But soon they recovered from their stupor, and lavished civilities on us. Our landlord was a fat, elderly man, who seldom ventured beyond the precincts of the kitchen. His wife was a rather pretty, lady-like woman, evidently well educated, who did not do much except go to mass, say kind things to her guests, and cultivate her geraniums, the finest of which she liberally gathered for us. There was a waiter, quite a young boy, who came when called, and received orders which he never executed; while all the work of the house was done by Manuela, the little lame and deformed chamber-maid. Her duties consisted of doing everything that the boy forgot, besides making the beds, cleaning the house (rather imperfectly, it must be owned), bringing hot water, waiting on the guests, walking all round the town with them as *commissionaire*, if, as was often the case, no other was to be had, running messages, doing all the needle-work, keeping the linen in order, dressing her mistress's hair in the most elaborate fashion, taking care of the birds, and petting seven black cats of different ages, from a week old upwards. She was always in good humour, never in a hurry, and sang merrily all day long; she had even time to find the

kittens when the old cat hid them, and forgot
where she had put them, as frequently happened.
Poor little Manuela! she was an orphan, she said;
had never known her father and mother, and
had no relations; but she had been a long time
with "la Señora" (the landlady), who was *so* kind
to her!

The inn was not exactly what would generally be
called comfortable, being rather dirty; and the cookery
was not particularly good. But there was so much
kindness and hearty good-will, that it made up for all
deficiencies.

We had been warned beforehand to beware of
talking English here; for most of the young students
at the great Segovian Military College dine in this
hotel, and all understand English, though nothing
will induce them to speak it. We thought this a
rather alarming prospect, and selected an hour for
breakfast when we supposed we should have the comfort of solitude. But when we opened the door, the
room was nearly full of students, sitting at breakfast
with their hats on. We need not have doubted
Spanish politeness, however; the moment they saw
us, they started up, threw their hats to the other end of
the room, gave us their chairs, and went to look for
others for themselves.

After breakfast, we went to the Alcazar, that superb Alcazar! It is impossible to imagine a more magnificent position, as it stands on that bold promontory formed by the two streams, the Eresma and the Clamores. Segovia is said to be a thoroughly Castilian city; but there is nothing Castilian in the view from the Alcazar: all is running water and fresh green leaves.

The history of the fire that made a majestic ruin of what was, till recently, one of the stateliest edifices in Spain, is curious, as illustrating the complete lawlessness which prevails in this extraordinary country. The students, all scions of noble Spanish families, found it dull in Segovia, and thought, if they could succeed in destroying the Alcazar, then the seat of the Military College, they might possibly be transferred to Madrid, and there amuse themselves to their heart's content. They accordingly set it on fire; and the Segovians say the sight of it blazing was something appalling. So far they succeeded in their intention, inasmuch as the building was too much damaged to be any longer used as the college; but they did not carry their point of being transferred to Madrid; another locality being found for them in the hated Segovia. No investigation was made, however, and nobody was punished; the families to whom the

culprits belonged being too powerful to be meddled
with !

But even in ruin it is magnficient, and the view
glorious. Its historical interest, too, is great. We
were shown the room where the thunderbolt fell,
close to Alonso the Wise, just as he was finding
out the starry secrets of which the Church dis-
approved. The learned monarch was dreadfully
frightened; and, to make amends for his too
prying researches, put up a rope of solid gold, in
honour of St. Francis, round the cornice of the
room ; vowing also to wear a hempen rope always
round his waist. The golden rope was melted by
the conflagration in 1862.

Here Isabella the Catholic took refuge in her
early troubles; and here she was residing when
she was proclaimed Queen of Castile. Here, too,
our Charles the First stopped for a night, 13th
September, 1623, on his Spanish journey, and
supped on " certaine trouts of extraordinary great-
nesse."

We were shown the window from which the
poor little Infante, son of Henry the Third, was let
fall by his attendant. It is indeed a fearful
height; down, down, among the rocks and bushes,
the hapless baby must have been dashed to pieces.

Of course, we went up to the very top; rather dizzy work, as in some places there is no parapet whatever, and you are occasionally warned not to step on this or that stone, as it is insecure. One terrace, in particular, our guide would not allow us to go on at all; he said it would break off, some day, and fall into the river below. When we were on the highest part, a tremendous thunderstorm came on; and the crashes were so completely overhead, that we began to think we were incurring much the same risk as Alonso the Wise. It was so grand that even this danger could not drive us away; the clouds stalked about among the mountains, blotting out one after another, and then rushing down and descending on Segovia; till, all at once, the storm rolled away over the great plain, and the hills were again sapphire and pearl.

When we came out of the Alcazar, we were much struck by the extreme beauty of the view of the Cathedral from this point. It stands high, and the rich yellow of the stone contrasts finely with the blue sky and bluer hills, with their pure white snows. I accordingly determined to sketch it, later in the day; but in the meantime we proceeded to the Vera Cruz, a little Templar church, which stands on the very edge of the green oasis of Segovia, where the dry, pale yellow desert stretches away as far as the eye can reach, with the little village of Zumarramala in the midst, looking like a heap of stones.

Unluckily, this being St. John's Day, there was nobody to open the church; the guardian having gone, it was supposed, to the gipsy fair. We had therefore to content ourselves with walking round the outside, and admiring the peculiar and beautiful west doorway, with its zigzag mouldings. Then we went on to Fuencisla, an exceedingly curious church, partly cut in the rock, which rises above it, and from which criminals were anciently thrown. In coming back, we passed a large cave in the rock, where a great number of the houseless poor live, or rather sleep; for their waking moments are probably devoted to begging, or possibly to stealing. We asked if there were any robbers there; and the answer was, "Sometimes it might be so." And indeed I should not like to pass that cave in the dusk alone, and with money in my purse.

We next went to the *Casa de Moneda*, or Mint, founded by Alonso the Seventh, in the twelfth century, and now no longer used. It is beautifully situated on the Eresma, in a mass of green foliage, with a pretty little garden sloping down to the river. All

was dilapidated, tangled, confused; the garden so
overgrown that one could scarcely get along the
walks; but, instead of weeds, it was a jungle of
splendid old-fashioned cabbage-roses that hindered
our progress. We were not at all inclined to find
fault with this sweet-scented wilderness, especially
when a great bunch of the very largest and
finest roses was bestowed on us. In the house,
the instruments for coining still remained, but
broken and dirty; not rusty, however, for in dry
Spain nothing rusts, nothing moulds. The spiders
were extremely flourishing, and their industry was
testified by many cobwebs. The Mint is now
established in Madrid.

Now, we began to climb the steep hillside leading
up to the town. It was exceedingly hot; for, though
the air of Segovia is remarkably pure and bracing,
the sun on St. John's Day has quite as much power
as is pleasant; and the Spanish veil, which we had
adopted, as being less conspicuous, gave but little
protection to the head on this shadeless ascent. We
were, therefore, very glad to go into the church of
Santa Cruz, whose coolness seemed icy coldness after
the warm outer air. In Italy it would have been dangerous to sit in a cold church after such a walk; but
in Spain, if you can manage to avoid sunstroke, and

don't mind being baked occasionally, nothing else
does you any harm; always excepting in Madrid, where
everything half kills you. So we rested comfortably
in this Arctic temperature, and then examined the
beautiful carvings round the doorway. The cloisters
are deserted, and exceedingly dull; which latter state
of things is rare in Spain. The adjoining convent
was Dominican, founded by Ferdinand and Isabella,
and bears their well-known motto, "Tanto monta,"
with their devices, the yoke and the bunch of arrows.
It was a Spanish custom, in the Middle Ages, for
husband and wife each to adopt a badge of which the
first letter should be the same as that of the beloved
consort's name; for instance, Ferdinand chose the
yoke, or "*jugo*," whose initial corresponded with that of
Isabel, then, strange as it may seem, frequently spelt
Jesabel; while Isabella took the *arrows*, or "*flechas*," for
her device, beginning with the same letter as Ferdinand.

Behind, on the other side of the garden, is a very
curious little church, San Domingo, where we saw an
interesting and exceedingly odd-looking genealogical
tree of St. Dominic and the Guzman family generally,
showing the saint to be descended from Robert,
Duke of Normandy, and consequently from Ganger
Rolf.

The convent of San Domingo is still occupied by nuns, so we could not get in to examine either the old Roman statue of Hercules nor the Moorish frescoes said to exist there,

On our way back to the town, we passed through the Plaza of St. Esteban, and entered the church. There is not much to see inside, but the exterior is very beautiful, with its graceful tower and curious open cloister, or *corredor*, as they call it, *outside* the church.

We next went to the old Roman aqueduct, which is superb. It is in perfect preservation, and still conveys to the town its abundant supply of coldest, clearest water from Rio Frio. The height is stupendous, and so fragile and fairy-like is it, that one marvels how those light arches should, for so many centuries, have resisted the winter's cold and summer's sun of Spain, not to speak of the hand of man. The grandest point is where it strides across the entrance of the town : it is supposed to have been built by Trajan, who, himself a Spaniard, did much for his native country ; but no record whatever exists on the subject. Wonderful tales concerning it are plentiful ; and as we wished to hear what our guide had to say, we asked him "Who had built it?" He replied that a great many extraordinary and incredible stories were told about it, and many of them he really could not believe; but it seemed to him extremely probable that it had been built by the devil! And what confirmed him in this supposition was that, as we might perceive, there was a portrait of the devil up in a niche, "and he must surely have done it himself, for what artist would like to take a portrait of the devil?" We suggested that some people said the portrait in question was that of a saint. "It was all very well to *say* so, but nobody could doubt it was the devil; and was not the aqueduct always called the devil's bridge? And had there not always been a statue up there, even in the old misbelieving times?" This was quite true, only the statue which then existed was supposed to be Trajan. Our guide scouted this last idea, and said it was, and always had been, the devil. Then he related the well-known legend of the devil building the aqueduct in one night, to win the soul of a Segovian girl, and how she cheated him by the legal quibble of finding that a single stone was wanting.

We wished to go to the Parral, once the great Geronimite convent, but being St. John's Day we were told there would be nobody to open it for us, and that it was very doubtful if we could get in, even on the following day. This was disappointing, the

Parral being one of the most curious and beautiful things in Segovia; but there was no help for it, so we went round by St. Millan, an interesting old church with cloisters outside, as is often seen in Spain. Afterwards, H. being very tired, she was left at the inn, while I went back to the Alcazar to sketch the Cathedral.

It was singularly quiet and pleasant. I suppose all the boys and other rabble of Segovia were occupied with the horse fair; for here nothing came near me, except two or three goats, who were as overpoweringly friendly as goats always are, poked me with their horns, jumped on the wall beside me, and looked gravely at my drawing, as if criticising it, and finally attempted to eat my colours, a proceeding which, in the interest of the goats, as well as in mine, had to be put a stop to. I sat there all the afternoon, till the blue hills grew lilac, and the rich golden hue of the Cathedral became brightest flame-colour; and then all melted into pale rose and purple.

Next day hopes were held out that we might possibly get into the Parral, so we started early and were soon in the beautiful Alameda. Here our guide left us, saying he was going to look for the key, which was supposed to exist somewhere at the other end of the town. Nearly an hour passed before he returned, and we began to think some insurmountable difficulty had arisen, and that he, weary of the obstacles, had gone to amuse himself at the gipsy fair. It was so pleasant, however, that we were not inclined to grumble; all was deliciously cool, and fresh, and green, with the pretty Eresma flowing swiftly away, and the willows weeping into it. From this point the view of the Alcazar, towering far up into the sky, is perfectly superb.

At last the guide returned, having in the meantime made an elaborate toilette, which was not altogether superflous, as at first he had been ragged and exceedingly dirty. With him came a most obliging and polite Segovian gentleman, bearing the key. He was a "botanico," which in Spanish does not mean a botanist, but an apothecary. He seemed an extremely well-informed and cultivated man, and was head of an archæological society. The funds of this society were very small indeed, and quite insufficient for the objects they wished to accomplish; but on our offering a donation in aid of it, it was politely but very decidedly refused, on the ground that they, Spaniards, could not think of accepting the money of strangers travelling through their country. It seemed very odd to us, after living so long in Italy, where strangers and their money are looked upon as natural prey, to be snared to any amount. On casually mentioning the circumstance, without comment, to a Roman, he .replied gravely, "The Spaniards are barbarians, and all mad."

Even in its ruin, nothing can be more beautiful than the Parral. Some time in the last half of the fifteenth century, in the palmiest days of Spain, Juan Marquis de Villena had to fight a *duel* with *three* antagonists, as the chronicle rather Irishly expresses it. He had the skill and good luck to overcome them all; and, to commemorate this feat, he founded the Parral, which was finished soon after the taking of Granada. He and his wife Maria lie buried here; and their tombs of elaborately sculptured white marble and alabaster are magnificent, having escaped in a great measure the destruction that has befallen the rest.

To this convent belonged the mountain-farm of La Granja. Surely those monks must have been much detested in Segovia; probably only because they were rich and comfortable. The first thing the mob always does in every one of the many revolutions that have lately taken place, is to rush out to the Parral and break something ; yet the Segovians seem a peaceable set of people in general. Now it is kept carefully locked up for fear of further mischief.

The kind "botanico" guided us through one beautiful court after another, all ruined and grass-grown, where exquisite pillars and cloisters and sculptured tracery are mingled with flowering weeds. We went up to the great balcony, or rather terrace, above the river, from which the view is glorious, with the stately Alcazar rising out of the masses of green foliage. Some part of the Parral is now used as a kind of poorhouse, several families of beggars being allowed to live there. We were not however annoyed in any way, all the poor people being out at their daily avocation of begging; there were no insects, and the rooms were perfectly clean, though dilapidated and almost unfurnished; a sack of straw in one corner, a pot for cooking, and a rope stretched across, on which their clothes were hung, was the whole. Those clothes were a very extraordinary spectacle; most wonderful old cloaks, of which it was difficult to conjecture the original colour or fabric, patched with blue, brown, yellow, grey, green, and black; and over all a sort of mellow russet nondescript hue that was extremely picturesque. I asked if they could not have found patches rather more similar to each other, if not to the original stuff, but was told that the beggars thought it looked much better to have them all different. How said beggars

got out and in, when the place was always locked, I
cannot imagine.

Our friendly archæologist now asked us if we
would like to go into the Vera Cruz, the Templar
Church, which we had found closed the day before.
We accepted with alacrity, and he took us there by a
short cut; the walk was very pleasant, across a dry
rocky field, where poppies and sweet-scented herbs
grew much at their own will. It was noon, and the
sun was hot, but the air had a fresh crispness in it
that our own beloved balmy Italy is without.

Inside the church there is a building two stories
high, which is said to be an exact model of the Holy
Sepulchre. As the church itself is very small, this
inner building fills it up almost entirely. Everywhere there is the Templar cross. There are some
curious inscriptions, one of them relating to the Ides
of April, 1240. The church was built in 1204.

In going back to the inn, we went into a very interesting old Jewish synagogue, in a network of back
lanes. It dates from Moorish days, and is of course
no longer used as a synagogue, there being now no
Jews in Segovia.

We bade adieu, with many thanks, to the obliging
Segovian who had shown us so much; and I set off
alone to finish my sketch at the Alcazar. It was an

odd sensation to walk absolutely alone through this strange Spanish town, finding my way as best I could. Nobody annoyed me; nobody even looked at me, except once when I stopped irresolutely where two streets diverged; then an old woman very politely asked me what I was seeking; and came with me a little way, to put me on the right track. At the Alcazar, I was even more undisturbed than on the previous day, inasmuch as one goat and two dogs were my only neighbours; and they were too much occupied making fun and chasing each other, to have any leisure to spare for me.

Next evening, we had hoped to get to the Escorial, but all the diligence-places were taken; and even for the following day the berlina was unattainable, and we were obliged to content ourselves, as before, with the whole coupé. Having this additional day, and being in hopes that the bustle of St. John's fair was nearly over, I resolved to attempt a sketch of the aqueduct. It was no easy matter, however. There were many idlers still hanging about; and at no time is a Spaniard unwilling to leave his work in order to stare at a stranger, and especially at a lady sketcher. Unluckily too, as often happens, the best view was precisely in the most ineligible place. However, this time I was provided with a guide, who, I hoped, would keep people off, and H. was a host in herself, having a peculiar and valuable talent for striking terror into boys. So I began boldly; and while I was merely drawing the pencil outline, which could be done standing, I did not attract much attention, but when I borrowed a chair from a shop, and sat down to colour, my woes began. As long as the crowd consisted only of those who took some real, though rather teasing interest in what I was about, I did not much care, and submitted patiently to tall youths standing between me and the particular arch I was busied with, and heavy girls leaning over and shaking my chair. But when the whole street filled, and fresh hordes came pouring down each side-lane, the guide began to remonstrate, saying, " Spaniards ought not to behave so rudely." " Si; en la calle," (" Yes; in the street"), was the discriminating reply. This distinction is thoroughly Spanish; I do believe each one of my tormentors would have been politeness itself if I had taken shelter in his house. But in the street it is most true that the obligation of courtesy too often ceases, as was the case here. Seeing therefore that matters had become intolerable, I retreated into a shop, and pulled the curtain (with which all Spanish shops are provided) before me, holding it a little open with one hand, while I drew with the other. It was certainly not the easiest imaginable way of accomplishing a sketch that would have been difficult even under more favourable circumstances. But, happily, the crowd soon got tired of contemplating the curtain, and dispersed sufficiently to allow me to venture out again. The good-natured shopwoman now carefully barricaded me with crockery; and when any boys came near, rushed at them with a stick, saying they were not to break her dishes.

In the afternoon, little Manuela took us to the Provincial Museum, where there was a very miscellaneous collection of objects, old engravings of the time of Louis Quinze, dedicated to " Monsieur le Duc de Choiseul," " Monseigneur le Cardinal de Rohan," and so on. They seemed oddly incongruous here, among the grotesque figures of the Passion Plays, and the wild dark fanatical saints, and horrible martyrdoms of the Spanish school of painting. The most interesting thing was one of the extraordinary granite bulls, like those at Avila. Here they call them pigs; and said there had been originally a pair, and that they. formerly stood in some Plaza or other, at the entrance of an old house. This was " el Caballero, " they said ; and " la Señora " had been sent to the Archæological Museum in Madrid.

Afterwards, we went back to the Cathedral to

examine it in detail, and walked up and down the cloisters, from which there is an excellent view of the whole building. In the sacristy they showed us a splendid silver *custodia*, on wheels, very like the Car of Juggernauth, on a smaller scale. Those *custodias* are used for carrying the Holy Sacrament at the Fête Dieu.

Towards sunset we made our way to the Alameda, always beautiful; but I think we liked it best earlier in the day. The morning light seemed more cheerful and brighter than even the glories of the setting sun. In Spain it always is so; there is no beauty and freshness like that of dawn.

Next day we had a specimen of thoroughly Spanish ways. H. had taken a fancy to a very tiny glass tumbler, small enough to fit into her travelling-bag. She wished to buy it; but on asking the price, it was instantly presented to her, and all payment absolutely refused by our hostess. She also gave us some pretty little devices of plaited paper, made by herself; they were religious subjects, the Cross, the Emblems of the Passion, etc., and were beautifully woven together.

We again mounted to our lofty places in the diligence, and very hot it was. We almost regretted not having come by night, and yet it would have been a pity to miss that lovely drive through the wild pine-forest and across the flowery Guadarrama. The slopes were so entirely covered with the golden broom, that the eye could scarcely bear the dazzling hue. The snow on the road had, alas! disappeared, and the snow-fields above were perceptibly smaller. We got on pretty well, however, till we arrived at the railway at Villalba. Here, as the station was being painted, and there was consequently no admittance, we had to sit in a shed, sharing a bench with dead calves and live bugs, dirty beggars and boorish peasants. Finally, we had to cross the line, and stand a very long time in the sun waiting for the train, which was greatly behind time. When it did come, the carriages were like ovens.

At last we arrived at the Escorial, hot, tired, dusty, and thirsty beyond description; and found rest, shelter, and cold water in the clean and comfortable little Fonda de la Miranda.

We had looked forward with fear and trembling to this visit to the Escorial, having always understood that one's sufferings from cold, dulness, and fatigue, were to be appalling. Everybody, without exception, rejoiced that they had "got it over;" and we had never heard of anybody paying a second visit. So next morning we screwed up our courage, and sallied forth manfully, resolved to go through with it and dare the worst. We soon perceived that whatever miseries from fatigue and dulness might be in store for us, cold was not likely to add to them. We crossed the white glaring road, and found ourselves apparently in the court of an ash-coloured penitentiary surrounded by buildings with small windows, all exactly alike, and all of the same ashen hue. "Those are the houses of the ambassadors," said the guide. For those ambassadors we felt intense compassion.

It was the custom in Spain, under the old régime, that all the foreign ambassadors must follow the Court wherever it went; and after all, dull as those pale grey houses looked, they were at least a place of shelter; whereas, at La Granja, it was exceedingly difficult, even for the diplomatic body, to find lodgings of any kind at any price. Of course, they had to take their own furniture with them in every case; beds, kitchen utensils, everything. How very odd it would seem in England, if all the foreign ambassadors and envoys had always to go to Osborne and Balmoral with the Queen! But in Spain, in those days, Court and ambassadors went to Aranjuez after Easter, stayed till the heat began, then went to cool La Granja for the summer months, and to the Escorial in autumn.

Once in the church all else is forgotten. Beautiful

it is not, for beauty implies something pleasant to look upon; but surely it is one of the grandest edifices ever planned by the mind of man. In its great size and perfect proportions it recalls St. Peter's at Rome; but St. Peter's cold, and grey, and frozen, without light, or life, or colour. Grander perhaps than St. Peter's in its excessive plainness; here there is no bad taste, no meretricious ornament: but it is the stern simplicity of death. It is like the strange wild tales of the northern mythology, of journeys beyond the Realm of Light, where there is no sun, no warmth, no brightness,—to vast, dim halls in the Kingdom of Silence, the very Twilight of the Gods.

There, beside the altar, kneels Charles the Fifth, with his fair and saintly wife, Isabel of Portugal, and their daughter Maria; there, too, are the sisters of Charles, Maria and Eleanor, the latter of whom married Francis the First of France, after the death of her first husband, the King of Portugal. On the other side kneels Philip the Second, with three of his wives: the first, Maria of Portugal, mother of Don Carlos; the third, the lovely Isabella of France, daughter of Catherine de Medicis, and mother of Clara Eugenia Isabella, Philip's best-loved child; and lastly, Anna, the Austrian princess, who was mother of Philip the Third. Mary Tudor's stiff figure and sour face is not among them ; because she was unloved, it is said : yet the still less loved Don Carlos, Philip's unhappy and hated son, is there. Truly, this is a magnificent Temple of Death, ; but oh ! for a grave in a churchyard beneath the blue sky, or a sculptured stone in some quiet, sunny cloister, rather than all this icy grandeur !

We turned from the kneeling figures of the mighty dead, and went up to the choir, which is here a gallery above the church, leaving the space below unbroken. Here Philip the Second used to glide in like a spectre, and seat himself among the monks, and here he received the news of the victory of Lepanto. The choir books are splendid specimens of illumination ; and the guide was most good-natured in allowing us to spend as long a time as we liked over them ; he even made no objection to my copying an initial letter that particularly struck me. The bright little daisies, and strawberries, and purple blossoms, looked strange and out of place, imprisoned beneath this sunless dome.

They showed us Benvenuto Cellini's celebrated white marble crucifix. It is thought very fine, and as far as workmanship goes, it certainly is so; and one is greatly struck with the perfect finish and graceful lines of the figure, after the rough-hewn,

angular Spanish sculpture. But after all, grace and
finish are not what one most wishes for in so sacred a
subject: the face has no divinity in it, nor is it even
a very sublime human type; and I began to think
that perhaps the ghastly Spanish crucifixes, with all
their awful reality, were greater proofs of, and aids to
devotion than this smooth and perfectly well-executed
work of art.

This crucifix was sculptured in 1562. In Benvenuto Cellini's autobiography he mentions how well-
satisfied he was with it (as indeed he generally was
with his own works); how he displayed it in his
studio, inviting everybody to come and see it; how
Duke Cosimo di Medici and his Duchess came also,
and complimented Benvenuto much, who thereupon
offered to give it to the Duchess. Finally, however
he sold it to the Duke for 1500 crowns in gold, and
it was placed in the Pitti Palace in 1565. In 1570
his son and successor, Duke Francesco, presented it to
Philip the Second. It was sent to Barcelona by sea,
and from thence carried on men's shoulders to the
Escorial. It is but natural that it should be so completely the reverse of all that is Spanish; for what
could be more unlike than the gay Court of Florence
under the Medici, and that of Spain under Philip the
Second ?

We now went down to the royal sepulchres. Strange to say, this dwelling of the dead is decidedly more cheerful than most other parts of the Escorial. In its wealth of rich marble, it recalls a little the Medicean Chapel in Florence, though on a smaller scale. There is no decay, no neglect; all is perfect, in which respect it constrasts most favourably with some other places of regal sepulture; for instance, with the pestiferous vault of the Capuchins in Vienna, where the Imperial family are buried, and in which, during the last century, smallpox lurked, and too often carried off the visitor.

I scarcely wondered that the Spanish sovereigns so delighted in descending into this peaceful vault to contemplate their future resting-place. In the Escorial Death seems better and brighter than Life.

Here the great Emperor rests who reigned over the widest and fairest realms of the earth, and who ended his days like a monk at Yuste. German legends tell how he is not dead nor buried, but sits in a cave beneath the Unterberg, with Charlemagne and Frederick Barbarossa, waiting to come forth, till Germany shall be "free and united." But Germany *is* free and united (tolerably so at least), and the cave is still unopened; and in truth, I think, whatever might be the opinion of Charlemagne and Frederick

Barbarossa on the subject, Charles the Fifth would find a great gulf somewhere between the state of modern Europe and the cell at Yuste.

The founder, Philip the Second, of course is here, with his fourth wife, the mother of his heir. The beautiful Isabella of France, whom he loved with such fierce jealousy, lies in the horrible Pudridero, as is the fate of every Queen of Spain who was not also mother of a king. All the little princes and princesses who died in childhood, however dearly loved, are excluded from this wholly regal burial-place, and all were thrust into the Pudridero; and not only those royal children, but Don John of Austria, the Emperor's gallant soldier-son, who won Lepanto.

Queen Isabella was very much shocked and distressed at this horrid state of things; and when one of her own children died, she could not bear the thoughts of such a fate for the little babe: so, in concert with the Duke de Montpensier, she began a new Pantheon, as they call it, for the younger branches of the royal family; and there all the bodies at present in the Pudridero were to be decently interred. This good work was put a stop to by the revolution; and only one monument was nearly completed when Amadeus was called to the throne. This one, oddly enough, is that of a prince of the House of Savoy; but what

prince, or how he came to be there at all, I could not
learn. They persisted in saying it was Emanuel
Philibert himself, he who won St. Quentin, in honour
of which victory the Escorial was built; but this was
clearly impossible, he being, as is well known, buried
in the Cathedral of Turin. The prince who is buried
here certainly appears to have been called Philibert,
that name being inscribed on the tomb; and he may,
possibly, have been husband of one of the Spanish
Infantas. One Philibert of Savoy, besides the hero of
St. Quentin, is connected with Spanish history; but he
died long before Philip the Second was born, or the
Escorial thought of. This Philibert married the
young widow of Prince Juan, Ferdinand and Isabella's
only son, and died a few years after; but there seems
no reason why he should have been buried in Spain
at all.

In the Pudridero is also buried the illegitimate son
of Louis the Fourteenth, the Duke de Vendôme, who
died at Vinaroz, on the east coast of Spain, of eating
too much rich fish. Philip the Fifth, who owed his
throne to him, had the body brought to the Escorial,
in order to do him honour; but surely any other
burial-place would have been better than this: and,
indeed, so little did Philip like the idea of it for himself, even in the royal vault, that by his own

directions he was buried in the little chapel at his beloved La Granja. All the other sovereigns of Spain, from Charles the Fifth downwards, are buried in the Escorial, except Ferdinand the Sixth.

We now proceeded to the Library, a most beautiful hall, in the style of the Vatican Library. The frescoes on the wall are curious, the subject being the different arts and sciences. Eloquence is represented by somebody drawing people after him by cords coming out of his mouth; music, by Orpheus subduing the beasts, who are all on their knees before him; grammar, by Nebuchadnezzar founding the first grammar-school, a fact concerning that monarch of which I was previously ignorant. We saw here Charles the Fifth's camp-stool, under a glass case; which glass case is a lantern or *fanal* of gigantic size, taken at Lepanto.

The manuscripts are, most of them, kept locked up. The Arabic ones are said to be particularly fine; and among them is the whole library of a king of Morocco.

In another hall is the celebrated Last Supper, by Titian; beside it is a very good Tintoretto, Queen Esther fainting before Ahasuerus. There is another good picture by Tintoretto, Christ at Supper in the Pharisee's house. Further on, in a different room, is a masterpiece of Luca Giordano, Balaam and his Ass. In general, I am not very partial to Luca Giordano's paintings; they are usually too slight and showy. But this one is excellent; the donkey is perfect, with an expression of shrewdness and intelligence that makes it seem not at all surprising that he should speak, and speak to the purpose, too.

The *pendant* to this is, Noah drunk, also by Luca Giordano, and very good, though we preferred the Ass. There is also a good Velasquez, the Sons of Jacob bringing him Joseph's bloody garment. The other fine pictures have all been moved to the Museum at Madrid, where we had already seen them.

We could not be admitted to the royal apartments, because they were being prepared for the Queen and the little Princes, who were at that time expected to spend the summer at the Escorial, a plan with which political events soon interfered. We were allowed, however, to go through as many of its thirty-six courts as we wished. Some are little quiet cloisters, most unlike a royal palace; one is a large garden, with quaintly clipped box-trees; others are grey, ashen, colourless squares, where one would naturally expect to see convicts at work, and to be told it was a new model prison.

In the afternoon we walked down to the gardens, which are pretty, but rather hot and shadeless on the 28th of June. Here also is a little toy-palace, which might be made comfortable in winter, but is too small for summer. Some of the rooms are furnished with most elaborate needlework; one in particular is hung round with a series of embroidered pictures, in old-fashioned satin stitch. These were really very beautiful, but the amount of labour was painful to think of. They were worked by a "caballero"—a Spanish gentleman—we were told, who had devoted many years to it. A strange life and occupation.

We then walked back through the long avenues much more quickly than our guide at all liked. He said it was always so with the English; they went along, never looking as if they were in a hurry, while he ran and panted behind them. Though not particularly active, he was an exceedingly intelligent man, who greatly deplored that Spain was, as he phrased it, "with its paws upwards"—"*las patas arriba*," this being a Spanish expression which means topsy-turvy. He had this further peculiarity, that he was the only person in Spain whom we ever heard speak well of King Amadeus. By his account, however, both King and Queen were much liked at the Escorial. He added, "In this place we are not like other Spaniards; we are always satisfied with the sovereign." I could not learn from what this eccentricity arose.

We returned to Madrid in the evening, and found the thermometer at 88° Fahrenheit in our room at night. We had also the disadvantage of finding out how much noise Spanish lungs can make. Everybody except ourselves had, probably, been asleep all day, and awoke, refreshed and strengthened, just as we arrived. The whole night did the shouting, singing, and driving about last; at length, after dawn, there was about an hour's peace.

Next day, unfortunately for us, was " San Pedro;" so, after toiling along the Alcala in the broiling sunshine, we found that all banks were closed. We had never thought of St. Peter's Day, and began to fear we should be detained in Madrid. Our landlord, however, obligingly changed money for us, and we secured our places in the diligence for Granada.

CHAPTER VII.

Madrid was now like a fiery furnace, though why it
should have been so hot I cannot understand, as the
thermometer in the shade never rose above 88° Fahrenheit, and was seldom more than 85°.   But the sun
blazed with a fierceness far beyond anything we had
ever met with in Italy, and crossing the street was a
serious matter.   However, we could have borne the
blinding splendour of the day; but the heat and
noise of the nights were almost unendurable.   With
closed windows, we were suffocated; with open ones,
deafened: so that we hailed with delight the prospect
of a night spent peacefully in a diligence, and longed

impatiently to begin our twenty-seven hours journey.

At 6 A.M., on the 1st of July, we left the hotel : the people were still asleep on the streets, on doorsteps, anywhere ; and in truth they must have slept much more comfortably than we had. The air was cool and fresh, though July had come ; the Prado had not yet lost its spring-like greenness, and oleanders had taken the place of roses. Altogether, Madrid was looking very charming, and we gazed regretfully at the Museum, and wondered if we should ever again behold those marvels of art, the masterpieces of Velasquez and Murillo.

Away we went, still looking back to Madrid, of which much the finest view is to be seen from the railway, in going southwards. When we had passed our old friend Aranjuez, the country was new to us, and we began to look about with interest; but nothing whatever of any kind was to be seen, only a brown plain. On, on we went ; still the same dreary, interminable plain. Now we were in La Mancha, which the Spaniards say means a *spot*, a blot upon the face of the country. The sun blazed hotter and hotter ; hour after hour, the fierce heat, the blinding light, the tawny plain, shadowless, treeless, tenantless ; a desert without grandeur. The windmills were some alleviation, for Don Quixote's sake; and indeed we could not but think of him, as he started also on a hot July morning, and rode all day on his first quest of adventures. Moreover, said windmills were not at all like English ones; they really did look a little like giants with lance in rest. But after seven or eight hours of this, the windmills failed to interest us; the burning atmosphere seemed to produce stupor, and even the water brought to the stations in porous jars had lost all coolness. Vainly did the vendors call out, "Water! water! who wants fresh water?" We all wanted it, but it proved a tepid fluid when we got it.

At last, we came to some low hills that screened us from the sun; we roused ourselves, and looked out; the dreary plain was past, and, as far as the eye could reach, we beheld a flush of brightest rose colour; the wild oleanders, covering miles and miles with brilliant blossom. A little clear stream was gushing merrily along, the low hills were purple in the sinking sunlight; and we were in Andalusia.

Soon it grew dark, and we fell asleep; as it seemed to me, only for a moment. Presently, I awoke, in utter darkness; for in Spain they rarely light lamps in the railway carriages. We stopped at a station, and, scarcely knowing why, I put out my head and lazily asked where we were. " Menjibar," where we were to leave the train, and take the diligence. Now, if I had not accidentally inquired the name of the station, we should inevitably have been whirled, or rather; dragged slowly (Spanish trains don't whirl) on to Cordova, nobody troubling themselves about the matter. The last thing that would occur to a Spanish official would be to open the carriage-door, or call the name of the station, even at an important junction. Everybody and everything in Spain is left to get on as best they can; and it is astonishing how seldom matters go very far wrong. There is, at any rate, a total freedom from interference; you are never told that anything is against the laws; you are never locked in, either in carriage or waiting-room; you cross the line, walk along it, jump out and in, and nobody finds fault. Petty regulations and worrying red-tapeism are utterly foreign to the Spanish character. According to their ideas, if any-body wishes to run into danger, it is tyrannical to prevent them; and I got quite to enjoy this lawless state of things. At first we were horrified at the idle people and beggars who had free access to the stations; but we found this had its advantage. There was always a boy at hand, ready to earn a few coppers by carrying small hand-packages; and, strange as it

may seem, nothing was ever stolen or lost, though
the beggars wandered, unchecked, among the luggage.
One only law of any kind did I see respected in Spain:
on almost all the lines there is a carriage set apart for
ladies; and, so inviolably is it kept that, if there are
no ladies in the train, this carriage goes empty,
although they may leave male passengers behind, for
want of room. This makes it very comfortable for
ladies travelling alone; and, as few Spanish ladies do
travel alone, the result, in our case, was that
we usually had it all to ourselves, and could change
our seats as the sun's rays pursued us. The
other carriages, on the contrary, are generally extremely crowded, and always full of tobacco smoke.

We got out of the train into nearly total darkness,
and had the utmost difficulty in finding the diligence,
it being nobody's business to show us the way. At
last, we descried a black object looming in the dark,
were shoved into the berlina, and away we went, as it
seemed, much faster than the railway. Spanish
diligences invariably go as fast as they can, and that
is often at a tearing pace; whereas the trains dawdle
in a most unaccountable manner, not only stopping
at all stations, but still more frequently in the midst
of a desert, where there is no station at all.

Once in the diligence, nothing could be more comfortable. We had taken the whole berlina, and thus had three places for two people; and indeed there might easily have been room for four, so commodious was it. The road was excellent, and so were our ten mules, which were changed every two hours. There was never a moment's delay; the mules were waiting on the road, and in an instant we were off again, whirling along in the moonlight. The scenery seemed fine, and we had a dim vision of a river flowing on its way to Cordova and Seville—the Guadalquivir. The only stoppage was at Jaen, where we arrived at 1 A.M., and spent half an hour, finding delicious chocolate and Savoy biscuits ready for us. We regretted not seeing the cathedral; had we come a fortnight earlier, we could have done so, as the diligence goes by day in winter and spring; in summer, as the heat would be unbearable, it goes by night. So we had to pass in the dark the place where the King of Morocco, the Miramolin, retreated after his defeat at Tolosa. It was at Jaen, too, that Ferdinand the Fourth of Castile died; he who, having condemned two brothers to death, without sufficient evidence, was summoned by them to appear, within thirty days, before the throne of God, to answer for this injustice. He died within the time, and was therefore called " The Cited One." Some commentators of Dante have thought it was to him, and not to Alonso the Wise, that the poet alluded, in the passage where he blames a Spanish sovereign for negligence in the affairs of life.

Off we went again; and now we felt that we were really on our way to the southern land of Moorish romance. We gazed eagerly onwards; but we saw little except the silvery distance, and the road with its ivory light and ebony shade. Then light and shadow and silver distance confused themselves in an odd way in my brain, and I slept; slept long and sound.

When I awoke, it was broad daylight, and we were scampering along through a wild and rather dreary country, all little stony valleys and bare ridges of rock. Now I was exceedingly glad that H. was still asleep, for our mode of progression, though probably perfectly safe, did not look so. In Spain there is always a horse before the eight or ten mules; on this horse the postilion rides, or ought to ride, and we had been especially warned on no account to permit the said postilion to leave his proper place. But how were we to prevent him? Here he was, sitting calmly beside the driver, enjoying a refreshing sleep, and paying no attention whatever to the eleven animals that, with ears laid back, were tearing up hill and down dale, turning sharp corners, and skirting precipices which, though not very deep, were quite suffi-ciently so to kill us if the diligence went over. It was, I well knew, useless to alarm myself or H., and worse than useless to remonstrate. There is no good in giving commands that cannot be enforced, so I re-signed myself to fate, and really it was wonderful how well we got on. The mules, even at full gallop, were as cautious as possible; and I soon saw that they were quite as intelligent as the postilion, and much more careful. Up we went, never ascending a very steep hill, and sometimes even descending a little way; still on the whole it was pretty steadily up, through scenery less dreary, but not beautiful.

At last, we saw sharp, cold, blue peaks rising before us, with more snow on them than one usually sees in a Spanish July. They were less white than I expected, or could have wished; but they were the Sierra Nevada, and Granada lay between us and them.

Now we gained the top of the ridge, and looked down on Granada, with its Vega; the mayoral turned round, and pointing to a huge, stern fortress, said, "The Alhambra!" It was a strange sensation; I have felt nothing like it since we glided into Venice, one starlight night, long ago. Once before, I felt the same, still longer ago, when we first crossed the Tiber on our way to Rome. Nor shall I ever again feel the like until I see Jerusalem. N

As the red towers grew more distinct, it was certainly very unlike what I expected. I had thought only of the little boudoir-like fragment at Sydenham, which gives about as comprehensive an idea of the whole as an oakleaf does of an oak. At the distance at which we were, the Moorish fortress looked like a small fortified town of the lower Apennines; when we drew nearer, it resembled Bergamo, the Alhambra being like the upper town, on a small scale, and Granada the lower suburb, on a very large one. But the Vega is far richer than the Lombard plain; and the snow-streaked mountains are so very near Granada, and moreover so exceedingly steep, that they look even more than their height—8000 feet above the sea, and about 5000 above the Vega.

We lost sight of the view as we descended; and got entangled in a wilderness of olives, orange-trees, agaves, Indian figs, and, above and beyond all, oleanders. It was less hot than we had feared; the air was fresh and light, quite unlike the burning atmosphere of Madrid, or the dusty Escorial. Not but what there was dust enough here, too, as the whitened leaves and flowers on each side testified; but it lay peaceably on the road and annoyed nobody.

It must be confessed that the entrance to Granada,

coming from the north, is not the best view of the
town; and we felt rather disappointed at first. It
was dusty, and exceedingly dirty; the air had lost its
morning freshness, and the streets looked mean compared with lordly Toledo. The houses, as is usually
the case in Spain, except in Madrid, are very low,
only two stories: the little, low doors, and almost
windowless walls, give them a dull appearance; and,
in this part of Granada, there are no Moorish remains.
I am not sure that we did not sigh for our leafy
retreat at La Granja.

The diligence stopped at the Hôtel Victoria, in the
town; and we were wondering how we were to get
ourselves and our property up to the Alhambra;
when, to our relief we heard, "Siete Suelos, ma'am?"
in a very English voice. "Siete Suelos," assented I
gladly; and soon we were in a carriage, driving
towards the Alhambra. "That ditch is a decided
disadvantage to the town," said H., looking into what
guide-books call "the gushing Darro." However,
the tumble-down houses leaning over it were certainly
very picturesque, and at the end of the street rose the
blue Sierra.

We now entered a large, irregular Plaza, with a
handsome palace of the time of Charles the Fifth; we
crossed the Plaza, and began to ascend a very steep

street, ill-paved and exceedingly hot. I shut my
eyes, to avoid the overpowering glare; to my surprise
a cold, moist wind blew freshly round us. I looked
up; a mountain of foliage rose before us; we passed
through a gateway, and found ourselves in a long,
dim, green avenue. Immensely tall elms met in an
arch high overhead, like some great cathedral-aisle;
long trails of ivy hung from the highest trees, and
nearly touched the top of the carriage. No ray of
sunlight penetrated the deep shade as we went slowly
up towards the Alhambra.

The Hôtel Siete Suelos is most delightfully situated
between the Alhambra and Generalife; the trees
grow almost against the windows, and before it is a
fountain, whose cool plashing is delicious in the hot
hours. At first we were so pleased to find ourselves
there, really and truly within these charmed precincts,
that it seemed as if we scarcely cared at that moment to
penetrate further. Besides this, we were rather tired
with our journey, which had proved nearer twenty-
nine hours than twenty-seven. So we went to breakfast, thinking contentedly of the wondrous Arab
palace now so near us. From the window of my
room I could almost touch the Siete Suelos Tower,
inhabited, as the legends say, by a headless horse and
a pack of hounds, who rush out, baying, at midnight.

Certainly, we heard a good deal of barking of dogs at night, but I think the only inhabitants of the haunted dwelling were a cat and her five kittens. It was from this tower that Boabdil issued forth when for the last time he left his lovely Alhambra. The towers and walls are in perfect preservation, and surrounded by a jungle of pomegranates now in full blossom.

After breakfast we went out, in spite of fatigue, and asked the way to the Alhambra. It was pointed out to us, and we walked up under the elms. We soon got to the unfinished palace of Charles the Fifth, of which the outside is square and the inside round. It is too low to be handsome, but the dark warm brown of the stone has a good effect. The myrtle hedges were delicious, with sweet-scented blossoms peeping out here and there. At the end rose grand, reddish-tinted towers, guarded by soldiers ; we supposed this to be the palace of the Moorish kings, and looked longingly at it. But the first time one goes to the " Arab Palace," as it is called, one must see it all in due form with the guide, and for this we were much too tired. Besides, we wished first to present our letter of introduction to the Governor, and get permission to sketch and to wander about as we liked ; and as the visit to the Governor would have to be paid in polite Spanish, to this also we felt unequal.

So, after resting a little on a bench under an oleander, we went up to the Moorish "Well of the Algives," where the donkeys come, and carry most picturesque jars full of cold, clear water down into the town. Underneath the level space at the top of the Alhambra hill all is hollow. A great cistern, like a cathedral crypt, is full of the water from the mountain source of the Darro ; it contains enough to last a year, and is cleaned out always in January. The water is certainly delicious, excelling even that of Rio Frio, and the well is constantly surrounded by wonderfully picturesque groups. We admired the curious Torre del Vino, with its beautiful arch; and then went down to the grander Gate of Justice, "the Gate of the Law," as the Moors called it. Here, under Moslem rule, the Cadi, or Alcayde, sat and administered justice; and here above the arch is the celebrated "open hand," the protecting talisman of the Alhambra. Above the inner arch is the key, also a talismanic symbol. As in all other Moorish gateways, one does not pass straight through, but, after entering, one turns to the right, and goes out by the *side* of the tower. This is an Oriental arrangement, to make the entrance more complicated. Then we went up and looked down on the Albaycin, the old Moorish town, gleaming white in the sunshine, and still whiter when the sun went down. But after dinner we were glad to go to bed, and leave even the glories of sunset on the Vega.

Next morning we called on Don Rafael Contreras, the Governor, who kindly gave us unlimited permission to do whatever we liked. On our way to his house we asked the boy who guided us, " Is that the Arab Palace ? " pointing to the tall red towers. No; that was the Alcazaba, the prison. " It had always been a prison ; and there was the Torre de la Vela," pointing to one where a bell hung. " Where then was the Arab Palace ? " " There," pointing to Charles the Fifth's. " But the Moorish one ? " said I doubtfully. " Yes;" this time indicating a thicket of oleanders. " But where is the entrance ? " Still the oleanders were pointed out, where there was only a little low wall, and no palace. So I asked the Governor's servant, who pointed quite in a different direction, into a myrtle hedge on the other side of Charles the Fifth's Palace, where one could perceive no building of any kind. It was puzzling ; surely it could not be so very difficult to find ; so we walked up and down and round and round in vain, till I began to think the genii of the place had rendered it invisible.

At length we condescended to take a small boy with us. I thought that after the fashion of those imps of darkness, Spanish boys, he was leading us all wrong ; for he first took us alongside of Charles the Fifth's palace, where I knew there was no other entrance ; only the low mud wall and the clump of oleanders. Next, regardless of my remonstrances, he plunged *into* that same palace, where we had already been, and in which we knew there was nothing to see; and then proceeded to dive into the bowels of the earth ! I really thought this was to turn out a stupid practical joke, if not worse, and very nearly refused to go on. But just then an official with a gold band round his hat appeared (at least, his hat did) as through a trap-door, and motioned us to advance. We did so, and found a flight of steps going down apparently into the earth ; but the friendly official, and the still more friendly apparition of a pleasant-looking grey cat, encouraged us to proceed. We ran down the steps, and instead of finding ourselves, as I had feared, in a dark cellar, we were in the Palace of Boabdil ! In the Court of Myrtles, with its hedges of fragrant leaves and white starry blossoms, enclosing the pale green water trembling in the golden light; and before us the slim colonnades and lace-like fretwork, so strange and yet so familiar.

Away we wandered to the Court of Lions, to the Hall of the Dos Hermanas, and looked into Lindaraja's garden ; then into the Hall of Justice, with

its solemn portraits of turbaned and bearded Moors
sitting in council; to the Hall of the Abencerrages,
where the dark red stains by the fountain recall a
bloody tale; up to the Tocador de la Reyna, and
looked out at the Sierra Nevada, and the Generalife
among its cypresses. Then, down through light, pillared galleries, with wondrous glimpses of the outer
world; down, down into the dim bath-rooms, all rich
gold and crimson and blue; up again into still, sunny
courts, full of bright orange-trees and tall, dark cypresses; then into the mosque where Boabdil worshipped. And ever that forest of slender columns, and
those marvellous arches, all pale yellow in the July
sunshine! At last we found ourselves in the Hall of
Ambassadors, with its glorious views of Vega, Sierra,
and mountain valley, and the exquisite frame of those
lovely pictures! But who can describe the Alhambra? It is the one thing on earth in which disappointment is impossible—the great Wonder of the
World.

When we left it that day, and stood once more in
the half-built modern palace, it seemed as if this
lovely Arabian dream had vanished, swallowed up in
the common-place, work-a-day earth. We could
scarcely believe that we might come back and back,
as often as we pleased, and still find it again.

Many a long, bright summer day did we spend there; sitting with books and drawing materials under the colonnade in the Court of Lions; or, when it grew too hot there, in the Hall of Ambassadors, which, with its unglazed windows to north, east, and west, and its seventy feet of height, could never be otherwise than perfectly cool. At all hours, in the early morning, at midday, and even by moonlight, we went out and in as we pleased. Always beautiful, I think it was less so by moonlight than at any other time; at noon, it seemed to us the most enchanting. One peculiarity of the Alhambra is, however, that everybody always thinks they themselves have seen it in its greatest perfection. Often have we been told, " Oh! but you should have seen it in spring when the violets are out, and the nightingales are singing, and the Sierra Nevada is white as the Alps." It is indeed a melancholy fact that the violets were over, and the nightingales silent, by the time we arrived; but one cannot have everything; if we had had violets, we should not have had oleanders nor myrtle blossom : and the strange dreaminess, the oriental charm of the Alhambra seems to demand the hottest blaze of July sun; then one feels all the luxury of its great, cool halls, and shady colonnades. Winter must, I should think, be much too cold at Granada; and autumn, with its falling leaves and its storms, is like a note out of tune: all decay, all fading, all imperfection, jars on one here.

Two things particularly struck us in the Alhambra; namely, its great size and its perfect preservation. We had expected to see an exquisite little ruin; instead of which, here was a very large palace in excellent repair. In a week it could be made habitable, and perfectly comfortable; and as to size, besides the great Hall of Ambassadors, there is the Court of Myrtles, a hundred and fifty feet long, and the Court of Lions, more than a hundred; and yet they look small, compared with the whole. The restorations are now most skilfully made; the greatest attention being paid to correctness in the Arabic inscriptions. This was not formerly the case; in the bath-room, which was restored about forty years ago, there are some inaccuracies, the restorer not having been an Arabic scholar, and having regarded the Cufic letters as mere ornamentation, without meaning. In particular, the letter *m*, in *Jumna*, or "felicity," is omitted, thereby making absolute nonsense.

The profusion of those Arabic inscriptions, and the curious way in which they are woven into ornamental patterns, is very remarkable. Some are obvious at the very first glance; and one soon gets so accustomed to the forms of the letters, that without any knowledge whatever of the language, one recognizes the frequent repetitions of, for instance, " There is no conqueror but God."

We were fortunate enough to be acquainted with an excellent Arabic scholar in Granada, who kindly came with us sometimes to the Alhambra, to show us how to read the inscriptions. Every part of it is covered with writing : some in letters so large that half-a-dozen of them cover a whole wall; some so small as to be almost invisible : some in the modern cursive Arabic; others in the old Cufic character, which bears about the same resemblance to the modern as black-letter does to the English of the present day. I do not think the Cufic character is ever used in merely poetical and secular incriptions ; it was probably considered too sacred. The peculiarity of these Cufic letters is their squareness and angular form, as distinguished from the flowing curves of the modern writing. It is, at first, much more difficult to distinguish from mere ornamentation, as it often looks like geometrical tracery ; and besides, the words are inverted and bent together at the corners, much in the style of monograms on letter-paper. But we at length learnt to decipher them ; and one of our great pleasures was to look for inscriptions in the most out-of-the-way places, high up on the roof, on capitals of pillars, on azulejos, everywhere. I do believe they are inexhaustible; our kind friend, who had spent four years in the Alhambra studying those inscriptions, one day, when with us, found a tiny one that he had never before observed.

It is like a fairy tale; as, indeed, everything in the Alhambra is. You look at a wall, thinking it covered with beautiful but meaningless ornament; gradually, flowers and leaves seem to bud and blossom before you, and finally they arrange themselves into words of welcome to man, or of praise and glory to God. "Blessing." "Felicity." "There is no conqueror but God." "God is our refuge in every trouble." Such was the Theism of the Arabs.

I need not say that the name of Mahomet is never mentioned, though that of Muhamed Abu Alahmar, the founder of the Alhambra, occurs in some of the merely secular inscriptions, written in the cursive character. He was born at Arjona, in the year of the Hegira, 591 (A.D. 1195), and was not of the royal line of the Caliphs. He was of the noble family of Beni Naser, and began life as Alcayde of Arjona and Jaen. Afterwards he took advantage of the troubled state of affairs, and, in 1238, got himself proclaimed King of

Granada. Though a usurper in the first instance, he seems to have been an excellent sovereign : building hospitals for sick, old, and poor ; and also schools and colleges. He used to delight in visiting the schools and hospitals unexpectedly, as Haroun al Raschid did at Bagdad. He also established shambles and public bakeries, and had the prices and quality of the food constantly inspected. It was he also who brought in the streams of rushing water that still make a paradise of the Vega. We used often to watch the irrigation of the Generalife. The perfect simplicity of the system is probably what has made it last so long, as it can scarcely get out of order. The gardeners merely placed or displaced a stone or a little earth with a sort of hook, or sometimes with their feet, and the little runnels turned in this direction or in that.

The only blot on Muhamed's reign was the disgraceful treaty by which he agreed to help St. Ferdinand to conquer Seville. It is true that he could not well do otherwise ; or Granada must have fallen then, as it did two centuries and a half later. And in that case the world would never have possessed the Alhambra, it being on his return from his expedition with St. Ferdinand, against Seville, that he began this fairy fabric. But it was the unhappy dissensions among the petty Moorish kings that finally involved them all in destruction.

Muhamed, however, having once, though unwillingly, made the treaty with St. Ferdinand, kept it faithfully, and even chivalrously. His reign was long, and, in all else, prosperous. He died in his eightieth year, and was buried in a silver coffin in the Alhambra.

This Palace, which looks as if it had risen from the ground at the stroke of an enchanter's wand, really, like the aloe, took a hundred years to come to perfection. It was finished by Yousouf, who came to the throne in 1333. So mild and benign was he, that he took especial pains to prohibit wanton cruelty in war, enjoining his soldiers not only to spare, but to protect all women, children, the old, and the infirm, and especially all friars and persons " of holy and recluse life." I am afraid his Christian adversaries would scarcely have done as much.

More patriotic, though less wise than Muhamed, he joined the King of Fez against Alonzo the Eleventh of Castile; and was defeated at the great battle of Salado, near Tarifa, which gave a crushing blow to the Moslem power in Spain. Cannon, made at Damascus, are said to have been used on this occasion.

Yousouf built the Puerta de Justicia, and finished the whole palace in 1348. His name also occurs in the inscriptions on the walls.

Strange to say, this mild and beneficent sovereign was murdered as he was praying in the mosque of the Alhambra; being stabbed by a madman.

During July and August, our long afternoons here were most delicious, spent in those airy halls, reading the old Spanish ballads, the Romanceros and Cancioneros, which tell of the Moorish and Christian feats of ancient days, of tournaments and bull-fights, and gallant knights and beauteous ladies, of love and war and bloodshed,—till the Dreamworld seemed the real one, and it felt quite strange to go back to the hotel and be offered the 'Times' and the 'Siècle.'

Here also we read Washington Irving's delightful tales. Most of the legends he mentions are really believed in by the people to this day. They are quite convinced that all tortoise-shell cats are Moorish princesses in disguise, who will one day resume their human shape; they are therefore much prized, and a tortoise-shell kitten is always reared, and treated with the utmost respect. I am not sure that they altogether believe in the enchanter who sits among his treasures below the Siete Suelos Tower, or the myrtle wreaths that become emerald and pearl; but when the trees take strange shapes in the moonlight, they rather think that the topmost branches are Moorish and Christians Knights on horseback, fighting in the air. Here Earth and Air are indeed haunted.

It would have been pleasant to stay always within this charmed boundary, and never go down to Granada at all. But there are many interesting things to be seen there; so one morning we started early and went to the Cathedral, a large building, supposed to be classical, and not quite so ugly as I expected. But when one thinks of the wonders of Spanish architecture, not only of Burgos, Toledo, and Avila, which are much older, but of Segovia, which was built about the same time, one is struck with amazement at the bad taste which could erect such a thing as this. In the centre of the church, above the choir, there is a flattened arch, of which the natives of Granada are very proud; it really is curious.

The most interesting thing in the church is the resting-place of Ferdinand and Isabella. She died far away, at dreary Medina del Campo, in old Castile; but was brought to Granada for burial. The white marble monuments are magnificent. On one lie Ferdinand and Isabella; her head weighs down the pillow, while that of Ferdinand rests on it without making any impression: the Spaniards say it is because she had more brains. On the other sepulchre lie Philip the Handsome (whose effigy has no particular beauty, after all) and poor Juana: Philip turns his head away from his unloved wife; characteristic also!

They are buried in the vault below, in rude plain coffins. The bodies have never been disturbed, and Philip's coffin is the same that Juana watched so long and would never part with. In one corner is that of little Prince Miguel of Portugal, the boy who was thrown from his pony in a square here in Granada, and killed; had he lived, he would have reigned over both countries, and thereby accomplished that union which has been ever the dream of the Spaniards, and the dread of the Portuguese.

We came back by the Alcaiceria, the Moorish bazaar, almost unaltered since the days of Boabdil; and then passed through the Zacatin, in whose name we again trace the Arabic *Zac*, a marketplace. It is a narrow, picturesque street, full of shops, where there seemed little but shoes and rather coarse silver ornaments. These two streets are too narrow for carriages, so one walks in great comfort. Here, for the first time, awnings over the streets began to appear; and indeed

they are very necessary, as it is not the custom, in
this part of Spain, to use a parasol. When we did so,
the people always called to us that it was not raining !
Now, as umbrellas were originally introduced into
England from Spain, it is remarkable that the natives
of such a very sunny and almost rainless climate have
not adapted the invention to keeping off the rays of
the sun. In England, at first, umbrellas were as much
laughed at as parasols are at the present day in Spain.

Another day we took a guide, and went off to the
gipsy quarter. We wished to walk, but the guide
would not hear of anything so beneath his dignity;
not to mention the fatigue. So away we rumbled, in
a most extraordinary vehicle, something between an
omnibus and a vetturino carriage ; the roads were like
dry, stony watercourses, and frequently the sharp
turns and the precipices would have been startling,
had we not been prepared for any amount of queerness.
I am rather surprised we were not upset.

The gipsy quarter, on the opposite side of the Darro
from the Alhambra, is wonderfully beautiful, and exceedingly odd. The gipsies live underground, in
caves covered with thickets of prickly pears, of which
the fruit is said to be the best of the kind in Granada,
owing to the heat of the houses. Most of the gipsy
aristocracy are blacksmiths, who keep up a large fire ;

besides which, the sun beats on those slopes all day long : so, what with the heat above and the heat below, the fruit is forced into a size and juiciness quite remarkable. We were told that at night those gipsy caves look absolutely demoniacal, with the red fire-light coming out of the ground, and the swarthy figures of the inhabitants flitting about ; but we never had courage to venture there after dark.

No carriage can enter this quarter, the road being too narrow ; so we were obliged to get out and walk. This we did rather nervously, as we had been told appalling stories of the ferocity and insolence of the gipsies. We need not have been afraid ; they were perfectly polite ; more so indeed than the *Castillanos*, as the natives of Granada choose, without the slightest right, to call themselves. The lower orders of Granada struck us as being usually less courteous and more ferocious than in any other part of Spain. Of course, to this there are exceptions : all the officials, gardeners, labourers, and peasants in general were politeness itself ; and the upper classes there, as elsewhere in Spain, are unrivalled in courtesy and kindness. But there seemed to be always a good many roughs hanging about, both in the streets and on the outskirts of the town. Perhaps this was partly owing to the seething republicanism, then at the very point of boiling over ;

we were told, however, by Spaniards, that the population of the kingdom of Granada, including Malaga and the Alpuxarras, had always borne a rather savage character.

We went into one of the gipsy caves, in spite of the remonstrances of our guide, who finally refused to come in with us. It was not so very dirty, being nicely whitewashed inside. It consisted of two rooms: we did not attempt to penetrate into the back one; but it looked tolerably tidy. There was not much furniture; consisting chiefly of several doormats, on each of which a child lay asleep. One of the great difficulties in civilizing a gipsy is that he cannot be cured of stealing doormats; if they gain admittance to any house, either as beggars, or, as is frequently the case, as models for the artists, they are sure to carry off the doormat. We were shown one splendid gipsy, up at the Alhambra, who had been a very popular model among the artists; but the consumption of doormats was so tremendous that they were obliged to give him up.

Here the gipsies were anything but splendid, seeming very poor and sickly. Of course they begged from us, but without importunity; and we gave them some coppers, with which they were quite satisfied. One woman held in her arms an exceedingly small baby, the size and colour of a black kitten, but by no means so lively. I asked, in the Spanish idiom, "How many days it had?" The answer was, "Seven months!" It did not look more than a week old. When we were getting into the carriage again, there was certainly rather a rush after us, in hopes of a shower of copper; but there was no insolence.

What an exquisite view there was up the valley of the Darro! It seemed a pity that it should be wasted on the half-savage gipsies, who do not at all care for the lovely landscape. Anywhere but in Spain people would build houses and live there; but, to be sure, if they did, it would lose great part of its wild charm. It is very well as it is.

Then we went to San Nicolas, in the Albaycin, for the view, said to be one of the finest of the Alhambra and the snowy Sierra Nevada; and indeed I think there cannot be anything lovelier on this earth. We went next to San Miguel el Bajo, where it is also fine; and in going down to which we seemed to be on the very point of driving over the precipice. We must certainly have done so, if it had not been for a friendly drove of pigs, which stopped us exactly at the right moment. We met several of those droves. They were rather nice-looking pigs, small, neat, and active ; generally smooth, and of the colour of black-lead : but sometimes chocolate-brown, with wavy hair. These latter were the prettiest. They all seemed cleanly creatures, and ran gladly into the river. Pigs and the like are here taken out to walk every day by a herdsman, who is paid a halfpenny for each pig, goat, or sheep, of which he takes charge. He makes a great deal of money by it; often five francs a day: but he must have an assistant ; for, when the herd is large, there should be a man behind and a man before, or the confusion becomes inextricable, especially when two droves meet. It is sometimes a serious matter to encounter the pigs going back at night. In their joy at getting home, they rush along, with small consideration for any pedestrian who may happen to be in the way.

We now proceeded to the Cartuja, of which the Granadinos are more proud than they are of the Alhambra, and are greatly surprised that English people in general care so little about it. It is really very magnificent, as far as marble, tortoise-shell, mother-of-pearl, and wonderfully large fine agates can make it. But there is no architectural beauty, nor is it interesting, though the ground was a gift from the Gran Capitan Gonsalvo de Cordova, himself.

The celebrated painted cross is extraordinary in its truthfulness; at first, it is impossible to believe it otherwise than a wooden one in relief. There are plenty of horrible frescoes in the cloisters, all representing the Carthusians tortured by the English under Henry the Eighth! The garden was a pleasant wilderness of fruit-trees; and our guide got so absorbed in endeavours to knock a fig off a high branch, that he became practically useless. I am bound to confess that the fig, when at last secured, was the best I had ever tasted; large, juicy, sweet as honey, and cold as ice.

The great object of this expedition was to go to the Casa de Tiros, belonging to the Marquis of Campotejar, the owner of the Generalife. At the Casa de Tiros we were to see Boabdil's sword, and there also we were to get a permission to go into the Generalife.

This permission is generally given for only one visit; but we resolved to endeavour to obtain a permanent one. The " administrador " of the Marquis of Campotejar proved, luckily, to be also Italian vice-consul, and was so delighted on hearing that we lived in Italy, that he not only gave us unlimited permission to go to the Generalife as often as we pleased, but also wrote on the back of the ticket an order to get into his own villa of Bella Vista, situated opposite the Siete Suelos.

This Marquis of Campotejar is better known as one of the Grimaldi-Pallavicini of Genoa; the heiress of the family is married to the Marquis Durazzo, and has never seen her lovely Granada estate. These Grimaldis or Campotejars are of Moorish race, being descended from an uncle of Boabdil, Cidi Aya, who became a Christian, and was afterwards called Don Pedro; to him the Generalife was given at the time of the Conquest of Granada. Thus it is that he possesses Boabdil's sword, a beautifully inlaid weapon.

He has truly an embarrassing amount of riches, as far as houses are concerned; the Generalife, the Casa de Tiros, the splendid Durazzo Palace in Genoa, the Pallavicini Palace, also there, and the beautiful Villa Pegli, by the Mediterranean.

The Marchesa Durazzo has only one child, a boy of eleven years old; failing him, the Granada property lapses to the Spanish crown.

In the Casa de Tiros are some very good pictures; in particular, a Shepherd Boy, by Rubens, which is excellent. It is a nice old house, and the wooden ceilings are curious.

Almost every morning we went to the Generalife,

from which the view of the Alhambra is superb.
Thence, and thence only, is every part of it visible,
in its circuit of red towers : even the little, low
brown roofs which cover the wondrous Arab palace
can be distinguished ; and here alone can one judge
of the enormous size of the whole.

Here we walked up and down, in the fresh morning, beneath the glorious oleanders.   Never did I
see such flowers !   The great, heavy masses of deep
rose-coloured blossoms almost weighed down the
trees.   Each flower was as large and full as the
largest double hollyhock.   The Spaniards say the
faint bitter perfume of the oleander is poisonous.
I thought it delicious, and never found any bad
effects from it.   So persuaded are they, however, of
its evil qualities, that they never give it to anybody,
nor do I think they ever gather it at all.   This
surprised us, for in general the Spaniards have a
passion for flowers, and do not object to the strongest
scents : a Spanish girl always puts a rose, a clove
carnation or a tuberose, among her dark locks ; and
if she gives a flower, as she frequently does, to a
lady friend, is vexed unless it is instantly placed in
the hair.   If you put it in water, she says, "Is it
not good enough for the hair?" and will generally
fasten it there for you herself.   And with what grace

she does so ! If any hairdresser could but arrange it like that ! But among all those flowers the pink oleander alone, which would look so well in the black hair, is never used.

Whatever its bad qualities may be, one of the merits of the oleander is that it lasts so long. In the end of June they were in blossom in Madrid, and they lasted till the middle of September when we left Granada. Even then the flowers were still to be found, though no longer in profusion. All the months of July and August they hung in rich luxuriance, with the little streamlets of clear water bathing their roots, the Spanish sun above them, and the dark cypresses behind. Till between 9 and 10 A.M., that cypress avenue was always in shade ; and very delightful it was, with the Vega stretching far away into the blue distance, and, below us, the vermilion towers of the Alhambra.

We often went into the inner garden, and lingered on its quaint terraces, all full of rare flowers, and myrtle hedges, and plashing fountains ; up to the great old cypresses of the time of Boabdil, where the air was laden with their hot, aromatic perfume. There the Sultana cypress still stands, where Zoraya met her lover, the Abencerrage ; and even then it was more than two centuries old. On a still higher terrace, the trellised vines are also of the time of the Moorish kings; the stems are thick like a tree, and the grapes most excellent, as we experienced one morning when the gardener's son, a fine boy of thirteen, climbed up, and cut huge bunches for us.

In the house are some remains of Moorish ornamentation, which, however, have been so pertinaciously whitewashed, as now to present a rather waterworn appearance. The outside has no architectural beauty, as indeed few Moorish buildings have. There are some interesting pictures in the principal hall. Boabdil, the Rey Chico himself, with a fair face and gentle expression; his uncle, much fiercer-looking, from whom the present proprietor of the Generalife is descended; the Moorish princess who was baptized, became a nun, and founded the convent of St. Isabel la Real; and several ancestors of the Campotejar family, who, on the whole, look somewhat as if they would rather have been Moslems, after all. Ferdinand and Isabella, too, are here; and the Gran Capitan.

But it is the gardens and terraces that are so enchanting. And up those terraces we wandered to the Mirador, with its marvellous view of the Sierra Nevada, which, by the way, is a view very seldom seen from the Alhambra side of Granada.

Either the lower hills or the dense foliage almost always conceal the serrated azure peaks, with their streaks of silver snow.

Truth obliges me to state that those same silver streaks were, for the greater part of our stay, the only claim the Sierra could make to be called snowy. But the Spaniards persist that it is covered with perpetual snow, and when you demur, and ask where it is, they say, "There! don't you see that streak? and the white spot yonder?" It is very meritorious of such a small quantity of snow to cool the air as much as it certainly does. I was told, however, by Englishmen who had explored those mountains, that there is very much more really than appears from a distance; that there are glacier-gorges quite full of ice and snow.

Once, after a night of heavy rain (the first for more than two months), we went up to the Mirador, and lo! instead of the blue Sierra, it was pure white like the Alps, and wondrously beautiful. In the evening we went up again, to show it to some friends, and it was gone; melted by the noonday sun. This was in September; in winter, spring, and early summer the snow-view must be superb.

From the Mirador, a door opens upon the wild hillside, and one can scramble up to the Silla del Moro;

that is, if the heat permits, for it is absolutely shadeless, and even late in the evening the ground is
burning. Occasionally we went up at sunset; it is
but a stone's throw from the Mirador, and there is a
kind of path. The view is magnificent; you look
straight down into the valley of the Darro, which
seems strangely lonely, though in reality peopled
with the gipsies. But as they live underground, you
don't see them; and it does not naturally occur to
the beholder that those tawny slopes, where nothing
is visible bnt a luxuriant jungle of prickly pears, is
really a populous suburb; the gipsy town, in fact.

Further up, the scene becomes wilder and wilder;
more like some lovely valley far among the Apennines, than anything Spanish. A little more to the
left the white Albaycin, or Moorish town, lies below
us; and beyond, stretches the rich Vega, bounded, in
the direction in which we are now looking, by the
Sierra Elvira, deep purple against the sunset.

Then we returned to the cypress avenue, light as
day in the moonlight, and generally lingered so long
that we were often locked in, and had to grope our
way out by some of the labourers' cottages, to the
intense indignation of a number of dogs, who barked
furiously, and nibbled at our heels, but, rather to my
surprise, never did us any harm.

One July evening, some of our Spanish friends came from Granada, and we went into the Garden of the Adarves, perched on the very edge of the high battlement, with six hundred feet of sheer precipice below. The courteous Governor, Don Rafael Contreras, accompanied us, with his wife and daughter.

"Let us make Tertulia," exclaimed one of the ladies. Now, "making Tertulia" consists in sitting all round, chatting in a very lively way, drinking water and eating azucarillos. Accordingly, Don Rafael sent to the Well of the Algibes, and the coldest, iciest water was brought, with a tray of azucarillos and méringues; and we sat there, among a profusion of flowers, many of which were new to me, and called by the Spaniards by very curious names. One magnificent shrub, completely covered with rose-pink blossoms, was called "Jupiter;" another smaller plant, somewhat like a petunia, with dark red, sweet-scented flowers, was "Don Pedro." Many old friends there were, too, among those brilliant strangers; oranges and citrons covered with fruit, as yet dark green; dulcamara, sweet-basil, lemon-verbena, and tall tuberoses. No chill ever comes in that wonderful climate; no dew, no damp. We never thought of shawls or wraps of any kind;

a thin muslin dress and the unfailing black lace veil was all that was necessary.

Then the deep crimson of the Vega faded, and the full moon rose slowly behind the Sierra Nevada like a great golden shield; and still we sat listening to talk of old Moorish days, and the almost unknown treasures of Arabic literature, and the strange legends that linger yet among the people, till our friends remembered the length of the way back to Granada, and we reluctantly rose to depart.

As we came out of the garden, the moonlight on the Plaza de los Algibes and the unfinished palace of Charles the Fifth was absolutely blinding, and the sudden transition to the pitch darkness of the Alhambra avenue made us grope and stumble. Don Rafael politely insisted upon sending a guard with a loaded gun to escort us home; I do not think it was at all necessary for protection, because we every night came home in utter darkness, and never met with any disturbance, except once. This one occasion was a Sunday night, when we were coming home from church, and a man flourished a stick over the head of a gentleman who was with us, requiring him instantly to state distinctly whether he was in favour of Queen Isabel the Second or not. Now the gentleman being of a peaceable disposition, and moreover perfectly indifferent to Queen Isabel, or any other Queen or King of Spain, was quite willing to agree with the man's politics, whatever those might happen to be. But the misfortune was that there were no means of ascertaining whether our assailant was Republican, Radical, Carlist, or Alfonsist. Luckily something diverted his attention, and he dashed off to the other side of the road, to join in an unearthly yell, supposed by its utterers to be a song. I dare say if we had been alone, he would not have attacked us; for I don't think that in the south of Spain they are yet quite sure that women have souls; and if they have no souls, why then they need not have political opinions.

CHAPTER VIII.

After the accession of King Amadeus, Spanish Protestantism was for the first time tolerated. Exiles returned, the prison doors were opened, and congregations were formed in the principal towns of Spain. In Granada it was a very small one, consisting chiefly of the poorer classes, though there were also some officers of the garrison, who used to come with their wives. I think there was a strong prejudice against it on the part of all classes; as we went in, the people sometimes called out to us that we were *Jews* and *Moors;* and even the more enlightened Spaniards, who were very far from being bigoted Romanists, and whose greatest encomium on anybody was, "They never have a priest in the house," opposed this, and said the pastor only wished to make money of it. The fact is that the great difficulty in Spain is, that there has been only too much of this making money of holy things, and that for many years religion and morality have ranged themselves on opposite sides; consequently all priests, and clergymen generally, are hated as such without further inquiry.

There being no English church in Granada, we were however very glad to have this Protestant service to go to. It was in the house of the pastor, who was a friend of Matamoros, and had shared in his sufferings; this pastor, Señor Alhama, had been, with his wife and his old mother, then seventy years of age, imprisoned, as many others were at that time, for reading the Bible. The representatives of the different Protestant powers remonstrated, and after some delay the sentence of imprisonment was commuted into banishment. The Alhama family then took refuge at Gibraltar, where the son and daughter were educated, and learnt to speak English. After several years' exile the revolution came, and allowed them to return; the mother was still alive, a quiet gentle old woman, with a pleasant but sad expression. The pastor himself was a burly, energetic, rather rough man, with the thick utterance derived from his Moorish blood.

For *Alhama* is a thoroughly Moorish name; and the daughter, a girl of seventeen, might have sat for a portrait of some of the Xarifas or Zaydas of Moorish romance, with her long, almond-shaped Eastern eyes, her fair skin, and raven hair. Altogether it was a curious combination: listening to the Bible read by a descendant of the Moors, and hearing Spanish children sing translations of well-known English hymns, set to old Scotch psalm-tunes; and all in the Moorish Zacatin of Granada!

The service was in the evening, at eight o'clock, as the heat by day would have been intolerable. It consisted of prayers translated into Spanish from the English prayer-book, a chapter of the Bible, a good many hymns, very heartily, 'if not very musically sung, an extempore prayer, and a very good sermon by the pastor. He was exceedingly fearless, and actually ventured one evening to preach against the bull-fight! Those who know Spain will appreciate his courage.

Miss Alhama devoted herself entirely to teaching.

Her school was in a pretty Carmen, or villa (the word Carmen in Arabic, signifies, properly speaking, a vineyard), on the slope leading from the Alhambra to the town. The family lived there during the summer months, only going in to their house in the Zacatin on Sunday evening for the service. We went one day to see the school, and it seemed very well managed. The children read very well indeed, rather fast, but distinctly and correctly; of course with the the sing-song tone, utterly unnatural, in which all Spaniards of every rank read aloud, even a common note or letter. They wrote most beautifully, both *Spanish* and *English* hand, as they call them, the Spanish having squarer, bolder letters, like the hand-writing of a clever practical English person; the so-called English being like a weak Italian hand, neat, sharp-pointed and tidy. They seemed to delight most of all in singing, which they did very loud and fearfully out of tune, but heartily and spiritedly, with nothing dragging nor dull about it, though much that was shrill and harsh. The needlework, both plain and embroidery, was exquisite, as it always is in Spain. Miss Alhama's own was quite artistic. She said the most difficult thing to teach the children was *manners,* but even in that she had succeeded pretty well. She very properly insisted that they should rise when strangers came to visit them; they not only did so, but said "Good morning" in English when we came in. After we had examined the children, we went into the garden, where we made acquaintance with a pet raven, and gathered the early pomegranates.

On the whole, the children near the Alhambra were not nearly so teasing as in some other places. They soon got to know us, and carried out all their pets to show us, puppy-dogs, kittens, birds, etc. They caught beautiful large rose-coloured moths for us, and were much surprised that we would not stick pins in them. One morning we happened to go out earlier than usual, and on passing the cottage where a little boy of five or six years old lived, whom we had already made friends with, a cry of "gatitos! gatitos!" (kittens! kittens!) arose. His cat had had kittens the evening before, and he was anxious to show us his new acquisitions. But, unfortunately, his toilet was not yet made, so somebody hastily wrapped him up in his father's cloak, and he dashed out of the house to meet us, with the garment, his only one, as it afterwards appeared, trailing on the ground. It was gracefully enough draped round him, but in his eagerness to display the new-born treasures, he held up his arms and let the cloak fall grandly behind him, in a manner that, though very picturesque, rendered it wholly useless for the purposes of clothing. I wished a sculptor could have seen the little bronzed figure, with the drapery falling back, and the arms stretched out holding up the kittens. It would have made a beautiful statue.

Even in sketching I was quite unmolested. I suppose they are accustomed to it, for they seldom made any remark. But one day when I was drawing the Gate of Justice, an old woman, a girl, and a youth came up to look at what I was about, and greatly amused me by their remarks. The girl expressed surprise that I did not rather occupy myself in embroidering trimmings like what I had on my dress. The boy replied, "Any fool can work trimmings; I dare say even *you* can do it" (very contemptuously to the girl), "but painting is quite another matter." The old woman thereupon said, "Yes, it is all very well for a man. I have seen a man paint, but for a lady it is *rara*." Now *rara*, in Spanish, means *odd* as well as rare, and is not altogether a compliment. "Well, if it is *rara*, it is all the more merit," said my defender, the boy. "Ah! but," said the old woman, "I have seen finer things than that,—a man painting with a large box!" This was an artist painting in oil, whom I had also observed. "A large box!" rejoined the boy, with infinite scorn, " what merit is there in that? Anybody can paint with a large box; why he could not even carry it himself; got a boy to do it You," (to the old woman and girl) " don't understand those things, but if you did you would have seen that there was *oil*, and anybody could paint with oil. And besides, he had everything ready-made. It is easy to put on blue or yellow when it is all there, but the lady has nothing but little bits of black earth; and if you would only look and not be so stupid, you would see that it comes blue or yellow, or green or red, off the same bit of black earth, just as the lady pleases. There now ! " (triumphantly, as I dipped my brush in the gamboge, and proceeded with the green trees) " I told you so."

We sometimes went into the Villa Bella Vista, in the evening. It was too hot there in the daytime, and even quite late it was warmer than elsewhere. But the flowers, especially the roses, were plentiful, and the gardener liberally bestowed them on us. The sunsets, seen from its Mirador, were glorious, the Sierra Nevada seeming quite at hand. It has quite a different view of the Alhambra from any other. The Arab palace is entirely concealed, and even Charles the Fifth's is scarcely visible; but the circuit of the red towers and walls, forming the outworks of the whole, are here seen to great advantage. One looks straight down into the Alhambra enclosure, with its yellow fields and agave hedges: a forest seems to intervene between this and the Torre de la Vela, which stands far off, quite black against the crimson sunset and the purple Sierra Elvira.

I could never look at that red circuit without thinking of the towers of the City of Dis, in Dante's 'Inferno;' and wondering if some tale of Christian captive among the Moors had suggested the idea. It is remarkable that Dante expressly calls the red towers of Hell, mosques or minarets. In truth, the scene here is more like Paradise than Hell; but in those old times, the followers of Mahoun, as they were called, were supposed by the orthodox, to be little better than demons.

Nothing is more remarkable than the extraordinary variety presented by the Alhambra from different points of view. From one, it is a classical façade, in a formal garden of myrtle hedges and oleanders; from another, it is a rude, stern fortress, whose vermilion towers have stood for a thousand years. Here, it is a large farm, with cornfields where they are gathering in the golden grain; there, it is a thicket of agaves and pomegranates, with only a reddish mud wall apparent: again, it is like a splendid fortified town, by the edge of a grand ravine, on some Apennine height. Without, the palace of Boabdil is like a collection of magnified swallows' nests, stuck on the hillside; within, it is a creation of the genii, too fairylike for this earth.

We were always finding something new; in almost every one of the many towers of the outer circuit there is something interesting. The Great Mosque has long since disappeared, and in its place stands the modern church of Santa Maria del Alhambra. But, besides the one existing in the palace itself, there is in one of the towers, a small mosque, which has lately been beautifully restored. There is a very curious slab let into the wall; it has a long Arabic inscription, and was brought from the ancient Moorish Mint, where it formed the key-stone of the entrance arch. The views from the little Moorish windows are lovely, and that from the garden still more so, looking down on Granada.

This mosque was exceedingly difficult to find, being approached by a narrow lane. At the garden-gate are two sculptured lions, also brought from the Mint; within is a mass of oleanders, roses, vines, and lavender. We were standing below one of those thick-stemmed, trellised vines, when we heard a rustling above us; we looked up, and saw a child about three or four years old, quite naked, riding on a branch, and trying to conceal himself among the vine leaves. His sister said that, not being yet dressed, he had clambered up there when we came in, being ashamed to be seen by English ladies without his clothes. It seems to be the habit of Spanish children to run out without taking the trouble to dress, on the fresh, cool mornings; and I have no doubt it does them a great deal of good. He looked very pretty among the vine leaves, with his bright eyes and merry face, putting one in mind of a Cupid upon an ancient Greek vase.

In another tower, the Tower of the Captive, lives a family of very poor people, and the beautiful tracery is all uncared for. We had wandered in, without anybody with us, and the inmates looked so poor and so wild, that I began to wonder if we were quite safe. But they received us civilly enough; saying, however, that they would expect us to give them something for showing it. We assented, and they took us up to the top, each story consisting of one room. As there were two of us, I think we were in no danger; had I been alone, I am not quite sure about it. It was a lonely place, and it would not have been difficult to take a purse, and then shove the owner off the battlements; an accident might so easily happen! But I dare say I did the poor man injustice, and quite misinterpreted his eager looks at our money.

Formerly all the towers were inhabited by poor people, labourers, and sometimes beggars; but they are gradually being rescued from this, and kept in repair. Another very beautiful tower, with the most exquisite *Turkish* or Moorish stucco-work, is uninhabited and kept locked up; but it is all blackened by the smoke of fires that have been lighted in those lovely rooms. This latter is the Tower of the Infantas, where the scene of one of Washington Irving's tales is laid; where the three princesses, Zayda, Zorayda, and Zorahayda were supposed to have lived, and from which the two elder escaped with their Christian lovers to Cordova, leaving the youngest to fade away in her beautiful prison.

These two towers are far away from the Adarves and the Arab palace, quite across the cornfields, and looking down on the ravine that separates the Alhambra from the Generalife.

One morning we went to the villa of Madame Calderon de la Barca, nearly opposite the Siete Suelos; it is beautifully kept, with very fine flowers, and extensive walks. Madame Calderon usually lives there in summer; but at this time she was at Biarritz, her son being a Carlist, and involved in the insurrection then going on in the north. We were surprised to hear that there was a dairy at this villa, and to see nice, English-looking cows. In this dairy most excellent fresh butter is made, which, in the absence of Madame Calderon, was sold to the hotel, and was a great dainty, butter of any kind being extremely rare, and fresh butter almost unknown in Spain. Indeed, in Spanish, there is but one name for butter and for lard; and salt butter, the only kind generally used, is called "Flanders lard," not a very attractive appellation. Madame Calderon is an Englishwoman, which accounts for the dairy and the cows.

One of the things we most wished to see in Granada was the Cuarto Real of San Domingo, as it is called. This was a sort of jointure-house for the Sultana-mother, in Moorish days. It still belongs to the noble family to whom it was given at the time the Christians entered; the Marquis Salar de la Conquista. This title, "de la Conquista," is given to those nobles who gained their estates at that time. This Marquis, however, does not seem to prize his interesting possession, and keeps wood in the beautiful Moorish hall. He is quite aware that he does not treat it as he ought; the reason he gives for obstinately refusing to show it to any English is, lest they should call him a brute for keeping it in such confusion!

Our kind friends, however, knowing how much we wished to see it, exerted themselves in our behalf. There were great difficulties; they could not ask it themselves, because, as they were known to have English acquaintance, it would certainly be refused. But they applied to a friend, who knew an officer of the garrison, who knew the Marquis, and, what was quite as much to the purpose, had probably never before seen any English person. Accordingly, we were taken there, receiving strict injunctions not to speak a word of English the whole time; and, above all things, to make no remark whatever on the untidy state in which it was kept. It was exceedingly well worth seeing; the Moorish hall is very fine, and not much spoilt by being used as a lumber-room: possibly it is better so, than if it had been badly renovated. There are most beautiful Cufic letters, pale green, with the background, leaves, and flourishes of a brownish hue; so that it was quite easy, in this case, to distinguish the inscription from the ornamentation. The azulejos are nearly unique, with gold letters on silver lustre. There was a pretty garden, not very well kept; but pleasant with flowers and fountains, arching bays and great myrtles. It was originally much larger, but the Marquis chose to part with a bit of it for a theatre !

Our friends then took us to the house of Señor Fortuny, the eminent Spanish painter. We were received in a large and very beautiful patio, arranged quite like a drawing-room, with piano, tables, chairs, etc. ; rich Persian carpets were thrown carelessly on the ground here and there ; in the centre was a mass of flowering shrubs ; and on a pedestal, among the bright leaves, a large Moorish vase was placed, also full of flowers. We were admiring this when we were told that it was coarse compared with one upstairs. We accordingly went up, and saw one that was magnificent indeed. It was very large, of beautiful form, with golden scrolls on silver lustre ; and is, probably, second in value only to the celebrated Alhambra vase. In that room also was the largest and finest azulejo that has ever been found ; it is oblong, likewise with golden scrolls and silver lustre, and was dug up in the Albaycin ; it bears the name of one of the kings of Granada. We were shown, too, some of the azulejos made at a later period, after the expulsion of the Moors ; they were quite different, and much coarser, with a gold ground, like the common Venetian glass mosaic, without any lustre at all ; being, indeed, more like gold leaf laid on under the surface than anything else. There were many basins and plates of Moorish ware; some with ruby lustre, some with gold, and some with silver. They said the ruby was produced by copper, the gold by a mixture of copper and silver, and the silver wholly by silver.

Another day we visited the Museum, in order to see the little portable altar that belonged to Gonsalvo de Cordova; it is of exquisite enamel, far the finest I have ever seen, with its beautiful gold lights. One subject was very Dantesque, small devils being eaten by a large one. I think it was meant for the swallowing up of death and hell. In the centre of the upper row was the Saviour enthroned, with the Virgin Mary on one side and St. John on the other; but both the Virgin and St. John were much lower than the Saviour, and were *equal;* the writing was "Even so come, Lord Jesus." Alongside of this is a representation of the crowned Saviour leading a great multitude up a golden stair; I think, in allusion to the text, "And after this I saw a great multitude which no man could number;" but, possibly, it might be the Ascent from Hades. On the other side is the Final Doom of Sinners. Below is the Crucifixion; one of the kneeling figures strongly resembles the portraits of the Duchess of Urbino, Guidobaldo's wife, and the head-dress is also similar.

In a room downstairs are some antiquities—Arabic inscriptions found, face inmost, in the wall of the Ayuntamiento, or Town-hall; they must have belonged to the old Moorish Town-hall, which stood on the same spot as the modern one. There is also a curious Moorish jar of very graceful form.

The picture gallery was deplorable, consisting chiefly of frightful saints from desecrated convents. One or two might have had some merit, if cleaned and properly placed; but none, in any circumstances, could ever be agreeable to look at.

One of the pleasantest of the many pleasant days we spent in our southern paradise was in the vineyard of our kind Granada friends. This vineyard is between two and three miles out of the town, on the other side from the Alhambra, and an afternoon there had been often talked of. On the 1st of September, the great heat being now past, and the grapes in their fullest perfection, we all went there together. It was a very garden of Eden; trees laden with the little golden figs which, by the bye, Rodriguez Borgia, otherwise Pope Alexander the Sixth, introduced into Italy from his native Spain—one good deed of his at any rate. The plums were such as only Spain can produce; in fact, nobody can form an idea of the capabilities of the greengage until they have tasted it at Granada; so much so that delicate children are brought here for a sort of "plum-cure," like the grape-cures of Tyrol and Switzerland, and eat them by the dozen. The variety and excellence of the grapes was quite bewildering; large, luscious, thick-skinned black ones; dim green ones, with a sharp, refreshing, pine-apple taste; muscatels with a flavour undreamt of elsewhere; pale straw-coloured ones with juice like thick honey; tawny, freckled ones like a mouthful of sunshine; greyish ones, tasting of perfume; and, most curious of all, pale rose-pink ones; the prettiest fruit I have ever seen, though not nearly so good as those of more sober hue.

Away we wandered through the vineyard, gathering what we chose in careless abundance, our friends saying, with the true kindly profusion of the Spanish character, "Oh! do throw those away, and gather that; it is finer. It is so pleasant to eat just two or three of the finest of each bunch." Our consciences, however, really would not permit us to fling delicious fruit away in this manner.

Then we sat under a tree till the sun went down, hearing all about the Spanish plans of agriculture, which, to say the truth, consist chiefly of giving the ground as much water as possible, and then letting the fertile soil and splendid sunshine do the rest. They do not like new inventions; indeed, why should they make any change? They don't want to make money of their land; it produces wine and oil, and fruit and vegetables in luxuriant plenty as it is. In the south few people are in want, and nobody is very rich; and, perhaps, it is happier so.

Certainly, whatever be the plans of cultivation, the results, as far as quantity and quality of fruit is concerned, are astonishing. The complete absence of damp is partly the cause of it. In the whole of the middle and south of Spain there is no such thing as mustiness or mouldiness. The grapes may hang on the vines, the melons may lie on the ground for any length of time; and sweeter and richer the melons become, and the grapes get encrusted with sugar and wither into raisins, but they never become spoilt nor mouldy.

From the fruit being so much richer and less watery than elsewhere, it is a chief article of food among the lower classes. In the fig season it is a common thing for a poor family to hire a tree. They then pitch some kind of tent under it, and live on the figs, with the addition of a little bread.

When the sun became lower, we took a walk round the vineyard, to look at the varying colours of the Sierra Elvira. Presently we came to an open space, where a table was set, covered with fruit of every description, and two large Moorish cakes. One of them, the largest, was called *Ayuya* (I spell phonetically, not having the slightest idea, save by the sound, of how it ought to be written); the other was *Hornazo*, and had whole eggs in their shells, like Easter eggs, baked into it. Both were very good, but the Ayuya was the best. We were told it was made simply of dough prepared for bread, and mixed with egg and sugar; but I should have thought it more complicated. They said both kinds had been made in Granada ever since the Moorish days.

Then our friends opened a cask of old wine for us, made of the grapes of this very vineyard, in 1834, before the grape disease had begun. It was delicious, like Malaga, but drier, and with a slight Tokay flavour. We drank it out of beautiful little slender tumblers with gilt patterns, like Turkish attar-of-rose bottles. The thick, broad boxwood hedges served as sideboards—not an uncommon use of hedges in this country. In the Generalife I often used a myrtle hedge as a sketching-table; it was perfectly steady and perfectly impervious.

We were taken to see the wine-presses, which were of the most primitive construction; by no means calculated to make the most of the grapes. But here again, if one judges by success, the result was fault-less. No such wine as that is ever produced in Italy, with all the attention now given to vine culture ; and as to quantity, they had a great deal more than they wanted.

A Spaniard likes this feeling of heedless abundance, and any appearance of economy or even making the most of things, causes him annoyance. He can perfectly well do without a thing altogether ; but to economise in the use of it is hateful to him. He can be very self-denying when kindness, politeness, or a feeling of what is due to himself or others prescribe it. The Spaniards bear hunger or thirst, heat, cold, fatigue, or any other discomfort, with perfect equanimity ; it would be beneath them to fret or complain. They are kind, hospitable, cour-teous, liberal, and magnificent in all their ways ; but thrifty they are not, and I think never will be.

The purple and golden light had faded, and now the stars were peeping out, so we prepared to return home. The street leading to the Alhambra-gate was under repair, so no carriage could get in ; our friends therefore walked up with us, the servant carrying an enormous basket of the finest fruit ; which made us extremely popular in the hotel, as long as it lasted.

When we got back to the Siete Suelos, we found a political dinner going on in the garden; noise, music, speechifying, and much applause of everything that was said. This lasted till they all grew hoarse; then they came into the house to have coffee and "*clow*," the housemaid told us. For a moment I was at a loss as to what "clow" could possibly mean; she said it was something sweet and exceedingly cold. At last it dawned upon me that this was Andaluz for *helado* or ice! My supposition was confirmed when the landlord appeared, bearing two plates of the dainty in question, which he begged us to accept.

This singularity of the Andalusian pronunciation throws considerable light on the much disputed question of the *assonance* or *consonance* of Spanish rhymes; the fact being that a very great proportion of those so-called *assonant* verses really rhyme perfectly well in the ordinary way, when read by an Andalusian, who always leaves out the consonant between the last two vowels, and often the whole of the last syllable. The letter *s* he hardly ever pronounces at all. Let anybody try to read the Andalusian ballads in this way, that is, as the Andalusians do, and it will be obvious that the rhyme is there, without explaining it by any peculiar laws of Spanish versification.

The cooler weather now allowed us to go down often to Granada to see our friends. Their house there was very Spanish, very characteristic. It was at the further end of the town beyond the Vivarambla; how strange it seemed to talk familiarly of the Vivarambla, with all its memories of Moorish romance! This is quite beyond the noisy, crowded part of the town. A long, quiet street stretches away in the sleepy sunshine to the trees and country beyond; the houses, like most others in Granada, are low, only two stories, and the lower stories have scarcely any windows to the street. The upper ones are grated, as well as glazed, and nobody ever appears at them. One knocks at a small, rather low door; when it is opened, one is admitted into a small room which leads to the *patio*. There the family sit, with an awning overhead, and a fountain full of gold-fish, surrounded by flowers, ferns, and birds, in the middle. From the patio open small rooms, which have no other entrance, and often no windows in any other direction. Upstairs are larger rooms, but they are not much used in summer, being much hotter than the ground-floor.

In one of those small rooms sat the old mother,

who had been left a widow at the age of twenty-three, and who for some five-and-thirty years or more, had scarcely crossed her threshold, always wearing deepest mourning. She was a great invalid, and suffered much ; but her face always wore the kindest, sweetest smile. Her life was spent almost entirely in prayer ; and her sole pleasure was in her grandchildren, two fine boys of eight and two years old. Another larger room was her son's library, full of treasures of learning, Arabic manuscripts, and books in the Castilian language, but in Arabic character (of which many exist in Spain), huge volumes of Spanish history and Spanish ballads; and, what seemed stranger here, much of the English literature of the day. In the *patio* the baby boy was generally to be found, petting his nightingales, of which there was a cage full of young ones, who were his great interest in life. When he met us out of doors, his usual greeting was, " The nightingales and mamma are quite well." (" Los ruiseñores y mama estan bien.") The elder boy, I think, found the patio too narrow a sphere for his energies, and went to fly his gorgeously painted kite (called a *comet* in Spain) elsewhere.

A few doors from our friends' dwelling is the house where the Empress Eugénie was born. It has the same quiet, old-world look that all this side of Granada has.

One of those fresh September mornings, we determined to go to Monte Sacro; but not knowing the way, further than that we had to pass through the Gipsy Town, we resolved to take our guide. Now began a pitched battle; the guide insisting that we were to drive, and we equally pertinaciously declaring that we should walk. Strange to say, we carried the day; the guide groaned, but gave in; and we started early one bright, cool morning. The walk was delightful; at least *we* thought so; but our guide evidently did not enjoy it. The air was crisp and bracing, and the poplars were just beginning to wear their golden autumnal tint. We passed through the Gipsy Town, and proceeded up the valley of the Darro. The last part of the way, with the fallen leaves rustling beneath our feet, was like the ascent up to some Tyrolese castle, and the views were very similar.

In the entrance of the church is a beautiful picture, Santiago preaching; they say it is by Alonso Cano; but whoever is its painter, it is very fine. In the church itself is a curious *retablo*, or altarpiece in compartments; there are also some tolerable pictures. One seemed to be a copy of a Juanes, the Saviour with his hand on the head of a boy, as if blessing or curing him; the heads are fine, and the modelling good. A Madonna of carved wood, by Alonso Cano, struck us by its strong resemblance to the Empress Eugénie, only it was less beautiful.

Then we went into the curious rock-chapels, which are small rooms cut in the solid rock, with so many little passages and turnings that I got quite confused, and should certainly never have got out, had I been left to myself. In one of those rock-cells we suddenly came upon a corpse, as it seemed, lying with a gash across the throat, and a calm smile on the face. It was strangely startling; but so beautiful as to inspire no horror. A little further, and there lay another dead form; but this time the wound was on the head. They looked absolutely real; but were waxen figures of the martyrs San Vito and San Leonzio. There was nothing horrible, nothing grotesque, nothing disgusting; only calm still beauty.

In curious combination with the figures of the saintly martyrs were the old Spanish glass chandeliers hung in those caves in the rock. They were like Venice glass, and seemed fitter for some grand old palace of the Queen of the Adriatic than for those rock-hewn cells.

We observed this inscription on a picture of St. Dionysius, in one of the rock-chapels :—"El Señor San Dionisio Areopagita, Obispo y Martir, primer Capellan de la Reyna de Angeles y hombres Maria S. S., y Patron de este Insigne Collex de Theologos del Sacromonte." "The Señor St. Dionysius the Areopagite, bishop and martyr, first Chaplain of the Queen of Angels and men the most holy Mary, and Patron of this distinguished College of Theologians of the Sacro Monte."

Dionysius the Areopagite, who heard St. Paul's sermon on the Unknown God, was believed, in the Middle Ages, to be author of the celebrated work on the Angelic Hierarchy, really, however, written in the fourth century. Thus he is here called by the quaint title of "First Chaplain of the Queen of Angels." The system of theology ascribed to him was greatly esteemed in mediæval times, so he was naturally chosen as patron of an ecclesiastical college.

The building is still used as a seminary of students for the priesthood.

Another inscription states that St. James, or San Tiago, as they here spell what we generally see as Santiago, was believed to have said Mass here ! and that San Cecilio, patron of Granada, and several of his companions and disciples were martyred and buried here, in the second year of Nero, some on the 1st of February, and some on the 1st of April. They showed us a stone beneath which they had found plates of lead giving the history of all this; and, among other things, stating that " Mary was without original sin." They also found sacred vessels for oil, for the bread and wine of the Sacrament, and (as far as I could make out) a *vinagrero.* But whether that meant a vinegar-cruet, a vinaigrette, or merely a wine-bottle, I did not at first understand. Afterwards I found that it was an Andalusian mispronunciation for *vinagera,* which is a stand for wine and for water, used at Mass. All this, they said, was buried in the second year of Nero, possibly on the 1st of April; on the same day of which month, I think, it must have been that the Archbishop, Don Somebody Castro, discovered them again.

The church and college were founded in 1595, in honour of these supposed discoveries, made in 1588. There is a kneeling statue of Archbishop Castro, which gives one the impression of being an excellent likeness.

The walk back was enchanting, with the magnificent view of the town, and the cathedral in the midst; and, crowning all, the red towers of the Alhambra.

But our cross and weary guide did not appreciate it;
he sighed and grumbled, and said times were changed
and greatly disimproved; formerly nobody walked
who could help it.

Another autumn walk was to the Fuente de los
Avellanos. The present name means "Well of the
Nutbushes," which abound near it; by some people
it is supposed to be the old "Fountain of Tears."
We first went down the steep, rugged ravine which
separates the Alhambra from the Generalife. This
ravine is called the Path of the Dead, because the
funerals generally come up it. Those funerals are
conducted in a manner that seems very strange to our
ideas. They usually pass at night, and, as there is a
small wineshop on the way, the bearers always stop to
make merry. The first month of our stay, they used
to come up the Alhambra avenue at midnight, place
the bier on a bench at the door of the hotel, and dance
and sing, if singing it might be called, for hours.
This was quite against the laws, but nobody interfered;
till one night, a lady who had just arrived from Malaga,
was wakened by the noise; and got so nervous at
this (as she considered it) bad omen so soon after her
arrival, declaring that she knew she should never
leave the place alive, that our landlord, who was a
magistrate, exerted himself to get this abuse put a

stop to; and from that time the funerals came up the ravine, and turned away to the cemetery without passing the hotel. One evening we met a funeral in the ravine; it was a little girl, with white dress and white wreath, lying on an open bier. She was very pretty, and looked like a wax image. In this case, they were carrying her quite quietly, without the songs and merriment that seem so incongruous. Very often a child is carried to its grave by children of its own age; but, sad to say, it is always the children who behave the worst, dancing and singing in the most boisterous way, and considering it all as a piece of amusement. Probably, the idea did not altogether originate in irreverence; it may have arisen from the belief that the death of a very young child, who has committed no sin, is a subject rather of joy than of sorrow.

In going to the Fuente de los Avellanos, one turns to the right, after descending the Path of the Dead, and goes up the valley, on the opposite side from the Gipsy Town; that is, without crossing the Darro. Then a little path through the nutbushes leads to the wells, of which there are three, at a short distance from each other. The water is delicious, and the view most beautiful, especially in coming back towards Granada; but the walk is rather too great a favourite with the rough lower classes, to be so agreeable as some others.

We were very sorry when the time passed on, and we felt that we must rouse ourselves from our dreamy life, and go out into the light of common day again. Not that it was to be the light of common day, either; for it was to Cordova, the city of Abdarrahman, that we were to go. But we had got so attached to our beloved Alhambra, that the thought of departure was very grievous to us. It is true that autumn was coming fast, and many of our friends had already gone in different directions; some to Malaga, some to Madrid, and some to Gibraltar. Even the parrot, whose apartment was on the first floor, just below ours, and who had been such pleasant company during the hot hours, had gone with his family to Alhama. He belonged to a lady who was ill, and who never left her room; so he found it rather dull. Accordingly, one day when H. had got tired of her Spanish lesson and was leaning out of the window, the parrot looked up with one eye, while he closed the other and screwed it up in a most comical manner, opening the conversation by addressing H. as "Juan!" "Si, bonito loro!" ("Yes, pretty Poll!") responded H., with promptitude. "Yes, *pretty*," assented the parrot approvingly. From that time the ice was broken, and the bird was ready to talk at all times; and very amusing he was. So when he departed to Alhama for the baths, we missed his lively conversation so much that we were quite ready to sing, "Ay de mi, Alhama!" The waiters admired him much, and said, "He speaks Castilian like ourselves:" the highest compliment a Spaniard can pay anybody.

Our life had indeed been very pleasant during those summer months; our morning walks in the Generalife, our Spanish lessons during the hot hours, in our cool room with the dark, metallic-green foliage growing almost in at the window, and ever the gay plash of the fountain; the still sunny afternoons in the Alhambra, where we were always greeted with the kindliest smiles by the civil door-keeper, who was very grateful to us for bringing bread every day for his favourite cat, and where the gold-fish in the tank of the Court of Myrtles had got also to know us and our bread-crumbs, and to eat out of our hands and swim through our fingers. At first, they were exceedingly timid, diving to the bottom if a shadow did but cross the water; but soon they grew so tame that, whenever we appeared, they all came towards us open-mouthed, with their heads up, and followed H. from one end of the tank to the other, till she looked like St. Anthony preaching to the fishes.

All the people near, too, had become quite friendly; the gardeners who gathered their finest roses for us, the peasants who cut great bunches of grapes and gave them to us as we passed the vineyards; the man at the little shop, who was always ready to bring out chairs when he saw me sketching, and who sometimes carried his civilities so far as to produce a watering-pot, and water the ground all round me— a piece of well-meant attention that I could have dispensed with. Though last, by no means least, there was the huge mastiff belonging to the hotel, who poked his ponderous head into our hands in token of affection, as we went out and in.

It was a trial to leave all this; but if we lingered here much longer, we must give up Gibraltar and Tangiers, so we set to work to see everything we had as yet omitted; and went up, one magnificent blood-red sunset, to the Torre de la Vela, the Watch-Tower, which juts out from the furthest end of the bold promontory on which the fortress is built. We went also to another, called the Vermilion Tower, though it is not by any means redder than almost all the others, and less so than some. It is one of the outer circuit, and stands near the Gomales-gate, which shuts off the Alhambra from the town. It is the oldest of all, being built long before the Arab Palace; indeed, more than a thousand years ago. From it, the name of Alhambra, 'the Red,' took its rise; Medinah Al-hambra, 'the Red City,' as it was called. It is mentioned as ' Khalat Al-hamra,' ' the Red Castle,' by an Arabian poet, in A.D. 864. This tower is inhabited by quite a respectable family, who keep pigs, and possess a dog, and are altogether superior people. They were very civil, and invited us into their kitchen-garden to examine the old walls. Indeed, all over Spain, if you get a glimpse of a pretty garden, or picturesque patio, through a half-open door, or if you have reason to suppose there may be a fine view from any window in any house, of rich or poor, you may fearlessly knock, and politely beg to be allowed to admire it. You will be received with the utmost courtesy, entreated to consider the house your own, and encouraged to ramble through every room. If the family happen to be at dinner or any other meal, they will ask you; " Do you wish to eat ? " You politely refuse, saying, probably, that you have already dined; they then say, " But won't you dine again ? " This also you decline, with many thanks, expressing a hope that the food they are eating may do them good. Even in the *salle-à-manger* of an hotel, a Spanish family will often ask strangers to share their repast; but, of course, it is not expected that they should accept the offer.

At last, it was time to go: we spent a last morning in the glorious bowers of the Generalife, a last afternoon in the fairy halls of the Alhambra, a last evening in the moonlit garden of the Adarves. We bade farewell, with much sorrow, to the kind and gifted friends who had made our sojourn so pleasant; and at 2 A.M., on the morning of the 17th of September, we left our Moorish paradise. Granada looked very beautiful as we drove through it for the last time, the railway station being quite on the other side of the town. Surely, there never was a more inconvenient hour for a start than two in the morning; it is neither one thing nor another, or rather, it is *both* one thing and another. It combines all the disagreeables of early rising and of sitting up all night. It is scarcely worth while to go to bed beforehand; and yet one cannot sit up till 2 A.M., with nothing to do, when everybody else is comfortably asleep. Yet such are the railway arrangements; it is the only train in the twenty-four hours, so there is no choice. And in the darkness we sped away to Loja, where, for the present, the railway stops, and one has to go in a diligence.

The motto of Loja is "a flower among thorns:" as far as we could judge of it in the dark, it seemed more to resemble a thorn among flowers, being an ill-paved and rather squalid town among beautiful scenery.

Much has been said of the terrors of that Loja road, and probably in winter and spring it may be very bad; but when we were there it was perfectly good, very comfortable, and quite safe. Our fellow-traveller in the berlina was an elderly Spanish gentleman, who had spent all his life in Peru, and looked as if he were made of india-rubber. He was exceedingly polite, and finally presented us each with a very large bright green apple, which he said came from Aragon. They were excellent, with the flavour of an American apple, from which we inferred that the original stock of the American apple was brought by the Spaniards from Aragon.

When we again took our places in the railway, the Peruvian came into the same carriage. Presently, the heat began, and I was sitting on the sunny side; and very different it was from cool Granada. But our amiable fellow-traveller insisted on changing seats with me, and sat heroically in the sun all the way to Cordova.

The country was wild and lonely, all broken into low, rugged hills. Every part of the way had some history of encounter between Moor and Christian, every rock had its romantic legend. One isolated hill, rising out of the plain, with an abrupt precipice on one side, is 'the Lover's Rock.' A Moorish maiden eloped with a Christian knight, and, when closely pursued across the plain, took refuge on the top of this rock; but the foe began to ascend it, there was no hope, no retreat, and they sprang from the top clasped in each other's arms.

We passed Antequera, celebrated in Moorish warfare, and soon after changed trains at Bobadilla, where the Granada line joins that from Malaga to Cordova. Now the character of the scenery altered; it was more open, with tawny slopes, agave thickets, and dark blue distances. We passed Montilla, noted for its vineyards; and, more recently, since we left Spain, infamous for some acts of horrible butchery perpetrated by the Republicans. It has another and better claim to celebrity; the Gran Capitan, Gonsalvo de Cordova, was born there, in the castle close to the town.

As we drew nearer Cordova, the prickly pears and agaves became more abundant; and now we were in a great plain, bounded by the dark purple of the Sierra Morena; we crossed the Guadalquivir, and entered the City of the Western Caliphs.

CHAPTER IX.

Tired as we were with our night-journey, we went
out without loss of time, and walked through the still,
silent streets, where one could almost hear the beating
of one's pulse. The heat was intense ; it seemed as if
the air were thick, like hot gruel ; and a thunderstorm
was evidently gathering. But what did that signify ?
Were we not walking towards the Mosque of Abdarrahman ?

And through the deserted streets we went, in the
overpowering heat, with the blinding white houses
round, and the inky sky above. The guide tried to
point out to us some objects of interest as we passed
on ; but we were, for the moment, totally incapable of

listening to a word he said. A boy on a mule and an old woman were the only living things we saw.

At last we came to the long, dead wall, with its flame-shaped battlements. We entered, and were in the Court of Oranges. There stood the palms, of which tradition says one was brought by Abdarrahman himself from his dearly loved Damascus; but, in truth, I suspect Abdarrahman's palm is a thing of the past, though he certainly planted the first that was ever known here. There, at any rate, was the fountain at which the Moslems were wont to wash before entering the Mosque; and there the great, old orange-trees, with their weight of dark-green fruit. It gave one the strange sensation which I have had elsewhere in Spain, as if I had seen all this before, in childhood or in a dream. It was like coming back to something well known, but half forgotten.

It has been much disputed whether there were or were not oranges in Spain in the days of the Caliphs; some people saying that they were only brought after Vasco da Gama sailed round the Cape. It certainly seems quite impossible even to imagine Cordova or Seville without the green and golden fruit; but this feeling by itself would hardly suffice to decide the point, critically or historically; and the theory that Andalusia was the Land of the Hesperides, and that here Hercules (a great Spanish hero) came for the Golden Apples, can scarcely perhaps be admitted as evidence. The first authentic mention of oranges is by Avicenna, in his cyclopædia, ' Kilât el Mainu; or, Book of the Sum Total.' Now Avicenna, or Ibn-Sina, was not a Spanish Arab, being a native of Bokhara. But the works of Avicenna were always studied in Cordova; consequently, the Spanish Caliphs must have known of the existence of the fruit; and that being the case, we may well believe that they, who possessed everything that luxury could give, would hasten to introduce the orange-tree into their adopted country. Besides, the wondrous palace, built by Abdarrahman the Great in the tenth century, was called Azzahra; and Azzaher, or Azaher, means *orange-blossom* in Spanish at the present day. The palace is said to have been named from Zahra, a favourite Sultana ; but the fact remains that this name also signifies the orange-flower. Possibly, the orange-tree was introduced into Andalusia in the tenth century, about the time that this palace was built; but in all probability this was only the bitter kind (of which the blossom is the principal charm, and is indeed the most fragrant of all,) while the sweet orange may have been brought from Portugal, after the voyage of Vasco da Gama.

Leaving the question of the oranges, we entered the

Mosque, as the Cathedral is always called, and rightly so; for it is still, to all appearance, as completely a Mosque as it was during the dominion of Islam. We wandered through that strange forest of low pillars, on and on, turning now here, now there; and still the endless vista stretched in all directions, before, behind, and on every side: it was like walking through a dim forest, where the branches enclose one bewilderingly. There was no one, at that hour, but ourselves; and our own footsteps startled us. We sat down; and, tired and sleepy as we were, it was all a delicious dream of the Arabian Nights. Always dark, to-day, owing to the gathering storm, it was more so than usual; and, as the gloom deepened, a lamp was lighted here and there, as if by invisible hands. One almost expected to see the 4700 lamps, which illuminated it in Moorish times, burst into radiance, and to behold the prostrate Moslems at prayer. But, instead, the white-robed choristers glided up, in the dim twilight, and the vesper chant began.

It has been said that the modern choir quite spoils the Mosque. Certainly, it does not improve it, and would be better elsewhere. But nothing can spoil it, short of pulling it all to pieces. In the first place, the Mosque itself is not exactly beautiful; it is strange, and vast, and weird, and altogether unlike anything else ; but you do not feel that proportions are spoilt, when you are so bewildered and awe-struck as to be incapable of observing whether there are, or ever were, proportions at all. Besides, the original plan was changed by the large addition made to the edifice of the first Abdarrahman, in the reign of Abdarrahman the Third. Another thing is that, so far from the choir obtruding itself, it is extremely difficult to find. Large as it is, it is lost in the enormous space, and you may walk about the Mosque half the day without ever falling in with it. When you do find it, it is certainly exceedingly beautiful ; so much so that I could scarcely quarrel with it for being there, more especially as, by turning in the other direction, I could as effectually get rid of it as if it had never existed.

Fortunately, too, all the finest part of the Mosque is untouched, and remains precisely as it did when the Caliphs worshipped here. The Holy of Holies is there still ; the *Ceca,* which was as sacred to the Spanish Arabians as Mecca to those of the East. Here the Moslems came on pilgrimage, and walked seven times round it. The pavement is worn by the feet of the many worshippers ; we felt the groove as we, too, stood there. On the outside of the Holy Place is the finest mosaic in the world ; it was a gift from Con-

stantinople, from the Emperor Romanus the Second.
They brought candles to show off the exquisite
colours; even in the broadest daylight, one could
scarcely, in that dusky chapel, see them sufficiently.

This mosaic must have been made expressly for the
Caliph, as it contains no representation of any living
thing; only the most graceful leaves and scrolls.
The colours are indeed unrivalled; deep, glowing
crimson, and rich, vivid green predominating, along
with the brilliant gold now being revived in Venice,
who originally learned her skill in this art from the
East. With regard to the avoidance of representation
of life, it appears that the Greek Emperor was, in
this case, more particular than the Moslems; for in the
Alhambra there are the portraits of Moors, and, moreover, sculptured lions frequently occur. The Ommiades were never so strict on this subject as other
Moslem races; and were in all respects less bigoted,
perhaps from their perpetual contact with those of a
different faith.

It seems strange that the Greek Emperor, the protector of Eastern orthodoxy, the successor of Constantine, should have been on such friendly terms
with the successor of Mahomet, as the Ommiades
claimed to be. But the Western Caliphs, being
always on bad terms with those of the East, were the

natural allies of the sovereign who reigned by the Bosphorus; who, truth to say, seemed always greatly to prefer the gentle, polished, learned Arabians of Spain, not only to the Persians, Syrians, and Turks, who were always harassing and menacing the Eastern Empire, but also to the wild Crusaders, who claimed alliance with the Court of Constantinople.

The *Maksurah*, or seat of the Caliph, is still there. It is a magnificent chapel, of the most gorgeous Moorish design; and must formerly have been seen to even more advantage, before they raised the floor, thereby diminishing the height of the arches. The path among the arcades by which the Caliph walked from his seat to the Holy of Holies is marked by the line of inscriptions on the cornice. Verses from the Koran, and "There is no God but God;" still do they remain, in large gold letters, untouched by white-wash. So far from obliterating this, the Cordovans are proud of it, and take every pains to prevent it being erased by time. The Mihrab, too, where the Koran was kept, is still as it was when it held the Book of the Prophet; and much resembled the recess in a Jewish synagogue which contains the Bible.

We stayed till the gathering darkness warned us to go. The storm had not yet come, so we lingered in the Court of Oranges, and then went out by the exquisite

Puerta del Perdon, the 'Gate of Pardon,' with its old Moorish door, inlaid with silver. Then, frightened by the intense blackness of the clouds, we hastened home.

That evening the storm came in good earnest; it hailed, and it rained, it thundered, and it lightened, as if heaven and earth were coming together in one crash. It had this good effect, that it cooled and cleansed the air, and checked the ravages of smallpox, which had previously been raging to a fearful extent.

Next morning the sun again shone brilliantly, and we hastened back to the Mosque. It looked even vaster by the fuller light; and the vistas in every direction seemed interminable. They are now taking off the barbarous whitewash, and the original painting of alternate red and cream-colour is visible. About a third of the Mosque is still white, so one can appreciate the difference; it is curious how much the absence of colour diminishes the apparent size.

Almost every one of its thousand columns has a marvellous history. Some are from the temples at Carthage, some are Roman, others from Constantinople. Two small yellow pillars are from Damascus, and were much prized by Abdarrahman, eleven hundred years ago. Some are said to be from the Temple at Jerusalem, and on them the Saviour may have looked. Truly, the memories here make the pulse beat and the eyes grow dim.

The columns are all monoliths, and of every imaginable variety of material : alabaster, granite, porphyry, verd-antique, and the rarest African marbles; finest of all are the jasper ones, which are solid, and I should think unequalled; but they are so dim and neglected, that it is only on examination that one sees how precious they are. Their shape and size are as various as the material : some thick ones are pared away at the base, where they are stuck into the ground; those that are too short are provided with very large disproportionate Corinthian capitals to make up the difference, while others have no capitals at all. Yet no sense of unfitness strikes one; all combine into this strange, petrified forest, and one would no more expect the pillars to be uniform, than one would wish to find all the trees of the wood exactly alike.

The sacristan had been prowling about for some time, looking exceedingly mysterious. He watched everybody out and in with intense interest; and at last, seizing his opportunity, when nobody was in sight, swooped down upon us. We naturally thought he was going to turn us out as heretics; but instead of that he inquired in an agitated whisper (quite unnecessary, as there was not a living creature in the vast Mosque but ourselves), whether we wished to see the Treasury. "Certainly," we were preparing to answer with alacrity; but, without waiting for our reply, he suddenly pirouetted round, and stood with his back to us. Thinking he misunderstood, I went after him, upon which he took to flight, and concealed himself behind a column. Presently, he came cautiously out, and began once more, "Would your worships like to see "—— but again he broke off, and gazed at the roof with an air of abstraction. "The Treasury," said I, innocently finishing the sentence. "Hush!" said he, becoming excited, and gazing nervously around. I began to think he was a lunatic, and got nervous also, not at all understanding the cause of all this. I looked about for an explanation, and saw three or four people advancing. They turned in a different direction, however; whereupon the sacristan instantly became calm, and again suggested the Treasury, adding that, as no Spaniards were now present, he could safely open it. "Do you never show it to Spaniards?" asked we. "Never," said he, "it would be ruin." He urged us to make haste lest any Spaniards should enter; and indeed, just as we got to the Treasury door, two girls appeared. In an instant he and his key vanished; but

now we understood his tactics; and presently he re-
appeared and unlocked the door.

No wonder they are careful how they let people in;
it is one of the richest treasuries I have ever seen.
There is a magnificent *custodia* of solid silver, and
wondrous workmanship; very like, on a smaller, but
not a very small scale, the Sacraments-häuslein at
Nürnberg. The graceful Gothic architecture tapers up
and up, like the spire of a cathedral, and ends in a
slender flower; and all in purest silver. There were
some beautiful episcopal crosses of silver, for carrying
in procession; and a profusion of lamps with silver
chains, and crosses, and crucifixes, and reliquaries, and
monstrances, and every conceivable cup and dish.
Really, as in the days of Solomon, silver seems to
have been nothing accounted of in that era of Peruvian splendour.

We should have liked to sit all day in the Mosque,
lapped in an Arabian dream; but there were other
things that we wished to see. So we went up the
tower, which well repays one. It is detached, like
the Giralda at Seville, or Giotto's Campanile in
Florence; or, indeed, like any Moorish minaret.
The roof of the Mosque is exceedingly curious, when
one looks down upon it, being much like the card-
houses children build. It is said that this roof was

originally flat; but at present it exactly resembles those of the Mosques in Tangiers at this day. From tho top of the tower one can also study the many different forms of the Moorish battlements. They were quite unlike any others we had yet seen: some were like pyramids cut in steps; others were singularly notched and zigzagged; in one place they were shaped somewhat like a fleur-de-lis; in another, they were the true flame-form, which is so beautiful.

As we came out, we passed a very fine flamboyant doorway, just opposite one of the entrances to the Court of Oranges, and next the Archbishop's Palace. It is the entrance to a hospital. Then we went away to the Guadalquivir, where the broad, pale yellow river comes down in a full flood of water, between banks fringed with pale green. In summer, I believe all is brown; but a few autumn showers had already changed the hue of the landscape. The bridge is grand, with its irregular arches; the foundations are Roman, but the arches are Moorish, built in 710. Just before one comes to the bridge is a modern gateway, of the time of Philip the Second, which, though classical (Doric), looks wonderfully well. The worn, worm-eaten look of the stone enables one to bear it better. Here was anciently the Moorish Bab-Alcantara, the Gate of the Bridge. What was once the

Alcazar is close at hand; the Castle of Roderic, the last of the Goths; there, till lately, was the dreaded Inquisition. It is now a prison.

On the opposite side of the river is a beautiful old fortified tower, intended to guard the bridge. It is exceedingly picturesque.

We rambled all round the town, and saw and sketched many bits of old wall, and enjoyed ourselves thoroughly. Everywhere those brown towers, and the violet-blue Sierra Morena, with its exquisite lights and shadows.

Then we came back through the silent streets, where the sunshine on the white walls was now blinding. It was utterly lonely, but quite a different character of loneliness from Toledo. There it seemed a city of the dead; and not only of the dead, but of the burnt-up: here, it was as though a deep sleep had fallen on the inhabitants, caused, as appeared quite probable, by the spells of an enchanter; and, some day, one might expect them all to rouse themselves, and resume the ordinary life and occupations of the ninth century, instead of those of the nineteenth. In the meantime one stepped lightly, for fear of waking them too soon.

As we passed along, we could often see into the patios, which were beautiful; quiet and dim, with bright flowers, and a fountain that plashed slowly, as if in a dream. But no living thing did we see in those lovely courts; the spell seemed on them all. Once or twice we saw an old woman sitting in a door-way asleep. The nearest approach to wakefulness was in a donkey, that stood thoughtfully at a door, to which he was tied with a rope; quite a needless precaution, as far as running away was concerned. But even the donkey did not look altogether like a donkey; he might have turned into anything else, if you had happened to hit upon the proper magical formula suited to the case.

We now went to an old house, where the guide said the Gran Capitan, Gonsalvo de Cordova, once lived. Through this we passed, and crossing a very large court, or rather garden, full of huge old orange and lemon trees, we entered the church of San Hippolito, where Alonso the Eleventh now lies buried. We had looked in vain, all over the Mosque, for his grave; and at length, on inquiry, we found it here. Why it had been moved from the Mosque, or whether it ever really was there, we could not learn. But there are very few graves in the Mosque, and a curious feeling seems to prevail among the Cordovans, as if it were scarcely a Christian church yet, except in the choir.

As we went home, we passed through the silver-smiths' quarter, which is very unlike what a silver-smiths' quarter would be anywhere else. Small, dingy houses, which nobody could possibly suppose contained shops of any kind, if there had not been a few tarnished silver buttons in the window, do not at all prepare one for the beautiful workmanship within. In true Oriental fashion, the merchant begins, especially if there be any peasants or common people in the shop, by saying he has nothing of the kind. At length a sudden thought seems to strike him, and he produces a drawer full of exquisitely worked silver. It is in the style of the Genoese work, but much more solid; and it has a glistening look that is quite peculiar. It is only the ornamental part that is well-made, however; the clasps are beneath contempt, and break the first time you touch them. This is partly owing to the extreme softness of the silver, which bends like leather. It is all made by women.

The silver once produced, the bargaining begins. At first, he asked a great deal too much; but, to my surprise, at once took off about a third of the price of some buttons, when I asked it. I was exceedingly proud of this; it being the first time I had ever succeeded in bargaining in any country. He was obdurate concerning a bracelet, however; probably because he

saw that I particularly admired it; but, in his eagerness that I should buy it, he ran to the door, and
begged the passers-by (of whom there were but few)
to come in and give their advice!

Close to the Hotel a very interesting mosaic had
been discovered a few months before. It is in, or
rather under, a carpenter's shop, but not in a dark
cellar, as I had feared. The carpenter, with much
public spirit, had broken up half the floor of his shop,
and put a ladder, so that one could examine it very
well. It represents the Four Seasons, and is in the
best period of Roman art, as far as one could judge.

The Hotel (Suiza) has a large patio, with the porti-
cos supported by beautiful fluted Corinthian columns,
dug up on the spot. On the capital of one of these
pillars an Arabic inscription is carved. On this site,
in the days of Roma Patricia, when Cordoba was
peopled by the poor and proud Roman aristocrats, as
opposed to the more democratic and thriving Seville,
the residence of the Roman Governor stood; and
afterwards here was the Moorish palace of Abdarrahman.

The Cordovans are very proud of their city, and of
the great men it has produced; and give their names
to the streets and squares. The Gran Capitan is
naturally their favourite; they dont seem to care much

about Lucan, but they greatly admire Seneca ; and, next to him, Juan de Mena, who lived in the dawn of Spanish literature ; he was the most distinguished poet of his time, and much esteemed at the Court of John the Second, who was a sovereign of cultivated tastes, and to whom Juan de Mena sent his verses to be corrected.

John the Second, father of of Isabella the Catholic, governed Castile, Leon, and Andalusia, from 1407 to 1454 ; and during his long reign was considered to favour poetry and poets " more than was wise," as his nobles thought. He himself made verses; he loved music, played, sang, and danced well. So say the historians. His nobles do not seem to have objected so much to the dancing and singing as to the verse-making. Some of them did him justice, however. " He was," says Perez de Guzman, " a man who talked with judgment and discretion. He knew other men, and understood who conversed well, wisely, and graciously ; and he loved to listen to men of sense, and noted what they said. He spoke and understood Latin. He read well, and liked books and histories, and loved to hear witty rhymes, and knew when they were not well made. He took great solace in gay and shrewd conversation, and could bear his part in it." He does not seem to have been altogether a bookworm either; for, as Perez de Guzman goes on to say, " He loved the chase, and hunting of fierce animals, and was well skilled in all the arts of it. Music, too, he understood, and sang and played; was good in jousting, and bore himself well in tilting with reeds." Such was the sovereign in whose favour Juan de Mena stood high.

All this poetry, and music, and learning was not generally looked upon with much liking by the warlike nobles. It was not in Castile as in Barcelona, where, though the palmy days of the Troubadours were past, the " Gaya Sciencia " was still cultivated. The Castilians, on the whole, inclined to consider poetry as nonsense; music sheer waste of time: while, as to learning, that was the worst of all, as the Black Art must certainly have something to do with it. Another learned man (not a Cordovan, however), of the Court of John, suffered from those grave imputations: Henry, Marquis of Villena, whose family, at the time of his birth, possessed the only marquisate in Spain, and who was cousin of both the King of Castile and the King of Aragon. He it was who first translated Dante's ' Divina Commedia ' into Castilian ; and the King was so delighted with it, and his curiosity so raised on the subject of Virgil, that he desired Villena to translate the Æneid also.

But Villena's high position, as Grand Master of Calatrava and near relation of the sovereign, could not save him from the suspicion of necromancy; and after his death his library was looked upon as something quite diabolical. In a letter concerning this library, written by John the Second's confidential physician to Juan de Mena, we read : "Two cartloads' of books were carried to the King, and because it was said that they related to magic and the unlawful arts, the King sent them to Friar Lope de Barrientos ; and Friar Lope, who cares more to be about the prince than to examine matters of necromancy, burnt above a hundred volumes, of which he saw no more than the King of Morocco did, and knew no more than the Dean of Ciudad Rodrigo " (who this illiterate Dean was I have failed to find out) "for many men now-a-days make themselves the name of learned by calling others ignorant ; but it is worse yet when men make themselves holy by calling others necromancers." He then goes on to beg Juan de Mena " to solicit in his behalf some of the surviving volumes from the King, that in this way the soul of Friar Lope might be saved from further sin, and the spirit of the defunct Marquis consoled by the consciousness that his books no longer rested on the shelves of the man who had converted him into a conjuror."

Lope de Barrientos was a Dominican, confessor of John the Second, and preceptor to his son, Prince Henry ; but it would appear he really did examine the books, as he afterwards composed a treatise against Divination, in which he says that among the books burnt was one called ' Raziel,' from the name of the angel who guarded the Gate of Paradise, and taught the art of divination to a son of Adam, from whose traditions the book in question was compiled. It is curious that Friar Lope should not have seen that magic learnt from an unfallen angel could have nothing diabolical in it. Any how, it is evidently from this affair that Cervantes took his delicious scene of the burning of Don Quixote's library.

It was not in Cordova that all these things happened ; yet this city seems to have been, according to monkish theologians, a very focus of necromancy. It was quite natural for people to suppose that what they did not understand must be dangerous ; besides which, the Moors had always been considered in a manner sold to Satan ; and after Cordova became Christian, the taint might linger still. Even Pope Sylvester the Second did not escape this imputation of necromancy ; and, Pope though he was, the question was seriously raised whether he was to have Christian burial or not : all because he had studied at Cordova.

In those schools, philosophy, medicine, arithmetic, algebra, mathematics, music, and astronomy were taught as they were taught nowhere else; to them we are indebted even for the common numerals now in use, so easily understood by all nations, and much simpler and better than the somewhat clumsy combinations used by the Romans, or the still more awkward system of the Greeks, which was practically useless to all unacquainted with the Greek language. Indeed, all the learning of the Dark Ages was Arabian; and so celebrated were the physicians of Cordova that Sancho, King of Leon, came here for medical advice, and was cured of dropsy.

Here Averroes translated and expounded Aristotle, while the writings of the Greek philosopher were as yet unknown to the rest of Europe; and they were first studied in the West through an Arabic translation. It may have been partly the frequent intercourse between the Eastern Empire and the Spanish Caliphs that facilitated the study of the Greek language in the schools of Cordova.

The Caliphs themselves greatly encouraged learning. Abdarrahman the Second was accustomed to spend his leisure in conversation with philosophers and poets. Music, too, he greatly delighted in; and sent to Bagdad for Ali Zeriab, one of the greatest musicians of the East. I wonder what sort of music that was, so prized by the Arabians! It could not have been like the Andalusian songs (melodies they cannot be called) of the present day; which latter, indeed, are thoroughly African.

The celebrated Library of Cordova is said to have consisted of 600,000 volumes. What became of all those treasures of knowledge? If only some potent spell could bring to light again all the lost libraries, all the scattered manuscripts, all the pictures that have vanished into the Land of Non-existence, all the Greek statues that have been burnt into lime or melted into money! That indeed would be a collection worth seeing. I should be well satisfied with one glance into the dim caves where the glories that have been are buried.

We had been advised to ride out three miles from Cordova to see the Hermitages and the site of the Palace of Azzahra, built by Abdarrahman the Third; but we preferred spending our few remaining hours in the Mosque, especially as the noonday heat was still very great; and, moreover, not a vestige of the splendid palace now remains, and even the site has been disputed.

All the tales of the Arabian Nights fade into nothing compared with the stories related of this palace. It was built by architects from Constantinople, and all the marbles were wrought and polished there, the Emperor presenting many of the columns. The walls of the Hall of Audience were encrusted with the finest marble, ornamented with gold ; in the middle was a fountain surrounded with figures of birds and quadrupeds, all of the finest gold, embossed with jewels ; probably in the style now termed Byzantine work. Above this fountain was hung an enormous pearl of priceless value, a gift from the Greek Emperor to the Caliph. In the garden was another fountain which flowed, not with water, but with quicksilver. Those gardens were said to be delicious, and one can well believe it. The most apparently incredible thing is, that at the great entrance there was a portrait-statue of the beautiful Zahra. This is very remarkable, not so much because the Koran forbids the making of images ; for, as we have seen, that was frequently disregarded in the West, and, at this period, even in the Eastern Caliphate, the coins were impressed with the figure of the monarch ; but because it is so contrary to Moslem ideas to allow all men to gaze on the face of a wife, and especially of a favourite Sultana. However, one gathers from Moorish ballads that there was not so rigid a system of seclusion in Spain as elsewhere in the Mahometan world.

Abdarrahman the Third, the possessor of all this magnificence, wrote thus: "From the commencement of my reign to the present moment, I have carefully numbered the days of pure and genuine happiness which have fallen to my lot; they amount to fourteen. I have reigned fifty years, beloved by my subjects, dreaded by my enemies, and esteemed by my allies. Riches and honours, power and pleasure, have waited on my call, nor does any earthly blessing appear to have been wanting to complete my felicity. In this situation, and during this long space of time, I have not been able to enumerate more than fourteen days passed without being imbittered with trouble and uneasiness. O man! learn to make a just estimate of this world and of the pleasure which it affords!"

Such was the experience of Abdarrahman the Great.

CHAPTER X.

Our journey to Seville was southern indeed, over the brown plain of Andalusia; we left the mountains, and soon the only break in the horizon was here and there the stately flower of the agave. When we drew near the station, we put out our heads to look for the Giralda, and were horror-struck to behold several tall chimneys sending forth volumes of smoke! This was appalling, and upset all our preconceived ideas. The Spanish proverb, "Quien no ha visto

Sevilla, no ha visto maravilla," signifies, in a free translation, that until you have seen Seville you don't know what it is to be thoroughly astonished; and this was precisely our case, for we were much and disagreeably surprised. Surely Seville was not going to be so utterly un-Spanish as to turn out a thriving manufacturing town! It was most disheartening.

Sadly we got into a cab (there were actually cabs) and drove through distressingly modern-looking streets, like those of some town in the south of France. A thousand years seemed to divide us from the sleepy, dreamy Cordova of the Caliphs.

We soon came to a small square, where a few orange-trees in some degree restored our equanimity. At the corner of this little square was the Hôtel de Madrid, to which we were going; and, on entering it, the beautiful patio effectually banished the smoky chimneys from our minds. All white marble and green leaves, and streams of water full of gold fish—it was indeed very splendid and very Spanish. Under the colonnades were most comfortable chairs and sofas, and tables covered with Spanish newspapers; and in the evening lamps were brought out here. The rest of the hotel by no means fulfilled this promise. Upstairs the passages were dirty, and the rooms dull, looking chiefly into a narrow and noisy street, exceedingly unlike our large, airy, and very clean room at Cordova, with its pleasant view over the Botanic Garden. The *salle-à-manger*, however, was very pretty; it was large and irregularly shaped, being much narrower at one end than at the other, and on the walls hung dark, old pictures. It opened on the patio on one side; on the other, there was a vista of courts and gardens, in one of which the servants dined under the trees; beyond that, one could see the kitchen, which was like a picture of Bassano's, with melons and cabbages lying about. But the great charm was the azulejos, with which the room was wainscoted up to a considerable height. They had been brought from old houses, and were singularly fine; the colours were chiefly blue, green, and bright orange patterns on a creamy white ground, and the combinations of form were endless.

Next morning we hastened to the Cathedral. We soon passed through the Frenchified street in which the hotel is, and entered a very large and perfectly regular square; an uncommon thing in Spain. The centre space was entirely filled with orange-trees, which, in spring, must be delicious with fragrance. This is the best situation for invalids in winter, it being very sunny. We passed out at one corner of this square, and found ourselves in one of the filthiest

streets I have ever seen. This is a rare evil in
Spain, where the streets are generally clean; in Cordova, especially, they were beautifully so. Small,
mean, dirty shops were on each side; nothing could
be more unattractive: when we turned a corner and
the Cathedral was before us. Huge, and grim, and
grey, it rose far into the deep blue sky, more like a
rugged mountain than a building in its stupendous
size. The outside is more grand and stern than
beautiful; the gigantic buttresses seem to oppress
one; and the cold grey colour looks strangely out of
keeping with the golden sunlight.

We entered; and stood in the most majestic cathedral in the world. There is nothing like it; it cannot
be compared with any other. Breathless and awe-
struck, we wandered among those magnificent aisles,
in the dim, coloured light of the wonderful windows.
I really almost felt that, in Spain, I had for the first
time seen what stained glass is. In many other
places there are some beautiful windows, but there
are so seldom enough of them! So often some dull,
badly restored window, or a dirty pane of white
glass, covered with cobwebs, mars the whole effect.
But in the Spanish cathedrals it is all perfect. I do
not think that in those of Seville or Toledo there is
one window that is not wholly of the most gorgeous

gem-like hues. It is very remarkable and exceedingly satisfactory that a Spanish revolution never takes the form of breaking church-windows. All here are fine : St. Peter is especially so, in a robe of deep and glowing purple ; but the finest is the Conversion of St. Paul. The peculiar iron-grey of the stone gives wonderful effect to the windows, which look like a mosaic of dark rich jewels.

At first one scarcely knows what gives the Cathedral its overwhelming grandeur. On a second visit one can observe the enormous span of the arches, the huge pillars that lose themselves in the dim distance, the stupendous height, and, above all, the extraordinary width, not only of the nave, but of the seven aisles. I have seen other Gothic cathedrals as long, or longer ; but never any at all approaching to it in width.

This peculiar form is owing to the Cathedral being built on the site of the old Mosque, whose plan it has in some measure retained. Nothing else remains except one most beautiful horse-shoe doorway, which leads from the Court of Oranges. The present edifice was begun under Ferdinand and Isabella, when the power of Islam was waning fast in Spain, just twelve years before the fall of Granada ; and was finished in the astonishingly short time of thirty-nine years.

But the old Mosque had more interesting historical associations than this, the most magnificent temple on earth. It was in the old Mosque that the funeral of St. Ferdinand took place, when the King of Granada sent a hundred of his knights to do honour to the royal dead; and for long after, when the last day of May came round again, the hundred Moorish knights again rode down the steep mountain paths from Granada, and stood, with lighted tapers in their hands, round the regal cenotaph, while the funeral Mass was sung, and the requiem sounded among the low pillars where so lately the Moslem had worshipped.

In a very different time, and by a very different sovereign, was St. Ferdinand laid in the splendid silver sarcophagus in which he now rests,—in the early part of the dreary eighteenth century, by Philip the Fifth, a King who was not even Spanish. But the original tomb is there still, with its epitaphs in Spanish and Latin, Hebrew and Arabic. I should have liked to have been there on one of the three days on which there is Military Mass, and the troops march into the Cathedral, and lower the colours to the dead monarch. The sword of the Royal Saint is still there, and the iron-gilt key of the city, given by the Jews, the day Seville surrendered. The

Arabian key, which was of silver-gilt, with the inscription, in Arabic, "May Allah render eternal the dominion of Islam in this city," has disappeared, but there is a model of it. I do not know if it had been stolen, or perhaps hid somewhere for safety. The Banner of Spain still hangs proudly above the grave of the conqueror of Seville.

In the same chapel are buried his Queen, Beatrice of Suabia, and his son, Alonso the Wise, who composed the epitaphs on his father's tomb. A hundred years later, Maria de Padilla, Pedro the Cruel's long unacknowledged wife, was also laid in that most regal of regal places of sepulture, among the greatest and best of her husband's race.

So occupied were we with St. Ferdinand, and all the chivalrous memories of those old days, that it was long before we could go to look for the many fine pictures existing in the Cathedral. And when we did, it was no easy matter to find them in the dim light; not that it was exactly dark, but the air seemed thick with glowing colour. At last we met a delightful old friar, who told us that now that he was turned out of his convent, he had no pleasure, except in the Cathedral. He stayed here all day, he said; and there was one altar that he always kept in order, with candles burning on it; not that he was paid for doing so, he was not a sacristan; but he saved a little of his pension to buy the candles. If we would only come to the other side of the church, we could see how nice his altar looked; but his great difficulty was to prevent people taking away the candles; not that perhaps they meant to steal them, but for some other altar. So we went with him, and it was indeed very well cared for. He then took us into the different chapels where the pictures were. One very fine one is Santiago on his white horse, when he fought at Clavijo, as Castor and Pollux did at Lake Regillus. It is by Juan de Roelas, and is really magnificent, as the saint dashes along, trampling down the Moors, and scattering them to right and left. Of course, it is in the Chapel of Santiago.

We were rather disappointed in the celebrated St. Anthony, by Murillo; the light is not good, and it is difficult to see it well. Not so with Murillo's Guardian Angel: it is perfectly lovely; the angel bends tenderly and anxiously over the child, who looks up, half obedient, half heedless. A long ray of light comes in from one of the doors, and strikes this picture, bathing the angel in a golden glory.

At the back of the High Altar is a good Luca Giordano, the soldiers throwing the dice for the

Saviour's coat. But the picture that pleased us most after the Guardian Angel, was a Madonna and Child, by Alonso Cano; it is the best of his that I have seen, and very, very sweet and still.

The old monk then pointed out a very curious lock on one of the doors; he was exceedingly proud of it, because it had been made by a friar. He then consigned us to the sacristan, who showed us the great candlestick used with the thirteen lights at the Miserere in Holy Week. It is bronze, of exquisite workmanship; the figures of the twelve apostles are at the top, alternately with the candles. We saw the massive silver Custodia, which is fine, but the form is not so graceful as that of Cordova. It was made about seventy years later than the Cordovan shrine. There were also very rich and splendid vestments; artistically inferior, however, to the delicately shaded needlework of those we had seen at Toledo, which were as fine as if they had been painted.

Under the pavement of the nave, midway between the great entrance and the choir, is buried the son of Columbus. The ship in which the great discoverer first sailed to America is sculptured beneath one's feet; a strange, high-prowed galley, or *caravel*. The inscription runs thus, " A Castilla y a Leon, Mundo nuevo diò Colon : " " Columbus gave a new world to

Castile and Leon.”   After all, when one considers all the wrongs of the Indians, all the sufferings of the negroes, all the dark pages of the history of that fair Western World, where there has been more wrong, more bloodshed, more cruelty, more tears, in the few centuries that have elapsed since its discovery than in a thousand years of our old hemisphere, one is inclined to doubt if Columbus was indeed such a benefactor to humanity.   To the Spaniards he certainly was not: all the gold of Mexico, all the silver of Peru was poor payment for the guilt they incurred in their treatment of their new-found subjects; and, from that day to this, the star of Spain has slowly but steadily waned.   Her best days were from the time of St. Ferdinand to that of Ferdinand and Isabella.

But, however, it is quite certain that, if Columbus had never existed, America would have been discovered by somebody else long ere now; and the natives must have disappeared gradually, as the New Zealanders are doing at this day, before the force of civilization.   There can be no far-off land now, beyond the setting sun; no “ Island of the Blest,” where steamers don’t touch at least once a fortnight.   So all honour be to the great Genoese!   He did his work nobly and well, amid countless sorrows and discouragements.   And one is glad to think that, in spite of all these discouragements, all those sorrows, he must have been, on the whole, happy in so doing. Such work as that is its own exceeding great reward, and the hour in which he first descried the distant shore, the moment in which his foot first touched it, must have been well worth all his toil; although he was afterwards obliged to write (in prison, too) a treatise to convince the Inquisition that the existence of America was not contrary to the Scriptures.

We did not go out by the great entrance, but through the old Moorish gate, and found ourselves in a dark corridor, where we were rather startled by the apparition of a crocodile hanging in mid air. This was the identical animal sent by the Sultan of Egypt to Alonso the Wise, in hopes of inducing him to give him his daughter in marriage. It was in pretty good preservation, and looked very well, though certainly an unusual feature of ecclesiastical architecture.

From this corridor one passes into the Court of Oranges, which is small compared with that of Cordova, and has not quite the same dreamy charm. Yet in spring, when the white, fragrant blossom is out, and in winter, when the trees are covered with golden fruit, it must be a pleasant place to linger in; but the great height of the Cathedral makes it seem insignificant. Those Moorish Courts of Oranges harmonize better with the low-roofed Mosque than with the lofty Gothic Cathedral.

We wandered about here for some time, looking in vain for the entrance to the Library; and, in our search for it, went into the Lonja, or Exchange. The patio is magnificent; but, finding out our mistake, we did not penetrate further. It was built the year after the first Royal Exchange of London; but the Archbishop of Seville, who advised Philip the Second to found it, nevertheless felt constrained to apologize for following, in this, the example of heretics. In the upper story are the Archives of the Indies, said to be a mine of yet unexplored information.

At length, as we could not find the Library, we had to go back into the Cathedral, and apply to the obliging old friar, who showed us the entrance, in an exceedingly dark corner of the corridor. It was not yet open; but they very good-naturedly unlocked it for us at the unusually early hour of ten minutes past eleven—eleven o'clock being the proper and legal time for doing so. We wished to see the manuscripts of Columbus, but they are too valuable to be left lying about, and the chief librarian was not there. "When did he come?" "Sometimes at one time, sometimes at another; possibly in five minutes, perhaps not for two hours." "Did he stay when he came?" "Sometimes he did, and sometimes he did not." This was not very satisfactory; but they brought us some fine illuminated missals to console us. After waiting a little, we began to think it hopeless, and went off to the Giralda, saying we should come back next day about one o'clock.

The ascent of the Giralda, in spite of its great height, is a very easy matter; as, for the greater part of the way, a mule or donkey could do it without difficulty. We did not venture to the very top, that being fearfully dangerous; it can only be done, at the last, by clambering up little steps cut on the outside, without any parapet whatever, at the height of 350 feet from the ground. The guide said nobody could get up there; it was not for men, it was only for birds ("para los pajaros"); but, of course, Englishmen could do that or anything else; he had seen a young Englishman go up, and he (the guide) had felt giddy ever since.

There is really no occasion to run the risk, as one can get so very near the top without either trouble or danger, and the view, where we were, is quite as good. The only thing that one does not see is the Giraldilla, that is, the figure of Faith, turning round and round with every breath of air. A strange and unfortunate symbol to choose for a weathercock! I suppose the idea was taken, with alterations for the worse, from the Moorish one at Granada, where an armed Moor turned, and pointed his lance in the direction of the wind. The tradition was that when the figure should be removed or destroyed, the dominion of Islam should be at an end in Spain; and so it really was. But the Moorish knight pointing to the wind was a happier thought than that of Faith, holding the banner of Constantine, and whirling round and round. Still, I should have liked to examine the figure.

As that was impossible, we had to content ourselves with admiring the great pots of lilies, in beautiful iron-work, at the four corners of the platform where we stood. The pot of lilies is one of the emblems sacred to the Virgin; thus one often sees it painted at the edges of pictures of the Madonna. Those here are very graceful; they are so large as to be in some measure distinguishable from below, yet the workmanship, though bold, is not coarse, even when quite near.

Strange to say, the view was what we cared least for. Seville itself lies as on a map below one, but the only architecturally striking buildings are this very tower on which we were standing, and which we, therefore, could not see; and the cathedral, which is too near. It was interesting, however, to look down on the roof of the cathedral, and thus more fully appreciate its enormous size; while far below us lay the Court of Oranges, which, on the contrary, looked exceedingly small. As to the country round Seville, nothing could be uglier; it is a great plain, with no mountain-horizon, no vegetation, no colour. It is not brown enough to look Spanish, nor yellow enough to look African, nor green enough to be pleasant to the eyes. Above all, it is not fertile; the inhabitants took good care that it should not be so, when they destroyed the Moorish system of irrigation. So the great river, the Guadalquivir, flows sluggishly along, with water enough to make the whole plain a paradise, like the Vega of Granada. As it is, it does not attain the dignity of desolation; it is only dull.

This Mueddin tower of the Moslems may have suggested the idea of the Campanile of Florence; but, beautiful as the Giralda is, Giotto's slender tower is far more so. At the time the Florentine Campanile was built, the Giralda was only 250 feet high, the additional hundred feet being a comparatively modern erection: Giotto's tower is 275, and, as originally planned, would have been 370 feet in height. The decree of the city of Florence commanded him to make a tower that should exceed in height and richness any in the world; thus it almost seems as if Giotto had wished to rival the famous tower of Islam, if indeed he ever heard of it.

The foundations of the Giralda are said to be fragments of Roman and Christian sculpture. At the time the Giralda was built (1196) the only Christian sculpture that could possibly have existed in Spain must have been executed between the time that Rome became Christian and the days of the Arab invasion; so that probably little of value was broken up for that purpose. As to Roman works of art, it is likely that the fragments in question were chiefly architectural, taken from the Roman city of Italica, close at hand.

On our way down we turned aside to look at the works of the great clock; the weight is a funny little figure of bright steel, with a crown on his head, and a long pole with a ball at each end, in his hand; he poises himself jauntily on one foot, and balances himself backwards and forwards, making a low bow one moment, and the next kicking up his heels scornfully, like some mischievous sprite controlling the destinies of Seville. This clock was made by a Franciscan friar in 1764; it replaces one that dated from 1400, which was the first ever put up in Spain.

We now went to the Alcazar, whose high dead wall

gives no promise of the beauty within. The Moorish palaces are not like those of Venice, "the wealth within them" does *not* "run o'er;" but, on the contrary, is carefully concealed inside. Here it is very rich and splendid, and has been well restored by the Duke de Montpensier, in the style of the Alhambra, but of much coarser workmanship; the colours, too, are rather raw and glaring. It was all whitewashed in 1813, and the restoration of the colours is not yet quite complete; they are still working at it, and the paint-pots were lying about. Consequently, what was white was rather too white, and what was red or blue was almost distressingly brilliant; very unlike the mellow tint of the Alhambra, where, except in the bathroom, the colours and gilding have not been retouched since Boabdil went forth from the Siete Suelos Tower.

Still, it was very beautiful and very gorgeous; and though restored, has been little altered since Pedro the Cruel lived and committed murders here. Some of his bloody deeds may be palliated by the circumstances of the time, but two were particularly treacherous: the murder of his brother, the Master of Santiago, whom Maria de Padilla in vain tried to save; and that of the "Rey Bermejo," the Red King of Granada, who sought shelter at his court and was put to death by Pedro's command, in order to take possession of his jewels. It is true that Abu Said, the Red King, was a usurper, and probably the jewels belonged rightfully to the crown of Granada, and not to him at all; but still, to receive a guest with feigned cordiality, and then murder him, was so contrary to all the laws of Oriental hospitality, not to speak of those of Christianity, that it was no wonder Moslem and Catholic alike looked upon him as a monster. The jewels that caused this horrible act were superb. Among them were three splendid rubies; one of them, called the " balax " or balas-ruby " of the Red King," is probably the finest in the world, and may now be seen in the Tower of London, as the centre stone of the royal crown of England. It was given by Pedro the Cruel to the Black Prince. This jewel was much prized by Queen Elizabeth; she showed it to the ambassador of Mary, Queen of Scots, and he describes it as " a fair ruby, great like a racket-ball." The Spanish chronicler says, those rubies were as large as pigeons' eggs; but the one in the English Crown looks larger, as it is now set. There is no record as to what has become of the two others.

It would be interesting to know when and how those gems came into the possession of the crown of Granada, and their previous history. Were they brought by Abdarrahman from Damascus ? or of what city, of east or west, were they the spoil ? Rubies are rather a rare stone in old collections; nor are they very often mentioned in history. Sapphires seem to have been the chief jewel among the Goths; and we read much also of emeralds of extraordinary size. Among the spoils brought back to Damascus by Tarik was an emerald table of prodigious size, and emerald cups were not uncommon; though some people, disbelieving the existence of such enormous precious stones, have conjectured that the table may have been of some sort of ancient glass. In the East *red* jewels were, during the crusading times, sometimes regarded as amulets; and this " exceeding great ruby " may, very possibly, have been considered to have magical virtues. It is strange that Pedro should so easily have parted with this stone, after thinking it worth while to commit a treacherous murder for the sake of obtaining it.

Whatever were his faults, Pedro was a staunch ally of England; and, it is said, regretted that the marriage which would have made him brother-in-law of the Black Prince never took place. The fair young English bride, daughter of Edward the Third, had got as far as Bourdeaux, and in a few days they would have met. But a more awful one than even the ferocious king received her first—the Black Death. She arrived at Bourdeaux late in the evening, and by next morning she was dead, a victim to that fearful pestilence.

It must be said also, in Pedro's behalf, that he had a miserable childhood and youth, with much to embitter him against human nature. His father, Alonso the Eleventh, chivalrous sovereign though he was, behaved extremely ill to his wife and son, treating them almost as prisoners, while he kept court with Leonora de Guzman, at Seville, in this very Alcazar. It was not then, however, the gorgeous Oriental palace it now is; those Moorish halls were built by the terrible Pedro, who seems to have been more Moslem than Christian in his predilections, though much more treacherous and bloodthirsty than any of the Spanish followers of Islam. But, at any rate, he had an excellent taste in architecture, and sent to Granada, where the Alhambra was but just finished, for Moorish workmen.

The gardens are perfectly enchanting, with flowers of every kind in profusion, tropical shrubs, orange and lemon trees, fountains and fishpools. Some of the fountains require caution, for the jets of water spring out of the gravel walks, close to one's feet, without the slightest warning. Here and there the paths are

bordered with little, low, broad walls, of which the
top is covered with Moorish azulejos, and forms a comfortable seat: in some shady spots it becomes a kind
of sofa, with a back to lean against; and in those
places the azulejos are in the form of a chess-board,
black and white; so that one could play at chess
or draughts in those delightful bowers. The terrace,
which opens from the window of the upper story,
must be pleasant in winter; but even as late as the
21st of September, the heat was so burning that
we could not stay there a moment.

Next day we went to the Museum to see the
Murillos. Our expectations were very highly raised,
and I think we were a little disappointed at first.
It is true there are twenty-one pictures undeniably by
Murillo, besides some others that are doubtful; but,
fine as many of them certainly are, not one can be
called a masterpiece. They are placed in the chapel
of an old convent, and the light is extremely bad: it
is only about noon that they can really be seen at all;
and even then but one at a time is distinctly visible.
One has to sit opposite each picture in succession,
waiting till the solitary ray of sunshine falls on it,
then for an instant it is bathed in brightness; the next,
all is again dark, and it seems blotted out. If one
misses the exact moment, there is nothing for it but

to come back next day and try again; and in
dark, wet weather it is no use to go at all. The
pictures are also excessively dirty; but they have this
advantage, that they have never been retouched nor
overcleaned.

The only others that struck us were the Zur-
barans, which are the masterpieces of this artist.
None but he could make such pictures out of subjects
so apparently unpromising. It does not seem as if a
group of Carthusians, with little variety in their faces,
no colour, no brilliancy, nothing to contrast with the
monotonous white of their robes, could be interesting
or beautiful. Yet such is the magic of this painter's
genius, that those cold shadowy figures attract one,
even among the glowing tints of Murillo.

In the court of the Museum is some Roman sculpture from Italica. The architectural fragments are
beautiful, consisting chiefly of very fine Corinthian
capitals: the statues are not remarkable in any way;
but they are so badly placed that it is difficult to
judge of them.

A far finer Murillo than any in this Museum is
'Moses Striking the Rock,' in the Hospital of La
Caridad. It is, indeed, a masterpiece, and one of the
finest pictures in the world. The Spaniards call it
'*La Sed*,' 'Thirst;' and it is well named. Each group

is perfect in itself, without interfering with the unity of the whole. In one, a woman pushes away her child, and drinks the water greedily herself. Yet, powerful as the picture is, there is nothing horrible; it is most beautiful, and pleasant to look on withal, because you feel that the terrible thirst will surely be quenched: you rejoice, as they do, in the abundant stream of water flowing from the rock.

Originally, here were the splendid Murillos that Marshal Soult carried away, which are now the glory of the Louvre. But the Miracle of the Loaves and Fishes, another good picture by the same artist, is here still. There are also two exquisite small ones, the little St. John and the Infant Saviour.

At the appointed hour we went back to the Library, and, to our surprise, found the librarian ready to receive us. He brought us the manuscripts of Columbus, and the book that he took with him to read on his first voyage. It is a description of the world (Tractatus Imagine Mundi), and has marginal notes in his own handwriting; in one he says, "No one is secure from adversity."

This library is called the 'Columbina,' and was presented to the canons of the cathedral by the son of Columbus. They seem to prize it much, and keep it in excellent order; but I do not think many people go to read in it. The memory of Columbus is greatly revered now in Seville, if that could make amends for the ingratitude with which he was treated when alive. Probably, jealousy of him as a foreigner and an Italian contributed to this bad treatment; no native of Italy has ever prospered in Spain. The French are disliked and feared by the Spaniards; the English are rather liked in some places, and very much respected in all; the Germans they simply know nothing about; but the Italians they wholly detest.

In the afternoon we went to see San Telmo (as they here spell St. Elmo), the palace of the Duke de Montpensier. It was formerly a naval college, founded by Fernando Columbus. It is a pretty house, and there are some beautiful pictures in the rooms. One of Murillo's finest is there, the Virgin de la Faja; it is very lovely. There are also many good modern pictures by German artists, especially by Lehmann. One room is entirely furnished with mother-of-pearl; chairs, tables, everything. The collection of Moorish pottery is fine; some of the plates have a ruby lustre, but none are so magnificent as those we had seen at Granada.

The gardens are quite different in character from those of the Alcazar, and much more like this everyday world. They have nothing Moorish about them, being planted only in 1682. But it is a pleasant place, with plenty of shady walks, and more oranges than I ever before beheld. In one part flowers are carefully cultivated, with tidy borders, and neat gravel-walks; not in the usual Spanish style, where a garden is generally a wilderness of sweet blossoms. The gardener showed us very triumphantly two young dragon-trees in pots; he said they were 'chiquititos,' an affectionate diminutive much used by Spaniards in speaking of any little creature they are very fond of, such as a child, a kitten, a puppy-dog, or a young nightingale. He appeared to consider them as sentient beings, and to treat them accordingly. In truth, the dragon-tree is no common plant: there are, as far as I am aware, but two full-grown ones in Europe; the very fine specimen in the Governor's garden at Gibraltar, and one in Lisbon. When they are young, like those at San Telmo, they are much like young palms; but the stem is quite smooth, instead of being scaly, and the leaves are more like those of the Yucca. When they grow old, they become more strange and weird than a fantastic dream; the branches are like huge, misshapen, swollen limbs, and the whole tree seems a creature half animal, half vegetable, as if it were under the spell of some evil magician, or malignant fiend.

They put us in mind of the doleful forest in Dante's
Inferno, where each tree enclosed the soul of a sinner,
and bled when the branches were broken off. In
this too they were like, for if the bark of the dragon-
tree be pierced, the sap flows crimson, like blood;
and when it heals, it leaves a scar exactly like that of
a wound.

In a shady space we came to three tombs of old,
grey stone, with trailing ivy growing about them.
The gardener pointed to the one in the middle, and
said, "That is the tomb of Don Juan Tenorio."
Probably we looked stupid; for he added, "Your
worships doubtless know his history very well."
Rather ashamed of our ignorance of the lives
of Spanish worthies, we replied that we did not.
"No!" said he, "do your worships never go to the
theatre?" beginning to sing the last act of 'Don Gio-
vanni!' It had certainly never occurred to us that
the hero of Mozart's opera was otherwise than
mythical; but here was his grave, a very handsome
sarcophagus, much prized by the Duke de Montpensier!

The gardener said the other two graves were 'the
Commendador and Doña Iñes,' as he called them,
and that all three had been in an old church now
pulled down, which had been anciently the burial-

place of the Tenorio family; the Duke de Montpensier had saved them from destruction and brought
them here.

These Tenorios seem to have been generally either
very bad, or very good and great. One of them was
Archbishop of Toledo in the fourteenth century, and
was a benefactor to the city, inasmuch as he repaired
both the bridges over the Tagus, one of which had
been completely broken down. He also built one of
the chapels in the cathedral, and otherwise beautified
it.

From the Garden of San Telmo we went out into
the Delicias, the public promenade of Seville. We
had heard much of its charms, but to us it appeared
only very moderately delicious. In spring it is probably in greater perfection; when we saw it, it looked
rather dusty and forlorn. It is close to the river; but
here the Guadalquivir is not beautiful; it is sluggish
and dirty, with shabby houses and workshops scattered about its banks.

After the first day or two our guide had become so
unbearable that, as we were to be ten days in Seville
and had plenty of time, we resolved to do without
him altogether. He was not stupid, but was intolerably lazy, and said we must not fatigue him!
He refused to go out except in a carriage, and,

finally, made such exorbitant demands in return for very small services, that we were glad to get rid of him. We now found that the cabs, which had distressed us on our arrival, had their bright side ; and the cabmen proved quite as intelligent, and much more civil and trustworthy, than the guide. Even when, as sometimes happened, they did not know some of the places we wished to go to, they took pleasure in finding them out for us.

One of the most interesting of the old houses of Seville is that of Murillo. It stands far away from all bustle and noise, in a little sunny Plaza, close to the wall of the town, and now belongs to Dean Cepero, a man of cultivated tastes, who takes pride in preserving all the memorials of the great artist. Here Murillo died, on the 3rd of April, 1682, of the injuries he received in falling from a scaffolding in the church of the Capuchins at Cadiz, while painting the Marriage of St. Catherine.

The house is charming, with a lovely patio and delightful garden, still, even at the end of September, a blaze of splendid flowers, on a background of thick, dark foliage ; there are curious fountains, too, and remains of frescoes, some of which are said to be by Murillo's own hand. On the other side, the windows look on the old city walls ; and, beyond that, over a wide plain covered with tall reeds. The view is not much; but with that intensely blue sky and golden sunshine, even the bending, whispering reeds had a strange charm. One was glad to think that Murillo had such a pleasant dwelling. The rooms were delicious, opening on the beautiful court; they were comfortably furnished, and full of plants and flowers. Upstairs were some good pictures, especially an Ecce Homo, one of Murillo's very finest works.

Another delightful place is the old palace of the Duke of Alva, all neglected and decayed though it be. The azulejos at the altar of the chapel are unrivalled with their glorious golden and ruby lustre. There is a charming tangled old garden, with thickets of myrtle and jungles of orange and lemon trees; the gardener gave us branches of the myrtle, and *sweet* lemons, which are a most disappointing fruit, quite without flavour of any kind. The fountains are broken and out of order, but robed in a drapery of the loveliest maiden-hair ferns. This palace is one of the *Casas Solares*, as those houses are called which were acquired at the time of the expulsion of the Moors, and was originally much larger, consisting at one time of eleven patios; but part of it is now inhabited by poor families.

The most Moorish of all those old houses is the

Casa O'Lea, which is in the same style as the Cuarto Real of San Domingo, in Granada. The Moorish stucco-work is in perfect preservation, and the rooms are inhabited and comfortably furnished. We hesitated about asking admittance, as the family were at home, and just going to breakfast; but the servant politely insisted that we should go in, and showed us everything. The house was still arranged for summer, the family inhabiting the ground-floor, which was furnished with slight bamboo chairs and sofas, and *esparto* matting; but they were on the point of migrating upstairs for the winter. There are no fireplaces in a Seville house; but the upper rooms face the south, and are provided with thick, warm curtains, carpets, and *portières*.

I have certainly never seen anywhere such delightful houses as those in Seville. They are all much on the same plan, though some are, of course, more richly furnished than others. All have the patio, as at Granada; but those at Seville are far more splendidly decorated: one peculiarity is, that, instead of the jealously-closed door prevalent elsewhere, there is a gate of prettily wrought iron in open work, so that, in passing along the street, one can quite easily see into all the houses. Sometimes there is a screen that is put up when the inhabitants are at meals; at other times they do not seem to care about being looked at by the passers-by. The peeps into those white marble courts, with their fountains, and shrubs, and flowers, are very picturesque, and unlike anything one sees in other places.

The most splendid modern palace we saw in Seville is that of the Marquis de Paramares, of the Alarcon family. Though new, it is built in the most perfect imitation of the Moorish style, combined with the utmost luxury of soft carpets, gorgeous damask hangings, and French mirrors. In some of the rooms the walls were covered with very good modern pictures, chiefly of wild forest-scenery, or winter landscapes, all snow and ice. Then one raised a crimson or pale blue satin curtain, and stood in an Oriental hall, ornamented with arabesques and delicate fretwork. The court was thoroughly Moorish, with its slender pillars and graceful arches. On the other side was a small but pretty garden, into which the drawing-rooms looked.

Half of Seville must be taken up with those gardens, for every house of any pretension has one; besides at least one court, and often three or four, all with flowers and shrubs. Consequently, the town covers a very large space in proportion to the number of inhabitants, and from a height looks more like a scattered suburb of immense extent than like a populous city. The distances, too, are very great, as we found when we walked to the Casa de Pilatus, it being exactly at the other end of the town from our hotel. We were, however, well repaid for our trouble. It is an exceedingly curious and interesting place, and the azulejos are very remarkable for their extraordinary beauty and variety. The little garden is full of bananas, and other tropical plants.

But a full account of Seville would be but a repetition of marble courts, and light colonnades, and fretted arches, and ruby-lustred azulejos, and great orange and lemon trees, and myrtle thickets, and flashing fountains, and every bright flower and fragrant odour; and ever the sapphire sky and the southern sunlight gilding the 'Marvel of Andalusia.' For such it really is, in spite of the slight disappointment caused at first by the smoky chimneys and the modernised streets near the railway-station. The more one penetrates into it, the more one sees its wondrous beauty.

But when it rains,—well, it does not very often rain, and it is better so; for, with the most cheerful disposition in the world, it would be difficult to appreciate Seville when the sky is black, and the streets are running like rivers, and the air feels like a hot, wet sponge. And if the stranger goes there, as we did, about the autumnal equinox, he must not be surprised if such is sometimes his experience.

One morning, after a night of heavy rain, which had cleared the air and cleaned the streets, we went to the market-place, where the fruit is an extraordinary spectacle. Huge piles of melons were the principal feature; and really I had no idea that there could be so much of that particular fruit in the world. The market-place was crammed with every variety of them. At a distance it looked as if further progress must be impossible; but, on coming nearer, we we found we could pick our steps among the heaps of yellow and green globes that lay like cannon-balls in an arsenal. The excellence and variety of melons in Andalusia is quite astonishing. Some are yellow without and green within; others, on the contrary, are green without and yellow within: some are rough, others are smooth and glossy, while many are spotted and speckled. The common water-melon, with its dark green rind and crimson pulp, is very abundant. The best of all is the musk-melon, of which the outside is greenish, and the inside palest pink. But all are good, and all are eaten to a startling extent. They are eaten at breakfast, of course; many people begin with one slice, and all end with two. At dinner it is usual to eat a slice after the soup, and two or three, or indeed any quantity, at dessert. Besides that, a slice of melon is refreshing at any hour of the day; and the poor people live upon them, with bread, almost entirely during the season, which lasts, more or less, for five months. The only time that a Spaniard never eats melon, or indeed any other fruit, is late in the evening; they consider it then almost poisonous.

From the melon-market we went to the shopping street of Seville, the Calle de las Sierpes, the 'Street of Serpents.' Why it has this unpleasant name I know not; at present there are no snakes, but only little shops like booths. The Spaniards call all shops *tiendas*, tents; and formerly, I suppose, the merchants did really pitch a sort of tent in the bazaar. We bought fans, which were very pretty and extremely cheap; and orange-flower water, *agua de azahar*, which is a speciality of Seville, and is indeed deliciously fragrant. The shop-people were much surprised that we did not rather buy Parisian perfumes.

On our way home a friend who was with us took us to see the new, or rather, newly-arranged Pres-byterian church. It is very beautiful, having been first a mosque and then a Roman Catholic church. We expressed surprise that the Catholics had made no difficulties about selling it to the Protestants, but were told that they had recently sold another church to be made into a theatre !

Protestantism seems to make more progress in Seville than elsewhere in Spain. There is an English church, and in connection with it is a school for Spanish children, which is well attended and very well taught. In the Presbyterian church there is service in Spanish every Sunday, and a great many Sevillians go. There seems to be much less prejudice against Protestantism here than in Granada; partly because there has for many years been a much greater influx of strangers in Seville, and partly because the Andalusians, properly so-called, are of a gentler disposition than the Granadinos. The harmony among the Protestants here is very remarkable; there are no bickerings, no heart-burnings. The Episcopalians are as proud of the splendid Presbyterian church as if it were their own, though their place of worship is only a small and simple room. This perfect unanimity produces the happiest effect among the Romanists, who in many places are greatly shocked at the disputes and quarrels which too often arise among the Protestants.

One afternoon towards the end of our stay in Seville we drove out to the Cartuja, now desecrated and made into a pottery. The roof is fine, but the church is so completely filled up with potters' wheels, that all else is quite spoilt; it makes one sad to see such ruin. At a short distance, on the other side of the road, is a little chapel surrounded with flowers; in it the *silleria*, or seats of the choir, are of most beautifully carved wood, by Cornejo, the Grinling Gibbons of Spain. But, on the whole, it is not worth the long, dusty drive through the disagreeable suburb of Triana.

Another day we spent at Italica, which well repays one for the still longer drive. But in this case it is only the first part of the way that is uninteresting, though even on the 28th of September the heat was burning, and the sun blazed with a fierceness that made one rejoice it was not one's fate to spend July and August in Seville. The country round is a great plain covered with stunted grass, more grey than green in colour, mixed with the glaucous tint of the agaves, and their yellow and brown blossoms, tall as a young tree. The sky was too completely saturated with sunlight to be blue; it was of a pale metallic hue, as if the heavens were iron. A faint line of azure marked the distant Sierra; the air trembled and quivered in ripples of heat, while the great yellow, sluggish river lay seemingly still as a lake.

We were glad to arrive at Italica, and seek shelter under the broken arches of the amphitheatre. Here Spain seemed to have sunk under the earth, swallowed up by the stroke of some necromancer's wand; and we were in Rome, among the Imperial ruins. We felt very much at home, and sat in the shade till the sun lowered; then we scrambled all over the rows of seats, which are still tolerably perfect. The door-keeper was quite a character. He asked much and eagerly about the Roman Coliseum, and then repeated a great quantity of Spanish poetry to us. His house was a curious little place, almost hidden by flowering shrubs, and we sat on a stone among them, joined by two dogs, that seemed to take a great and intelligent interest in the poetry and conversation.

The amphitheatre is in a lonely situation, quite apart from the almost invisibly small village which now occupies the site of the city founded by Scipio Africanus, the birth-place of Trajan and Adrian. It is quite possible to go to Italica and also to the convent of St. Isidoro, not far off, without perceiving that there is a village at all, or a house of any kind.

At St. Isidoro we had great difficulty in getting in; but at last we found some white-washers, who were at work in some part of the building. One of them very good-naturedly went to look for the door-keeper and key of the church; but neither of them were apparently at hand, for we waited long. At last the door was opened, and we entered. There are the tombs of the noble Guzmans; and amongst them that of the founder, Alonso el Bueno, the hero of Tarifa.

It is still a grand castellated pile, and looks strangely lonely in that great plain; for, as I before said, the village, if there be one (of which we had no ocular demonstration), is invisible from the convent.

The drive home was delightful, in the cool of the evening, with Seville lying before us, all pale rose-colour in the dying light, and the deep purple haze stealing over the wide horizon.

This was nearly our farewell to Seville. On the last day of September we left it, and sped away to Cadiz.

CHAPTER XI.

Cadiz—Church of the Capuchins—Murillo's last Pictures—Cathedral—Polite Boys—Journey to Algeciras—Sugar-canes—First view of Gibraltar—Rambles on the Rock—Monkeys.

THE approach to Cadiz is somewhat like that to Venice, inasmuch as, after crossing the level plain, one gets among the lagoons, and has a general impression of going out to sea. But here the fields are covered with low, bushy clumps of fan-palms, instead of the reedy grass of the Adriatic shores, and the hedges are agave instead of acacia. The snow-like salt-fields are a curious feature in the landscape; and finally one seems to leave the land entirely behind one. The causeway on which the railway is made is in the form of a half-moon, white and shining as silver; at the end of this silver crescent lies Cadiz, like a pale pink sea-shell.

Unlike many other maritime towns which are beautiful only from afar, Cadiz is as bright and fresh and clean when entered as when seen from a distance. It is one of the few towns in Spain that has really handsome streets. The houses are very high, which is unusual in Andalusia: they are said to be whitewashed every year; but, as far as we saw, they were washed certainly, but not white, being generally of different shades of pale yellow, pink, and lilac. They have not, however, the beautiful *patios* of Seville; the fact being that Cadiz, built on what is practically, though not really, an island, cannot afford room for the oriental courts and gardens of the rest of Andalusia. This want of space accounts also for the great height of the houses.

There is not a great deal to interest in Cadiz, but we were never weary of the beautiful Alameda, with its three or four tall palm-trees, and its wide view over the violet sea; and the port, full of shipping and boats of every kind, with the glittering houses looking like white sea-foam.

Of course, we went to the Church of the Capuchins to see the picture Murillo was painting when, in his anxiety to judge of the effect of his work, he retreated back and back, till, at last, one step too much, and the old man was lying on the pavement below, not killed, but sorely hurt; never more to touch the canvas with magic colour, but to be carried back to his sunny home in Seville to die.

This fatal picture, the marriage of St. Catherine, is very beautiful; it is exactly as Murillo left it, nearly finished, but not quite. Another superb picture by Murillo, in this church, is St. Francis receiving the Stigmata. We preferred it to most of those in the museum at Seville. In San Felipe Neri is a very fine Concepcion, also by the same artist. But one of his most interesting, though not one of his finest pictures, is a work that he had in hand at the time of his death. It is in the church of the Merced, and represents San Gaetano. The head of the saint only is by Murillo; the rest by his pupils. It is a curious little church altogether; the sacristy has the roof beautifully painted with garlands of leaves, and lovely angels peeping out. The angels are, however, much more like cupids, and recalled some of Albani's bright creations. The whole thing looked so little Spanish, and so extremely Italian, that we were amazed. On inquiry, it turned out that they were by an Italian artist. How different the genius of the two nations is! The doll-like, over-dressed Madonnas, the crucifixes in petticoats, and the dark, fierce, wild-looking saints of the Spanish school are indeed unlike the chubby, dimpled, merry little angels we were now looking at.

We went to the cathedral, which is handsome in its way; somewhat in the style of that of Granada, being classical, and excessively ornate Corinthian. The woodwork of the choir is exceedingly beautiful, having been brought from the Cartuja at Seville.

In the Museum are some beautiful white-robed Carthusians by Zurbaran; and one or two tolerable pictures by other artists. This was not, however, enough to detain us long from the pleasant Alameda. Strange to say, this charming walk was generally quite empty; being deserted for the more fashionable Plaza de Mina, where the band plays. This Plaza is a pretty garden, with very large pepper-trees and plenty of seats; but we thought the Alameda much more delightful.

Of Cadiz a remarkable fact must be chronicled; namely, that the street-boys are politeness itself! When I was sketching on the Alameda, a few of them came up; they did not tease, however, taking care to stand behind me, and punctiliously stoning any smaller child who came between me and the view. They were chiefly anxious as to whether I was going

to put "the Saint" into my drawing; this so-called
saint being in fact a copy of the Faun of Praxiteles.
At last, a few drops of rain began to fall. whereupon
some of them helped me to close up my paint-box,
while another held my umbrella carefully over me!
And all this without asking, receiving, or seeming in
the least to expect any recompense.

Pleasant as Cadiz was, we were anxious to get on
to Gibraltar.   But that is not always an easy matter;
Spanish steamers are very uncertain; and the land
route, if it existed, which seemed doubtful, was by
all accounts frequently impracticable.   Of course, we
were told that the best steamer on the line had sailed
the very day we arrived; and at first we could get no
information about any other.   At last we heard that
one was to sail next morning; but by this time the
wind had risen so much that H. began to look grave,
and it was reported that the steamer would not venture out.   We now made serious inquiries about the
land route, but were solemnly assured by everybody
that it did not exist, or at any rate existed only as
far as Tarifa.   The unanimity of opinion on this subject was remarkable: usually, false witnesses differ;
but, in this instance, they agreed in the minutest
particular.   The diligence went only as far as Tarifa;
after that, one had to ride.   All this exactly tallied

with what people from Gibraltar had told us was the
case.　We naturally believed it; but as we were
walking along one of the streets, I happened to look
up, and saw "Office of the Diligences between Cadiz
and Algeciras" written over the very door we were
passing.　This was precisely what we wished to ascertain about; and here we were assured that the
carriage went the whole way without change.　The
truth, as we afterwards discovered, lay somewhere
between those two extremes.　We found, to our annoyance, that we could not have the whole berlina,
as we wished; one place being already taken.　We
were told, however, that this unwelcome occupant
was a "caballero de edad, muy apreciable," that is,
a highly respectable elderly gentleman; so, as the
storm was increasing every moment, we took the two
remaining places.　When we got back to the hotel,
everybody, landlord, landlady, and waiter, were in as-
tonishment, and said they had never heard of this
diligence, and hoped, for our sakes, it might be so;
but they evidently disbelieved its existence.

Next morning at five A.M., when we heard the wind
howling, and other travellers departing, we congratulated ourselves that we were not obliged to get up
and face the storm.　But very soon it calmed, the
day was faultless, and we began to doubt if we had

acted wisely. On rising from dinner, a Spanish gentleman, with the lowest of Castilian bows, expressed, in a well-turned speech, the hope that we might make our journey "with as little inconvenience as possible, and *without novelty*." Novelty, in Spanish, is synonymous with misfortune: " No hay novedad," literally, " There is no novelty," means that nothing disagreeable has happened. Truly, there is much of the character and history of a nation to be found in the peculiarities of its language.

Late in the afternoon we started on foot (as is the Spanish custom), with a porter carrying our luggage. When we got to the railway station, having hurried prodigiously, we found we were an hour too soon; so we went and sat on a log near the port, sketching. Though October it was as hot as summer. From Cadiz to San Fernando, where we were to find the diligence, is about half an hour: there our troubles began; the diligence was small, what professed to be berlina was but an open coupé, and our fellow-traveller looked clumsy and cumbersome. But he could not help being clumsy, and he was inclined to be polite, and anyhow there was no remedy; so we took our places. No sooner had we, with great difficulty, got ourselves and our possessions in, than the carabineers appeared, and requested the keys of our boxes, to open them. These we distinctly stated we should on no account give; whereupon they begged us to get down and open the boxes ourselves. To this also we objected, and a *peseta* soon settled the matter.

We started, and after about an hour's drive got to the entrance of Chiclana. Here we were told to get down and walk, as the street was full of holes. And full of holes it certainly was. I cannot imagine how they got the diligence along. *Holes* is a mild expression; they were trenches, pits of unknown depth. We walked to the other end of the village, and then stood waiting for the diligence to come up. It seemed a very long time; at last a sausage-seller, whose shop was not yet closed, kindly brought out a small bench, on which H. and I, with a Spanish lady, who was one of our fellow-passengers, found room.

Chiclana is a very fashionable watering-place; so it is the more remarkable that the principal street should be in such a lamentable condition. On asking why no attempts were made to fill up the holes, the answer was, " What would be the use of that when the government may be changed to-morrow ?" We suggested that the next government, whether Republican or Carlist, would not dig up the holes again; but we were told, with a solemn shake of the head,

that it was not easy for strangers to understand those
things, in which latter opinion we quite agreed with
our informant.

At length the diligence came up, and we again
mounted. To sleep was, however, rather a difficult
matter. The road was rough, and the carriage so
badly hung, that one's head was knocked about like a
shuttlecock. The "respectable elderly gentleman"
smoked perseveringly the whole night, and burnt
large holes in my dress, but he did not mean to
annoy us; on the contrary, he politely roused me up
when we were passing Trafalgar, to compliment us, as
English, on the victory.

We rattled on, the horses occasionally sticking fast
in some more adhesive pit than usual, till daylight
dawned on our sleepy heads and bruised limbs. A
grand, rugged outline of mountains rose before us,
not dim and distant, but seemingly close at hand. I
asked the *mayoral* what Sierra that was. "Africa"
was the laconic but very satisfactory reply. It was
delightful; there it was, Mount Abyla, the "Mount of
God," the southern Pillar of Hercules, rising magnificently into the clear sky. Clear, but very cold;
it seemed hard to be frozen in sight of Africa; but
such was likely to have been our fate if the mayoral
had not kindly wrapped us up in *mantas*.

We soon arrived at Tarifa, and were once more summoned to descend. Here we were to change diligences, and get into a smaller one, though it was not easy to see how a smaller one could contain us. We, however, got down, though no other diligence was visible; and now recommenced the process of waiting in the street. No inn, no buffet, nothing to eat or drink; fortunately, the weather was fine, but if it had rained, or if the noonday sun had been burning us up, it would have been all the same; we must have waited without shelter. A good-natured woman brought out one chair, on which we both sat, at the gate of Tarifa, with all the luggage lying heaped up in the middle of the road. Our fellow-passenger meanwhile feeling cold, had attired himself in a huge railway rug, with broad black and yellow stripes, and walked up and down, looking like a Bengal tiger on its hind legs. After a long delay the new diligence came up, not apparently very much smaller than the other, but with no place for luggage. As we got into the coupé we anxiously inquired what was to become of our property. "Oh! it will come on *with cavalry*," was the answer. We felt grave, never having contemplated leaving our possessions in this manner, at the gate of Tarifa; but there was nothing else for it, so we drove off, and abandoned them to their fate.

The drive was now very pretty, and exceedingly pleasant. We began to thaw a little in the morning sun, and the diligence, being less heavily loaded, did not swing so much. Besides, the road was decidedly better than anything we had yet experienced since we left San Fernando. I asked why the carriage had been changed, as the road was so good. The *mayoral* only shook his head and pointed onwards. We still proceeded along in great ease and comfort, when all at once every vestige of a track stopped. Now there was nothing before us but a very steep hillside, interspersed with bushes, stones, and young trees. In some places, but not everywhere, the way was faintly traced out, and that was the utmost that could be said of it. I am now quite convinced that it is impossible to upset a Spanish diligence; if the thing could have been done, it must have happened us that morning. Rattle, swing, bump, jump, we went down the hill; the scenery was pretty, but by no means so " glorious" as the guide-books describe it. There were cork-trees, but scarcely enough to be called a forest; nor did we see any wonderfully fine ones. We observed very curious ferns growing luxuriantly on the trees, and should have liked much to examine them. Afterwards we learnt that it was the hare's-foot fern, and found some of our friends at Gibraltar making them grow on flat pieces of cork.

Presently, we were again requested to descend, in order "to walk across the river." "Certainly," said we; "where is the bridge?" "There is no bridge," said the man, looking as if he thought we were lunatics for proposing such a thing. After all, the river was not broad, nor very deep, and there were stepping-stones: still if we had fallen in, which might easily have happened, we should have got exceedingly wet; and, moreover, I don't suppose it was anybody's duty to pull us out again. I wonder why, in Spain, they so seldom combine bridges with rivers. We saw many bridges without rivers, and still more frequently, as here, rivers without bridges. But except in the cases of the Guadalquiver, the Tagus, and the Ebro, we rarely saw the two things in juxtaposition. We had to walk a little way, after crossing the stream, and it was very pleasant in the bright morning sunshine among the wild flowers. In spring they must be lovely; for even at this season we found abundance; among others, great quantities of heather.

When we got back into the diligence, our travelling companion grew eloquent on the subject of sugar-canes. He was going to Algeciras to lay out sugar plantations on the at present bare and rugged slopes immediately above the little town. He pointed out to us a few patches already planted with the " sweet canes," as the Spaniards call them. I never saw so vivid, yet delicate a green. Everything else pales, or looks russet beside it. We were told it kept so always, never fading nor changing, and that soon the whole hillside would be covered with it, an English Company having bought the ground for the purpose. As yet those slopes wore a very scrubby appearance : no flowers, no grass ; absolutely nothing but brown earth and a few coarse weeds. As we drew near Algeciras, the scene was very strange. This brown uncultivated land reaches almost to the entrance of the town, or rather, large village ; for it is unwalled, and looks as if somebody had thrown down a quantity of rubbish and stones in that wilderness by the sea-shore. There is only one road to it ; and that would, elsewhere than in Spain, be considered anything, rather than a carriage-road. On the other side there is not even a path : the streets end in a field ; not a very green one, certainly, but still a field. Near the entrance to the town we got among the sugar-canes, the only green things visible ; and the road was bordered by a thicket of wild castor-oil plants, with their great russet leaves. The little inn is on the port, next door to the diligence-office. It did not look very inviting, having rather a seafaring appearance; but it was really very comfortable, with its English landlady, excellent tea, and delicious fish.

The great attraction was the view of Gibraltar, which we now saw for the first time. It was not at all like what I expected. Somehow, I had imagined a bluff promontory ending a line of rocks, with its whole top surmounted by fortifications, all stony masonry and bristling cannon. In short, I thought it would be like any other fortress, but larger and stronger. Then I was not at all prepared for its being so exactly like an island. From Algeciras, the neutral ground is invisible, because it is level with the sea; and the Rock seems completely detached from the Spanish coast. I was also much surprised at the wildness of the scenery; its beauty does not become apparent till one gets nearer. The clear atmosphere deceives one too as to distance; and consequently the Rock looked lower than I expected. At night the effect of the lights in Gibraltar was very curious and beautiful; it was exactly like a gigantic necklace of diamonds.

About an hour after our arrival, our luggage appeared with "the cavalry," which consisted of two very nice-looking mules. The boxes were neatly packed in huge rope-nets, and looked a great deal safer than when on the rickety diligence. The mules did not seem at all tired; as soon as they were freed from their burden, they began to caper about like kittens.

After breakfast we went out to look about us, and came to the conclusion that Algeciras was a very odd place. The streets, tolerably wide and regular, and pretty well paved, all things considered, end abruptly, as I before said, in a field where there is not even a track. On one side is the sea; on the other, the only road, a very bad one, among the sugar-canes and castor-oil plants; all else is a stony field, on which the late rains had brought out a few tufts of grass here and there. Behind, the brown uplands, without a leaf or blade of vegetation of any kind; beyond, the jumble of hills over which we had just passed. There, indeed, the colour was wonderful, almost fierce in its wild grandeur; dark stormy purple, burnt-up yellow, ashen grey. It had that look which I have observed in some other parts of Spain, as if it lay under the weight of some awful doom. Countries have an expression, as the human face has ; and Spain, truth to say, even in her beauty sometimes wears a frown.

Next day we went over to Gibraltar in a little steamer. We were delighted at being required to declare ourselves British subjects ; when we offered to show our passports, the reply, in undeniable English, was, "All right, ma'am ; no occasion." What a bustle and hubbub there was at the Waterport ! and how very unlike Spain it was ! and yet with a Spanish sky and Spanish sun, and almost African vegetation. We proceeded to the Clubhouse Hotel, where everything was quite comically English ; a mixture of comfort and dinginess, worthy of an old-fashioned London hotel. A *very* old-fashioned one, though ; for the march of railways has changed all that. The only other place I have been in for many years that in the least approached this antiquated state of things was the inn at Hanover, with its dingy furniture of the time of the Georges. It was very comfortable, though, and the views from the rooms are magnificent ; one of ours looked over to Africa, Mount Abyla, and the whole range of the Riff ; the other, up the Rock to the old Moorish Castle and the fortifications.

We spent some delightful days, taking long walks on the Rock ; up to the Signal Station, with its uninterrupted view in all directions; to the Rock Gun, where the precipices are really appalling ; but our favourite was the wild, steep, lonely path behind Europa Point, among the fan-palms. Our sketching-permit enabled us to ramble unquestioned wherever we pleased. We often lingered, however, in the lovely Alameda, the most beautiful public walk in Spain, or perhaps in the world, with its enormous stone-pines spreading their thick shade over the undergrowth of scarlet and pink geraniums (which here grow wild), and its magnificent views of Europe and Africa. The English fleet was lying in the bay, and greatly added to the interest of the scene.

One day we walked round to Catalan Bay, through the deep sand, where the stones hang on the almost perpendicular precipice, and where one is warned to walk quickly and gently, for fear they should roll down on the passers-by. It was less pleasant than the other walks about Gibraltar ; not so much on account of the sand and the rolling stones as from the excessive dustiness of the road at the North Front. There is not a blade of vegetation of any kind ; and the day we were there the wind was extremely high, so much so that it was sometimes difficult to get on, or even to stand, against it. When we got to Catalan Bay, it was quite sheltered and very beautiful;

of course, perfectly without vegetation; but the little fishing-village nestles under the cliff, and the deep ultramarine blue waves break pleasantly on the yellow sand. Even if Catalan Bay were not so pretty, it would be worth while to take that walk, if only to see the stupendous precipice. At the North Front it goes sheer up the whole height of the Rock like a wall.

We made acquaintance with the great dragon-tree in the Governor's garden, and also with a small one that had not yet begun to branch, being too young, only a hundred years old! With the monkeys we were not so fortunate, never having the luck to see any. Everybody else saw them. If we went up in the morning, the monkeys were sure to remain obstinately hidden till the afternoon; if we waited till the afternoon, every ape on the Rock had taken his walk early in the day. Once we were told that, a few hours before, a large monkey had been sitting on the very gun we were leaning against; another time, some people we knew saw nine all together; seven full grown and two babies. The mothers carried the little ones, and now and then put them down to jump about. It must have been a beautiful sight! But we never met with such good fortune.

I am afraid they are not very amiable creatures.

A few years ago, as fears were entertained that their numbers were diminishing, some were procured from Barbary, and let loose on the Rock, but the Gibraltar monkeys instantly killed them all!

In spite of this regrettable incident, they are greatly esteemed and beloved. They never attack human beings; so we went to every place we could think of in search of them. In vain! The absence of the monkeys was the one dark spot on our stay at Gibraltar.

CHAPTER XII.

ONE of the most delighful parts of a visit to Gibraltar is the trip across the Straits to Tangiers; but, like many other pleasant things, it is often rather difficult of attainment, owing to the extreme uncertainty as to when the steamers sail. As far as we could understand, they arrived when they could, and departed when they were ready. Sometimes there was a placard put up at the hotels; sometimes not. Generally the post-office authorities knew, but occasionally they did not. Abraham, the Jew *commissionaire*, was about the best person to apply to; but even he was not infallible. We had made up our minds to go over by the first practicable steamer, and on Saturday, the 11th of October, we were told one was going. But just as we were all ready, the steamer sent up to say that though it would be very happy to take us, and we might come on board immediately, it must first tow out two American fruit ships to Cape St. Vincent. This we could not encounter; the wind had been very high for three or four days, and the sea in the Straits was likely to be quite sufficiently rough without going out into the Atlantic. So we gave up all thoughts of it for that day, and went off to Europa Point and the Governor's Cottage. At the lighthouse, when we saw the furious sea outside, and found how difficult it was even to stand, we were rather glad that our voyage was, as we believed, deferred.

When we came back, quite leisurely, we found the whole hotel in a state of excitement, and everybody, landlord, waiters, *commissionaire*, and guests good-naturedly running about in all directions, looking for us. A very large steamer had just come in, bound for Mogador and the Grand Canary, touching at Tangiers, and was to sail at five o'clock. It was now nearly four, so there was a hurry to get off. The boatman who had landed us begged us to take his boat, which we inconsiderately did. It was much too small; and

the two rowers could hardly make head against the
heavy sea. They wished to put up a sail, but this we
forbade. I rather think we were wrong, and that it
would have been safer with than without it; for there
were no squalls, only a heavy sea, and the sail might
have steadied the little cockle-shell of a bark. As it
was, we were tossed from one big wave to another;
the men did not row very well, and the steamer was
lying halfway across the bay. It was exceedingly
beautiful; the long line of black and golden waves,
stretching far out into the sunset, seemed interminable. We got so knocked about that we sat down in
the bottom of the boat to avoid being jerked out; and
then those same black waves looked uncomfortably
high as they came towards us. At last we were near
the steamer, but the worst was yet to come; she was
coaling, and we had to go round to the seaward side,
at the risk of being dashed against her. Then there
were on that side no steps; and we had our first
experience of a rope ladder, by which we climbed
over the bulwark. Once on board, she was so large
that no motion was perceptible, and we flattered ourselves that it would be smooth on the Morocco coast,
where we hoped to arrive before nightfall.

But coaling and taking in cargo lasted so long that
we did not sail till 8 instead of 5 P.M.; and it soon

became apparent that we were not likely to reach
Tangiers that night. It was really not very uncomfortable, except that all the berths were occupied
by people going to more distant places on the coast of
Morocco, or to the Canaries; and in the cabin there
were so many casual passengers like ourselves, that
there was no room to lie down. But everybody was
very good-natured; and we were cheered, soon after
starting, by the appearance of the steward and a small
white kitten ("my hanimal, ma'am," he said) who
busied themselves getting tea. After which we slept
(at least I did) most comfortably, sitting bolt upright
on a very narrow, slippery haircloth sofa. About
5 A.M. I awoke, and went upstairs to see how we were
getting on. We were now a good deal rocked about,
but did not appear to make progress. My first impression in the dim morning light was, that we were
still lying off Gibraltar, so quiet and steady had we
seemed all night. But soon I saw that the ghostly
white houses on the long point of land were very
unlike the Rock; we had anchored three hours before
off Tangiers.

There it was, Africa, the mysterious land I so
longed to see; but there, too, were the black billows
between us and it. As at Gibraltar, the great size of
the steamer prevented her getting in-shore; and though

the port of Tangiers is generally pretty calm, we were
lying far out with nothing between us and America,
I fancy; and the long, steady roll of the Atlantic,
not by any means softened down by the late storm,
looked so appalling that had the steamer been going
straight back to Gibraltar, I think we should have
been tempted to go back too. The Grand Canary,
however, though in some respects an interesting
island, was decidedly out of our way; so there was
nothing for it but to hope that the sea would
calm down before 6 A.M., when we were to land.
The time came, and so did the boats, full of
wild, dusky Arabs, shouting and shrieking. I
asked the captain if it was safe to land in such a
sea. He replied, doubtfully, "I *think* so; if you
don't slip in getting down, and if the boatmen keep
well off the steamer." We got down the side somehow,
amid cries of "Stop!" "Go on!" "Now!" "Not
yet!" "Wait!" "Jump!" "Don't move!" and so
on; all of which we disregarded, for the excellent
reason that, even if our minds had been sufficiently
clear to understand the instructions given us, our legs
were totally beyond our control. Very glad we were
to find ourselves on all fours in the bottom of the boat;
then a great wave seized it and sent it against the
steamer. A minute of fearful confusion followed;

the captain swore, the boatmen yelled, the spray
dashed over us, everybody called out, "Keep her off!"
"Keep her off!" which was much easier said than
done.   I shut my eyes; and the next moment the long,
steady pull of the Moorish boatmen was taking us
wonderfully easily through that wilderness of black
water.   Certainly, the Arab boatmen are capital; far
better than the Gibraltar men.   We soon got under
the lee of the long low point that does duty for
a breakwater; and now, as it grew shallow, wild-
looking Arabs rushed into the water, seized us,
and carried us to shore.   We felt as if we were being
carried off by pirates; but they were very careful, and
put us down safely on the slippery stones.   A
splendid, white-turbaned Moor, strongly resembling
Solyman the Magnificent, stepped forward, and in
perfectly good English announced himself as Muhammed, the interpreter of the Victoria Hotel.   But
first we must go to the Custom-house.   "What
Custom-house?" said I, bewildered, not expecting
that disagreeable feature of civilization in the land
of Ham.   "The Emperor of Morocco's," was the
overwhelming reply.   Now, the Emperor of Morocco
had always appeared to me a semi-fabulous potentate.
I knew he existed; yet, ever since childhood, he had
occupied the same place in my imagination as Jack

the Giant-killer, the Great Mogul, ogres in general, and such like. So now it was startling to find he had a custom-house, like ordinary mortal sovereigns.

After all, it was much better than the Spanish custom-houses. Grave, clean, turbaned Moors sat solemnly, cross-legged, surrounded by half-a-dozen most beautiful cats, equally clean and equally solemn; and overhead waved the blood-red flag, the pirate banner once so dreaded on the sea. I felt as if it were highly probable my head should be cut off at a sign from one of those dignified Mussulmans, for was I not an unbeliever?

But they were extremely courteous, as all Moors are; they scarcely opened our box, and we soon proceeded up the steep street to the hotel. Tired as we were, we had a cup of coffee, and immediately went to the market-place. On Sunday and Thursday a fair is held there, and it is the very strangest sight that can be seen within three hours of Europe. It is a stepping back into an earlier world, into the days of the Prophet; yea, further back than that, to the old Biblical times, to the patriarchal age, to Abraham and Isaac and Jacob. It is very unaccountable, but never did I fully realize the Old Testament history as here, among the Mahometans. Even the New Testament seemed to stand out in clearer light. If it had been Syria or Egypt, it would not have surprised me; but here, in Tangiers, with no Biblical associations, it could but be the similarity of manners and customs.

We went on through a crowd of magnificent white turbaned Moors; wild, tawny Arabs of the desert; date merchants from the far oases of the interior; peasant women with huge palm-leaf hats, large as a cart-wheel; negroes black as coal; white figures all hid save one long, sleepy, dark eye, not brilliant like the Italian eye, but soft and liquid; Jews with dark blue kaftan, red sash, and shrewd, keen countenances; beautiful Jewesses in bright purple, with white head-dresses and uncovered faces; camels, donkeys, sheep, and goats, all bleating, braying, running round, before, and behind us. In the crowd there was no rudeness, though it was often difficult to get along: nobody looked at the two English ladies; not a remark was made. With that excellent Oriental principle of minding their own affairs instead of other people's, they bought, sold, haggled, and called out continually *Bal-a-a-ak*, as they drove their donkeys through the throng. *Bal-a-a-ak* means "get out of the way," apparently; at least, it is always prudent to do so when you hear it shouted, as, otherwise, the nose of a donkey instantly pokes your back, or the cross face of a camel towers right over your head.

The market is held just outside the southern gate, which leads out to the country, away to the desert. Of course, there is nothing that answers to our idea of a road, without the walls; but the bright green uplands stretch away towards the Riff, and paths may be found if one looks for them. The chief attraction at present, however, was the gateway, with its endless stream of picturesque comers and goers.

The Moors of Tangiers are certainly most superb specimens of humanity. Their great height and broad shoulders struck us all the more after having lived for some time among the Liliputian Spaniards; it was like coming among a nation of Newfoundland dogs, after spending a summer among toy terriers. Their costume is perfection, the upper classes all wearing the white *haik*, which is the very most graceful garment that ever man arrayed himself in. I could not exactly make out how it was made; it is not the bournous, but is more like the Roman toga. It is made in different kinds of stuff, the most usual being the *kooskoos*, which is somewhat like a very fine, soft, creamy white Turkish towel. The magistrates and other people of distinction wear it much lighter and finer, more like the stuff of which the Algerine bournous is made. There is another kind, with alternate stripes of kooskoos and silk. In bad weather, or when they are about any work that is likely to soil the white haik, they wear one of a coarser blue stuff, or with very narrow stripes of dark blue and white. The middle classes, such as shopmen, for instance, wear this latter. The trousers are always white; not gathered in like the Turkish trouser, but wide, like those worn by the peasants of the Danube. Only the upper classes wear stockings; the others shuffle along in a wonderful way over the rough stones with their brown heels sticking out of their yellow slippers. Those yellow slippers always gave me an uncomfortable sensation, recalling how, in Miss Edgeworth's story, they gave the plague to Murad the Unlucky; which really was an extra piece of bad luck, inasmuch as, rightly or wrongly, it is popularly believed that shoe-leather does not usually communicate infection.

Of course, the true Moor always wears the white turban; the Jews have a sort of fez; the Arabs from the interior, a kind of bournous of coarse brown stuff, with the hood drawn over the head. Indeed, a considerable part of the Arab population wear only a coarse sack, of which so large a portion is drawn over the head to protect it from the sun, that exceedingly little is left for the body. Consequently, the length and brownness of the legs one meets at every turn, is something quite astounding. The negroes from Soudan generally have a red turban, which is very becoming to their coal-black faces; but many of the black slave-boys have only their frizzly hair, woven into a funny little plait that sticks straight out from the top of the head. The natives of Soudan are extremely black, which strikes one all the more, as they have not in general very decidedly negro features; when they waited on us at dinner, I could not at first get over the idea that the blackness would come off their hands on the table-cloth !

We returned to the hotel to breakfast, and then went to church to the British Legation. After which, we were too tired to do much except stand by the sea, looking at the marvellous effects of light and shade in that purest, clearest of atmospheres; the dark, blue-green sea, the pink and azure mountains; and the picturesque groups sitting with that strange, Oriental stillness so unlike the bustle of European life. Repose! that seems the great charm of Eastern life; and a wonderful charm it is.

By the way, it seems very absurd to use the expressions *Eastern* and *Oriental* in speaking of a place that is considerably further west than most European countries. Yet one must always think of Tangiers as Oriental, inasmuch as it has the old civilization, utterly

without mixture of Western habits or ideas. There
is not a carriage, nor indeed anything with wheels in
Tangiers; the Frankish dress is, happily, as yet un-
worn by its grave, dignified denizens; its mosques
are yet unprofaned by European foot.

We were told that, some years ago, a young English lady, who was spending a few days at Tangiers,
said she was resolved to go into one of the mosques.
And she did so; but at the entrance a grave Mussulman rose from his knees, took her by the hand, and
led her politely out. She said she was a great deal
more frightened than if they had made an uproar.
Probably, they thought she had made a mistake;
otherwise, courteous as the Moors are to strangers,
and especially to all women, she might have fared
badly. I was always very much afraid of entering a
mosque by mistake.

In the interior of Morocco, they are even more rigid
than at Tangiers. There is one place, Sallee, the
Holy City, of which it was always said that no Christian might set foot in it; and it is quite true that,
till very recently, no Christian ever did. But this
was a mere arbitrary regulation, not founded on any
real law or precept. I could not find out that there
was anything peculiar about this city, except that it
contains an unusual number of mosques.

The first day or two in a Mahometan country gives one a very strange sensation.	I believe I should rather say *Mussulman,* for they never call themselves Mahometans ; nor does, as I have already said, the name of Mahomet ever occur on inscriptions, nor, as far as I could see, in any form whatever, anywhere. It was really grand to hear Muhammed, our interpreter, say, " I am a Mussulman." And when we asked him the date of a building, he always replied, "In such and such a year of the Prophet." We found it very inconvenient not to have the Hegira at our fingers' end.

The servants in the hotel, with the exception of the two interpreters, old Muhammed and young Muhammed, were either Jews or Soudan men.	The housemaid was a handsome Jewess, called Rachel, very obliging, with soft, pleasant manners ; in which latter respect, it must be confessed, she greatly excelled the Andalusian damsels we had lately had to do with.	Some people say they do not like the Jewish servants, but prefer the Arabs ; as far as our experience went, nothing could exceed the civility of both.	When we went out and in, all the servants and interpreters who were sitting, Oriental fashion, in the court, rose and stood respectfully, as we passed : a piece of politeness quite bewildering, after the

“I’m as good as you” manners of waiters and house-maids in the south of Spain. I should say the fashionable politics of Morocco are extremely conservative. Speaking of Spanish affairs with Muhammed, he said, “What can you expect of a republic?” “But it is a monarchy” (which it was, for the moment), suggested we. “A *constitutional* monarchy, which is the same as a republic,” replied Muhammed loftily.

Our great wish, naturally, was to visit a hareem; and, on mentioning this to the English Minister, he kindly promised to do all in his power to procure us admittance to one. The Pasha’s wife does not like to receive visitors; she is ugly, in very delicate health, and particularly dislikes the idea of being criticized by European ladies. But Sid Absalom Aharem, a magistrate, and a man of high position, was said to have a very beautiful house, which he liked to be admired; he was also believed to have a young wife, but it was difficult to ascertain this, as, in Mussulman countries, no man can speak to another about his wife. But he could be asked to show us his *household;* and there would be no impropriety in *our* asking him to introduce us to his wife. “What language does he speak?” we asked. “Arabic, of course.” “But we don’t understand that," said we, feeling keenly, as we had done even in Spain, what a miserable thing it is to have had one's education so neglected as to be ignorant of Arabic. " Oh ! but you have your interpreter," was the reply. The name was given to us in writing; and when we asked if Muhammed would be able to find Sid Absalom's house, we were told that he was as well known as the Lord Mayor in London. So we went off in high spirits; when it all at once occurred to me that the interpreter could not possibly ask Sid Absalom about his wife, far less enter the hareem. This word *Sid* is the same as *Cid*, and means simply *gentleman ;* the Spanish *Don*, in fact.

When the time came we proceeded up one of those quiet, narrow streets, with their windowless walls all blinding white in the sunshine. The Sid, with true Moorish courtesy, was waiting for us in the street, and walked up along with us. He was an excellent specimen of a Moorish gentleman, tall and handsome, and much fairer than most Spaniards or Italians. He was entirely enveloped in the finest white raiment. I presume he wore the turban, but it was not visible, as a flap of the soft, white, silky stuff, after being thrown round across the shoulder like a Spanish cloak, covered the head also. Would it not be better, and more historically correct, to represent Othello like this, on the stage, than to make him a negro, dressed like a Turkish janissary ?

To our very great relief we found our host could speak a little Spanish, so we were at our ease immediately. He conducted us upstairs, leaving the interpreter behind. I began to wonder if he had a wife, and how we were to ask for her ; when we found ourselves in a small upper court, exquisitely paved with azulejos, precisely the same as those of the Alhambra : at the present day they are made at Fez. Two ladies stood there, bowing very low, and laughing a little nervously. The first was partly veiled ; that is, she had the thick white stuff wrapped round her head and shoulders, but her face was uncovered. She had a bright, kind expression, but was not pretty. When I bowed to her, she drew back, and indicated the other lady, as much as to say that the latter was the principal one. So I turned to bow also to the other, who was one of the very loveliest creatures I have ever seen. She received us extremely gracefully, and led us into the reception-room. It was long and narrow, with the whole of one side opening to the court, but partly closed with a curtain. There were no windows whatever ; yet it was not at all dark, the rays of the African sun pouring full into the court, and being reflected by the bright azulejos. At each end there seemed to be recesses curtained off. The floor was carpeted with the thickest, softest, richest, brightest of Turkey carpets, far finer than I have ever seen in any World-Exhibition. We felt quite uncivilized as we walked over it in our high-heeled boots. Had we anticipated this visit, we should certainly have put on over-shoes, in order to take them off at the entrance. Our host put off his shoes, and walked about the room in his stockings; our hostess left her red velvet, gold-embroidered slippers in the court, and her small, bare, white feet looked quite comfortable in the yielding carpet. Her foot was very much prettier to my taste than the fat, short Spanish foot; being long, slender, delicate, and as flexible as her hands.

The divan, running along one side of the room, was also covered with rich carpets; and behind it the wall was wainscoted, so to speak, with crimson velvet, embroidered with gold-coloured silk, in a pattern of arches. In the middle, three of the arches were embroidered in thick, heavy gold; and there the place of honour seemed to be.

Sid Absalom had been in Gibraltar, and thus was accustomed to English habits and peculiarities. So three long-legged cane chairs were brought, on which

we, however, declined to sit, placing ourselves on the
divan beside our hostess. Our host, to show how
English his sympathies were, sat on one of the cane
chairs, and I think must have been uncomfortable,
though he looked wonderfully at his ease.

A very nice, respectable-looking, middle-aged
Jewess now made her appearance. She seemed to be
an upper servant, and spoke Spanish extremely well,
so that the conversation went on more briskly. She
interpreted for her young mistress, who said all sorts
of pretty things in pretty Arabic, which were duly
translated and replied to. The lady was full of
apologies for her appearance: had she known earlier
that we were coming, she would have put on a better
dress to do us honour; she was ashamed to be seen
so. Now there was really no need for all this,
because she was very prettily attired. She wore a
long kaftan or pelisse of pale bluish-green cashmere,
edged with gold braid, and confined at the waist by a
very broad cloth of gold sash; and white trousers,
not gathered at the ankle, but so wide as to look like
a petticoat. Round her forehead she had a diadem of
black velvet, and a very long silver gauze veil fell
from it over the back of her head. The hair, long,
black, and straight, hung loose, mixed up with the
fringe of a black silk handkerchief, apparently put on

iu order to make the hair seem more abundant. Very lovely she looked, with her slender, supple figure, great dark eyes, fair skin, and sweet smile. The only defect was her teeth, which were nearly as black as her eyes; so much so, that I think they must have been blackened artificially. She had no false hair, no rouge, nor paint of any kind, nor henna; but I suspect there was some black pencilling under the eyes; not on the eyelid itself, but as if a finger with black-lead had been drawn below the eye.

Nothing could be sweeter or kinder than her manner; there was no curiosity, no asking questions, no remarks on what must have seemed to her strangely different from all that she was accustomed to.

Her husband was very proud of her, especially of her slim figure, and seemed rather to regret that she had not dressed more magnificently. "She has very good clothes," he said, and made her a sign to show us them. She accordingly went into one of the curtained recesses, and brought out a profusion of splendid brocades. Violet, gold-coloured, crimson, the richest products of Lyons' looms; but what pleased us most was a kaftan of gold-coloured Broussa silk. This had been brought from Constantinople for her, and was an old fabric, such as could not be procured

now. The sashes, six or eight inches broad, of cloth
of gold shot with red or purple, with a long gold
fringe, were so heavy that I could hardly hold
them.

Then the Sid said something to her in Arabic, and
threw her a key; whereupon she produced one of
those curious many-coloured boxes peculiar to Tangiers, and showed us her jewels. Long strings of
pearls like rosaries, of which the larger beads were
great, uncut sapphires and emeralds; huge gold earrings, and diamond and ruby rings rolled over the
floor. We asked how the earrings could possibly be
worn, for at first we had taken them for bracelets;
and indeed they would not have been too small for
her wrists. They were as thick as one's little finger,
but she took out those she had in her ears, and thrust
the thick piece of gold into the hole. I think it hurt
her, for she winced a little, but persevered in pushing
it through. There was a short string of pearls,
divided by emeralds and sapphires, attaching the
earring to the head-dress, and another longer one to
fasten it to the shoulder. It was very becoming, but
must have been exceedingly uncomfortable.

Presently her child came in; a lovely little girl of
three years old, with rich chestnut hair, great black
eyes, and cheeks like pomegranate blossoms. She

was very funnily dressed, her clothes being wrapped so tightly round her legs that it was surprising she could walk, while her shoulders were swathed in fold upon fold, till she presented the appearance of a wedge. For all that, she was the most perfect specimen of childish beauty I have ever seen. Her father was immensely gratified with our unfeigned admiration of her, and said proudly, " Yes! she is even better than the mother."

The child had evidently been bribed to come in by having a pair of new purple velvet, gold-embroidered slippers put on for the first time; and so pleased with them was she, that instead of leaving them at the entrance, she came in with them on, pointing them out to her father with great glee. When she saw us, she hesitated for a moment: her mother said something, apparently desiring her to come forward and speak to us, but still she drew back; upon which her father called to her, and bade her take off the new slippers and offer them to one of us. It was a terrible trial. She looked exceedingly grave, but at once obeyed, and timidly offered the precious slippers. Poor little thing! She seemed very much relieved when they were refused with thanks. I suspect Sid Absalom was always obeyed in his own house; yet he seemed very much loved too. The child jumped about him with the greatest fondness, and did not appear at all afraid of him. His wife looked at him with the most devoted affection; her whole face brightened when she spoke to him, and everybody, servants and all, seemed to like this mild paternal despotism.

In a short time we attempted to take leave, but they would not hear of it, the lady even holding us by the dress to detain us. She seemed to enjoy the visit, and begged her husband to explain to us " how very much she liked us." It was quite surprising how well she understood what we said, and often answered by signs before it was translated to her. For instance, when we asked the child's age, she instantly held up three fingers; and when we spoke of the jewels she was delighted, because the Spanish names of sapphire, diamond, emerald, ruby, are almost the same as the Arabic.

It was a strange and beautiful scene; more like the Arabian Nights than anything I had ever expected to behold. The splendid brocades and costly jewels thrown carelessly on the rich, soft carpet, the lovely child playing with the strings of pearls, the beautiful mother sitting cross-legged on the divan, while the brilliant sunshine lighted up all the crimson and purple, the sapphires and emeralds, the silver veils and cloth of gold, and the child's dark eyes and glowing cheeks; what a picture it would have made !

After some more conversation, we again endeavoured to depart, but in vain. The lady now clapped her hands, and a little black slave appeared. An order was given in which I thought I distinguished a sound like *atsa* or *atsan;* that, or some word resembling it, meaning *tea*, in Arabic. "Are we going to have afternoon tea in a harcem in Morocco ?" thought I, much surprised. My forebodings were correct; for presently a silver tray and tea-pot, with tea-cups, were brought. They were placed on the floor, before the lady, there being no table in the room, nor indeed in the house. I was a little disappointed that it was not coffee, fancying that the tea had been brought because we were English. Such was my ignorant supposition; for we afterwards learnt that tea is as much the national beverage of Tangiers as coffee is of the East in general; and it was adopted in the days when Portugal ruled here, before Katharine of Braganza introduced it into England. I do not know if it is used in other parts of Morocco.

A large, soft, white Turkish towel was brought by way of table-cloth, though table there was none; and the lady spread it on her lap and proceeded to pour out the tea. It was very unlike anything I had ever tasted, but exceedingly good, being made of the finest Russian golden tea, flavoured with leaves of lemon-verbena and mint, and sweetened almost to a syrup. In fact, it was rather too sweet; but it was very hot and refreshing. Seven cups had been brought, from which we gathered that we were expected to take two each. Afterwards, we were told that it is a piece of politeness to take three; but we regulated our proceedings by the number of cups on the tray; as, in those countries, they always give you a fresh cup with more tea. Our host took two, our hostess one, which disposed of all the cups.

The third time we rose to take leave, the Sid proposed to show us the house. It was not at all what is commonly called Moorish in style with respect to the decorations; but the shape and disposition of the rooms was thoroughly so; and thus we could quite understand how the Alhambra must have been furnished and arranged. There have been many disputes on this subject, and much has been written about it; all which might have been spared if the combatants had taken the trouble to cross the Straits and visit a Moorish family.

We also went up to the housetop, but there the lady could not accompany us, as she was not veiled;

the Sid politely saying, in order that we might not feel in the wrong, "Every country has its customs." I hope she sometimes had the pleasure of going up and enjoying that glorious view over the dark blue sea and white Tangiers, with its minarets and solitary palm-tree.

The absence of flowers in the house struck us very much, after Spain, where they are in such profusion in every room and patio. Even in a small, high-walled garden which we were shown, there were none. There were also no pets of any kind. Dogs, of course, we knew there could be none, in a Mahometan country; but we had always heard of the Moorish love of other animals, and were surprised not to see any. One cannot, however, judge of the tastes of a nation from a visit to one household.

One thing we could certainly judge of, namely, the extreme and polished courtesy of the Moors; and this not merely in set forms of politeness, but with a delicate and graceful tact such as I have rarely seen. We were begged to stay longer, to come back often, and repeatedly thanked for our visit. I noticed they were especially careful to avoid expressing surprise, or seeming to imply disapprobation with respect to European customs. We particularly observed this politeness in the little girl; she never stared at us, nor laughed, nor looked awkward, nor asked questions, nor touched our dresses, nor made any remark whatever on what, I should think, must have been quite new to her. Few children of any nation would have shown such perfect good-breeding in the circumstances.

Of course, we were told that the house and everything in it was ours; the Spaniards having learnt this expression from their Moorish enemies. When we at last got away, Sid Absalom walked downstairs with us, shook hands (having evidently learnt this at Gibraltar), expressed the hope of seeing us very soon again, and left us with a most agreeable impression of Moorish hospitality.

Next morning we resolved to ride to the Roman Bridge, and desired Muhammed to order donkeys. When we came downstairs, I was much alarmed at the sight of the saddle I was expected to sit upon. They were pack-saddles of the most rudimentary description; being simply a very large, high sack, stuffed with some hardish substance, and without any attempt at pommel or saddle. There was no bridle, only a halter to hold the creature by.

I at once saw that this would not do for me, and determined to walk; foreseeing that I should certainly be thrown over the donkey's head, and probably alight on my own, going down the steep street. H. boldly mounted, and said she felt perfectly comfortable and quite secure. But she did not look either the one or the other; so I was very glad I had decided to walk, though it was rather fatiguing.

We soon got out of the town and on to the sands, which are very soft and very deep; and though the donkey appeared to be walking slowly, all my powers were taxed to keep up with him. It was exceedingly hot, too, in the noonday sun, and I felt as if we were on pilgrimage to Mecca, as he solemnly proceeded along. Before us were camels going back from the market, the shadows of their long necks projected on the sand; and wild Bedouins returning to the interior. Soon they diverged to the right, away across the plain, and we wound round by the edge of the sea. And what a colour that sea was! A curious combination of blue and green; not by any means bluish green, but bright green and bright blue mixed, but not mingled; the sands, deep golden yellow, without any vegetation except here and there an agave. All was solitude; not a human being, not a living thing to be seen.

The remains of the bridge are curious. The water must have encroached on the land since it was built; for at present it is quite at the mouth of the river,

almost in the sea. I should have liked to get across
but there was no means of doing so. Probably there
is a bridge higher up, but we had no interpreter with
us; the donkey-boy knew scarcely a word of Spanish,
and we now, as ever, felt bitterly the want of Arabic.
As it was, the water was exceedingly rapid, brim-
ming full, and apparently very deep; in short, quite
unfordable. So H. dismounted and rambled about;
I sat down to sketch, and the donkey gave himself up
to the enjoyment of eating aromatic and thorny herbs.

There was a lovely view of Tangiers, with its white
houses, from this place; the sea rolled onward, in
long green-blue waves with white foaming crests, the
azure river gurgled down to meet it, and the dark
brown masses of old Roman masonry stemmed the flood,
and looked as if they must be swept away in another
moment. Yet they have stood there for 1871 years;
since the time when Tiberius ruled the Empire of
the World, deeming himself and his vast realm the
grandest things on earth; and a little Child had but
just been carried down into Egypt, before whose
might Rome, with her gods and her godlike emperors,
was to change utterly, to pale into purer light. But
so far from feeling the evanescence of human life
and human power, here it was the complete unchang-
ingness of the older civilization that struck one.

The Roman Empire seemed to be but a little episode, that had gone by like a dream, and we were once more in the Patriarchal times, in the days of Abraham, and Isaac, and Jacob.

Long did we sit there in the utter loneliness. Once only a solitary figure passed along, an Arab with brown skin and brown raiment, gliding noiselessly on the soft sand. Boy and donkey had disappeared, and no sound was heard save the gurgle of the river, and the plash of the waves on the shore.

At last it was time to depart, but the first difficulty was to find our guide, and after that to waken him. He had fallen fast asleep, face downmost, in a clump of thorns, which he seemed to find comfortable. The next thing to be done was to find and catch the donkey, which was not easy. He had got into great spirits, and careered away much faster than could have been expected, judging from the previous solemnity of his demeanour. He would not allow H. to come near him, having taken a dislike to her because she had ridden him. He did not object to me at all, thinking me a nice person who never rode donkeys, and who could therefore be trusted. After he was caught, I had to hold him and coax him, while the donkey-boy, by a sudden *coup de main*, seated H. on her elevated position on the pack-saddle. I shall never forget the donkey's look of reproachful indignation at me, when he found how he had been cheated. I really felt quite guilty of betraying his confidence, poor thing! But he ought to have been grateful for having such a very light weight to carry.

As we were returning home, we met a party of the Riff men, on their way back to the mountains. It was rather alarming; there were about thirty of them, and they looked very wild and fierce, with their long guns, and dark, turbaned faces; and the place was exceedingly lonely. But they saluted us courteously with "Salaam alikam," which we were told meant "Peace be with you." We heard afterwards that there is now perfect security for strangers in Morocco: "A great deal safer than London," was the expression used. Everybody was surprised that we did not go into the interior. Why did we not go at least to Tetuan? And, indeed, we should have much liked to do so; but the season was rather far advanced, and we could not well spare sufficient time.

A visit to the Pasha's palace is by no means to be omitted. We did not see the Pasha, as he was in the country; thus we saw only the outer courts, which have some beautiful Moorish decorations. A number of soldiers were hanging about, all as black as coals; I suppose they were from Soudan. A jet-black woman came forward to show us everything; she spoke only Arabic, which rendered conversation difficult, and she fell into such raptures with the fringe of my jacket, that she became incapable of receiving any other idea.

Eleven beautiful cats were in the first court; the twelfth reigned in solitude in the inner one. I tried to find out if so many were kept merely for pleasure, or if the Pasha suffered from mice; but the only explanation, as far as I could understand, was, that the cats being there, they remained there! This was true Mussulman obedience to the decrees of fate.

Business was being transacted in one of the courts. There was a man, like the scribes of old, with an ink-bottle at his girdle, and a large reed-pen in his hand; piles of papers lay about, covered with most beautifully clear writing. I don't know why seeing letters addressed in Arabic should have made such an impression upon me, it being naturally the language of the country; but the whole scene was a glimpse into an elder world. In Tangiers it seemed as though one were always looking through a mental telescope that brought the dim and distant Past close to one's eyes.

Among more modern things, we went to see the Belgian Consul's house, which is very pretty, and most obligingly shown. The Swedish Consul's villa, too, just out of the town, is worth a visit. I believe this latter no longer really belongs to the Swedish Consul, but it still goes by his name. I rather think, when we were there, it was let in apartments which must be pleasant to live in; the views are beautiful. There is a very large dragon-tree in the garden, quite as large as the celebrated one in the Governor's garden at Gibraltar, but not of so perfect a form. The obliging Arab gardener gathered great bunches of pink amaryllis for us. I asked what the name of the flower was in Arabic. "Susanna," was the reply. Then I remembered having been told, long ago, that Susan and Lily were the same name; one Hebrew, the other English.

In the afternoon, Muhammed said we ought to walk to Marchann. (Probably I spell the name wrong, for I have never seen it written; but that is what it sounded like.) So the Jewish waiter was summoned, who called his brother David, and desired him to accompany us.

We started, passing out by Bab-el-Suk, "the Gate of the Market-place." They were bringing in great loads of branches of sweet-bay. We asked what it was for. "It is for us," replied David shortly. "For what purpose?" said I. "To make the *cabanas*," answered he. We could not think what he

could possibly mean; and just then a picturesque
group distracted our attention, and we inquired no
further.

We went on, through lanes bordered with agave
and prickly pear, and overhung by tall, whispering
reeds. In Italy I had often heard the rustle of
the reeds, but never before did I so distinctly
hear it like voices. It was almost impossible not
to believe that they were really whispering, speaking to each other. It gave one a strange, haunted
feeling; I am not sure that I should have liked it
had I been alone.

Presently we came to a little gate through which
we passed, and found ourselves in a little country
place of our landlord's, where he kept his poultry.
It was very wild and very pretty, hanging right
above the sea. There was a very tiny house for
the poultry-man to sleep in; but it could have been
made charming. At the end of the garden was a
rickety seat, with two broken legs; the view from
which was magnificent, away over the sea to the pale
pink peaks of the lower Atlas.

Then we went on again, through the narrow lanes
among the agaves and prickly pears, till we came
out into an open field, also with a glorious view.
This was Marchann; and all round there were

country houses, where the Moors go in summer.
Here I could scarcely believe that I was in Africa:
the yellow sand and the wild, desert look had disappeared; the grass was intensely green, and the
rich vegetation and leafy woods stretched away
towards the Riff. David beckoned us on, and in a
few steps we were again standing just above the
sea, much as if we had been on the Sussex Downs;
only that the sea was a far deeper blue, and the light
was strangely vivid. When I looked round again,
it was quite startling to see the white-robed Moors
and the brown figures of the peasants passing along.

David now proposed returning home a different
way, that we might see more of the country; and
we struck across the fields inland, as if towards the
mountains. It was a most beautiful walk; and
presently we came to a pretty villa belonging to
the Belgian Consul. The flowers were splendid, and
again the rosy Atlas gleamed in the sunset sky.
But the dew was so heavy, that we thought it
prudent to return, especially as we were at a considerable distance from the town. So we took a
short cut through the fields, which, even in October,
were carpeted with wild flowers. There were great
quantities of white narcissus, with black hearts and
a most peculiar perfume, not at all like that of any

narcissus I have ever seen. It was aromatic, and
rather pungent, with somewhat of the faint, bitter
smell of the oleander. It was not at all heavy, as
the jonquil is; and at first we thought it delicious.
But in a short time it seemed to fill one with horror;
not that it was disagreeable, nor did it make one's
head ache, but one felt as though it were a sweet,
subtle, deadly poison. I do not know if it really is
a poisonous plant

By the time we got back to Tangiers, the rose-
coloured minarets had faded into cold, bluish white;
and it was already dusk. I have no doubt we should
have been perfectly safe, in any case, but it would
have been something new to us to be benighted in
Morocco!

A morning was naturally devoted to shopping in
the bazaar. There sit the shopmen, cross-legged, on
the board where they display their wares, and which,
I believe, serves as a shutter when they close their
shop. In a short visit to Tangiers, it is well to avoid
Friday and Saturday, as on the latter day the Jewish,
and on the former the Mahometan, shops are closed.
The old Jews, with their silvery beards and mild,
rather cunning faces, had nothing patriarchal about
them; it is the Mussulman that brings Abraham to
one's mind: while the Hebrew recalls, not Isaac the

Patriarch, but the Jew of the Middle Ages; in fact, old Isaac in ' Ivanhoe.'   Jew and Moor, however, were equally courteous.   They are also said to be almost equally rapacious; but we did not think them particularly greedy.   Of course, we probably paid too much for everything; we expected that: still, I think, in Italy the over-charging would have been greater.

The most attractive things were the different kinds of kooskoos, and the brass trays.   These latter are very pretty and very peculiar.   We did not care for any of the embroidery we saw; what comes from Constantinople and Algiers being much finer.   There were pretty cushions made of bits of different coloured cloth or leather, sewn together in patterns.   We also rather liked some of the coarse, bright-coloured pottery.   They spoke a little Spanish in most of the shops.   Indeed, Spanish, in Morocco, is like French in Europe; one can always get on by means of it.

After a good deal of haggling, we completed our purchases; a quantity of kooskoos, a brass tray, a cloth cushion, an earthenware jar, and a rush basket full of dates.   I don't think we paid too much for anything except the basket of dates, in which they cheated us iniquitously.

But the whole thing was so like the Arabian Nights that it was well worth the money.   If the interpreter had not been with us, we must certainly have hired a porter to carry home our purchases, as was done in Bagdad in the days of Haroun Alraschid.

One day we went up alone to the bazaar, and enjoyed wandering about by ourselves, and making a few small purchases. Nobody stared at us, nobody made any remark. The merchants who had tried to cheat us the day before were, naturally, exceedingly glad to see us; those who knew a word or two of English wished us " good morning " in that language; the less learned greeted us with the Spanish " buenas dias ;" while the utterly illiterate said the same thing in Arabic ; but all were equally polite.

The only exception to the general friendliness was in one instance. We were looking in at a shop, when a woman put her hand on H.'s shoulder. She turned round, thinking it was an importunate beggar; the woman suddenly withdrew her veil with a mocking laugh; she was a leper. Her malignant expression was more fearful than the disease. Probably she thought we must be Jewesses, because we were not veiled, and that we would shrink with peculiar horror from leprosy.

The night before we were to depart, Rachael, the pleasant Jewish housemaid, begged that we would excuse her if anything should be amiss the following morning, as she was going to the "cabanas." We remembered the sweet-bay which David had said was to make those cabanas, and eagerly asked for an explanation. "The Feast of the Cabanas;" it was the Jewish Feast of Tabernacles!

The housemaid entreated us to go; they liked to show it to strangers; and if she should not be at hand, was not the waiter's brother, David, always there?

Next morning, despite the glories of the previous sunset, the wind had changed; the air was thick, hot, and oppressive, and a drizzling rain had come on. Moreover, nobody knew exactly at what hour the steamer was to sail; it might be at any moment. Nevertheless, we rushed out in great haste to see the Tabernacles, escorted by the unfailing David.

In the bazaar we had the comfort of seeing the broad shoulders of the captain of the steamer, and thus ascertaining that we had plenty of time. So we went more leisurely up to the Jewish quarter, through exceedingly narrow, badly paved, but perfectly clean streets, or rather lanes. I felt a little afraid to go into the houses, thinking it might be considered an impertinent intrusion, and not knowing how, as Gentiles, we might be received in the midst of a religious ceremony. However, everybody invited us in, and seemed quite delighted to see us.

In each patio was a booth or tabernacle of branches of sweet-bay, very large, filling up nearly the entire court, and exceedingly high, so that the whole family could sit in it, eat, and live there, for the time. They seemed to be preparing a feast under the shade of it.

The Jewish houses were very clean and tidy; indeed, they had just finished washing all the floors, which were of coarse blue azulejos. Yet they did not at all object to our coming in, and walking about with muddy boots, which I should have thought they would have considered a pollution. But neither Jew nor Mussulman seem to make those kind of difficulties.

The only occasion, for many years, on which there has been risk of a serious disturbance at Tangiers, was caused by pigs. The Christians persisted in keeping myriads of pigs, which must naturally be always an abomination to both Mussulman and Jew. Not only were the pigs kept, but they were allowed to go at large; not, of course, in the streets, which could not have been tolerated for a moment, but on waste pieces of ground, of which there are many. But the pigs, instead of remembering they were in a

Mahometan country, and therefore keeping modestly in the background, as pigs of any tact or delicacy would have done, perpetually made their escape, and rushed about, running against the legs of true believers in a manner that was quite unendurable. Diplomatic interference was necessary; and an edict was issued that nobody, on any pretext whatever, was to keep more than two pigs, and that even those were to be strictly shut up.

We went also to the new synagogue, of which David was evidently very proud. We hesitated about going in, as the Jewish women never worship along with the men; but he said they would not mind strangers. However, we stayed near the door. There was not much to see; it was all clean and freshly painted, with a new and very ugly lamp: nothing picturesque, compared with the curious synagogue, or, rather, cluster of synagogues in the Roman Ghetto, or the magnificent Moresco one at Pesth; or, the most interesting of all, the little old, old, dark building at Prague, where the Hebrews have worshipped for more than a thousand years. Yet the earnestness of the people, and their pride in their persecuted faith, could not but interest one. I was sorry, however, to hear from good authority, that since the Jews in that part of the world are no longer

persecuted, they have greatly disimproved; become
pretentious and disagreeable, in fact. We were also
told that this persecution was never by authority of the
Emperor of Morocco, and that it was even quite against
his wish. It was the mob who rose now and then
against the Jews, and maltreated them ; and though,
of course, the Mussulman population was greatly to
blame for so doing, yet there was generally some pro-
vocation on the part of the Jews. In Tangiers itself
there has always been more toleration than in the
interior.

We accomplished our visit to the Tabernacles by
the time the captain had finished his purchases in the
bazaar. The weather had improved for the moment,
but the white houses of Tangiers do not look quite so
well against a grey sky as with their usual azure
background ; and the change of weather had produced
change of costume. Most of the white *haiks* had
disappeared, and were replaced by blue; and I saw
one Arab arrayed in a mackintosh and nothing
else.

However, on our way to the shore, we saw a grand-
looking, white-draped Moor pacing slowly before us.
"Oh! who can that be? What a magnificent dress!"
said we. "It is a great man, a magistrate," replied
Muhammed. At this moment the white figure

turned, and lo! it was our friend, Sid Absalom. He
came up to reproach us for not having come again to
see his wife, who had been expecting us. Then he
walked down to the port with us, and the bystanders
did not seem at all surprised at this, nor at the
cordial shake of the hand with which we parted. It
is curious that, though the Moors are so completely
free from all mixture of European habits or ideas,
they are so very tolerant of what is utterly unlike
themselves. In Tangiers nobody remarks anything
strangers do; in Spain, on the contrary, the slightest
departure from the usages of the particular village
you may happen to be staying in, calls forth much
comment, and even in some instances, I have been
told, showers of stones; though this was a form of
interference we were lucky enough not to meet
with.

The tide was in, so that we were not obliged to be
carried out by the Moors. They drew the boat up to
the shore, and we got in easily; the port was perfectly
calm, and the steamer, being a very small one, was
lying quite near. As we pulled off I felt very sorry
to leave Morocco; it was stepping out of an enchanted
world, half fairy, half biblical. I had often longed to
get on a wishing-carpet that should, as Carlyle
suggests, take one not only any *where* but any *when*;

and really here my wish had been as nearly gratified
as possible. I really felt as if I had seen

> " Bagdad's shrines of fretted gold,
>   High-walled gardens green and old ; "

and I do believe that if I had actually visited the
banks of the Tigris at this day, I should have
found more changes, more jarring discords than
here, inasmuch as more foreign influences have passed
over that country.

But we were now on the deck of the steamer which
was to act as wishing-carpet on this occasion, and
transport us back to Europe and the nineteenth
century. We were rejoicing in the calmness, and
establishing ourselves on camp-stools, when the
captain said we had better have mattresses. This
idea we spurned with indignation ; the day was calm,
why should we lie down ? The captain shook his
head ominously, and pointed out to sea. We saw
nothing except some grey mist ; but the mattresses
were brought, and we set off. I was looking so
intently at Tangiers, on which a sudden gleam of
light had fallen, that I never observed what was
coming, till we rounded the point. All at once the
camp-stools flew in every direction, and the human
beings pretty much followed their example. Ladies,

children, and chairs, were brought under the same
levelling process, and a good deal of salt water equal-
ized the thing even more, while provision-baskets
floated and hand-bags were swept away. Everybody
tried to run to the rescue of their property, but
running, or even standing, was not easy under the
circumstances. Going on all fours was the only available mode of progression; and that, in two or three
inches of salt water, cannot be agreeable to any living
creature but a dog, especially as it was quite impossible to direct one's course to any given point. Just
as one thought one was getting on extremely well,
and had stretched out one's hand to grasp whatever
one was in quest of, the tiny steamer toppled off a big
wave into the trough of the sea, and away one went
in the wrong direction, accompanied by an extempore
cold bath, and a few sea-sick fellow-creatures.

This being the case, I thought perfect repose the
most comfortable and dignified line of action, and
established myself in the very centre of my mattress
which, being hair-cloth, and raised several inches
above the watery level of the deck, kept, for the most
part tolerably dry. It was really enjoyable; the
little steamer, having wind, tide, and current in her
favour, flew like a swift bird; and as I supposed this
kind of weather to be the normal condition of the

Straits, it did not at all surprise me when she tumbled and rolled about in a way that we had never met with anything approaching to, in all our voyages on Mediterranean, Baltic, or North Sea. Once or twice it did seem paradoxical that she should ever right again, but she floated like a cork whatever happened.

It seemed but a moment till we got across to the Spanish coast, and then it was less rough, though still blowing hard. Presently we saw a great English steamer coming round by Tarifa, very slowly. Long before she was in mid-channel, she turned and went back much faster than she had come. "What is the matter?" said I; "why does she go back?" The captain shook his head. "No steamer that ever was built could get to Cadiz to-day," said he; "nor over to Tangiers either." And it was quite true; few attempted it, and those that did had all to put back. Out at sea there had been a gale from the west for some days, though quite calm at Tangiers; and when this happens, the force of the current is overpowering, even after the wind has fallen, which in this instance it had not.

We got to Gibralter a few minutes within the three hours, and landed easily, as the steamer could run almost ashore. Everybody was surprised we had ventured to come, for they had seen more of the gale than we had on the Morocco coast; and we were told it was the worst day that had been in the Straits for five years.

It was very homelike at Gibraltar; and perhaps all the more so, as a thick mist had settled on the top of the rock, and a drizzling rain, worthy of a London November, had set in. We were therefore very glad to find ourselves once more at the comfortable Club-house Hotel.

CHAPTER XIII.

Our voyage from Gibraltar to Malaga was most unlike that across the Straits, being indeed on a summer sea. We sailed very early in the morning, and the saffron-tinted sunrise behind the Rock was magnificent. Far the grandest view of Gibraltar is from the Mediterranean side; it rises like a wall, seeming to bar all further progress westward. No wonder the ancients feared to pass that awful gateway, and tempt the wild ocean beyond.

Our course lay in the other direction, and all was

smiling, perfectly calm, with sky and rippling waves like azure. We glided past Marbella, which deserve its name of " beautiful sea "; and along the coast rose mountain behind mountain, of every shade of colour, from palest pink to deepest purple.

The view of Malaga from the sea is superb. Here the scenery is grander than on any other part of the coast. A break among those peaks and precipices marks the valley through which the railway runs up to Cordova; on the other side, the rugged Sierra de Antequera rises to a great height, while all along the shore are the vivid green sugar-canes, contrasting beautifully with the rich violet and crimson background.

This is all that can be said in praise of Malaga; for the rest, tall chimneys were sending out dark clouds of smoke, a bitterly cold wind was blowing down that grand mountain-gorge, the port was filthy, the boatmen careless, the porters insolent, and the custom-house the worst I have ever seen. Not that they examined our things much; they were too incompetent and lazy even to do that; indeed, they seemed to care for nothing but pillaging us. Will it' be believed that in this, one of the most prosperous mercantile cities of Spain, there is actually no place

whatsoever in which to open luggage, which yet
must always be searched? The whole examination
goes on in the street, whatever the weather may be,
without shelter of any kind. There is a little railing
at one place, to keep off the beggars, and that is all.
The exorbitance of the porters was something quite
astounding: besides charging enormously for everything that they carried, they endeavoured to make
me pay a *peseta* for my parasol, which I had in my
own hand all the time. How we longed for the
civilization of Morocco!

When we got to the hotel, matters did not
materially improve; it was excessively dirty, the
food was bad and insufficient, and the attendance
simply did not exist at all. The much-boasted
Alameda was dirty, dusty, and forlorn, with no view
of the sea; in fact, it is but a broad street, not particularly handsome, with a few trees growing by the
pavement. The cold was bitter; neither out of doors
nor in could we find shelter from the fierce north-west
wind; the streets were dirty and evil-smelling, the
shops like those in a fourth-rate English town, with
nothing Spanish about them. They were, however,
'full of excellent woollen stuffs, blankets, and the like,
which, judging by the severe cold in October, must
be very useful in winter. It is surprising that

invalids should come to Malaga, when there are so many more attractive places in Spain and elsewhere.

The steep walk up to the Castle, the Gibalfaro, is very beautiful. Besides the view over the sea, there are some lovely peeps through the rents in the old wall. Malaga, surrounded with the brilliant green sugar-canes, and backed by purple mountains, is seen through a frame of bright orange sandstone. At the fortress they made no difficulty about admitting us; but they did not seem quite to like our guide accompanying us, and made him write his name. When we got down again, we found there had been a *pronunciamiento*, that is, a riot in the principal square during our absence. We had heard some firing, but supposed it to be merely a review, or something of that kind. I believe nobody was hurt, and no harm done.

There is very little to see in Malaga, and that little not particularly interesting. We went to the Cathedral, which is said to be in wretched taste; it is not very beautiful, but it is extremely well kept, and its great size makes it rather handsome. In Malaga, it is well not to expect much from the architecture, or indeed from anything else except the surrounding scenery. We went up the Cathedral tower, in spite of the high wind, which was terrific on the top; but the view at sunset was very fine.

In passing through the streets, we observed the very prominent position which raisins occupy here, the boxes lying everywhere in the sun at the doors of the warehouses. They looked very good, but those we had at dinner were a mixture of stalks, skins, dust, and small gravel; the sweepings of the warehouses probably. Malaga raisins are here called "raisins of London!" All the finest are exported. The best thing we had at the *table d'hôte* was the *batata*, or sweet potato; it is boiled in a sugary syrup, and is excellent. We had them also at Cadiz and Gibraltar.

We left Malaga without regret on the 23rd of October. The railway to Cordova passes through magnificent scenery; the gorge of the Guadalhorce is stupendous, with extraordinary ravines, precipices, and peaks of grotesque form. There is one bridge on the route that is extremely insecure; so much so that the trains no longer pass over it; everybody has to get out and walk across. This is perfectly safe, but it looks uncomfortable; the bridge is at a great height, and being made for trains, and not for foot passengers, the rails are laid on a sort of openwork, through which it might be possible to slip, or at least one might very easily sprain one's ankle in some of the gaps. The train meanwhile goes with the luggage by a temporary line round a corner of the precipice, making a fearful curve, and looks exceedingly unsafe in so doing; of course it goes very slowly. This provisional arrangement, like many other things of the kind in Spain, will probably last for some time; that is, as long as the unsteady bridge and the little temporary railway keep out of the ravine below. In the meantime everybody congratulates themselves and their neighbours when it is passed without accident.

One last visit to the Mosque and Court of Oranges at Cordova, and next day we were again in the train, bound for Alicante. It is a long journey of twenty hours; for there is no possibility of stopping for the night anywhere on the way. Those who do not dislike the sea would probably prefer to go by the steamer from Malaga, as by the land route one must go half-way up to Madrid, and then back again to Alicante.

When morning dawned we were passing through a strange desolate country, with curious detached hills and yellow slopes. There was no vegetation, except dry aromatic herbs, which are considered by cullers of simples to possess such virtue that the Moors sometimes come over even yet to gather them; and the air felt deliciously pure and light after the atmosphere of Malaga, which was at the same time cold and depressing. On some of those isolated hills wonderfully picturesque castles are perched. One of the finest is Villena, which belonged to that learned Marquis of Villena who was accused of witchcraft, and of whom it was said that he was so occupied with the stars that he neglected the things of earth. The most beautiful is the ruined Alcazar of Elda.

Alicante, on entering it, seems a very odd place indeed. The castle rises grandly on its huge yellow rock; but the town, not a very small one either, is at the first glance nearly invisible, inasmuch as the houses are exactly the same colour as the rock, and they nestle so close to it as to be difficult to distinguish. Everything is the brightest yellow; castle, rock, houses, shore, and the surrounding plain, all look as if they were made of fine yellow sand. The houses are high, but not handsome; the streets are broad and tolerably regular, but have no beauty, and are exceedingly dull. The Alameda is like that of Malaga, only a broad street, with a few trees, and no sea view. There are no fine churches, no Moorish remains, not a picturesque building in the place.

Yet Alicante has a strange fascination. The castle

is superb, rising over the deep blue sea, and morning, noonday, and, above all, sunset, kindle it into golden glory. It scarcely looks of solid earth, so living seems the light. At sunset the tints were the brightest; but at noon it looked quite ethereal, with its pale azure shadows in that transparent atmosphere.

The great attraction was the palm-shaded esplanade close to the sea. The clear pure water is so deep that large ships can ride at anchor, almost touching the shore; the palms brought from Elche are not very tall, but they are in profusion : there are hundreds of them of different sizes ; the whole undergrowth is palm, surrounded with roses and every bright flower. Here we used to sit for hours, looking across those great smooth-rolling waves to the horizon, where there was always a' warm vermilion flush. The climate is enchanting; breathing becomes a luxury in such air: it seems as if neither heat nor cold, fatigue nor pain could touch one in that intensely pure atmosphere. There is no vegetation, except the palms and the flowers; but that is enough : one feels that a blade of grass would be an intrusion.

The Hôtel Bossio is one of the most really comfortable in Spain. The Italian landlord was civility itself, the rooms were very pretty, and the *cuisine* faultless. There are a great many different kinds of fish, all excellent, and the fruit is perhaps the finest in Spain ; the melons rival those of Seville, while the pomegranates excel all others. Sometimes they were brought to table whole, sometimes peeled and broken into crimson lumps ; but the prettiest way was when they were all crumbled to pieces, and one helped one-self to a spoonful of rubies. At breakfast they always brought us six different kinds of fruit ; and so liberal were they that we had the fine white Aloque wine at the *table d'hôte* without any additional charge.

We went up to the castle, and, strange to say, encountered in this rainless climate a heavy shower when we were on the top. The officers of the garrison were extremely civil, gave us shelter in the guard-room, and, Spanish fashion, brought us some very cold water from the castle well. They said it was dreadfully dull up there, and down in Alicante was not much better. They asked us if England or Spain was the best country, and the most prosperous. In order to combine truth with politeness, we replied that Spain was much the largest and had the best climate. With this they were satisfied.

The main object of our visit to Alicante was to go to Elche. We went in the diligence ; it is said to be

two hours' drive, but was really nearer three, with
the wretched horses we had. The greater part
of the way was through a desolate country; but as
we approached Elche, here and there light tufts of
feathery palms broke the horizon; then, near a
labourer's hut, rose a group of three or four; on the
other side, by a gateway, one, tall and slender,
towered into the sky; next, a well, with twenty or
more, recalling the old Biblical narrative. Then we
entered the long palm-avenue; and now we were in
a forest of thousands on thousands. The wind was
tossing the long leaves of the ever graceful, ever
restless trees, that rustled with the peculiar sound so
unlike any other, the voice of the Palm-tree.

They grow not only round, but in the town.
Everywhere there are gardens, and every garden is
full of palms; some straight as an arrow, others
bending low, the trunks crossing each other in all
directions: from some hung the great, rich bunches
of bright orange-coloured fruit, while others were tied
up in a point to blanch the leaves for Palm Sunday;
and everywhere was the thick undergrowth of the
young trees. It was difficult to believe oneself in
Europe.

We were left at the little *Posada*, and the diligence
rolled away to Murcia. Now, this was our first ex-

perience of a posada; everybody had assured us we could not sleep at Elche, but must go and return the same day; so we were not quite sure how it might turn out. We went in by the low, broad, roughly-paved entrance used by the carts. This led to a court, with open galleries running round, as one sees in many parts of Italy. In the bedrooms there was a mud floor, and the very smallest possible amount of furniture, consisting mainly of a truckle-bed, a broken chair, and an exquisitely graceful water-jar. But everything was perfectly clean, and there were no insects of any kind whatever. Probably we were the only English who had ever ventured on this little inn; certainly, I should think, the first English ladies who had done so; but nothing could exceed the kindness and attention of the people. When we came to dinner, after scrambling down the pitch dark stair, we passed through the kitchen, where the red firelight gleamed on swarthy faces: then there was a large, half dark room, full of muleteers from Murcia, with their wide white trousers and bright-coloured mantas; off this was the little room where we were to dine. It was brilliantly lighted, almost dazzling us after the semi-obscurity we had been stumbling through; the table was prettily arranged, with an extremely clean and white table-cloth, crystal bottles

of glowing red wine, and tall cut crystal dishes full
of splendid grapes, melons, and pomegranates. I
must confess that one of those dishes, being broken
through the middle, always fell to pieces at the
slightest touch ; still the whole effect was very pretty
I am not sure that this room had a door; if it had it
could not be shut; but yet we were considered to be
in absolute seclusion, and nobody on the other side of
the threshold took the slightest notice of us. Theo-
retically, it was supposed they did not see us.

When we entered the room, a dark turbaned Oriental was sitting at the table. He was in Eastern
costume; Syrian, not Moorish. Presently, when he
was trying to explain something to the girl who
waited on us, some words of Italian slipped out in his
struggles to speak Spanish. Now, the girl's native
tongue was Valencian, which is a dialect of Provençal, and not Spanish at all; and though she understood a little of the latter language, it was not to the
extent of enabling her to comprehend every attempt
made by a foreigner to speak it; and the Oriental's
half Italian, half Spanish, was pronounced with an
exceedingly strong Arabic accent : the consequence
was, that she did not understand a word, and the
perplexity was great. Seeing that it was hopeless,
I offered to interpret; he was delighted to talk

Italian, which he spoke fluently, and told us that he was a Christian from Bethlehem, who was selling rosaries from the Holy Land. He said that Spain was the only country he had travelled through where they seemed to dislike his Eastern dress, and that nobody would believe that he was a Christian. This was natural enough, as they, of course, thought he was a Moor.

At night, the muleteers slept in the court, in the moonlight, wrapped up in their great *mantas*. The Murcian manta is a sort of white woollen blanket, with stripes of very bright colour. Their carts and mules were also decked with tufts and tassels of gay-coloured worsted, generally yellow, red, and orange.

Before the door of the Posada grew the largest pepper-tree I have ever seen. Its trunk bent over a good deal, and there was a stone below to stand on, so I contrived to measure it ; and found that at eight feet from the ground it was nine feet in circumference. It was very tall, too, and wonderfully full of leaf; its branches fell in a cataract of bright green foliage. There were many smaller pepper-trees also. But the palms were the great charm of the place ; we went into one of the gardens outside the walls, and the gardener climbed the tree in a very curious way, and gathered dates for us. He fastened himself loosely to

the tree with a rope, and then ran up like a monkey
and gathered the fruit. The dates were scarcely
ripe; they were small, and we did not think
them very good: after keeping them a few days, they
became moist and began to wither; they were then
much sweeter, but had a slight taste of fermentation.
We were told that if we had kept them a little longer,
they would have become very good; but we could not
carry them about with us, with the sugary sap running over everything. In this date-garden the chairs
they brought us were particularly pretty, being made
of beautifully woven palm-leaves.

From the top of the Town-hall the view is very
extraordinary. The flat roofs and dark blue, glittering dome peep out of the palm-forest, which extends
in all directions, as far as the eye can reach; except
southward, where it is bounded by one gleam of the
wine-coloured sea. The top of this building is, however, not a very safe place to wander about on, for it
is at a great height, and there is not an inch of parapet
of any kind.

We walked to the upper end of the town to look at
the grim tower of the old Alcazar; it is now used as a
prison. At one of the small grated windows we saw
a hideous face. Our guide said this was a murderer,
who had killed his father, in order to secure some

small sum of money.   He was under sentence of death ;
but when it would be carried into effect, if ever, was
doubtful.   In the meantime he was singing merrily.

The population of Elche have the character of
being ferocious and sanguinary, but they are not impolite to strangers; their savageness taking the form
of feuds among themselves, often ending in bloodshed.
They are also much given to stabbing the owners of
the date-gardens; the consequence is that all the
great proprietors live at Alicante or elsewhere, leaving
the management of everything entirely to the gardeners.

Perhaps the finest view of Elche is from the opposite side of the Rambla.   This Rambla is not, as one
might suppose, a gay and handsome street, with shops
and shady trees, like that of Barcelona.   Here it is a
water-course of pale yellow sand, though which a
little stream runs down, sometimes blue and sometimes
dust-coloured, as it happens to reflect earth or sky.
The long shadows of the palms fall across it; those
tall palms which were many of them planted by the
Moors, centuries ago, being the oldest trees of the
kind in Spain.   This ravine does duty as a road,
when not occupied as a river; and the children drive
the pigs and goats along it.   When we were sitting
on the edge, we saw a specimen of the violent temper

of the natives of Elche. Some girls were playing among the low sand-hills, and certainly were spoiling their clothes a good deal; whereupon the mother of one of them rushed out of a cottage, seized the girl, shook her, kicked her, beat her furiously, and dragged her screaming away. I dare say she deserved punishment, but it was horrible to see such brutal rage. It was pleasanter to turn to inanimate things—to the glorious sunset hues, now touching houses, ravine, and palms, with vivid rose-colour.

Next morning we had to rise very early to return to Alicante. The stars were just fading when the pale pure saffron of the dawn began to light up the eastern sky, growing richer and brighter till the feathery trees stood out black against a sheet of gold. Never did I see such a sunrise as that, while we turned away across the desolate plain from the beautiful oasis, the City of Palms.

From Alicante we went by land to Valencia, through what is probably the richest country in the world. The railway passes through orange groves for miles, and the train seems to push its way through the golden fruit. Here and there rise groups of palms round the Moorish water-wheel still used for irrigation. Nor is it merely a fertile plain; the mountain views are superb. The most beautiful part

of this lovely journey is about Jativa, the birthplace of
Pope Alexander the Sixth. The Borgias, or Borjas,
were a noble family of Jativa; and Gandia, from
which they took their title, is quite near.

The heat was intense. A peasant woman brought
a basket of pomegranates down to the train, and the
passengers devoured them like famished wolves. By
the time the basket arrived at the carriage we were
in, only one pomegranate remained. It was bright
green, but we bought it, thinking it better than
nothing. Never did I eat such a fruit. The refreshing crimson juice was the most delicious thing I ever
tasted, on that exceedingly hot November afternoon.

It was dark when we reached Valencia, and drove
to the Fonda del Cid. The name is tempting, but
there is not much else to recommend it. There is
great civility, and the bedrooms are clean and prettily
furnished in the French style; but the situation is
extremely dull, the house is cold and dark, and the
cookery very bad. Everything, including the fish,
which would otherwise have been excellent, was
floating in rancid oil; the fruit was the only article of
food really free from it.

The town, on the whole, is rather disappointing,
being dull and by no means picturesque. The cathedral is really hideous; it is dirty and dilapidated, and

the architecture is in the worst possible taste. Most
of the good pictures have been moved to the Museum,
but the very beautiful door-panels of the altar still
remain. They were painted by Italian artists, pupils
of Leonardo da Vinci, and were gifts of Alexander
the Sixth to the city, of which he had been the first
archbishop. Valencia had previously been only a
bishopric, but was raised to the rank of an arch-
bishopric for the Borgia family.

We saw some other interesting small pictures, but
it was impossible to learn by whom they were painted
or anything about them. The guide and the sacristan
were both equally stupid and ignorant. Their reply
always was that they did not know; it was a very
old picture, for it had been there as long as they
remembered; the painter was dead, and they thought
he must have died before they were born, for they
had never seen him. They had never heard of any
of the great Spanish artists; at last, they professed
some knowledge of Ribera, but it was the archbishop
of that name, not the painter, whom they meant.
This was sufficiently hopeless; but a Spanish gentleman, seeing our perplexity, came up, told us that in
the Museum we should find some of the pictures we
were in quest of, showed us one or two others, and
then said that, as he saw we liked paintings, he would

advise us to go and see some of the private galleries
of Valencia, at the same time writing down their
names, and instructing our guide where to find
them.

In the meantime we went to the Colegio del
Patriarca to hear the *Dies iræ*, it being All Souls'
Day.   The ladies were invariably in black, with black
veils.   It is not permitted to enter this Colegio
except with the veil, which indeed it is always best
to wear in Spanish churches. The chanting was
better than is usual in Spain, very wild and sad,
The church was exceedingly dark, and the black
figures, flitting about or prostrate on the ground, had
a strange mournful effect.   The people seemed
exceedingly devout.

We went into several other churches, all darkened,
draped with black, and full of those black veiled
figures.   It was impossible to look for the pictures
or to examine anything, owing to the great crowds;
besides which, we did not like to interrupt the
funeral masses.   In some respects we should have
seen Valencia better had we come at another time;
yet those wailing requiems, and funereal forms
gliding about the dim churches were perhaps more
impressive than if we could have examined everything in the full light of day, especially as there

is no architectural beauty and no richness of decoration.

In the Museum all the best pictures, formerly in the churches, are now placed. There are some very good ones, the gem of all being the masterpiece of Juan de Juanes, the celebrated 'Purisima.' And exquisitely pure it is; a faint moonlight tint pervades it. The Virgin wears a white robe, with undersleeves of pale pink; the mantle is a silvery green. Her hands are folded; and the expression is unlike any other, recalling a soft light falling on snow. The tint of the background is greenish, and the mottoes and emblems of the Virgin, the pot of lilies, the rose of Jericho, the "garden enclosed," the Star of the Sea, and others, are represented round the edge in darker green. Here and there the green seemed to flush into palest pink. I never saw anything so strange or more lovely; it is like a dream. There are some other fine pictures by Juanes in this collection, but they are terrestrial; very good, but nothing more; not like this wondrous moonlight vision.

There is a Virgin and Child by Leonardo da Vinci; and a charming picture by some old Flemish master, a Holy Family. The Virgin is at work making a pinafore; her work-basket stands beside her with her scissor in a sheath: the infant St. John and the

Divine Child are playing together; the Child turns round to His mother with an expression of delight, because the lamb has put up its fore feet on his shoulders: St. Elizabeth, in the background, looks on with pleasure; and St. Joseph, at one side, is busied with carpenter work. It is very sweet, very simple and German.

In the afternoon we resolved to avail ourselves of the list of private galleries which had been given us; and fixed on that of the Marquis de Casarojas, as being the nearest. We went along the Calle de Caballeros, the only very handsome street in Valencia, and found the house we were in quest of at the corner of the Glorieta, a pretty little promenade, full of flowers and pepper-trees. Supposing that this gallery was open to the public at stated hours, like those of Rome and Florence, we boldly rang the bell and asked if we might see the pictures. Instead of showing us in, or telling us we ought to come at such or such a time, the servant disappeared into the house, and presently returned, begging that we would come again in half an hour, as the family were at table; so we took a walk in the Glorieta. When we came back, the carriage of the Marquis was at the door, and I feared we were too soon, but they made us go in. To our amazement and consternation we

found him waiting to show us everything himself, the
pictures not being in a gallery, but in the drawing-
rooms, dining-room, and even in his own room. We,
of course, apologized much for our intrusion ; but he
overwhelmed us with civilities, said it gave him the
greatest pleasure to let strangers, and especially the
English, see his pictures ; took them down from the
walls to put them in the best light, and finally offered to
come with us if we were making any stay in Valencia,
and show us everything remarkable in the town.

The pictures were exceedingly well worth seeing.
Among them was a splendid Leonardo da Vinci, the
Virgin and Child ; a fine St. Laurence by Ribalta ;
and San Vicente by the same. There was a most
interesting portrait of Charles the Fifth in his latter
days at Yuste, broken down, mind and body. How
unlike the magnificent portrait by Titian, of the young
hero, the favourer of Protestantism, the gay and
gallant sovereign of the Field of the Cloth of Gold !
One can hardly believe that the life of Charles was
but one life ; it seems many. I wonder how it
appeared to himself ! The father of Don John of
Austria and of Philip the Second ; the protector of
Luther, the besieger of Rome, the thwarter of
Clement the Seventh ; the Prince who spent his childhood in the quaint old Flemish towns, his youth

among the grand Imperial free cities, Augsburg, Nürnberg, Ratisbon; whose early married life was passed in the glorious halls of the Alhambra; whose old age—in the convent of Yuste. Successor of the Cæsars, Emperor of Germany, Sovereign of Spain, of Flanders, of Austria, of Naples, and of the beautiful new-found world beyond the Atlantic:—and all to end thus! Gifted too in mind and body, warrior and states-man, loving Art and Science, and at one time Truth. Ay, but there was the dark taint inherited from his mother; the awful retribution for the sins of Spain towards the Jews, towards the Indians, towards the noble Moors: a curse resting, I do believe, on the land to this day, and on all who attempt to rule it. When shall it be purified from its bloody stain?

But whatever may have been the sins of Spaniards in the olden time, they have, at the present day, much that is worthy of praise and imitation; among other things the great and unfailing courtesy of the upper classes to strangers, as evinced in the case of this our intrusion into a private house. We took leave of the kind Valencian with many thanks, and proceeded to the tower of the Miguelete for the sunset view. Nothing can be more lovely. Valencia lies in a garden; and one looks over the orange and mulberry trees, with an occasional tall palm, to the blue and glittering sea.

The beauty disappears in a great measure when one descends into the town, the streets being, for the most part, dull and uninteresting. The Lonja de Seda, or Silk Exchange, is very beautiful, however; and the market-place near it was exceedingly picturesque, with the groups of peasants in gay Valencian costume, who had come in for the religious ceremonies of All Souls. They wear the many-coloured *manta* across the shoulders, wide white trousers like those of Murcia, and a red silk handkerchief on the head. They are much taller and slighter than the Andalusians, and instead of having short, curly hair, their locks were long and lanky. They walked with a light, swinging step; and the expression of their faces was exceedingly merry, in spite of the mournful commemoration of the day. They have the character of being more gay and light-hearted than other Spaniards; in fact, properly speaking, they are more Provençal than Spanish.

The next day we went in a *tartana* to the Grao, or Port of Valencia, three miles from the town. The tartana is an odd-looking vehicle like a covered cart, painted dark green. In it one sits sideways; but the better sort, such as this at Valencia, have springs and comforably cushioned seats. We were drawn by a pretty little sleek black pony, of which the driver was so

fond that he stopped continually to caress it, and feed
it with carouba-beans out of his pocket. The animal
was as tame and intelligent as a dog.

The drive is disappointing, through a dusty suburb,
where all the fine trees have been cut down. From the
port there is a beautiful view of the mountains, and
a rocky point running far out to sea; the bathing is
said to be good. But it looked dull and dirty, and is
totally shadeless. We came back by the Alameda, a
pleasant shady promenade by the river. It was
thronged with carriages, and presented a very gay
spectacle. At one end is a charming garden, which,
even in November, was full of all kinds of flowers,
and bright-blossomed shrubs. We admired especially
a most beautiful kind of tree-mallow, which, in fact,
was quite a large tree, covered with gigantic flowers
of the brightest rose colour. There was a double row
of them all along the garden, forming a line of rosy
blossom. In all directions there were pretty walks,
with fountains. On our way back to the hotel we
passed what was, till lately, the Bab-el-Schecher, the
gate by which the Cid first entered Valencia when he
took it from the Moors, in 1095. Why this old gate
should have been taken down is inconceivable. On
the tower Albufat, close to this, the Cross was first
placed in Valencia. The church to which the tower

is attached belonged to the Templars, and the street takes its name from them.

We went also to see the bull-ring; when it was empty, of course; for nothing could induce us to repeat our Madrid experiences. It is a magnificent building, and exactly like an old Roman amphitheatre. We went over every part of it. At the entrance is a stone screen for the attendants to run behind, in order to escape the bull's charge in case he should turn aside instead of going in. The bulls are kept in dens with trap-doors in the roof, so that those who are interested in them may go and see them beforehand, and poke them up with poles; a pastime in which the Valencians greatly delight. They are very proud of their splendid bullring, and say triumphantly, "Spain is the only country that has bull-fights!"

The following day we left Valencia for Tarragona.

CHAPTER XIV.

The scenery between Valencia and Tarragona is very beautiful, but quite different in character from that between Alicante and Valencia. The first object of interest is Murviedro, the ancient Saguntum. We had wished much to stop here; but gave it up, in order to have more time for Monserrat; in this also, as will be seen later, we were doomed to disappointment. Meanwhile we contented ourselves with the very good view of the remains of the old Greek city from the railway.

We had now left the region of oranges and palms, and entered that of olives and caroubas. Both these last-named trees grow here to a size unknown elsewhere. Even on the Riviera of Genoa, the olives, with a few exceptions, are but shrubs, compared with the magnificent specimens one sees on the eastern coast of Spain ; while the carouba is here a mountain of thick, almost black foliage. Presently, we left the olives behind, and got among the pines. The railway passes close to the sea, which stretches its calm blue expanse away to the horizon ; not a sail breaks the loneliness ; the ripple washes lazily into sheltered sandy coves ; the rocks are covered with heath, palmitos, thyme, and all kinds of aromatic herbs ; and the stately pines give a peculiar repose to the landscape.

Now, as often before, we wondered much that so many people choose to pass this lovely country by night ; and then, because they have not seen it, they say there is nothing to see. This is one of the many mistakes made by travellers in Spain. It seems almost unnecessary to mention that if one wishes to see a place, one cannot do so in the dark ; if one does not wish to see it, it is surely better to enjoy comfortable repose at home. Another mistake made by English tourists is to travel second-class. This ought never to be done in Spain, especially by ladies. The Spaniards of the upper ranks invariably travel first-class, and cannot understand anybody doing otherwise. There is nothing, in ordinary circumstances, to prevent English ladies from travelling, with comfort and safety, in almost any part of Spain, and meeting as we did, with kindness and courtesy from high and low; but it is well to remember that Spain is a very different country from Germany and Switzerland. The natives are not accustomed to so many tourists, and consequently those who come attract more attention; they are treated with much more kindness and hospitality, but any departure from the Spanish code of what is or is not suitable to be done, would be severely commented on; thus it is best to learn what are the usages of the country, and, as far as possible, conform to them.

We passed Vinaroz, where the Duke de Vendôme died. Not far from this is Peniscola, where Pedro de Luna, the Spanish anti-Pope in the beginning of the 15th century, spent his latter days. It is said to be a rock wholly inaccessible by water, and approached only by a long, narrow strip of sand, on the land side. The most beautiful place on the route is Tortosa, on the Ebro, which is here truly a magnificent river. The town lies piled irregularly on both banks, and the view from the station is enchanting; the purple hills, a group of cottages peeping out of a garden of foliage, and in the midst a palm-tree.

Tarragona stands high on its cliffs, and the little port, with a few brown fishing-boats, nestles below. No steamer touches here; there is no commerce, no bustle. The sea is without sails; the land is an aromatic wilderness; the air is perhaps the purest and most exhilarating in Spain. Our first impression of the Rambla was that it was very forlorn and uninteresting. It is a broad street, running not alongside of, but inland from the sea; the houses are neither picturesque nor handsome. But at one end is the glorious sea-view; at the other, one turns aside into the bright market-place, and goes up a long flight of steps leading to the cathedral. Indeed, a great many of the streets in Tarragona strongly resemble steep stairs; the town being full of ups and downs.

The Cathedral is one of the oldest in Spain, being built between 1089 and 1131. It is small, comparatively speaking, but is exceedingly striking in its stern simplicity. The organ is splendid; and, strange to say, most beautifully played. It was the only place in Spain where we heard really good church-music. Every morning we went there for the musical mass at ten o'clock ; afterwards the organist often played for a long time, and we could never leave it as long as the soft waves of sound were surging among those dark grey piers.

The cloisters are among the most interesting in Spain, with a very beautiful doorway leading into the cathedral. It is round-arched, and covered with sculpture. A small Moorish mirhab, or recess for the Koran, is still here, with a Cufic inscription ; the date is 349 of the Hegira, or A.D. 960. As usual in Spanish cloisters, there is a garden in the middle, luxuriant with flowers and shrubs. Some of the capitals of the pillars are very quaintly carved : one is a garland of fighting cocks ; but what pleased us most was a cat and rat funeral. They are solemnly carrying a cat to his grave ; he is stretched on a bier, which is borne on the shoulders of four rats ; a rat heads the procession with a holy-water brush in his paw, and a most devout expression on his countenance, while another, carrying a spade, walks alongside.

In the church are some curious rude sculptures, let into the walls ; especially the peculiar cross which is the badge of the cathedral. It is more like the letter T, or Thor's hammer, than a cross. All here is hoary with antiquity; it seems to belong to an older time. It was quite startling to come upon the tapestry hangings of old St. Paul's, in London; they were sold by Henry the Eighth at the same time as those which we had vainly searched for in Valencia.

The outside of the cathedral is beautiful, but not at all like a church; the low, round, machicolated tower and the protecting wall make it look more like a castle. Behind it is the little church of San Pablo, said to be the most ancient in Spain. Indeed, the natives go so far as to assert that it was built in the lifetime of St. Paul, to whom it is dedicated. At any rate, it is very, very old; this is apparent at a glance. It is very small; being about the size of a chapel in an ordinary church.

Everything in Tarragona seems several centuries older than anywhere else; and oldest of all are the Cyclopean walls: those are pre-historic, and their history was lost in the mists of antiquity, before Augustus Cæsar held his court in Tarragona. In many·places they are quite perfect, to the very top of their enormous height; in some, there is but one row of gigantic stones apparent, surmounted by more modern work; the greater part of the circuit has from three to six courses of the huge blocks still remaining, below the masonry of later times. In

1868, an old gateway was found in this wall, behind some shabby houses that had been built against it. It is Cyclopean; and the lintel is one stone, more than ten feet in length. The thickness of the walls here is more than sixteen feet. No cement is used.

The drive to the Roman aqueduct is delightful, and was perhaps not the less so, as the worthy Italian landlord would not allow us to go in a tartana; for, as he said, what was the use of breaking our bones? The Tarragonese tartanas are springless, and altogether very unlike the more civilized vehicles of Valencia; and the experience we had had, the day we arrived here, did not induce us to contest the point: so we started in one of those great heavy carriages, half diligence, half omnibus, which are frequently the only kind to be had in Spain. The best thing to be done was to take possession of the coupé, and fancy ourselves in a light open carriage, completely ignoring the lumbering omnibus behind; this settled, we got on very comfortably. After about three miles' drive, we had to get out and walk across the fields. It was quite charming; the slopes were covered with heath, myrtle, palmitos, thyme, dwarf oak, and a few last lingering wild flowers. Those little oaks are very curious; they grow quite low on the ground, and are entirely covered with prickles; even the acorn cups are thorny. The aqueduct is superb, with its line of deep orange arches striding across the ravine. It looks quite perfect, but is no longer used. It is possible to cross the ravine by means of it, but it is rather dizzy work, as the height is great. Of course there is no parapet, but it is worth while to go for some distance, in order to judge of its great size and of the depth below.

From thence we made the circuit of great part of the walls, and drove to the Tomb of the Scipios, which is quite on the other side of Tarragona. Lonely it stands near the dark blue sea, with the pines overhead, and the heath and myrtle around; while its two mournful figures seem to keep watch and ward. Nothing is known of its history; there is no record, save the one remaining word of the inscription, "perpetuo."

In the Museum of Antiquities we saw many interesting things. There is a fac-simile and translation, by Gayangos, of a grant made (as far as I could make out) in 1216, by a Moorish Emir, to the monks of Poblet, giving them permission to pasture their flocks, and drink water at the wells in a certain territory. It is couched in the most courteous and liberal terms; I am afraid the Spanish chivalry would scarcely have acted in so Christian a spirit as those their Moslem enemies. Here, too, are the remains of the tomb of Don Jaime the Conquistador, brought from Poblet; it must have been splendid. A medallion is on each side: one represents Jonah being ejected from the whale's mouth; the other is the Resurrection. The collection of coins is very good; among them is a fine gold one of Vitellius; also a silver one of Titus, and another of Vespasian. A Roman lamp particularly struck us; it was a sort of chandelier of little lamps, a circle of probably eleven of them, but only four of the ancient ones remained: one had been put on in a gap, but I think the space was intended for two. We saw a small bronze Athor, with Horns; fragments of ancient glass, among them being a glass ring; and a very beautiful gold ring of Roman workmanship. There were many specimens of flint arrow-heads, and weapons of different periods. The sword of Don Jaime the Conqueror was there; and beside it a long slip of paper containing portraits of the kings of Aragon, all more or less like each other, and, moreover, all closely resembling kings of spades and clubs. One of the finest things in the collection is a Roman mosaic found under the Palace of Augustus; the head of Medusa is particularly good.

This Palace of Augustus is a total ruin; indeed,

with some mistaken idea of beautifying the town, the
authorities were carting away a great deal of it. It
is on the slope, halfway between the town and the
sea, in a splendid position, with a most beautiful
view; here Augustus was living when he issued the
decree commanding the gates of Janus to be shut.

Tarragona was the capital of Roman Spain, and
here was the winter residence of the prætor. The
Tarragonese, although they are taking down the
Palace of Augustus, exult in the ancient Roman
glories of their city; they are particularly proud of
Pontius Pilate having been born here, and point out
a very old massive tower on the wall as the " Cuartel
de Pilatos."

We looked about a long time in vain for the Roman
amphitheatre. In Tarragona there are no regular
guides ; and our landlord's young brother, who acted
in that capacity, knew nothing about it, though he
was otherwise an intelligent youth. At last, not at
all where we expected to find it, I descried the unmistakable oval form, on the shore below, apparently
within the precincts of the prison. We went down ;
and the soldiers on guard civilly let us in to examine
it. Little now remains, except some rows of seats,
which are not built, but cut in the sloping ground.

This day was to have been the last of our stay, as

we wished to get to Barcelona that evening; but not being quite sure of the hour of the afternoon train, we went into the railway station, which we were at that moment passing, to inquire. The answer was, that no trains could go at all, as the Carlists had cut the line. We asked if the stoppage was likely to last long: they replied that it was impossible to say; probably three or four days, perhaps a good deal longer. We now inquired about steamers, as we were really anxious to get on; "There are none," was the succinct answer. Was there a diligence? No. Was there a good road, and could one get post-horses? The road was excellent, but there were no horses; and even if we could procure any, the Carlists would certainly take them from us. The other line of railway, by Reus, had long been impracticable on account of the disturbed state of the country, as we knew; having been obliged to give up our excursion to Poblet, for that reason. There seemed but two courses open to us; either to go back to Valencia, and try to get a steamer to Barcelona, or to stay quietly at Tarragona, and hope for the best. We chose the latter alternative, as involving less active exertion; and, since we could not get away, walked round the landward part of the wall, which we had not previously examined. On this side also there is a

Cyclopean gateway, but it is built up. The archbishop's palace is on this part of the wall, and the view from it must be superb.

We remained out so late, first watching the sunset, and then choosing photographs, that it was dark when we got into the Rambla. A crowd of people and a guard of soldiers were at the door of a church, opposite the hotel; and we went in, expecting Benediction, or some other religious service. The church was in nearly total darkness; presently, from a side-door a number of soldiers came out with torches, and among them the priests carrying the Host under a canopy. They were taking it to an officer who was dying. The effect, in the gloom, was very awful. As they came out, the long roll of the drum and the martial music began. Then far up the street the music grew faint, and the torches disappeared in the darkness.

In the evening the landlord sent down to the railway to make inquiries about the trains; none could go, and the Carlists had taken possession of one of the stations on the line. We therefore resigned ourselves to the prospect of passing some days, if not weeks, at Tarragona.

Next morning, at a quarter to six, we were wakened by a tremendous noise and knocking at our door. This was a message from the railway to say that we could go now, but we must be at the station at six o'clock; otherwise it was impossible to say when we could get away. The haste was fearful! We got ready somehow, and the horses galloped the whole way down the hill, the heavy omnibus swaying round the corners, in a most appalling manner: the landlord came with us, and we paid the bill while in the carriage. Somebody got our tickets, and we were pushed into the train, which waited seven minutes for us. At seven minutes past six A.M., we were off; very glad to be on our way northward, for the political horizon of Spain was growing exceedingly black. Wherever we were, in every hotel, at every *table d'hôte*, the conversation grew more and more revolutionary. Carlists and Republicans for the moment forgot their differences, and united in disparagement of the dynasty of Savoy. Even officers in uniform did not scruple publicly to talk downright treason; while among the lower classes the muttered threat of "Remember Maximilian of Mexico!" began to be heard. We therefore thought that the sooner we were out of Spain the better; and flattered ourselves we should find a steamer at Barcelona, to take us to Marseilles.

In the meantime, there was a good deal of uncertainty as to whether we should reach Barcelona or not. There was some idea that the Carlists were at Martorell, one of the small towns on the line; but perhaps they would let us pass. We looked eagerly out, at the different stations; but nothing was to be seen except basketsful of broken telegraph wires. We passed Martorell in safety, and greatly admired the beautiful bridge over the Llobregat, near this. It was first built by Hannibal, but the great central arch is Moorish. Now rose the exquisite wavy peaks of Monserrat, pale blue, crested with snow. It is, really, much more like "a wave about to break" than Soracte is; but Monserrat is an exceedingly large billow, compared with the little ripple-like hill of the Roman Campagna. We had hoped to spend some days at this, one of the wonders of Spain; but the Carlists had possessed themselves of both the points of access, and we thought it best to give it up. Not that we really feared anything but inconvenience and delay; still, in the month of November, we had no desire to be detained for weeks, or even for many days; so that this and all excursions in the country had to be abandoned.

Even beautiful Barcelona was seen more hastily than we could have wished; for there was always the risk of an insurrection in the city itself. Gladly would we have lingered here; for it is an exceedingly attractive place, with its busy Rambla, where the great oriental planes, still in fullest leaf, shaded an array of shops, splendid as those of Paris. It is by far the handsomest town in Spain ; wealthy and prosperous, gay and brilliant, yet quite Spanish too.

Then one leaves that glittering Rambla, and, through quiet, solemn-looking streets, one reaches the venerable cathedral. On entering it, the first impression is that of looking through a gigantic kaleidoscope. It is so dark that, except at noon, literally nothing is visible but the glorious stained glass, which is richer and more glowing here than anywhere else.

The walls are almost black ; and, even in full daylight, so dim is it that, after leaving the outer sunshine, one has to wait a little before one gropes one's way to the choir—that choir where Charles the Fifth held an installation of the Golden Fleece. The arms of all the knights are on the stalls, and among them those of Henry the Eighth of England.

Saracens' heads occur frequently in this cathedral ; it seems they were, in crusading times, considered to be a cheering spectacle. A particularly ferocious one hangs below the organ.

To the Spaniards the great attraction is the tomb of St. Eulalia ; but to us the sepulchres of Ramon Berenguer and his wife Almudis were more interesting. The arrangement of the arches behind the High Altar of this cathedral is very singular and exceedingly beautiful. The cloisters, too, are charming, with the quaint fountain surrounded by flowers and orange-trees. On the pavement are some badges of the different guilds; we observed a boot for the bootmakers, a pair of scissors for the tailors, and so on.

In a private house near the cathedral are some very fine Roman remains; gigantic Corinthian columns imbedded in the walls, which are built without the least reference to those ancient fragments: thus the base of a pillar is seen near the roof of one room, and a capital sticking out of the floor of another. But all over Barcelona there are bits of Roman wall, and fragments of Roman arches and gateways. If we could but have had time to study them more!

We of course went up to the celebrated Monjuich. The walk is lovely; quite in the country, among the wild flowers. It is an exceedingly strong fortress, and most beautifully kept. There is no well, and the rain water is the only supply; but the tanks are so admirably contrived, that even in this dry climate, there is always abundance. The view is glorious.

On our way, we had gone into the little Romanesque church of San Pablo del Campo, with its small deserted cloister, sunless and icy cold. It looks wonderfully old, with its little clustered pillars; and indeed the tiny church has existed for 960 years.

One of the most interesting things in Barcelona is the Casa de la Disputacion, which has a very beautiful outside staircase in the court. Inside is St. George's Chapel; and there we were shown exceedingly fine embroidered vestments and illuminations. In another part of this building the archives of Aragon are kept; and in one great hall are the portraits of all the Aragonese sovereigns. We were particularly struck with the extraordinary width of the staircases, doors, and archways here and elsewhere in Barcelona. It gives quite a peculiar character to the streets and palaces.

One more old building we went to see: in a quiet little Plaza, away from the gay quarter, is what remains of the Palace of the Counts of Barcelona, of the time when this was the home of poetry and the " Gaie Science." Then, with my head, I must own, rather confusedly full of jewelled windows, dark Gothic arches, and Corinthian capitals; cloisters, fortifications, and Roman gateways; Goths, Moors, and Troubadours; we went to walk at sunset on the beautiful Muralla del Mar, and to wish that we had weeks instead of days to spend in Barcelona.

But the state of affairs was getting so rapidly

worse that our main object now was to get out of Spain
as quickly as possible. There, however, was the difficulty. It was not very easy to get into Spain; but
getting out seemed likely to be even more perplexing.
The land route was infested by brigands; besides
which, the Carlists were out in all directions, and the
diligence had been stopped a few days before. We
then thought of going by sea; but the English and
French steamers touch at Barcelona only in coming
from Marseilles, and not in returning. The only
means of going was by the little Spanish river-
steamers that come down the Guadalquivir from
Seville, and which, as we had been warned by the
English consul at Alicante, were not fit for the Gulf
of Lyons in a storm. In this instance, however,
there was no storm, the weather having been for a
long time dead calm; so we very nearly decided to
go by sea, and if we could at the moment have found
the *commissionaire* to send for our tickets, should certainly have done so. Then, I scarcely know why,
we changed our minds, and went to the diligence-
office to secure places; there we were assured it was
perfectly safe by day, the robberies occurring only in
the dark. Quite satisfied, we returned to the hotel;
and, while waiting for dinner, took up the newspaper;
the diligence had been stopped again, the conductor

killed, and an Englishman wounded. There was no remedy now, however, so we resolutely put away all thought of danger.

We were to go by railway as far as Gerona; but the system in Spain is that you take your ticket, for both train and carriage, a few days before, send your luggage to the railway and diligence-office the evening previous to your departure, and walk there in the morning, with anybody you can procure to carry your hand-packages: from thence an omnibus takes you to the railway. This is in some respects very convenient, as one is not obliged to stand in a crowd taking tickets, or making fruitless efforts to get one's luggage weighed in a hurry. On the other hand, the diligence-office is generally uncomfortable and dirty, and one can rarely find a seat; besides which, the omnibus frequently takes second- and third-class passengers, and thus the contents are rather miscellaneous. On this occasion, we did not seem likely to have many fellow-travellers; but a box containing a heavy bar of silver was put at our feet. We did not much like this; as, if the Carlists heard of it, they were pretty sure to come down and rob the diligence.

But the fresh morning air, and the pretty journey up to Gerona, effectually banished all forebodings; and we were soon so occupied with regrets at the

disappearance of orange-trees, mulberries, olives, and
agaves, that we forgot the brigands. Now there were
none but deciduous trees, whose leaves were falling
fast; and by the time we got to Gerona, we might
have been in one of the lower valleys of Styria or
Tyrol. The town looked exceedingly tempting; but
we could not stop; this, like many other things in
Spain, must be left for a future time. We accordingly
got into the diligence, and sped away up the Pass.

Cheered by the bright sunshine, we laughed at our
fears, and congratulated ourselves that we had
arranged so as to make our journey by daylight.
This was all very well as long as the daylight lasted;
but about sunset we stopped to change horses at the
little town of Figueras, which is the most dangerous
part of the route, being indeed a nest of brigands.
Here the delays were unaccountable; our driver
chattered and smoked, and drank coffee and brandy,
till it grew dusk. There was no use in grumbling or
scolding; we dared not, even to each other, allude to
the danger of robbery; so we too got down and went
to have some coffee. The people were very civil,
even kind; but they looked wild, and rather as if
they might possibly harbour brigands.

It was quite dark when we left Figueras, and we
knew we had nearly three hours of a very lonely

road, before we could be out of danger. The other
diligences had long gone on, and the road was
perfectly solitary. It lay through a gorge, with the
river and some copsewood on one side, and a precipice
rising above us on the other. Here there certainly
could have been no escape; but at last I grew weary
of straining my eyes in the darkness for imaginary
brigands and fell sound asleep.

I was awakened by the carriage stopping, and
several men came up. "What is it?" asked we
anxiously. "The French custom-house, madame," was
the reply. "Oh, how glad I am!" exclaimed H.,
springing joyfully out. The *douaniers*, not being
in the habit of hearing people express such delight
at finding themselves in a custom-house, were
immensely flattered, considering it all a compliment
to the French nation, politely supposed madame was
French, and did not open our boxes at all. They
were greatly interested in our journey, expressed
considerable surprise that we had not been robbed by
" ces messieurs là-bas," and assured us we were now
quite safe, as the road was patrolled.

A few days afterwards, the diligence was stopped
by a band of two hundred Carlists, who intimated
that it would have to pay black-mail for the future.
It was therefore discontinued, the letters being sent

round by Irun. We were really fortunate, for we were afterwards told by a gentleman who had gone in the very steamer we had hesitated about, that they had encountered a frightful storm which beat them back to the Gulf of Rosas; there, after having been three days at sea, they had to land, and go by the brigand route after all; besides having to pay both their sea passage and the land journey, and losing nearly all their luggage.

All this we did not learn till some time after. Meanwhile we pursued our way, rejoicing at our escape. But we had now come into a northern land. The cold was bitter, the wind was howling wildly, the sky was black and lowering, the trees were leafless. We had left warmth, and flowers, and sunshine behind us; and sadly we felt that happy memories were all that now remained of our delightful Spanish Summer.

THE END.

PRINTED BY TAYLOR AND CO.,
LITTLE QUEEN STREET, LINCOLN'S INN FIELDS.

THE CONQUEROR AND HIS COMPANIONS. By J. R.
PLANCHE, Author of "The Recollections and Reflections of J. R. Planché,"
etc. *[In the Press.*

THE RECOLLECTIONS AND REFLECTIONS OF J. R.
PLANCHE (*Somerset Herald*) : a Professional Autobiography. 2 vols. 8vo.

" Besides illustrations of social and dramatic life, of literature, and of authors, Mr. Planché gives us record of travels, incidents of his *other* professional life as a herald, and reflections on most matters which have come under his notice. . . . There are few men who have amused and delighted the public as long as he has done ; and perhaps there has never been a dramatic writer who has been so distinguished as he has been for uniting the utmost amount of wit and humour with refinement of expression and perfect purity of sentiment."—*Athenæum.*

" So many and so good are the anecdotes he relates, that two or three could not be taken from the rest by any process more critical than the toss of a halfpenny."—*Saturday Review.*

Beethoven, Handel, Haydn, Malibran, Mozart, etc.

MUSICAL RECOLLECTIONS OF THE LAST HALF CEN-
TURY. 2 vols. 8vo.

"And music shall untune the sky."—*Dryden and Handel.*

" Such a variety of amusing anecdotes, sketches of character, bits of biography, and incidents in the career of famous *artistes* have never been crammed in a couple of volumes before. . . . ' Musical Recollections of the Last Half Century ' is the most entertaining and readable book on musical matters that has been published for many years, and deserves to become very popular."—*Era.*

The Life and Times of Algernon Sydney.

THE LIFE AND TIMES OF ALGERNON SYDNEY, Re-
publican, 1622-1683. By ALEXANDER CHARLES EWALD, F.S.A., Senior Clerk of Her Majesty's Public Records, Author of "The Crown and its Advisers," "Last Century of Universal History," etc. 2 vols. 8vo.

" We welcome this biography as the means of making an illustrious Englishman better known to modern readers, and because it will bring the noble letters and other writings of Algernon Sydney within the easier reach of a great mass of people.—*Athenæum.*

The Life and Adventures of Alexander Dumas.

THE LIFE AND ADVENTURES OF ALEXANDER
DUMAS. By PERCY FITZGERALD, Author of "The Lives of the Kembles," "The Life of David Garrick," etc. 2 vols. 8vo.

" If the great object of biography is to present a characteristic portrait, then the personal memoir of Dumas must be pronounced very successful."—*Times.*

UNEXPLORED SYRIA. By Captain BURTON, F.R.G.S., and
Mr. C. F. TYRWHITT-DRAKE, F.R.G.S., etc. With a New Map of Syria, Illustrations, Inscriptions, the " Hamah Stones," etc. 2 vols. 8vo. 32s.

" The work before us is no common book of travels. It is rather a series of elaborate, and at the same time luminous, descriptions of the various sites visited and explored by the authors, either together or singly, and of the discoveries made there by them."—*Athenæum.*

" While these magnificent volumes, with their original plans and sketches by Mr. Drake, the unrivalled map of Northern Syria, and the luxurious print, are triumphs of typography, they are at the same time enduring monuments of the energy and enterprise of our countrymen."—*John Bull.*

" The book must be pronounced to be valuable for its information."—*Spectator.*

TINSLEY BROTHERS, 8, CATHERINE STREET, STRAND.

TINSLEY BROTHERS' LIST OF NEW BOOKS.

Court Life in the Reign of Napoleon the Third.

By the late FELIX WHITEHURST. 2 vols, 8vo. [*In the press.*

Madame de Sévigné : Her Correspondents and Con-

temporaries. By the COMTESSE DE PULIGA. 2 vols. 8vo, with Portraits, 30s.

"There are always amongst us a select few who find an inexhaustible source of refined enjoyment in the letters of Madame Sévigné. The Horace Walpole set affected to know them by heart; George Selwyn meditated an edition of them, and preceded Lady Morgan in that pilgrimage to the Rochers which she describes so enthusiastically in her 'Book of the Boudoir.' Even in our time it would have been dangerous to present oneself often at Holland House or the Berrys' without being tolerably well up in them. ... Madame de la Puliga has diligently studied her subject in all its bearings; she is thoroughly imbued with the spirit of the period of which she treats; she is at home with both correspondents and contemporaries; she has made a judicious selection from the embarrassing abundance of materials accumulated to her hands; treading frequently on very delicate ground, she is never wanting in feminine refinement or good taste."—*Quarterly Review.*

The Life and Times of Algernon Sydney, Repub-

lican, 1622—1683. By ALEXANDER CHARLES EWALD, F.S.A., Senior Clerk of Her Majesty's Public Records, author of "The Crown and its Advisers," "Last Century of Universal History," &c. 2 vols, 8vo, 25s.

"We welcome this biography as the means of making an illustrious Englishman better known to modern readers, and because it will bring the noble letters and other writings of Algernon Sydney within the easier reach of a great mass of people."—*Athenæum.*

BEETHOVEN, HANDEL, HAYDN, MALIBRAN, MOZART, &c.

Musical Recollections of the Last Half-Century.

2 vols. 8vo, 25s. "And Music shall untune the sky."—*Dryden and Handel.*

"Such a variety of amusing anecdotes, sketches of character, bits of biography, and incidents in the career of famous artistes have never been crammed in a couple of volumes before. . . . 'Musical Recollections of the Last Half-Century' is the most entertaining and readable book on musical matters that has been published for many years, and deserves to become very popular."—*Era.*

Cartoon Portraits and Biographical Sketches of Men

of the Day. Containing 50 Portraits, with Short Biographical Sketches of each. 1 handsome 4to vol. cloth gilt, 21s.

Lord Lytton; C. R. Darwin, F.R S.; John Everett Millais; Dion Boucicault; Robert Browning; G. E. Street, R.A.; "Mr. Speaker;" J. L. Toole; Gustave Doré; William Morris; Dr. Garrett Anderson; William Hepworth Dixon; Professor Owen; the Right Hon. B. D'Israeli; John Hollingshead; A. C. Swinburne; J. C. M. Bellew; Henry Irving; Charles Reade; Tom Hood; Benjamin Webster; Anthony Trollope; C. E. Mudie; Lionel Brough; Wilkie Collins; Alfred Tennyson; Norman Macleod; Andrew Halliday; Canon Kingsley; George Augustus Sala; Professor Huxley; Charles Lever; J. R. Planché; Edmund Yates; Captain Warren, R.E.; John Ruskin; W. H. Smith, M.P.; Thomas Carlyle; J. B. Buckstone; Frederick Locker; Mark Twain; H. M. Stanley; J. A. Froude; Shirley Brooks; Dean Stanley; Matthew Arnold; Harrison Ainsworth; J. B. Hopkins; George Macdonald; William Tinsley.

The Life and Adventures of Alexander Dumas. By

PERCY FITZGERALD, author of "The Lives of the Kembles," "The Life of David Garrick," &c. 2 vols. 8vo, 25s.

"More amusing volumes than these it would be difficult to find."—*Standard.*

Wickets in the West, or the Twelve in America.

By R. A. FITZGERALD. With Portrait and Illustrations. 1 vol. crown 8vo, 5s.

History of France under the Bourbons, 1589-1830.
By CHARLES DUKE YONGE, Regius Professor, Queen's College, Belfast. In 4 vols. 8vo. Vols. I. and II. contain the Reigns of Henry IV., Louis XIII. and XIV.; Vols. III. and IV. contain the Reigns of Louis XV. and XVI. 3*l.*

The Regency of Anne of Austria, Queen of France,
Mother of Louis XIV. From Published and Unpublished Sources. With Portrait. By Miss FREER. 2 vols. 8vo, 30*s.*

The Married Life of Anne of Austria, Queen of
France, Mother of Louis XIV.; and the History of Don Sebastian, King of Portugal. Historical Studies. From numerous Unpublished Sources. By MARTHA WALKER FREER. 2 vols. 8vo, 30*s.*

Zanzibar. By CAPTAIN R. F. BURTON, author of
"A Mission to Gelélé," "Explorations of the Highlands of the Brazil," "Abeokuta," "My Wanderings in West Africa," &c. 2 vols. 8vo, 30*s.*

Explorations of the Highlands of the Brazil; with
a full account of the Gold and Diamond Mines; also, Canoeing down Fifteen Hundred Miles of the great River, Sao Francisco, from Sabará to the Sea. In 2 vols. 8vo, with Map and Illustrations, 30*s.*

Wit and Wisdom from West Africa; or a Book of
Proverbial Philosophy, Idioms, Enigmas, and Laconisms. Compiled by RICHARD F. BURTON, author of "A Mission to Dahomé," "A Pilgrimage to El-Medinah and Meccah," &c. 1 vol. 8vo, 12*s.* 6*d.*

Memoirs of the Life and Reign of George III.
With Original Letters of the King and Other Unpublished MSS. By J. HENEAGE JESSE, author of "The Court of England under the Stuarts," &c. 3 vols. 8vo. £2 2*s.* Second Edition.

The Newspaper Press: its Origin, Progress, and
Present Position. By JAMES GRANT, author of "Random Recollections," "The Great Metropolis," &c., and late Editor of the *Morning Advertiser.* 2 vols. 8vo, 30*s.*

Baron Grimbosh: Doctor of Philosophy and some-
time Governor of Barataria. A Record of his Experiences, written by himself in Exile, and Published by Authority. 1 vol. 8vo, 10*s.* 6*d.*

The Court of Anna Carafa: an Historical Narra-
tive. By Mrs. ST. JOHN. 1 vol. 8vo, 12*s.*

The Public Life of Lord Macaulay. By FREDERICK
ARNOLD, B.A. of Christ Church, Oxford. Post 8vo, 7*s.* 6*d.*

Lives of the Kembles. By PERCY FITZGERALD, author of the "Life of David Garrick," &c. 2 vols. 8vo, 30s.

The Life of David Garrick. From Original Family Papers, and numerous Published and Unpublished Sources. By PERCY FITZGERALD, M.A. 2 vols. 8vo, with Portraits. 36s.

The Life of Edmund Kean. From various Published and Original Sources. By F. W. HAWKINS. 2 vols. 8vo, 30s.

Our Living Poets: an Essay in Criticism. By H. BUXTON FORMAN. 1 vol., 12s.

Memoirs of Sir George Sinclair, Bart., of Ulbster. By JAMES GRANT, author of "The Great Metropolis," "The Religious Tendencies of the Times," &c. 1 vol. 8vo. With Portrait. 16s.

Memories of My Time; being Personal Reminiscences of Eminent Men. By GEORGE HODDER. 1 vol. 8vo, 16s.

Biographies and Portraits of some Celebrated People. By ALPHONSE DE LAMARTINE. 2 vols. 8vo, 25s.

Under the Sun. By GEORGE AUGUSTUS SALA, author of "My Diary in America," &c. 1 vol. 8vo, 15s.

The History of Monaco. By H. PEMBERTON. 1 vol. 8vo, 12s.

The Great Country: Impressions of America. By GEORGE ROSE, M.A. (ARTHUR SKETCHLEY). 1 vol. 8vo, 15s.

My Diary in America in the Midst of War. By GEORGE AUGUSTUS SALA. 2 vols. 8vo, 30s.

Notes and Sketches of the Paris Exhibition. By GEORGE AUGUSTUS SALA. 8vo, 15s.

From Waterloo to the Peninsula. By GEORGE AUGUSTUS SALA. 2 vols. 8vo, 24s.

Rome and Venice, with other Wanderings in Italy, in 1866-7. By GEORGE AUGUSTUS SALA. 8vo, 16s.

Paris after Two Sieges. Notes of a Visit during the Armistice and immediately after the Suppression of the Commune. By WILLIAM WOODALL. 1 vol. 2s. 6d.

Judicial Dramas: Romances of French Criminal Law. By HENRY SPICER. 1 vol. 8vo, 15s.

The Retention of India. By ALEXANDER HALLIDAY. 1 vol. 7s. 6d.

Letters on International Relations before and during
the War of 1870. By the *Times* Correspondent at Berlin. Reprinted,
by permission, from the *Times*, with considerable Additions. 2 vols.
8vo, 36*s.*

The Story of the Diamond Necklace. By HENRY
VIZETELLY. Illustrated with an exact representation of the Diamond Necklace, and a Portrait of the Countess de la Motte, engraved
on steel. 2 vols. post 8vo, 25*s.* Second Edition.

English Photographs. By an American. 1 vol. 8vo,
12*s.*

Travels in Central Africa, and Exploration of the
Western Nile Tributaries. By Mr. and Mrs. PETHERICK. With
Maps, Portraits, and numerous Illustrations. 2 vols. 8vo, 25*s.*

From Calcutta to the Snowy Range. By an OLD
INDIAN. With numerous coloured Illustrations. 1 vol. 8vo, 14*s.*

Stray Leaves of Science and Folk-lore. By J. SCOF-
FERN, M.B. Lond. 1 vol. 8vo, 12*s.*

Three Hundred Years of a Norman House. With
Genealogical Miscellanies. By JAMES HANNAY, author of "A
Course of English Literature," "Satire and Satirists," &c. 1 vol. 12*s.*

The Religious Life of London. By J. EWING RITCHIE,
author of the "Night Side of London," &c. 1 vol. 8vo, 12*s.*

Religious Thought in Germany. By the *Times*
Correspondent at Berlin. Reprinted from the *Times*. 1 vol. 8vo, 12*s.*

Mornings of the Recess in 1861-4. Being a Series
of Literary and Biographical Papers, reprinted from the *Times*, by
permission, and revised by the Author. 2 vols. 21*s.*

The Schleswig-Holstein War. By EDWARD DICEY,
author of "Rome in 1860." 2 vols. 16*s.*

The Battle-fields of 1866. By EDWARD DICEY,
author of "Rome in 1860," &c. 12*s.*

From Sedan to Saarbrück, viâ Verdun, Gravelotte,
and Metz. By an Officer of the Royal Artillery. In one vol. 7*s.* 6*d.*

British Senators; or Political Sketches, Past and
Present. By J. EWING RITCHIE. 1 vol. post 8vo, 10*s.* 6*d.*

Prohibitory Legislation in the United States. By
JUSTIN MCCARTHY. 1 vol., 2*s.* 6*d.*

The Idol in Horeb. Evidence that the Golden
Image at Mount Sinai was a Cone and not a Calf. With Three Appendices. By CHARLES T. BEKE, Ph.D. 1 vol., 5*s.*

TINSLEY BROTHERS, 8 CATHERINE STREET, STRAND.

Ten Years in Sarawak. By CHARLES BROOKE, the "Tuanmudah" of Sarawak. With an Introduction by H. H. the Rajah Sir JAMES BROOKE; and numerous Illustrations. 2 vols. 8vo, 25s.

Peasant Life in Sweden. By L. LLOYD, author of "The Game Birds of Sweden," "Scandinavian Adventures," &c. With Illustrations. 1 vol. 8vo, 18s.

Hog Hunting in the East, and other Sports. By Captain J. NEWALL, author of "The Eastern Hunters." With numerous Illustrations. 1 vol. 8vo, 21s.

The Eastern Hunters. By Captain JAMES NEWALL. 1 vol. 8vo, with numerous Illustrations. 16s.

Fish Hatching; and the Artificial Culture of Fish. By FRANK BUCKLAND. With 5 Illustrations. 1 vol. crown 8vo, 5s.

Incidents in my Life. By D. D. Home. In 1 vol. crown 8vo, 10s. 6d. *Second Series.*

Con Amore; or, Critical Chapters. By JUSTIN McCARTHY, author of "The Waterdale Neighbours." Post 8vo, 12s.

The Cruise of the Humming Bird, being a Yacht Cruise around the West Coast of Ireland. By MARK HUTTON. In 1 vol. 14s.

Murmurings in the May and Summer of Manhood: O'Ruark's Bride, or the Blood-spark in the Emerald; and Man's Mission a Pilgrimage to Glory's Goal. By EDMUND FALCONER. 1 vol., 5s.

Poems. By EDMUND FALCONER. 1 vol., 5s.

Dante's Divina Commedia. Translated into English in the Metre and Triple Rhyme of the Original. By Mrs. RAMSAY. 3 vols. 18s.

The Gaming Table, its Votaries and Victims, in all Countries and Times, especially in England and France. By ANDREW STEINMETZ, Barrister-at-Law. 2 vols. 8vo, 30s.

Principles of Comedy and Dramatic Effect. By PERCY FITZGERALD, author of "The Life of Garrick," &c. 8vo, 12s.

A Winter Tour in Spain. By the Author of "Altogether Wrong." 8vo, illustrated, 15s.

Life Beneath the Waves; and a Description of the Brighton Aquarium, with numerous Illustrations. 1 vol., 2s. 6d.

The Rose of Jericho; from the French; called by the German "Weinachts-Rose," or "Christmas Rose. Edited by the Hon. Mrs. NORTON, Author of "Old Sir Douglas," &c. 2s. 6d.

The Bells: a Romantic Story. Adapted from the French of MM. ERCKMANN-CHATRIAN. 1s.

TINSLEY BROTHERS, 8 CATHERINE STREET, STRAND.

TINSLEY BROTHERS' NEW NOVELS

AT EVERY LIBRARY.

London's Heart. By B. L. Farjeon, author of
"Grif," "Joshua Marvel," "Blade-o'-Grass," and "Bread-and-Cheese
and Kisses." 3 vols.

Home, Sweet Home. By Mrs. J. H. Riddell,
author of "George Geith," "Too Much Alone," "City and Suburb,"
&c. 3 vols.

A Fair Saxon. By Justin McCarthy, author of
"My Enemy's Daughter," "The Waterdale Neighbours," &c. 3 vols.

Murphy's Master: and other Stories. By the author
of "Lost Sir Massingberd," "Found Dead," "Gwendoline's Harvest,"
"Cecil's Tryst," "A Woman's Vengeance," "A Perfect Treasure," &c.
2 vols.

My Little Girl. By the author of "Ready Money
Mortiboy." 3 vols.

Lady May's Intentions. By John Pomeroy, author
of "A Double Secret," "Bought with a Price," &c.

Only a Face: and other Stories. By Mrs. Alex-
ander Fraser, author of "Not while She lives," "Denison's Wife,"
"Faithless, or the Loves of the Period," &c. 1 vol.

The Cravens of Cravenscroft. A Novel. By Miss
Piggott. 3 vols.

Legends of the Jacobite Wars—"Katharine Fair-
fax," "Isma O'Neal." By Thomasine Maunsell. 3 vols.

Masks. A Novel. By "Marius." 2 vols.

The Yellow Flag. By Edmund Yates, author of
"Broken to Harness," "A Waiting Race," "Black Sheep," &c. 3 vols.

A False Heart. By J. Edward Muddock. 3 vols.

A Woman's Triumph. By Lady Hardy. 3 vols.

Not Without Thorns. By the author of "She was
Young, and He was Old," "Lover and Husband," &c. 3 vols.

The Misadventures of Mr. Catlyne, Q.C.: an Autobiography. By Mathew Stradling, author of "The Irish Bar
Sinister," "Cheap John's Auction," &c. 2 vols.

Eve's Daughters. By E. Dyne Fenton, author of
"Sorties from Gib," "Military Men I have Met," &c. 1 vol.

TINSLEY BROTHERS, 8 CATHERINE STREET, STRAND.

Boscobel: a Tale of the Year 1651. By WILLIAM HARRISON AINSWORTH, author of "Rookwood," "The Tower of London," &c. With Illustrations. 3 vols.

At His Gates. By Mrs. OLIPHANT, author of "Chronicles of Carlingford," &c. 3 vols.

The Vicar's Daughter: a New Story. By GEORGE MACDONALD, author of "Annals of a Quiet Neighbourhood," "The Seaboard Parish," &c. 3 vols.

A Waiting Race. By EDMUND YATES, author of "Broken to Harness," "Black Sheep," &c. 3 vols.

Valentin: a Story of Sedan. By HENRY KINGSLEY, author of "Ravenshoe," "Geoffry Hamlyn," &c. 2 vols.

Two Worlds of Fashion. By CALTHORPE STRANGE.

The Pace that Kills: a New Novel. 3 vols.

A Woman's Triumph. By Lady HARDY. 3 vols.

Erma's Engagement: a New Novel. By the Author of "Blanche Seymour," &c. 3 vols.

Dower and Curse. By JOHN LANE FORD, author of "Charles Stennie," &c. 3 vols.

Autobiography of a Cornish Rector. By the late JAMES HAMLEY TREGENNA. 2 vols.

The Scarborough Belle. By ALICE CHARLOTTE SAMPSON. 3 vols.

Puppets Dallying. By ARTHUR LILLIE, author of "Out of the Meshes," "King of Topsy Turvy," &c. 3 vols.

Under the Greenwood Tree. A Rural Painting of the Dutch School. By the Author of "Desperate Remedies," &c. 2 vols.

Coming Home to Roost. By GERALD GRANT. 3 vols.

Midnight Webs. By G. M. FENN, author of "The Sapphire Cross," &c. 1 vol. fancy cloth binding, 10s. 6d.

Sorties from "Gib" in quest of Sensation and Sentiment. By E. DYNE FENTON, late Captain 86th Regiment. 1 vol. post 8vo, 10s. 6d.

TINSLEY BROTHERS, 8 CATHERINE STREET, STRAND.

The Pilgrim and the Shrine, or Passages from the
Life and Correspondence of Herbert Ainslie, B.A. Cantab. 3 vols.

Oberon's Spell. By EDEN ST. LEONARDS. 3 vols.

Under which King. By B. W. JOHNSTON, M.P.
1 vol.

Under the Red Dragon. By JAMES GRANT, author
of "The Romance of War," "Only an Ensign," &c. 3 vols.

Hornby Mills; and other Stories. By HENRY
KINGSLEY, author of "Ravenshoe," "Mademoiselle Mathilde,"
"Geoffry Hamlyn," &c. 2 vols.

Grainger's Thorn. By THOS. WRIGHT (the "Jour-
neyman Engineer"), author of "The Bane of a Life," "Some Habits
and Customs of the Working Classes," &c. 3 vols.

Church and Wife: a Question of Celibacy. By
ROBERT ST. JOHN CORBET, author of "The Canon's Daughters."
3 vols.

Not Easily Jealous: a New Novel. 3 vols.

Rough but True. By ST. CLARE. 1 vol.

Christopher Dudley. By MARY BRIDGMAN, author
of 'Robert Lynne,' &c. 3 vols.

Love and Treason. By W. FREELAND. 3 vols.

Tender Tyrants. By JOSEPH VEREY. 3 vols.

Loyal: a New Novel. By M. A. GODFREY. 3 vols.

Fatal Sacrifice: a New Novel.

Old Margaret. By HENRY KINGSLEY, author of
"Ravenshoe," "Geoffry Hamlyn," &c. 2 vols.

Bide Time and Tide. By J. T. NEWALL, author of
"The Gage of Honour," "The Eastern Hunters," &c. 3 vols.

The Scandinavian Ring. By JOHN POMEROY. 3 vols.

The Harveys. By HENRY KINGSLEY, author of
"Old Margaret," "Hetty," "Geoffry Hamlyn," &c. 2 vols.

Henry Ancrum: a Tale of the last War in New
Zealand. 2 vols.

She was Young, and He was Old. By the Author
of "Lover and Husband." 3 vols.

A Ready-made Family: or the Life and Adventures
of Julian Leep's Cherub. A Story. 3 vols.

Cecil's Tryst.   By the Author of " Lost Sir Massingberd," &c. 3 vols.

Denison's Wife.   By Mrs. ALEXANDER FRASER, author of " Not while She lives," " Faithless; or the Loves of the Period," &c. 2 vols.

Wide of the Mark.   By the Author of " Recommended to Mercy," " Taken upon Trust," &c. 3 vols.

Title and Estate.   By F. LANCASTER. 3 vols.

Hollowhill Farm.   By JOHN EDWARDSON. 3 vols.

The Sapphire Cross: a Tale of Two Generations. By G. M. FENN, author of " Bent, not Broken," &c. 3 vols.

Edith.   By C. A. LEE. 2 vols.

Lady Judith.   By JUSTIN McCARTHY, author of " My Enemy's Daughter," " The Waterdale Neighbours," &c. 3 vols.

Only an Ensign.   By JAMES GRANT, author of " The Romance of War," " Lady Wedderburn's Wish," &c. 3 vols.

Old as the Hills.   By DOUGLAS MOREY FORD. 3 vols.

Not Wooed, but Won.   By the Author of " Lost Sir Massingberd," " Found Dead," &c. 3 vols.

My Heroine.   1 vol.

Sundered Lives.   By WYBERT REEVE, author of the Comedies of " Won at Last," " Not so Bad after all," &c. 3 vols.

The Nomads of the North: a Tale of Lapland. By J. LOVEL HADWEN. 1 vol.

Family Pride.   By the Author of " Olive Varcoe," " Simple as a Dove," &c. 3 vols.

Fair Passions; or the Setting of the Pearls. By the Hon. Mrs. PIGOTT CARLETON. 3 vols.

Harry Disney: an Autobiography.   Edited by ATHOLL DE WALDEN. 3 vols.

Desperate Remedies.   3 vols.

The Foster Sisters. By EDMOND BRENAN LOUGHNAN. 3 vols.

Only a Commoner.   By HENRY MORFORD. 3 vols.

Madame la Marquise.   By the Author of " Dacia Singleton," " What Money Can't Do," &c. 3 vols.

Clara Delamaine.   By A. W. CUNNINGHAM. 3 vols.

Joshua Marvel. By B. L. FARJEON, author of "Grif." 3 vols.

By Birth a Lady. By G. M. FENN, author of "Mad," "Webs in the Way," &c. 3 vols.

A Life's Assize. By Mrs. J. H. RIDDELL, author of "George Geith," "City and Suburb," "Too much Alone," &c. 3 vols.

The Monarch of Mincing-Lane. By WILLIAM BLACK, author of "In Silk Attire." "Kilmeny," &c. 3 vols.

The Golden Bait. By H. HOLL, author of "The King's Mail," &c. 3 vols.

Like Father, like Son. By the Author of "Lost Sir Massingberd," &c. 3 vols.

Beyond these Voices. By the EARL OF DESART, author of "Only a Woman's Love," &c. 3 vols.

Bought with a Price. By the Author of "Golden Pippin," &c. 1 vol.

The Florentines: a Story of Home-life in Italy. By the COUNTESS MARIE MONTEMERLI, author of "Four Months in a Garibaldian Hospital," &c. 3 vols.

Hearts and Diamonds. By ELIZABETH P. RAMSAY, 3 vols.

The Bane of a Life. By THOMAS WRIGHT (the Journeyman Engineer), author of "Some Habits and Customs of the Working Classes," &c. 3 vols.

Schooled with Briars: a Story of To-day. 1 vol.

A Righted Wrong. By EDMUND YATES, author of "Black Sheep," &c. 3 vols.

George Canterbury's Will. By Mrs. HENRY WOOD, author of "East Lynne," &c. 3 vols.

Phœbe's Mother. By LOUISA ANN MEREDITH, author of "My Bush Friends in Tasmania." 2 vols.

Saved by a Woman. By the Author of "No Appeal," &c. 3 vols.

Nellie's Memories: a Domestic Story. By ROSA NOUCHETTE CAREY. 3 vols.

Clarissa. By SAMUEL RICHARDSON. Edited by E. S. DALLAS, author of "The Gay Science," &c. 3 vols.

Tregarthen Hall. By JAMES GARLAND. 3 vols.

PAMPHLETS,
ETC.

The Bells. A Romantic Story adapted from the French of MM. ERCKMANN-CHATRIAN. In Illustrated Wrapper, price One Shilling.

True to the Core: a Story of the Armada. The T. P. Cooke Prize Drama (1866). By A. R. SLOUS, Esq., author of "The Templar," "Hamilton of Bothwellhaugh," "Light and Shadow," &c. Price One Shilling.

The Wren of the Curragh. Reprinted from the *Pall Mall Gazette*. Price One Shilling.

Poll and Partner Joe; or the Pride of Putney and the Pressing Pirate. A New and Original Nautical Burlesque, written by F. C. BURNAND, author of "Ixion," "Black-eyed Susan," "Military Billy Taylor," "Sir George and a Dragon," "Paris, or Vive Lemprière," &c. Price Sixpence.

Manual of Salmon and Trout Hatching; or an Explanation of the Fish-hatching Apparatus at the Royal Horticultural Gardens, the South Kensington Museum, Zoological Gardens, &c. By FRANK BUCKLAND, M.A., M.R.C.S., F.Z.S. Price Sixpence.

The Battle of Berlin (Die Schlacht von Königsberg). By MOTLY RANKE McCAULEY. Price Sixpence.

The Cruise of the Anti-Torpedo. Price Sixpence.

TINSLEY BROTHERS, 8 CATHERINE STREET, STRAND.